T0323161

THE BLACK EDEN

by the same author

fiction
CRUSADERS
THE POSSESSIONS OF DOCTOR FORREST
THE KNIVES

film
ALAN CLARKE
THE NAME OF THIS BOOK IS DOGME95
SEAN PENN

non-fiction
KEEGAN AND DALGLISH

as editor
TEN BAD DATES WITH DE NIRO

THE
BLACK
EDEN

RICHARD T. KELLY

faber

First published in 2023
by Faber & Faber Limited
The Bindery
51 Hatton Garden
London EC1N 8HN

Typeset by Faber & Faber Limited
Printed in the UK by CPI Group (UK) Ltd, Croydon, CR0 4YY

All rights reserved
© Richard T. Kelly, 2023

The right of Richard T. Kelly to be identified as author
of this work has been asserted in accordance with Section 77
of the Copyright, Designs and Patents Act 1988

*All characters, names, places and events in this book are fictitious
and any resemblance to persons living or dead, places or events
is entirely coincidental.*

A CIP record for this book
is available from the British Library

ISBN 978-0-571-34658-5

Printed and bound in the UK on FSC® certified paper in line with our continuing
commitment to ethical business practices, sustainability and the environment.
For further information see faber.co.uk/environmental-policy

2 4 6 8 10 9 7 5 3 1

For Stuart, James, Pat, Gordon and Mike

We are here moving into what are largely uncharted waters. This oil business is all new and our experience of it comparatively short. I think we still have, as it were, almost a love-hate relationship with it; we want the oil, but we are a little frightened of what we shall do with it and what it will do to us.

Lord Polwarth, in the House of Lords, 13 December 1972

Contents

Author's Note

This is a work of fiction, and so none of it is true. It is set, though, during a real passage of recent British history, with a chronology that maps approximately onto the real timeline of exploration for and discovery of hydrocarbons under the UK section of the North Sea. Various real people, places, businesses et cetera are mentioned, but quite often in the company of other names and markers that are made up. I have taken great liberties with parts of the topography of Scotland – and one or two dramatic licenses, too, with regard to a number of its institutions and traditions – for which I beg the indulgence of any readers from that great nation. With regard to the made-up characters, no identification with actual persons, living or deceased, is intended or should be inferred.

PART I

FRIENDSHIPS

April 1956

Aaron and Robbie and the Sea

Under the water he feels he is concealed, set free in the way that concealment allows. There, too, he finds that things formerly hidden are revealed to him; and as if to him alone. As a child he had the child's fear of sea monsters, evil creatures of the deep. But now he is fourteen, and diving has helped him to put away childish things.

Down in the blue limbo, with the world's unhappy surface left to itself and the seabed shadowy below – there, he worries for little more than the air in his lungs. And in this twilight world he feels a strange, new, delighting grace about his movement, gifted to him by a skill he hadn't believed he could possess. He begins to feel special, capable. Not so apart as was feared, perhaps, from other fourteen-year-old lads who – he keeps hearing tales – are smoking and drinking and exploring sexual intercourse. Under the water, at least, another life starts to look possible: one in which he is a more considerable figure than his peers seem to believe.

They are done diving for the day; but Aaron Strang stands stock still on a rock, staring out at the spangles on the surface of the sea, waiting for Robbie to finish his *one more go*. Robbie's like that – his stamina and appetite are simply of a higher order than Aaron's. As smaller boys they learned to swim together, to hold their breaths together, to don mask, fins and snorkel together. But between the two of them Robbie is clearly the superior diver. To Aaron's eye he just hits the water better – carving it apart then vanishing clean, the blue restoring coolly in his wake.

Aaron is in his wet trunks, a towel round his shoulders, rough against his skin. The high gorsy cliffs all around him form a basin of sandstone – an amphitheatre of a kind. The vast overhead has but a few stately clouds and a kittiwake whirling. All is quiet save for the shir of the sea and a low whistling wind.

Aaron shivers slightly; folds his arms. The haar, the old sea fret, is in the air. He can smell salt on himself, the pads of his fingers are puckered, his nipples small and purplish. He finds this sensuous, somehow.

But the longer he stares at the water, the more he is pervaded by unease he knows all too well. He can't make it stop, not once this tide has come in: the special wistfulness of four o'clock. More than once in school his class have been told – and by Aaron's own father – to write poems of the sea, paeans to the Dornoch Firth, the source of so much local piety. And never has Aaron come up with a single line fit for sharing.

The sea doesn't care. It just doesn't care what it does.

His strongest feeling, really, is that there's something in the lapping of seawater – in its strong odour, and its steeping of his bare skin as he enters it – that stirs him in the region of his groin. But that's not the stuff of sea-poems for reading out in class. He is a good pupil, but he doesn't tell the truth at school, God forbid – he is the dominie's son. Rather, he passes himself off, for it has long seemed essential to him that he give nothing away – not one bit of the fleeting strangeness in his head which, in fairness, doesn't tend to outstay its welcome.

His feet teeter a little on the rocky crest. He imagines falling, into the sea, but this time swallowed whole, vanishing clean away – sinking and not resisting. Oblivion. The image in his head has a certain lonely appeal. But then Aaron imagines his throat glutted by saltwater, his lungs bursting . . . No: it pleases him to suffer only a little, a small measure under his mental command.

Now he hears a tread at his back but doesn't react, plays it cool – a little mindful of his own moodiness, how it could look daft, him stood at the water's edge staring out to sea like some loon in a storybook, some mystery lady with a windswept lover.

'Aaron! Eh!'

He turns and Robbie Vallance is coming straight for him, bounding from rock to rock, covering the sort of terrain where Aaron would tiptoe. But Robbie never stumbles. For such a strapping lad he is awfully graceful.

'Eh? What you thinkin', ye gowk?'

Aaron only smiles, abashed. He and Robbie never have to say that much to get along: they are best friends, which is to say neither has met another body they like better, the local choices being what they are. Always they fall in with one another easily enough. *'You up for such-and-such a thing?' 'Are ye up for it?' 'Aye.' 'Right enough then.'*

Robbie has reached Aaron's rocky crest, and gives him a friendly shove, such that Aaron struggles to keep his footing.

'What are ye gawkin' at?'

'What's it look like?'

'Aye but why?'

'Dunno. The sea. It's like . . . it's pure. Y'know? Pure just how it is.'

'Pure bollocks,' Robbie scoffs. 'My da says a big load of shite gaes i' the sea.'

Aaron laughs. No reproof; just the lightness pals have with one another. And that, he knows, is good for him. His pal Robbie is good for him.

Aaron's da has called them 'a fine pair', which discomfits them both just a bit. But Aaron is quite sure he would sooner die than fall out with Robbie. While not minding his own company, Aaron has always known: *You have to get along with someone.* Solitude, if not intolerable, is somewhat disreputable. He has needed a friend with whom he can nearly be himself.

And Robbie, while made of more robust and outgoing materials, is also a fellow who will, at times, turn abashed at the talk of certain difficult things – will bite his lip a bit and say *Aye*, he's *bothered a bit by that an' all*. Aaron knows that with Robbie, as with himself, there is surely a lot going on under the surface.

They take up their bicycles and head home from the rocks, in the direction of the Vallance cottage, where they can expect a mug of tea and a piece. Aaron's devout hope is only that Robbie's visiting cousin Morag will have gone to her dancing lesson, and won't be mooning about, trespassing on their leisure.

They follow the grassy coastal track north, above the sea, trundling a way by the ragwort and fireweed and harebells. Aaron's eye is caught by a rock that intrigues him – a bit of jasper? – and he stoops to gather it for his collection, knowing, of course, that he won't be asking Robbie's view on it. Ever since the first occasion Aaron was moved to share his feeling for 'interesting rocks', Robbie has never quite let the oddness of the hobby pass without comment.

Still, it's a fact: around the outcroppings of this coastal bluff Aaron has found what he can identify, courtesy of his father's encyclopedias, as cretaceous rock fossils and gastropod shells. Each item in his collection is adhered carefully to a cardboard sheet, with a hand-inked marker. His father has been oddly unenthused by these studies; but then David Strang teaches geography – his son's favourite class – nearly begrudgingly, as though it were an affront to the faith he professes less by churchgoing than by cryptic reference to theological tomes in his library, those bookshelves running all round the chalky walls of the Strang cottage. At any rate: Aaron knows how queer his private passion can appear to others, but it is a deep-lying part of a self that he plans one day to reveal.

Now the boys pass the schoolhouse, shut for a few days since it's the tattie-planting time and the hands are needed. But a light is on within – Mr Strang, no doubt, sat there correcting exercises still, under his yellowed old map of the world, with the frowning brow on which veins are sometimes visible.

They pass the Ferry Hotel, and the painted gables of fishermen's cottages. They pass the nature reserve, and the squat concrete outposts that are relics of the war. They pass, too, within sight of the implacable whitewashed church of the Reverend McVey, a kirk tall and pale like its incumbent, a plain cross set high atop the birdcage bellcote.

And then the big Gallagher property – the old stone fortress remodelled as a handsome home for a moneyed man's family, the perimeter of its long garden rolling powerfully down the incline toward rocks and sea. Aaron knows that Robbie's gaze will scour that lawn and that facade as they pass – he will be after a glimpse of Marilyn Gallagher. But Aaron also knows better than to tease. Girls tend to look at Robbie a certain way, as if he were something to consider, and Robbie is surely right to be pained that the girl he likes best won't pay him the same homage.

Aaron's sense of his own looks? A troublesome business. He sometimes feels he sees himself, painedly, in the plate section of his biology textbook: a little neanderthal caveman, albeit too lithe and bony to have survived long as a hunter-gatherer. When he tries out his smile in the mirror his teeth look like tombstones, his whole head somehow squashed underneath his monkish haircut. His brow, his nose . . . they just stick out too much. 'It's where you fit all them brains,' Robbie told him loyally, the one time Aaron shared his unease. But then Robbie is a superior specimen, his face long and chiselled, pleasingly dark round the eyes and lips – a mirror of Marilyn Gallagher, one might say. Meantime Aaron has wondered glumly what sort of a girl would be a match for him. Some cavewoman, maybe.

Soon they are passing fenced fields of black cattle, doddies and humlies. A couple of beasts dawdle over to inspect the intruders, and Aaron shouts to send them packing. The modest Vallance croft is in sight.

Mr Vallance is a crofter shepherd; and this, Aaron knows, is the man Robbie is meant to become. Robbie has grown up in a kitchen shared with Shetland lambs – he has sheared, and he has helped his da to slaughter. The boys step across the shared grazing field, its trodden way so laden with dung that each step is measured. Aaron has to smile when twin lambs go spryly by his side, as to say hello. He and Robbie carry on forward in step, down the path obvious to them. But Aaron has got to thinking that this can't go on forever, indeed must be at an end soon.

There is this sense – it gets said – that Robbie's 'people' are not Aaron's 'people'. It's not something they can talk about. But it seems to have a great deal to do with school – Mr Strang's school – and how pupils are being weighed and measured and forced to choose. Certain doors are opening, others may be shutting.

It's a reputable school, and his father has made it so by his cares, enabling an extra couple of buildings besides, the better to accommodate a few more taught subjects and a few more teachers. Always, there have been boys who never turn up, farming or fishing instead. But then there are top-stream boys and top-stream girls; and that is why Aaron knows that come the autumn he will ride a bus eight miles or so to the Academy, while Robbie will be for the farming. Possibly Robbie would be already by his father's side for keeps had David Strang not taken special pains to see that his son's great pal passed all examinations.

The Vallance cottage is nigh – only a haystack and a henhouse between the boys and their mug and piece. It's dusk and there is light in the window. Aaron hesitates.

'Whit's it now, Aaron? Scared of my wee cousin Morag?'

Aaron is not happy that Robbie can read his mind and, worse, make a laugh of it. 'Get away, Robbie.'

'Never known a lad so shy of a lassie with a shine on him . . .'

Aaron, stuck for words, resists the obvious riposte – that Morag is not any lassie but a relative of Robbie's, which is hardly ideal.

Robbie, though, persists. 'You think you'll ever be gettin' interested, then?'

'What do you mean?'

'Y'know. In the lassies, Aaron.'

Now Aaron cannot speak: the inappropriateness is so colossal. Yes, it's a fact there are things Robbie is up for and Aaron isn't, and that includes the lassies, of whom Aaron is indeed scared, and not just Robbie's cousin, neither. But Aaron can't comprehend why Robbie has elected to harry him for it right here and now.

'Or you'll mebbe not?' Robbie shakes his head, chuckles into his chest.

'What's that about, Robbie?'

'Dunno. You tell me. Jist sayin'.'

'Saying what? Eh?'

Aaron has hardly raised a hand to another soul ever. But nor he has ever felt quite such a wounding indignity. So he shoves Robbie right in the chest, with such unbridled force that the palm of his hand hurts. Robbie is rocked on his heels, his face instantly black with affront.

Then Aaron feels a hard and dizzying smack to his cheekbone, and next he's staggered and fallen to the mucky ground. Then he is struggling under Robbie's full weight.

He slaps and kicks out as best he can, feeling this is horribly unreal, painful, painfully stupid, too. And yet Robbie is breathing fiercely and issuing blows more effectively.

'*Robbie!*'

They fall apart as if shot, and scrabble to their feet, since the word of the Lord has come down. Robbie's father, a man of inarguable proportions, is ten yards away and wears the look of one coming as near to a scene as propriety and repugnance will allow.

'Robbie, in God's name get inside now.' Aaron has, in truth, heard Mr Vallance sound off a lot louder. 'Aaron, you need to get off, we've had bad news, get yon home. Robbie, your uncle's here, son. Heed me now.'

Robbie looks more than chastened as his father shepherds him away: he seems suddenly and awfully unsure. For Aaron, too, unease has supplanted embarrassment. As soon as is decent he follows their steps a little distance toward the farmhouse; and from behind the haystack emerges the ominous sight of a parked car, the black Wolseley of the local constabulary.

Aaron's return home is so premature and his manner so subdued that David Strang regards his son with a familiar fretful look before getting on the telephone directly. Then Aaron, fearing the worst, needing to know, watches his father stand there listening in a sombre silence punctuated by low, soft exhalations.

David replaces the receiver and bids Aaron sit. It is Robbie's cousin Sandy, elder brother of Morag. He went out to fish on an early morning boat, but he did not come back. The coastguards have now found wreckage off the cliffs at Tarbat – part of the ship's hull sheared away, and of Sandy not a sign.

'They fear he's gone. Lost at sea, Aaron.'

Aaron feels something now in the room, in the air, between he and his father, invisible but tangible, as if they have been joined by another – an oppressive presence. He is desperately sorry for Sandy, sorrier still for his dear friend Robbie. He feels a strong urge to flee this moment and be gone himself – back in time, back to the blue, beneath the water. But the gravity of the moment he feels all too firmly, and it weighs on him and nails him to the spot.

May 1956
The Reformed Church

Aaron trudges by his father's side through the churchyard gate, onto the estate of chapel and burial grounds enclosed all around by long borders of drystone wall. The array of weathered gravestones always provoke in Aaron a haunted feeling – for children who died so young; husbands and wives buried together; his own mother, and Robbie's. And today the village buries Sandy Vallance.

Aaron sees up ahead the Reverend McVey watching and waiting at the steps of the kirk while his funeral congregation draw near. Through his gates the serried and black-clad mourners proceed, in the shadow of the harled walls, watched by the high lancet windows.

Robbie's uncle is first to gravely accept the Reverend's handshake. While Aaron and his father wait their turn, Aaron is conscious that the Gallagher clan are behind them – Mrs Juliet Gallagher the councilwoman, and their illustriously dark-haired fourteen-year-old daughter Marilyn, slides in her glossy hair, her black woollen coat skirting her ankles. Aaron is careful not to turn his head, but when at last he shuffles indoors he can hear Mrs Gallagher greeting the Reverend with that peculiar authority of hers, as if she knows everyone's business as well as her own, and might organise it for them if asked.

Vallance family members lead mourners-in-chief to the pew bench at the front, beneath the large dark pulpit and the three long windows in the south wall. Aaron and his father are reasonably close to the front, if not as near as Aaron would have wished. But, feeling unseen to that degree, Aaron now steals a glance at Marilyn. Ordinarily he would no sooner look at her directly than stare at the sun but, from where he is seated, her fair profile is given to him freely.

He is pulled from reverie by Reverend McVey mounting the creaking steps to the pulpit so as to initiate the singing from psalter books. The Reverend has a head that makes one uneasily aware of the skull beneath the skin: his eyes have a milky cast, his tombstone teeth prominent, his bald crown fringed by white wisps. He emanates austerity, the air of one who subsists on little and wants no more. Holding his Bible proprietarily to his chest, he surveys the hushed gathering, and then he speaks.

'Brethren, today we witness as a community the consigning of a body to the earth. We are bred to such loss – we have suffered it before. And still we may ask, why did this have to happen? Why should a father be called on to bury a son?'

Fixed to his hard pew by the bleakness of the Reverend's oration, Aaron is put in mind of McVey's own son – the truculent Torrance, 'Torry', font of much local gossip. Even Aaron's father, known to give every pupil a careful assessment and a second chance, has been heard to wonder aloud about what is to be done with such a hallion.

'. . . men go to sea, and while they are away their wives may meet in the street, and speak of the weather, and of children, and of anything but the thing that is perhaps most powerfully on their minds – that their husband or father, or son, might not return but instead be lost.'

Reverend McVey looks up and pauses, surveying many a slow nodding head. Other heads remain fixedly low.

'And yet we must go on, as does this world, however changed. All who mourn shall be comforted – by the power of everlasting life over death. Death, meaning separation, but not an end. Recall how Jesus wept over Lazarus. "The dust returns to the earth and the spirit returns to God . . ."'

Aaron hears all of this, but he is experiencing a guilty sensation, familiar to him in churchgoing. Even a day of mourning, and for his friend's cousin, has caused it to rear. It is a base discomfort in the weight of pieties ordained by his elders – as pinching as the collar and tie round his neck. *You're forever made to kneel before things you can't know, things you can't change.* He feels bad about this feeling, especially sat amid hardy men and women who make him so conscious of his own slightness and selfishness. But he feels it nonetheless.

Then, from the back of the church, an unwelcome noise of rusty hinges. Aaron turns as others are turning, and he notes, as do they, the belated entrance of Torry McVey.

Briskly facing the front again, Aaron notes that the Reverend has surely seen his son, for all that he could not have looked any sorrier. In the next moment Aaron realises that the nearest place for Torry to be seated is right by Aaron's side.

As the youth settles, so tall and black-clad, Aaron shifts a few inches and feels himself shrivel inside. Torry is lean like his father, his face under a pompadour haircut curved like an axe handle, and he is known not to suffer those he rates as fools. For now, though, only a sullen look comes Aaron's way, and Aaron hopes that Torry has other things on his mind today.

'. . . for another of us is now with the master. And so we must turn to the work that lies ahead of us, each one of us – which is the work of the soul. There is the end we all must face, the lesson we must heed. "It is appointed unto men once to die, but after this the judgment." Therefore, the question of what is it we are to do with such life as we have left? Are we prepared?'

Aaron wishes very much that this peroration has put an amen to the matter. Indeed, McVey now asks the congregation to join in a hymn: 'Lead us, heavenly Father, lead us o'er the world's tempestuous sea.' Aaron only mouths the words into his chest, not looking at Torrance McVey, who stands and broods but remains likewise silent.

The elders and ministers lead mourners out to where Sandy's coffin has been positioned ready. The women take up their decreed places by the doors, forbidden to go further. The men will process the

13

short walk up the slope to the graveside. Aaron is anxious about what must follow – for Robbie is carrying, alongside Mr Vallance and his brothers.

At last the coffin is hefted onto four pairs of tall shoulders. Aaron nearly envies Robbie for the stalwartness with which he bears this duty. For sure, Aaron on his own feels reduced and exposed.

The Vallance men lead off and, as is custom, other men process behind, ready to take a turn in shouldering the coffin. David Strang is among them. So Aaron feels a small relief when his classmate Ray Bodie sidles up and walks apace with him past the mossy headstones.

'I'll keep you company, Strang. You having no pals.'

Aaron nods, not minding the jibe – Bodie often comes out with stuff that others mightn't, but matter-of-factly, as if it won't wait and can't be helped. At school Bodie is known to be a rare spark, as oddly assured in class as if he were stood up at the front of it. He has a spring to his stride and is forever glancing about him, as if he were *en route* to some private and furtive bit of business.

'You're a one for the diving, Strang, isn't that so? Would you have an interest in a scuba set? Aqualung, y'know? I've come across one, I could make you a deal if you fancy?'

Typical Bodie, thinks Aaron. At break-times or beyond the school gates he is often found selling knock-off toffees, coveted 45 rpm records, cigarettes both single and in packs. Aaron knows an aqualung is surplus to his needs; but in the act of mulling a polite response he is spared by the rude rasp of an engine exhaust. He and Bodie turn as one to see, beyond the stone perimeter, Torry McVey powering off down the coast road on his Matchless motorcycle.

Aaron feels as he suspects others do – an unspoken rule that no one is to note this spectacle or give it time of day. Still, he and Bodie stand and look a shade longer than others.

Bodie whistles. 'That used to be Sandy's bike, as I heard. Loved bikes, did Sandy. The Reverend might have said something of that.'

'I suppose he's not meant to say very much,' Aaron murmurs.

14

'Aw there's plenty he'd not have the nerve to say. See his face when his boy just rolls in bold as you like?'

Aaron has decided such talk is improper, and motions that he and Bodie should press onward. Some instinct, though, causes him to glance back to the church door, to seek out Marilyn Gallagher – thus to see that her sights seem fixed on Torry McVey burning away toward the village in the distance. It's only a moment; and then, surely conscious of being observed, Marilyn turns her back. But Aaron is sure he saw a sending sort of a look. He has seen it before, on the faces of girls who look too long at his pal Robbie.

'You can stop with that, wee man.'

'What?'

'Don't be saying you're soft on that one?'

'No chance.' Aaron winces.

'No chance is about right.'

Trudging on, feeling for the first time a real dislike of Ray Bodie, Aaron takes heart from a certain intuition that Robbie at least is well clear of 'that one'.

The sky has darkened. At the graveside the coffin has been lowered into the dug hole, and already Sandy's relatives are taking turns to scatter handfuls of earth upon it. Shovels are being passed from man to man. And now Aaron sees Robbie, taking hold of a shovel, his head down and one hand across his face, fingers spread as if to hide visible distress. Loss is something else he and Robbie share without speaking; they have never spoken of their mothers, and he has never seen Robbie cry. Even now Robbie is containing himself staunchly, and the other menfolk pay him no mind. But Aaron's heart goes out to his friend.

May 1956
Joe Killday and His Clan

In the grey light of dawn Joe Killday is done shaving, and he studies his handiwork in the mirror's misted reflection, tapping his jaw with the flat of the straight razor. Sixteen and game, he doesn't mind the look of himself – dark eyes, dark locks, a kind of hangdog handsomeness? Today, though, he must make sure none of that self-regard counts against him in the harder eyes of older men. A test lies ahead. *Steel yourself*, he tells his reflection.

'Joseph!' his father barks from the foot of the stairs. 'Breakfast, son!'

Andrew Killday rose at six, the custom he requires for all the males of the house, since all must get to business. He will have fired the Primus stove to boil water then repaired to the bathroom for a brisk trim of his beard. Lying abed, Joe knew all this was afoot by the familiar sound of a razor gaining its edge on a leather strop, and by the mug of steaming tea already deposited at his bedside.

But this is a day unlike any before: Joe's first deep-water excursion, on a stern trawler loaded with big nets and bound for foreign fishing grounds. In honour of the occasion Andrew will skipper a boat for the first time in ten years. Usually he is dressed for work in a suit and shoes with a high shine, but today Joe goes down to find his father at table in a thick Aran rollneck. Today Andrew is a skipper again.

Breakfast is fried eggs, sausage, white pudding. The dining room is as soberly dressed and clean-swept as every room in the family home known as Netherdown. The light is improving but still the lamp is lit. Mother Winnie serves and the Killdays scoff in the styles to which they're accustomed. Walter, ramrod straight in his chair, makes hardly a sound in buttering his toast, while frowning over his steely spectacles at some correspondence brought home from the office. Joe

16

has not much appetite but forces himself, hoping a full stomach might drive out butterflies. Garth, though, feasts like a hunter who's already laboured a long day, head low to the plate, a race between shovelling and chewing. Eleven-year-old Angela, who takes only porridge in the morning, averts her eyes from Garth's grossness.

Joe checks his Seamaster watch and when he looks up he sees his father studying him: Andrew's forehead pointed straight at him as if in the scrum, his blunt, fleshy features foreshortened. Joe looks away from the scrutiny. Andrew's hair and beard are angel-white, his eyes pure blue, but while the line of his mouth is often buried by that beard, Joe usually imagines something critical in it.

At the door Winnie helps the men into their pea coats. They will drive to the docks as four but only Andrew and Joe are going to sea. The boys must never be out in one boat – that is Winnie's rule; seeing it obeyed she waves them off with a minimum of fuss, off to the daily business of the family firm.

'We'll be back in four days, Winnifred,' grunts Andrew. 'Full to the gunnels with fish.'

Joe gazes out through the car window as Aberdeen streets go by. There is a promising brightness to the day, lifting the austere aspect of the black granite facades, the mica glistening in early light.

He is thinking now of how Winnie used to gather the children on the stark promontory of Portlethen Bay, near to Netherdown, so they could catch sight of Da's trawler, a quarter-mile in the distance, heading out to the deep grounds. Joe even now can seem to feel the whistling wind that would sink long fingers into him. That, and getting his go on the binoculars – panning to locate the boat, seeing it suddenly atop a wave before alarmingly pitching from sight as if down to the depths.

Garth nudges Joe. 'You hoping to spot a minister on the street so we can turn back? Home to your warm bed, eh?'

17

Joe smiles tightly, as to say he cares not a jot for sailors' superstitions. 'Aye, Garth, if you say so.'

Garth is chewing baccy, with the calmly predacious look of someone looking to land a catch for his plate or, worse, having already landed it. But he's always chewing on something that might – if one is unlucky – get spat out in someone's direction. Even Walter – eldest and tallest brother, if physically the least imposing – can snap and give out at Garth for his needless, needling jibes.

Joe knows better than to take the bait. They all got sea-legs as boys going out on Andrew's lobster-creel boat. Joe has been on inshore trawls, taken tours of the coast, seen catches of that size. He has helped to haul nets aboard, has scrubbed fish-boxes and had a go with a gutting knife, under his father's watchful eye. If he didn't love the experience – if Andrew seemed to see as much – Joe knows at least that he acquitted himself gamely. Are four days out to the Faroe Islands so much taller an order?

Andrew parks in his customary place at Albert Quay near the Killday company office, with its prime vantage on the dock, and the berthing points of Killday ships amid a crowd of hundreds of moored vessels – trawlers and line-boats, herring boats all in a row as if one might hop from one to another for a laugh. Joe climbs out into the salt air, full of the mingled noises of gulls, distant engines, hooting horns and shrieking derrick blocks. He retrieves his kitbag from the boot. Garth trudges off toward the quay without a word of cheerio. But Garth as ship's runner has the task of getting the crew onboard before ropes are thrown off – trawlermen being not so easily wrangled.

Indoors, Andrew is immediately in huddled conference with Sheila, his secretary of fifteen years. Walter takes up the high-backed chair before his roll-top desk and fills his ink-pen. The catching of fish is less Walter's concern than are the other arms of the Killday operation: ship repair, rigging and supplies. Joe, feeling spare, slips into the grasp of his father's burgundy leather chair and swivels idly, feeling that assurance he always takes from the dark wood panels and brass fittings of the office, their aroma of well-seated success.

Then once more he feels the drill of his father's gaze. Andrew is heading straight for him, nodding, clutching his 'black book', the weathered calfskin notebook fat with loose enclosures, navigation readings and the like.

'Right, then, son. Shoulder that bag and let's have you.'

Walter has got to his feet, all sympathy, and thrusts out a hand. 'Good luck, Joe. Sorry we saw no minister to save you.'

Even as Joe struggles to stay in step with his father on the way to the dock, the sky seems to turn rain-dark by the second. The seawater has assumed a mirroring murkiness.

'Och, we could yet see some weather,' Andrew mutters.

The *Reaper* is before them: a hundred feet of trawler, its tanks being topped with diesel and fresh water while deckies load gear aboard – tubs of ice, coils of rope, sheets of corrugated iron. Joe looks the ship over, fore and aft, shuddering slightly at the starkness of those metal stanchions for the towing blocks that he knows as 'gallows'. Then he follows Andrew in clambering aboard over the rail that touches the pier. But Andrew, without a word, heads directly through the roped-open door that offers a way up to the bridge; and Joe knows – has been told – he is not to follow; not a deckhand, even the skipper's son.

Feeling spare, Joe stands and watches the bosun at work, his scant hair trailed like weeds over the beach of his scalp, his complexion blotched as if the sea has sucked and nipped at it too long. But a well-built man, by God! As are they all on the *Reaper*. Even the smallest deckie, if short of leg, is long of arm, coarsely hairy like a little ape, and he puts both paws into his heavy lifting.

Then Garth is at his side, hefting a crate, and trailing in his wake one more deckhand hauled in from the Tap.

'Do they not stay sober for a day like this?' Joe keeps his voice low.

Garth shoots him a scorning look. 'Never you worry, young John Knox. You'll see they're sober enough to do their work once you're out at the grounds.'

Garth heads to the roped door, flicking a hand as to say Joe must follow. In turn they descend a steep creaky ladder to the foc'sle. It is a cold and fetid-smelling corridor, wet cardboard duckboards underfoot. Garth gestures to various gloomy thresholds.

'In there's the wet gear for a'body. Pick your own set. Shitter's there – it's what it is, door just about sticks. Kitchen there – Tam's no' a bad cookie . . .'

Joe peeks into the galley, sees a tattooed man in a greying apron smoking a fag; a big iron stove with rails round its hob; a lump of pale meat marooned in ice on a tin tray.

'In there's where you eat . . .' Joe notes eight hinged seats round a Formica table bolted to the floor. 'And you bed here.'

Joe stares at four double-bunks, eight stained and pocked foam mattresses. The floor is a graveyard of cigarette butts, spent matches and sodden sports pages. The reek – of damp, diesel and fish – is stronger still.

'You've your pick, so throw your bag and claim it while you can – I'd go the one on the top? Be sure and get your sleep between hauls, right? Sleep when you can, not when you want.'

'I know that, Garth.' Garth's sternness, as if he were Andrew incarnate, has begun to irritate Joe royally.

'You're not a passenger, Joe. Da can't watch you. You have to pull your weight.'

'Garth, I *know* that, I'm not some rabbit in headlights.'

Garth winces as sharp as if he had tasted rat-poison. 'Touch cold iron!'

Joe groans inwardly. *Aw God, the damn seamen's superstitions!*

'It's no' a joke, Joe. Get in Tam's kitchen, get your hands on that stove.'

20

Back up on deck Joe sees the crew lining the whale-back, rummaging their pockets for coins to chuck to a gaggle of kids on the pier. Garth punches Joe's arm, but gently, then he's off and away over the side. Joe watches his brother's departing back. The engines start up, vibrating the ship, vibrating Joe's spine. Casting off commences. The ship reverses, squeezes out and heads at five knots for the harbour mouth – for the sea. The sun is pale, nearly negligible, the waves undulating, the trawler lurching as it ploughs its furrow with great jarring heaves across the murky water. There are gannets, kittiwakes, eider birds in the air. To the north Joe can make out a dark bank of low cloud: a basking presence.

The deckies set to their prep for the first trawl, clearing the deck, coiling up ropes and wire. Two men are engaged very diligently in the patch and repair of the vast net. Then Joe is summoned – 'Eh, boy, geeza haun!' A hefty metal covering needs shifting from port side, and the wash-tank setting up just aft of the mast. Joe takes a share of the weight.

Then the men move on, Joe straightens up – and knows at once his problem. His knees are unsteady, there's a sourness in his throat, and when his eye falls on the horizon it looks to him askew. He knows the churn and pitch of being at sea; but he realises he has stopped keeping his usual composing eye on that horizon. And now, unlike everyone else on deck, he is not feeling well.

He heads directly below, so as to be unseen, feeling the thump of waves on the hull and the vessel's sickening heave, hearing the incensed chunter of the engine, the odours of fuel and shite in his nostrils. He lies down on a foam mattress, stares at lagged pipes over his head, feels his innards gripped ever more tightly by rising nausea. The hatred he feels for being so predictably unmanned is not going to help; cannot be mastered by any effort of will or measured breathing. Rapidly his whole being has become just a gullet hooked to an oesophagus, an exit point for the foul stuff churning around down there, of which he is helpless host.

Why did he eat breakfast? What use in thinking that now? He lurches from the bunk to the toilet, across the crazily unstable floor, and manages – just – to get his mouth over the filthy edge of the bowl.

He is shaken awake by Tam the cook: shaken most persistently, told that he can't just curl up like a bairn. Eventually he feels himself hauled up and out by both of his arms, frogmarched to the kitchen, a *chunka-chunka* engine din rising steadily with the fetid diesel fumes – though Joe is aware, even in his stupor, of the odour coming off himself.

A beaker of water is pressed into his fingers, then some piece of dry matter he recognises as ship's biscuit. Joe has an urge to ask if there is ever weather so foul that a trawler might turn back. At once he knows better than to make a bigger fool of himself. He is in prison now, the key is turned.

He knows he must redeem himself, somehow. When Tam shouts to tell him that the grounds are reached and the first haul is afoot, Joe makes haste and struggles to insert himself into boots and oilskin, desperate to master his disarray.

Four crew are on the main deck as he clambers up, and his father is in the wheelhouse. The great metal trawl doors are being hoisted, the vessel is turning broadside to the weather, the sea is vast and turbulent. The floor rolls wildly under Joe's feet; its slickness feels lethal to him. He clutches the side, appalled by the seeming ease with which the hulking trawlermen are weaving their way across the treacherous deck.

They push and shove the bulk of the wide-mouth net over the side, then the gears start to lower it so that it sinks under the surface.

The floor rolls again, Joe grips the side and sees one deckie has noticed him and is gesticulating sharply, as if Joe should turn about. Turn his back?

Then he is struck by a gout of water, knocked clean off his feet, and his shoulder and forehead collide hard with cold iron.

He knows he is hurt. He slips and slides back up, struggles down to the shitter, to see the damage. He is cut at his hairline, yes. But the cut is already clean, washed out by salt, for all that its puckered edges have a shocked look to them.

By the time Joe returns there is a deckie manning each of the port and starboard tracks, another at the net drum, and he hears his father's voice barking from a tannoy. The net is rising, pregnant from the deep, winches reeling it in. The doors clang against the gallows, the headline of the net breaks the surface. The deckies move swiftly to add muscle to the effort, hauling the bulging folds over the side, the net's rolling bellies. The winch gets to work again, hoisting aloft until the bloated, silvery mass of the captured haul sways suspended, its cod-end dangling a few feet above the deck.

The hatch of the hopper is thrown back. Andrew emerges from the wheelhouse in overalls and seaboots as if this turmoil were made for him, and he hurls a grapnel at the net where it hooks; then he yanks and yanks such that the cod-end is swung over the hopper, whereupon the net is unknotted and vomits forth its slip-slapping horde.

Do something, Joe hears in his head. *Get to the fish hold.*

Back down to the depths he goes, following others, to the hold, grey and stark, sinister as a prison laboratory, every inch of it slimy. Already the fish from the chute above are flopping onto another nylon chute and dropping out onto a sorting table. He sees and smells skate, dogfish, something slithering and eel-like. He knows the drill – they are to be sorted by type and size, gutted swiftly, packed in the iced boxes that are piled in every spare space.

The men are unsheathing red-handled blades, pulling on rubber

23

gloves, and then they fall to gutting – slice, scrape, toss, entrails everywhere. Joe gloves up, chooses his weapon, and grabs hold of a big greenish codfish, pointed spurs on its gill arches. He drives the blade into its guts and knows instantly, painedly, that he has sliced also through his glove.

'Ach, son!' The mate has been watching him.

'What can I do?' Joe asks, nearly too numbed for panic.

'S'good fucking question.'

At three in the morning, down in his dungeon, Joe is awake while others snore. He is no longer sick, merely miserable. At mealtime he was not mocked but – maybe worse – ignored, by older men who chewed noisily and groused about their lives, their enormous grievances, every insult they had endured from every person with whom they had sailed. Resentment was the theme; against which acrimony toward the skipper's eejit son with no business being on a boat had seemed like small beer.

He slips off his mattress and clambers through the dark up to deck. They are far north, but still the coppery light in the sky takes him by surprise. In the wheelhouse he finds his father, face lit ghost-like by the radar screen. When Andrew turns to look Joe's way his expression is not the worst, but perhaps the toughest Joe has seen, because of its pitying cast. Joe finds he has to avoid Andrew's eye.

'Sit there, Joseph.'

There is silence. Andrew reassesses the radar. Joe understands how well his father knows these grounds, these beds, these fish schools. The fruits of long and exacting labours and calculations. Joe can see all too clearly the man his father is – a man complete out here, in his element.

He is not looking at Joe when next he speaks. 'Joseph, I ken this is hard on you. I've seen all sides of this life, son. I understand. You ken I did this with your granddad. When I first went to sea . . . you'd not even the electric, no radios. No safety gear. Just men, doing their best for each other.'

None of this is consoling to Joe; but he isn't sure that is even the intention.

'I just got on and did it. But I'd the sea in my blood. Your granddad, though – he wouldnae have minded if I'd something different in mind for my life.'

At this gesture, at least, Joe feels able to nod glumly.

'Aye . . .' Andrew turns again to reconsider the radar, as if that will do for the small talk. Yet he murmurs still, almost to himself. 'It's not easy to put men through this. But, if you're the skipper, you must. That could be your brother Garth one day, if it ends up that he wants his skipper's ticket.'

Joe grasps his father's total disappointment in him. Poorly as he feels, there is a flare of antagonism in his chest – knowing full well he has been judged. But he does not accept the judgement: he will not apologise for himself. Garth, Walter, too; they can be their father's boys if they wish. Joe is decided to hand back the ticket.

March 1957

Mark and Ally on Match Day

And it's close, tight, together!
Never back we will go!
Cos we'll always be playing,
Innnnn the front row!

Mark Rutherford smiles at these sentiments, roared so lustily by his teammates as they wait in light rain by the portico at the top of their school's winding driveway. But he doesn't join in. To him, the singing speaks less of exuberance than jangling nerves before the big game: a common ailment, but one he believes his peers prefer to mask.

Mark is not so nervous. He feels fairly sure the game is going to go well – for himself, at any rate. Rugby is a team sport, and Mark will say he is all for the collective spirit; yet in his heart he feels that nothing else in life is quite so sweet as an individual style. He knows he can get things done by a solo stroke of flair while others bound to a group might toil to no end. He is confident of what he can do if he is given the ball and can stay on his feet. *Give me a chance and I will score.* The rest, he believes, is not in his hands so much as in the engineering bulk of those big scrumming forwards beside him, boisterously blaring their song – though slipping down now to a whisper for the rude bit.

Ref cannot stop us, we don't give a fuck!
Cuz we are the boys for a fast forward ruck!

They await a minibus to come and carry them to the Schools Cup semi-final, Kilmuir against Strathairn. A game at Murrayfield is the

26

prize for victory. Their holdalls are at their feet, stuffed with kit and boots and embrocation oils.

Other pupils passing by wear looks of envy and awe. Kilmuir has a fever for rugby, and the first fifteen are gods of a sort. It has occurred to Mark that when you're the pupil of an Edinburgh private school built like a French Gothic palace, on the verdant fringe of the city and yet a world apart, you could easily get some lofty ideas about yourself.

Mark unfurls and peruses his copy of the *Scotsman*, curious to read about the reopening of the Suez Canal, an affair that he hopes might somehow prove as harmful to the new Tory Prime Minister as it was to his fallen predecessor.

'Rutherford!' blares big Ed 'Reeker' McCreadie. 'Why you reading that boring shite, you buftie bastard?'

'Good sports page,' Mark bats back. Yes, his peers prefer the *Record* and the *Express*, which they read back to front, but he reckons it good for folk to get the news, in whatever form. He's aware the lads accuse him of excess brains. Already he suspects he is a writer – but he keeps that to himself. It's just a good job he is six feet tall and rangy; a bloody good job, moreover, that he is 'class' on a rugby pitch.

'Eh! It's Ally the Cat!'

Better news from Reeker. Mark's best pal has sloped into view, hailed by the first fifteen. Here comes Ally Drummond, smiling wryly from under his floppy crow-black fringe, his laconic, loose-jointed posture at an ironic angle to everyone else. He's 'The Cat' because he's sly, because he's cute. But Ally is proven 'class' just like Mark: so suave that he gets parts in the school musicals even though he can't sing – they just let him talk his way through the songs.

Mark steps toward Ally's side but Reeker gets there first, seizing the new arrival by both shoulders.

'Ally! We're gonna *fuck 'em up*, those Strathairn *cunts*!'

In the gentlest way possible Ally gets Reeker's hands off him and turns to address the wider group. 'Thank you, Reeker. Is that perchance a quote from Shakespeare?'

Ally gets the hoots he expected, with a line Mark wouldn't have risked. This is how you get to be everyone's friend and role model: with a light touch. That, and being a dependable hooker at the sharp end of Schools Cup season.

Now Ally inclines to Mark, sotto voce. 'How we suffer, tovarich, locked up with these savages . . .'

Such is their bond. Housemates from the start at Kilmuir; both A-students, and neither has yet been beaten. Indeed, as a pair they have had invites to tea in the thick-carpeted study of their housemaster, Dr Magarshack, the talk chiefly of rugby, since old Magarshack played once – only once, but once! – on the wing for Scotland.

They have boarded other buses to inter-school debating heats, there to argue about nuclear weapons or Scottish independence. Ally is a Unionist and Mark is Labour, but Ally voted loyally for his mate when Mark stood in the school mock election of 1955 – even as other boys catcalled Mark for a 'dirty commie'. That, in Mark's eyes, is Ally all over: the dependable ally with whom one can scorn the fools and the bores. One such, as Mark sees it, is team captain Gordon Fyfe, now clapping them aboard the minibus one by one, with an earnest shake of the shoulder as each goes past. 'Ready, men! Courage, Davie! Courage, Alastair! Mark, courage!'

'Such a numpty,' says Mark to Ally once they have seats together on the cold vinyl.

'The skipper? Let him have his way. He means well.'

Mark recalls that Ally has been a guest for dinner at the Fyfe house, where the father works in finance and has something to do with oil and gas in Texas, the glamour of which Mark reluctantly concedes, having lately seen – and been mesmerised by – the late James Dean being compellingly moody in the movie *Giant*. Mark suspects that Ally – son of a Lanarkshire tailor who has inherited little by that beyond a fondness for smart waistcoats – has his head a little turned by conspicuous wealth and privilege. Mark, son of an insurance seller, admitted to Kilmuir by scholarship exam, prefers to see himself as instinctively suspicious of the rich folk.

'Gordon's keen but he makes *us* keen.' Ally is still musing. 'Makes us want to fight on the pitch. It's leadership, tovarich. Don't knock it.' The wry smile resurfaces. 'Don't knock the rock.'

'I'm too tired to rock, Ally.'

That is nearly the last of the banter: the mood on the bus has turned steadily quiet and focused. There is no general certainty of success today against Strathairn. And in the silence Mark, too, begins to feel a mite more trepidation.

The contest does not start off as Mark had hoped, played in cold, persistent drizzle with the turf squelching underfoot, and the red-faced hectoring crowd very much behind Strathairn. Not uncommon conditions, but Mark feels them especially, given the size of the opposition – their massed weight and thoroughgoing fierceness. The tackles are crunching, and even when Mark makes his runs he feels the claggy mud clinging and sucking on his boots. Worse, the Strathairn forwards have no little skill: a tidiness to their heeling, a crispness to their distribution, which is bloody annoying in such a horde of obnoxious big bastards.

As for Kilmuir – their passing lacks fluidity, their running dogged but not penetrative. Mark can see his teammates as bedraggled as him, in their mud-soaked magenta hoops. Even Ally looks unusually breathless and anxious, like a lieutenant-colonel concerned for his troops in a land assault gone ragged.

'*Look to the creative players, Kilmuir!*' cries Dr Magarshack from touch. But Mark keeps finding his way impeded, all through a wearying half at the fag-end of which only a late penalty kicked by Fyfe keeps Kilmuir respectably in the game, seven points behind.

In the half-time huddle Fyfe seems incensed, demanding of greater efforts. Mark falls to moody private thoughts drawn from his classical studies, of Greeks striving without end to roll boulders up the sides of mountains.

Then Fyfe grabs his shirt collar, hard, taking some skin: 'Rutherford, do you *want* to win? Are you bloody well *bothered*?'

'Christ, yes, Gordon . . .'

'Then stop fucking about on that wing!'

Four minutes into the second half Strathairn score their third try; Kilmuir's deficit is now twelve. Three minutes later delivers Mark the moment for which he has hankered all afternoon, and hotly so since Fyfe humiliated him. From the scrum a sequence of clean passes puts the ball into his grasp, and he feints, then springs forward such as to leave his opposite number grasping air.

Now Mark pelts full-pace for the corner-flag, blood beating in his ears above the howling crowd. Strathairn's number eight is coming straight at him, another big bastard, bent on blocking and suppressing. But he's only a brute: Mark is sure he is defter and smarter, and Mark has a plan that has worked before and will work again with this sort of a brute – yes, he is going to use his boot and he will chip that number eight, chip the ball clean over his head and run round to collect on the other side, a touch of Rutherford class to get Kilmuir right back in the game, just as soon as he crosses the line. It's all in the execution, not revealing intent too fast – and now Mark executes.

Even as the ball leaves his boot he sees his error, his debacle materialising before him: that number eight's salmon-like leap and fingertip-deflection of the ball that then falls back into his grasp – a remarkable feat of anticipation and agility, totally uncalled for in the circumstances.

Mark lurches as if to recover, but already the ball is being recycled and Strathairn are hurtling down to the Kilmuir end. As their number eight surges over the try-line on his belly, Mark is ten yards back and can do nothing but curse at the sky. In his heart, he knows, he should be hanging his head.

Two minutes after the restart Mark is gored again to hear his name called, and he jogs for touch, substituted from the game that Kilmuir will now try and fail to salvage. At the final whistle Mark watches Ally exchange some words with Fyfe, at which Fyfe nods and claps his shoulder. In the changing room Fyfe slams the door viciously then tears off his filthy shirt. Mark has long marvelled at how startlingly hirsute is Fyfe all over his body.

'Listen, you lot. When you're beaten fair, it's one thing. When you're beaten by your own mistakes it's quite another.'

Mark has his head in his hands but he knows Fyfe is standing directly over him.

'Some of you know you put in a shift. Others should reflect on their failings.'

The bus back to school is largely silent. There will be no celebratory pints tonight, no bantering dares to drink bitter beer out of Reeker's boot.

'C'mon, no use lying there moping,' says Ally to Mark from the dormitory door. 'Let's bunk off. I'm buying at Larkin's, if you put the coins in the bloody jukebox.'

At Larkin's Café Ally does indeed stand a couple of Coca-Colas, and for the laugh Mark selects 'Don't Knock the Rock' on the Rockola. Its toe-tapping restlessness puts a bit of spirit back into him. Still, Ally can see his struggle to raise a smile.

'I know, tovarich. We have had disappointments to contend against.'

He lifts Mark's glass and slips from his blazer a silver flask which he very deftly uncaps so as to tip a ginger drop of hard stuff into the fizzy cola, before repeating the trick for himself.

'If we're going to the devil let's go in style. I know you appreciate the finer things. And I'm sorry you took that lashing off the skipper, there was no call for it.'

31

'Was that leadership, too?'

'The skipper . . .' Ally slumps back in their booth, shaking his head. 'He means well, loves the team . . . But there's something not right about him. He thinks everything here is life or death. I bet you, he'll get to fifty and still be asking everyone he meets what bloody school they went to.'

'I did mess it up today, but.' Mark sighs.

'On a different day, another inch and who knows? You're still a bloody classy footballer.'

'Thanks, Ally. So are you.'

'Ach.' Ally waves him away. 'You've an awful lot going for you, Mark. And the life you're going to have, it's not going to be rugger, is it?'

'I think we've seen that . . .'

'No, you and me, tovarich, we are natural aristocrats, don't you think? Where we excel is using our minds, and speaking them, too, so people listen. That will reap its rewards. I'm sure of it. That's why our *puir wee faithers* sent us into this bloody exile from the rest of Scotland. Because we are going to do well.' He raps the Formica table for emphasis.

Amid the chrome and plastic decor of Larkin's, among so many sullen lads with duck's-arse haircuts, Mark is not much feeling marked out for glory. 'I'm a bit less sure than yourself about that, Al.'

'Trust me. You will do things, Mark. As a writer, of some kind. Getting ideas across, to thinking people. That is you. I'll bet you that right now. Fuck the Strathairn first fifteen.'

Mark, somewhat abashed, has certainly begun to feel better. 'Thanks, Al. I wish I could say all the great things I think you'll do . . .' Mark is, in fact, more or less certain that his pal will take some straightlaced job that earns him good money; but it seems a little banal to reply as much in this heightened moment.

'Dinnae fret.' Ally winks and lifts his whisky-and-Coke. 'Whatever I do, I will surprise you.'

Mark doesn't believe that for a second, but he will happily drink to it – in the spirit of friendship, feeling sure he will always want to be by this man's side somehow, whatever goes down.

July 1959
Deeper Water

Aaron Strang waits for his ride, feeling that with each passing minute he cuts a yet more forlorn figure. He sits tensely, backside cold, at the top of the stone steps to the granite obelisk on the village green that is the gateway in and out of Tarnwick village. His view is that Robbie is pushing his luck; perhaps even standing him up.

He suspects it could have something to do with Robbie's latest girl, Mae Mackay. Lately she and he have been very invested in their private time, rather to the detriment of the long-standing Robbie-and-Aaron axis.

And the pair of them are due at the lifeboat station in Inverness in barely more than an hour, and a forty-mile drive is before them, followed immediately by an examination that won't wait on them to present themselves. Pass today, sure, and their open water diving certificates are in the bag. But that's enough of a challenge to be fretting over – the depth, the correct use of air, the business of resurfacing by stages – without a whole other fuss about getting there.

Aaron shudders: not just from the stony cold under him, but this unnerving site, the one where Billy Gow died. The obelisk has been a doomy place in local lore since the night of the accident the year before, when the Reverend's son Torrance McVey – worse for drink, some said – had tried with his mate Billy to scale the monument's eighty feet by handholds and footholds. In the end, firemen came out to pick Torrance off the barred window to which he clung; but Billy had already slipped, fallen and fractured his skull, fatally. Glancing up now at that stone elevation, that same barred window, Aaron tries to imagine whatever possessed McVey to risk the ascent; and what made poor Billy follow.

34

Resisting the dark thoughts, Aaron begins to mutter to himself – trying out what excuse for a no-show that he could beg his father to offer to the head of the sub-aqua school. Then he hears the fast-approaching rumble behind him. And then Robbie is screeching to a halt at the wheel of his father's Ford Woodie. Aaron snatches up his bag and makes for the passenger side.

'Sorry, Aaron, honest. It's Mae. You know what's she like.'

Rattling down the Inverness Road on a brightening morning Aaron starts to feel his mood lifting. Robbie is flooring the pedal as if to redeem his previous tardiness, and the turn-off to Invergordon brings to their left a lovely vantage on the waters of the Firth, broad and placid, glimmering silver.

'You feeling okay about today?' Aaron ventures, sensing that Robbie is a mite too fixated on the speedometer.

'No bother. You?'

'Can't wait.'

Aaron supposes the bigger share of nerves today is his. They have progressed their diving together in step, each getting hold of vintage twin-bottled cylinders, learning open-circuit and the proper use of the demand regulator. They have ventured ever deeper, thirty metres then forty, and have practised the sharing of air and the slow-kicking return to the surface. Throughout, Robbie has remained the superior diver.

It's Aaron, though, who really covets the qualification on offer today: a curriculum vitae item, for the betterment of his ambitions. While Robbie stares at the road ahead, Aaron wonders if this trip is really just for his sake.

Come September he will be at Aberdeen University to read geology, while Robbie will be helping his father to assess the testicles of rams and the bellies of ewes, tupping season close at hand. So a separation is coming; though they have hatched a cheery plan that Robbie might drive Aaron down to Aberdeen, for a gander at the city and to help him settle. Mulling it now, Aaron worries that this excursion might force an issue that, perhaps, worries him more than his friend: namely, what Robbie intends to do with his life – something to which Aaron really wishes Robbie might give some harder thinking. His friend's reserves of physical energy and ability to rouse himself to action are almost exhausting to Aaron. If only he had anything like the same impetus in his mind! And yet, Aaron knows well, there are things going on in Robbie's hollow-cheeked head to which he has no access.

'So, are you . . . things okay, then? With Mae?'

'Mae? Aye. Aw, aye . . . It'd be a sight easier if she'd see sense sometimes, but . . .' Robbie emits a strangely mirthless laugh.

'About what?'

Robbie gestures as to say it's neither here nor there. 'We've just had a spat on a thing. We'll figure it out.'

Aaron drops it, sits back: unsettled by what this 'spat' might be, but well aware that the course of romance is not a subject on which he could pass even the most cursory exam.

Instead, after a while, he remarks: 'The obelisk, it gave me the willies a bit. Got me thinking of Billy and Torry.'

Robbie nods. 'Wonder where Torry's at now, poor critter.'

'My dad's said similar. "He'd never take a lesson, that one, but he's had no end of a lesson now" . . .'

They share in a commiserating grunt, and Aaron feels a familiar companionable silence settle over them both in the contemplation of one clearly far worse off than themselves. It has never been clear to Aaron or anyone whether Torry fled Tarnwick of his own accord after the accident, or whether his father expelled him. But even Aaron had heard the rumours before of some dalliance between Torry and the much-coveted Marilyn Gallagher. And since the accident Marilyn has seemed to be in purdah of sorts, imposed by her parents – out of sight and, seemingly, out of Robbie's mind, which Aaron rated a handy thing, at least until that Mae came along.

—

By the time Robbie parks outside the lifeboat station they have only five or so minutes to present themselves; but Robbie wants a cigarette, and Aaron wants to be a pal, not a nag. So they both stand leaning on the Ford, and Aaron watches Robbie smoke.

'You well set for Aberdeen, then?' Robbie taps ash.

'Reckon so.'

'That's the thing for you, eh? The geology?'

C'mon, thinks Aaron even as he smiles and nods. He has told Robbie as much of his ambitions as he's told anyone; but maybe that has not amounted to so many words. It's true, moreover, that Aaron's deeper forages into 'interesting rocks' have been solo; like last summer's trek to Siccar Point on the Berwickshire coast, so that Aaron could observe the rocky promontory known as Hutton's Unconformity, its piecrust of rusty sandstone atop bony ribs of greywacke. Likewise, his pilgrimage to the foreshore at Eathie Haven on the Moray Firth, the rocks formed during what Aaron now assuredly knows to be the Kimmeridgian period of the Late Jurassic.

None of the appeal of this can he summon into words for his friend. Still, Robbie is studying him over the red tip of his Woodbine.

'Why, but? What d'you see in them rocks?'

'Well, I mean . . . it's the history of the world, Robbie. Before we were in it, right? For millions of years. It does my head in sometimes, I swear . . .'

Aaron could add that he has found a passion that seems to reward the patient excavation of certain truths that feel inarguable; or that human life often feels awfully limited to him next to the enormities ingrained in rock and stone. But with Robbie he reckons such high-flown stuff is for the birds.

So he delves into the pocket of his corduroys and brings out a trilobite fossil he has rather treasured for luck – found at Ardwell Bay, borne home and identified by its blackened weathering, then

37

chipped and finicked away with his penknife's smallest blade, so as to reveal the ribbed, insectoid shape now bristling in his palm.

'This, see? I look at this. Millions of years old, right? And it makes me think.'

Robbie peers, then grins. 'That's great. Funny. The wee critter.'

'This might not even be the critter. Just the shell it left behind. The exoskeleton?'

'That's mad, that. That's dead good.'

Aaron can believe he and Robbie are feeling the same charm, even if the notion of shedding an outer shell is maybe more appealing to him.

'Thanks for doing this, Robbie.'

'The dive? Eh, I'm all for it.'

'No, but driving us and all. Listen, when we go to Aberdeen I'm in the chair, I'm treating, okay?'

Robbie only stares at his boots for a moment, then flicks his Woodbine down to the gravel and grinds it underfoot.

'Aaron, listen. I'll not be going with. To Aberdeen? I know it'd be a good rake and all. But there's things I'm gunna have to take care of. Like this bit of trouble with Mae, y'know? So I jist don't think I can. Sorry, pal.'

'It's fine, Robbie, I understand.' Aaron absorbs the blow; he had seen it coming. But that word 'trouble' is like a scratch on his mind. He has heard it said of young couples – whispered, rather, as a rumour – in a case or two where a certain girl had to go away for a while.

'We'd best be getting in now, eh?' Robbie gestures, handing back the fossil.

'Keep it,' Aaron hears himself say.

'Aw naw, Aaron, I couldnae.'

'Go on. When I'm off doing my mad thing in Aberdeen you can look at it and have the laugh thinking of me and my bloody rocks . . .'

Robbie shakes his head, but then closes his fist on the fossil. 'That's brilliant of you, man. Thanks. I should given you something and all.' And Aaron realises that the headshaking was just self-reproach.

The diving instructor is named McPherson, a big Lanarkshire tough nut in a black tracksuit. He gets the candidates lined up on the quay, air cylinders at their feet, and he paces back and forth before them, hands clasped at his back. After a minute or two of McPherson's havering Aaron begins to feel like he has joined the army.

'I want to see fit men out there, men who are focused, who respect the water and get in it like they mean business, you hear? Disnae matter what you say you can do, or anyone else has telt me. I need to see it in ye's if ye's are to get past me.'

Aaron is reluctant to steal a look at Robbie's face but trusts his pal is also finding this ridiculous.

'This is no' a competition between you or any other guy. Just you and the water. And in the water you are responsible for yourself – how you manage your air, and the pressures on your bodies. Right? Your decisions are your own – aye, and your mistakes, too. If you make a mistake, the test is how you manage it. What you don't do is panic like a goat.'

Now Aaron steals that look. But Robbie looks perturbed, head elsewhere. Worry resurfaces in Aaron, for that 'trouble' his pal might be managing. It's worry of a sort he hasn't had since Robbie quit mooning over Marilyn Gallagher.

'What did I just say, pal?'

Too late, Aaron realises that Mr McPherson is right in front of him, breathing a sausage-meat odour right into his face.

'Aye, you, skinnymalink.'

'Sir, you were talking about air valves, about not wasting air . . .'

'Ach!' McPherson grimaces. 'Don't you be wasting my air, son.'

They ride the boat out from the dock and, once it is anchored, the candidates take their turns to plunge into the Firth from a short ladder, thence to kick out and head deeper into the dark waters.

As Aaron descends from the boat – following Robbie, feeling the metal rungs hard under his flippers – he is newly uncomfortable. He has ceased to feel up for this today. He will just have to get through it.

Then he is down in the blue, girding his concentration, observing his own gas coming out in bubbles while keeping an eye on Robbie's bubbles below, lacing past his mask as the two of them move down the shot-line.

But, deeper still, Aaron is feeling none of the old release: he is not transported. Wanting the day already done with, he also cannot shake off the encumbrance of the thoughts that have weighed on his mind over the preceding hours.

They are nearing maximum depth when Aaron has the strangest creeping feeling that his air supply isn't flowing quite as it should – that it is straining and thinning, somehow. But that just cannot be. Too soon, surely, to encounter such trouble.

Then he hears a click, like a closure, behind his head. His mouth-piece tightens round his face.

Dry tank.

Cold dread. *Don't panic.*

He fumbles for his equaliser valve. No air.

Now the inner voice is blaring at full volume: *Emergency! Come up!*

Has the tank failed? Has *he* failed? Frantic, he asks himself how deep, how wasteful were his intakes during descent, when his head was elsewhere? And instantly he knows.

Whatever he was told and half learned about sharing a mate's tank: absolutely no time for that. Everything in his body tells him *Go, surface, breathe!*

His floundering has alerted Robbie, and Robbie in a flash unclips him from the buddy line. Now Robbie is gesturing, making shapes with his body that Aaron sees as a dumbshow, meant to instruct. But Aaron has started to thrash upward, for the surface, already feeling a heaviness within. A roaring noise is blasting through his mask. He can taste his own dread.

In the frenzy above and around him he realises: *Must slow down. Can't be faster than the bubbles.*

But now his head is above water, he can see the team boat through the mask's blear, and he swims for it, hearing harsh cries.

Big arms haul him up over the side, and he feels stiff and sick, a sensation in his chest like a fracture. He needs very badly to lie down on the deck of the boat, and those hands lower him there. In the commotion he knows he must look a broken thing, a pitiable creature. Failure. How bad will this be?

The loudest voice over his supine figure is McPherson. 'Aw damn it, he's for the Grampian, he'll need the oxygen chamber, *goddamn it to hell!*'

Now at McPherson's back Aaron can see that Robbie, too, has emerged dripping onto the deck. McPherson is pacing over him again.

'You're an *idiot*, son. You endangered yourself *and* your pal here.'

Then, stupefyingly, Robbie's voice, no less irate: 'Will ye belt up, man? He coulda died!'

'*Eh!* Don't you be speaking to me like that, son! Ever!'

Aaron believes he could be hallucinating from where he lies: the pure black umbrage on McPherson, as he advances on Robbie with a prodding finger that looks like a fist, and then seizes Robbie by the collar of his wetsuit. But it is surpassingly strange to see Robbie throw off that grasp, and shove McPherson so hard that the great bulk topples back onto the wet deck – nearly squashing Aaron. Now there are roars, more pushing, pandemonium. But Aaron – even prostrate, frightened, in pain – can feel something else in his chest, more extraordinary still, because of what his best and only friend has just gone and done for him.

July 1959
Launch of the Andrew Killday

'No word from the heiress, Joseph?' Andrew enquires, not unpleasantly, but with a certain chide about it. In his burgundy office chair the patriarch appears restless.

'I'm not expecting word.' Joe is careful to smile, to project calm.

'I see. You expect her to walk through that door, heedless of the time . . .'

Joe is trying to keep his eye off the office clock above the fireplace, even while the eyes of his gathered family seem rather fixedly on him. It is 8.17 a.m., and the ceremony set for 10. The Killday clan are smartened and ready. Today even Ma has visited the office, sitting in her best hat and coat, hands in her lap, sipping tea with Angela at her side.

Belinda Morland, though, is coming to them overnight from Aix-en-Provence, where her family have a chateau and from which she travels as lightly as she moves between two languages. Travelling today, moreover, to be at Joe's side and perform the duty of launch mistress on this fine occasion – the ceremonial launch from Devane's Shipyard of a new diesel-powered steel trawler, to be christened the *Andrew Killday*.

Joe could feel easier, for sure. But the wait will be worth it to see Belinda's cherry-red smile, to hear the witty thing she will say whenever she does present herself – to observe the charm she will surely exert on the crotchety Killday men while she is adorning Joe's arm.

'This woman of yours, brother . . .' Garth shakes his head as he crafts a roll-up. 'You'd wonder where she learned her manners. She needs to know who's in charge.'

42

Garth is now twenty-one but sometimes seems twice that in his demeanour: whiskery and sea-dog-like as his da, but his delivery more of a goading drawl, his distressed hat and tweed a bit more rakish.

Joe today has donned a sports coat, narrow slacks and penny loafers, and this has just about passed Andrew's approval. Not that Joe is bothered. Studying economics at Edinburgh University has led him to endorse Adam Smith's idea that a man has 'natural liberty' to develop his own interests so long as others are not molested. Joe wants only to be his own man – and that his family recognise as much, without having to make an awful fuss about it.

The phone rings, everyone jumps.

Andrew's secretary Sheila, as dressy as any today, lifts the receiver and gives it her finest Morningside. 'Good day, Killday Fishing Company . . . ?'

But it's just the company's head fish salesman, Malky, phoning in the news from the harbour market.

'Does this young woman know what's expected of her?' queries Ma to no one over the lip of her teacup. As often, Joe is a mite irked by his mother's mimsy ways. By custom she might have been called on to perform the ceremonial smashing of champagne against the bow of the new vessel. But Joe had extended the invitation to Belinda even though it was not strictly in his gift; and then seemed to see a certain pride in his father at the thought of the youngest Killday squiring the daughter of the boss of Scotland's leading luxury cruise operator. It bothers Joe a little that he perhaps overvalues the charm of status; and yet he knows that Andrew, for all the grizzling, is not immune to it either.

Now, though, as the clock moves inexorably, Joe does grant that Belinda's timekeeping is a problem.

He met her at the university's Cosmopolitan Club: a regular Sunday night in an upstairs room where students might hear an invited speaker on a burning issue: the fallout from the Léopoldville riots, say, or the usefulness of the CND's Aldermaston March.

From the start Joe liked best to hear the carefully expressed, most discerning contributions of Belinda; while admiring also her lithe figure and dark bob, the pear-freshness of her scent and the chic of her evening outfits – a dress of grey lace crochet, a twinset and skirt of dark blue velvet.

Joe had asserted himself in the customary squiring of Belinda back to the door of her apartment below Calton Hill. And with him, he felt sure, her mood was different than with others. At that door he tended to look very directly into her eyes, but she didn't turn away, meeting his gaze and smiling her cherry smile. He worried at times that she glanced too often in the direction of Charlie Barrowclough, the son of a major-general; but then Charlie paid Belinda no notice in return, preferring to sound off about the size of his family's estate outside Winchester.

So Joe had taken Belinda to the Christmas dance and given her a rose that she tucked gaily behind her ear. After the Club's Easter conference on The Global State of Food and Agriculture – at which Joe spoke assuredly about fisheries – they had climbed Arthur's Seat to greet the dawn like collegiate druids. Carrying her shoes, he picked his moment to ask her if she might do the honours at the launch of the *Andrew Killday*. She had grinned and exclaimed that it would be 'a lark'. He had reminded her of the duty, more than once, through the summer term just gone.

At 8.57 a.m. the silence is broken again by the ding of the bell at the street-level door. Garth rises from his chair, but Joe is faster.

He opens the door to the telegraph boy from the Post Office, redheaded and red-faced. Joe accepts the buff envelope, knowing it to be of a dreaded kind at times. Then he sees this telegram is addressed to him, not to Andrew. He rips at it to get at the printed message stuck onto the slip with gummed tape.

44

DEAR JOSEPH MOST DREADFULLY SORRY COMMA
PLEASE FORGIVE ME COMMA BUT SLEEPER TRAIN
FROM LONDON CANCELLED STOP I AM STUCK
EXCLAMATION MARK DEARLY HOPE YOU CAN
REPLACE ME AND THAT FAMILY DAY IS NOT
SPOILED STOP YOUR UTTERLY DISGRACED AND
VERY CONTRITE FRIEND COMMA BELINDA

An awful pang in his chest, the force of revelation: she must have had entirely other things on her mind of late, in the measure of which the business of smashing a bottle on a trawler boat must have seemed a meagre lot. For a moment he can't quite move, can't think how he will face his family and deliver the news.

At length, once he has mumbled through it, Andrew only shakes his head.

'My Bryony will break the bottle, no bother,' offers Garth.

'So this queen's not coming?' Ma tuts.

'Naw, Ma.' Garth chuckles. 'You can have the bouquet.'

They all stand now to leave in some haste. To business, spilt milk and all that. Unseen, Joe risks another read of the telegram to see if there is possibly any part of it that he has failed to compute. All he observes anew is that the sending office stamp is Winchester.

Garth's girlfriend Bryony – about whom there is no nonsense – is very happy to deputise as the bottle-breaking belle. She looks grand in her flowery frock, and the easy-grinning manner in which she and Garth incline to one another – his whispers in her ear, her throaty laughter – seems to repair the spirits of the day, while causing Joe a lancing, envious pain.

At Devane's Shipyard the main party proceed up a gangway to the scaffolded ceremonial platform, while the yard's labourers mill around below where the *Andrew Killday* rests on the slope of a well-greased launch way, lashed by rope to wooden trigger poles at either side of its hull. It is, Joe grants, a smart-looking vessel, with its jaunty lantern wheelhouse and striped funnel: a change from the veteran rust of those old survivor ships in which the company (even he) has gone to sea for years.

He is nudged by Andrew. 'It's a cut above, is it not, son? All change for the modern world. I'd bet you'd feel a bitty more comfort aboard this 'un.'

Joe winces inwardly to be reminded of his younger self, that imposter. 'You'll maybe miss the old, Da? You'd rather be aboard the *Reaper*?'

Andrew appears to weigh this seriously. 'Well, in business, Joseph, always, you make change at the point of a sword. But, if it turns out for the better then you tell everyone change was what you wanted all along . . .' Andrew taps at his nose, then pats Joe's arm as to say it is time to look alive.

Gay flags are a-flutter and there are bouquets for all the ladies, albeit one too many, the handing-out performed by a bashful Devane apprentice and observed by newspaper photographers.

Looking out at the onlookers, smiling fixedly, Joe is surprised to spot two faces he has not seen in some years – Andrew's older brother Allan and his wife Grace. Amid the gaiety, though, they seem dowdily incongruous – two stooped figures, Darby and Joan, sore-eyed and grey-clad. Joe catches his father's eye to lead it toward where the couple stand; but Andrew merely nods.

Once the photographing is done, it is Walter, finally, who lays a light hand on Allan's shoulder to coax him forward. 'Came just to pay my respects, Andrew . . .' The handshake between the brothers has, to Joe's eye, a rather stiff, engineered look.

The naming ceremony proper is augured by a piper who plays 'Leaving Port Askaig', and then Andrew addresses the throng.

'Our family has been in the fishing business since 1893. In that time many a vessel has been called into service. We've made use of some badly beaten old things, barely fit for purpose. But, I'll say no more of myself.'

The audience gives Andrew the appropriate ripple.

'Today my company has done me the honour of naming our new ship the *Andrew Killday* – built to the best modern specifications by the best of craftsmen here at Devane. It leaves today in the charge of our trusted skipper John Cutter. So I call upon our launch mistress, Miss Bryony McIntyre, to perform the usual honours.'

And yet, Bryony is still made to listen and nod politely a while longer as Andrew mutters some instruction in her ear while holding on to her, as if to direct her hands in the grip and release of the cradle holding the champagne bottle. Finally he steps aside, and Bryony grins.

'Hullo, everyone! And thank you, Mr Killday. I know this ship bears his name, and rightly so. Though I'm told by Garth that the seamen always think of a ship as a woman!'

This doesn't get quite the reception Joe feels that it merits. Again it strikes him wistfully that his brother has done well.

'Anyhow! I name this ship the *Andrew Killday*, may God bless her and all who sail in her.'

Bryony swings the bottle and it connects with a plump, lathery smash, to cheers from all on the platform and yard workers below. Instantly the ropes to the trigger poles are severed, and those poles hastily shifted aside. The smart steel bulk of the *Andrew Killday* begins to move forward in a stately manner under its own weight, taking with it great mounds of drag-chain attached to the hull, now drawn down the slip, screeching all the way. In the ship's wake elements of the crowd are already moseying to catch a better view of the vessel afloat. It accelerates now and hits the harbour water to louder approval.

Joe recognises all the pride and satisfaction on display; but he simply cannot share it, and he doesn't wish to linger. Soon he is striding back down the quay, thinking he will stop on Market Street for a dram – a drop of hard medicine.

Noticing two stooped and shuffling figures ahead of him, he realises he was not even the first to flee the scene. It is Uncle Allan and Grace, Allan availing of a walking stick while also supporting his wife. Momentarily Joe wonders if it would be a disloyal thing to acknowledge Allan, given the curious oddness of earlier? Then he decides he doesn't care.

'Good day to you, Uncle Allan. Grace.'

Joe strides onward, even as he hears Allan calling to his back.

'You'll be having no more of this business then, Joe?'

'It's not my intention, Uncle.'

On Market Street, passing the shadowy window of an insurer's office, Joe catches sight of his reflection and doesn't like it one bit. Evidently, going away to university, whatever he imagined, has not changed him so much: he remains the indistinct youngest male of the fishing Killdays. Today has been, in essence, a painful public puncture of private hopes. How could he have read a situation so wrong? After such care in his approaches to Belinda, he had ventured something substantive, only to see it taken terribly lightly. That feels now like a heavier judgement upon him, and he can't bear the thought it should prove final.

November 1959
The Ministry of Power

A dirty dog of a night. Rain lashes the window as if some fury were flinging it by the bucketload, such that it courses down the pane like streams in the urinal stall.

'Fair is foul and foul is fair,' mutters the Minister For Power to his own smeary reflection in the glass. He is not much of a one for the theatre, but his wife surely is – so many bloody evenings spent in the upper circle, rigidly timed, with dress code. And tonight there are tickets booked for another bloody thing. He wishes to leave the office; and yet he does not. Work remains to be done, and home feels a distant project, as if separated from him by sea, given the hour and this deluge.

His party are newly returned to office, the Suez debacle safely in the rear-view. Here he stands at the centre of power. And still, he feels himself to be somehow on the subs' bench, the game passing him by. *Nothing I do is directive*, he thinks. Small mercy, at least, to have a PM who, however badly winged in the war, can carry himself erect – unlike Winston, unlike Eden, at their poor bloody ends.

And yet, the Minister feels a malaise around this government, its mandate too much dependent on the usual disorder of the other lot. It breeds the sense of running a business in decline. He has grown accustomed to putting in late shifts of ministerial scheming, just so that the civil service doesn't just bloody do all the scheming instead, while he's not looking, safe in the knowledge that the Minister will take the blame for any major miscalculations of theirs.

He awaits the day's final round of the Ministry tea-trolley. In truth, he is also thinking quite fixedly about the whisky bottle in the cabinet, but that is *verboten* when there are still people to see. He would also like very much to have a solid session on the porcelain throne, with the evening paper and a cigarette. But the Ministry lavatories appear to be out of order, and no bloody plumber has yet attended; thus even that low-level gratification is deferred.

His private secretary, Welland, appears at the doorway, neat and tidy as ever, with the look of a solemn bespectacled cherub.

'Mr Kynaston is coming up to see you from Petroleum, sir.'

'And what is troubling Mr Kynaston?'

'The North Sea, sir. Those enquiries we've had about license to explore for oil?'

'Oh God yes . . .'

Welland has some files to set down upon the ministerial desk, but first he produces a white handkerchief to rub briskly at what the Minister now sees are some crumbs and spit-spots from an earlier tea and biscuits. Welland is quite a one for a good appearance; the Minister has deduced that he is of the sort who went with other chaps at school and enjoyed the pursuit sufficiently to carry it on in spite of its many difficulties. The Minister, his own sap now pretty well spent, has a certain respect for his adjutant's devotions.

Welland requests that they first, if briefly, address the latest rumours and worries about the miners going out on strike.

'Well, nothing surprises me, Welland. But the ingratitude is galling. We've protected coal for bloody years, at great cost. We kept out the American coal, kept out the Russian oil . . . What we cannot do is wave a hand and endorse a glut of production here. Will these people ever understand?'

'You say ingratitude, sir. But I daresay it's not always easy to accept a favour – if it feels like charity, a handout, as it were, only postponing the problem for tomorrow.'

The Minister does not appreciate his secretary's irenic sentiments. 'These are wicked issues, Welland, the kind where no one solution is obvious. We keep trying the same things we tried before, and surprisingly they never bloody work. Do we ever have an actually new idea in this place? Or the stomach to do something about it?'

The Minister knows he has no such ideas of his own to offer – but, by God, he could endorse such a thing if he ever caught sight of it!

'Sir, perhaps then we might anticipate the matter on which Mr Kynaston wishes to speak?' Welland slides the box-cut folder into a precise spot in front of the Minister. 'It is occasioned by this recent discovery of gas in the north-eastern Netherlands?'

'I'm aware of the speculation, Welland. Royal Dutch Shell are enquiring, yes? Wanting a permit to look if there's oil out under our sea at the same longitude?'

Welland nods. 'They have identified an area of sixteen thousand square miles.'

'My God, not much, eh? Well, of course they can't have it. We don't know enough for ourselves yet. Hard not to suppose there won't be more claims to consider in due course.'

'Quite, sir.'

'So we must first weigh up our own interest.' The Minister slumps back in his chair. 'The North Sea, though. My Christ. Shell must have a bold notion of pouring a great deal of money down a hole. If you found oil that far down, by what bloody miracle would you get it out? The Yanks have been dipping their beaks here since the Great War and they've never found a drop worth the investment. No, unless they put down a big wager on this I won't believe it's serious.'

The Minister is surprised to find himself more expansive than he had been feeling. Welland, stock still and unblinking, seems to await an amen.

'But, of course, Kynaston knows all of this – he was a proper geologist, he's had postings in Washington, he knows any number of those Texan oil boys.'

'I believe Mr Kynaston is outside, sir.'

'Let's be having him then.'

Kynaston enters and the Minister prepares to pay close attention to the top civil servant in Petroleum. His chin is strong and prominent, his mouth a stern line, his hair swept back and across as if by one inarguable stroke of a brush. The Minister knows him to have served honourably in North Africa; but Kynaston's manner does tend to make lesser types flinch.

'So, what's your opinion of this Shell request, Kynaston?'

'Minister, I am not at all surprised they express an interest. From what I understand, the geological structures of their Groningen gas field share striking similarities with what we think we know of the Southern North Sea, its structure and stratigraphy.'

'But we'd be unwise to oblige them, no?'

'Simply, sir, it cannot be done. There are legal opinions pending – the treaty still to be ratified as to how the boundaries of the continental shelf are drawn between ourselves and our coastal neighbours? Norway will have its claim there.'

'Norway claims more than it ought,' the Minister grouses, his image of the Norwegian coastline being tolerably clear, and inclining him to scepticism of any grandiose assertions of Norwegian sovereignty.

'Be that as it may, a legal argument on the matter might take years. And be lost on our part.'

The Minister feels gloom descend anew. 'Kynaston, I trust we're in agreement that were any oil ever found in the North Sea it would have to belong to the Crown. Or else under a highly specific licence to our favoured local licensees.'

Awaiting Kynaston's nod, the Minister instead sees his subordinate, eyes clouded, evidently preparing to venture a different sort of opinion.

'Where oil is drilled for, sir, it is won only by great expenditure and risk. In the case of the North Sea this truism would apply many times over. I admit, I struggle myself to imagine what sort of technologies could withstand that environment – certainly not the ones at hand. However, any party that sets itself to such a titanic endeavour should, I think, enjoy a measure of our encouragement.'

The Minister weighs up how much he fancies an argument; before deciding that at this late hour he might offer a measured deference to an expert.

'Very well, Kynaston.' And he raises his Conway Stewart pen for emphasis, hoping to appear decisive. 'In due course I expect we might get some of your old Texan friends in and hear them out – look to see who is credible, who we can trust. But, we look also at all times to favour our own.'

'That seems to me a sensible stance, Minister.'

'Good. At ease, then. Welland, pour me a glass of the Glenlivet, will you? Will you take a drop, Kynaston?'

'I think not, sir, thank you.' And with that he is gone.

Rolling the amber around his crystal tumbler, the Minister begins to feel spirits lifting. 'My God, Welland, there's the stuff of dreams, what? That one fine day we might be an oil-producing nation. Not stuck paying five hundred million a year to get the bloody stuff off the Arabs.'

'A dream, sir. Perhaps also a . . . wicked issue?'

The Minister grunts. 'Why so?'

'I'm no economist but I understood that countries with oil all seem to suffer a rather overvalued currency? And a problem, therefore, in exporting very much else?'

'Welland, when I consider this country's horrific balance of payments, I might rate that a luxurious problem to have. "If it were done when 'tis done, then 'twere well it were done quickly . . ." The Scottish play, you know.' And, at that, the Minister's reverie is broken. 'Oh bugger. This bloody thing. Welland, would you care for a ticket to the Royal Court Theatre tonight?'

'*Serjeant Musgrave's Dance*, sir?'

The Minister sees he has piqued his bagman's interest. 'I believe so. You might take a friend if you like, so long as you will brave the telephone call to my wife with a suitable excuse for why it's not she and I who are attending.'

As Welland moves to the receiver, the Minister closes his eyes. He knows he would only have fallen asleep not long after the house lights went down; and he feels that for one day at least he has already entertained sufficient fantasies.

PART II
OPPORTUNITIES

April 1963
Something Transformative

How long wilt thou forget me, O Lord? For ever . . . ?

Aaron Strang is waiting again, on a distressed wooden seat adjacent to a gravely silent door, and he has begun to feel that his patient, weary vigil is making him ridiculous – sufficient to call to mind his churchgoing childhood, and the scratches left there by innumerable Biblical verses, despite his felt indifference at the time.

The Geology corridor is not busy this time of year, but a couple of Professor Munro's colleagues have stepped past him in the last ten minutes, their expressions projecting plenty of busy but also a little pity. *'Waiting for Hugh?'* This key tutorial meeting was undoubtedly in the diary. Hugh Munro could not have been unaware that this meeting was to consider Aaron's prospects for doctoral study – the whole matter of his future. Knowing himself to be not much to look at, Aaron has nonetheless attired himself as if for interview, collar and tie and tweed coat. But now, he wonders if Munro might have forgotten him, or happened on some other bit of business more deserving of his attention?

Ever since Aaron's arrival at Aberdeen he has craved the approval of this man – the department's 'star' professor who, more than anyone Aaron has met, gives a high sheen to the image of the life of the mind. Not in the literary manner of his father, founded on groaning bookshelves of great old books; rather, a man of bold current research in his field, restless, bearing an air of controversy and combustibility, an energetic hum about his presence.

In the quest to impress Munro, though, Aaron has been given little encouragement; save for one prized hint, offered in casual refectory conversation by a doctoral student who worked a summer in

57

the faculty office at the time of Aaron's enrolment. *'Professor Munro noticed you right off,'* this chap confided. *'He'd say, "And that bright boy from Tarnwick, how is he getting on?"'* Aaron, though, has always wondered if that was anything more than a collegiate tease. Now, from his wooden seat, he is resolved: he will give Munro five more minutes. Then he will march to the rock physics lab and put his head round the door. But he no longer believes anything meaningful can happen in his life today.

His rap at the lab door, though, elicits a sound of stirring within.

'Yes? Come!'

Upon entering warily, Aaron must navigate a shadowy space lit only by a scattering of table lamps. His host is not yet visible to him; merely a voice engaged in a telephone conversation.

'Of course, Mr Paxton, but that's why I ask —'

This lab has to Aaron the feel of a lair: strange objects piled up in the murk, minutely organised yet overwhelming in number, phalanxes of specimen trays and specimen cabinets and wheeled specimen tables, everything labelled in tiny script. He steps between big white-top work benches with their measuring cylinders and scales, flasks of acid and petrographic microscopes. At last, peeking round a wheeled partition, he finds Professor Munro sprawled in a swivel-chair, absently stroking his five-o'clock shadow.

'Aaron. It *was* round about now, right? I do apologise. Some business just won't wait. Pull up that chair and tell me what's on your mind.'

'I suppose, Professor, I was hoping to discuss the possibility, after my masters, of pursuing the doctorate—'

'Do call me Hugh, Aaron. And that's a perfectly proper ambition for you.' He raises one bushy black eyebrow. 'Remind me of the general subject matter of your thesis?'

Aaron wonders anew how much attention Hugh has hitherto paid to his supposed brightness. But, of course, he has a text prepared.

Though yet to alight on a truly consuming passion, he has selected some local research of a sort he hopes will prove worthy of the master's blessing.

'Volcanic regions and igneous activity – they've become rather a focus for me. The volcanic rocks on Skye and Rum? I've had a very rudimentary look but I'm interested in a closer look at the deposits and the arguments about origin . . .'

Conscious of talking to his shoes, Aaron looks up now to the familiar sight of Professor Munro appearing to have his mind on something a hundred yards down the line of what's so far been said.

'You could do that, Aaron, you certainly could . . . I'd a fancy you might want to test yourself a little further. Tell me, what do you really see yourself doing in this life?'

Put on the spot, Aaron summons his standard answer. 'I've thought that – subject to satisfactory progress, of course – I might teach and follow the path to, ideally, professorship? If, even, right now there was a chance of combining study with some teaching—'

'Rocks are well and good' – interjects Munro, nodding – 'but given this clear interest of yours in thermal maturation, my question really is – how much *deeper* might your research go?'

Aaron is momentarily quite nonplussed: he would not have described his 'clear interest' like so. Yet Munro motors on.

'If we set ourselves to years of study of the changes in rocks due to heat over, oh, ten million years or more – we would do well to focus on what sort of work could be truly transformative? To consider, let's say, not just the strata and how and why they change, but also – what lies between them?'

Aaron is none the wiser; Munro clearly sees this.

'Forgive me, I was just talking to a man on this very matter. I appreciate it's maybe not what was on your mind when you walked in . . . But will you let me show you something? Shall we take a drive?'

Munro is on his feet. Aaron follows, snapping to it, for this feels like as much of the man's undivided attention as he has ever enjoyed.

Hugh's car, while shinily new, is smaller than Aaron had expected, and its fire-engine red surprises him, too.

'Please do strap yourself in with that belt,' the professor advises. Moments later they are ripping a way out of college grounds and down leafy streets, Hugh raising his voice perforce as Aaron grips the veneer of his seat.

'She'll do eighty, would you believe? Funny wee contraption. But anything new is fun. They make them at Linwood, of course, and I like to support homegrown innovation. You drive?'

'Not yet.'

'Learn! It's good to be a roving man. To accelerate . . . God knows I feel better the minute I'm out of Aberdeen. "Cosy corner", you know? "This is how we do things and no other!" Never a good outlook.'

'I suppose not.'

'What you were going on about back there? I just don't think it's best for you, Aaron. Understand, a lot of academic geologists are just dry-as-dust pedants. Don't get stuck in that box, look for the breakout! In our game you want to be in the coming field, where there's potential for change. That's why I stress the word "transformative", you get me?'

'Oh, for sure. Can I ask where we're going?'

'To the docks!'

Hugh strides ahead down the quayside's cobbled way and Aaron struggles to keep up; also to hear the words the professor throws back over his shoulder and into the stiff wind, amid the harbour din of clangs and hammerings, horns and shouts. Aaron has never much fancied Aberdeen's waterfront, and he sees no charm now in the lines of weathered boats, the rusting rails and faded capstans, the long, iron-roofed goods sheds and rank sea odour all around. Rather, to him it all amounts to a rollcall of the most clapped-out things known to man.

'Ah, now there she blows . . .'

Hugh is pointing keenly and Aaron follows his direction to one moored vessel that is most definitely not like the others.

Its hull is boldly red but with a globe insignia etched on the bow; its wheelhouse is white, its tall mast topped by a strange vane like a television aerial; and a modest American flag flaps nearby. Moreover, the crew busying about the deck, loading goods and chattels aboard, do not look to Aaron's eye much like Aberdonian trawlermen. Rather, in their crewnecks and windcheaters, some toting big cardboard boxes, they would not seem out of place were they restocking one of the university science labs.

Aaron answers Hugh's expectant look. 'That's a funny sort of a fishing boat.'

'It's a geological boat, Aaron. For making a survey of what's under the seabed out there. It'll have been chartered by a company hunting these parts for oil.'

Now two of those collegiate-looking young men are hefting the opposite ends of a wooden box, as solemnly as if it were a coffin; and on its side Aaron is alarmed to read the clean-stamped legend DUPONT EXPLOSIVES.

'What,' Aaron murmurs at last, 'would *that* be for?'

'Oh they're going to be making a hell of a racket once they're out, but that's the whole point. They've been told where to hunt by a geologist, Aaron – across a big stretch of sea, hundreds of miles, but once they get there they will lay some clever little listening devices in the water. And then they'll blow it up.'

'I don't understand.'

'Well, think. The shockwaves of a blast will bounce back off whatever rock is under the seabed, depending on density, right? So, if you listen close, with good equipment, and record those shockwaves, you get a kind of map – from which any decent geologist can hazard something meaningful about the subsea geology. These people need us, Aaron. We're like the x-ray chaps in the hospital, telling the surgeon where to insert the scalpel. Or, in this case, the drill.'

'Not nearly so precise, though?'

'Of course not. It's more sticking a pin in a map. That's why you start by working big stretches of sea. But then you review the data and your guesses get better, just like anything else.'

To Aaron this notion of extracting oil from leagues under the sea remains about as probable as colonising the moon. 'It just sounds a very risky bet . . .'

'Not at all, Aaron! If you know anything about the North Sea, there is a perfectly solid wager to be made on finding hydrocarbons under the Jurassic rock.'

'But surely the cost would be enormous . . .'

'Yes. You'd spend millions before you sunk a single oilwell. So, on balance, what do you think? Let's not do it, eh? You're right. Best leave it be.'

Gosh but he's mercurial, thinks Aaron, more bewildered by the moment.

'That's right, just let the sea have it. Millions of barrels of oil and what that resource could do for us, the power of it. No, let's just forget about it and sit and drink our bloody cups of tea in Cosy Corner . . .'

Now Aaron is feeling lectured, and not kindly: victim of a classroom trick. In the next instant, though, Hugh's mood appears transformed anew, from vexation to consolation, in the hand that he places on Aaron's shoulder. 'Aaron, look, please try to see the bigger canvas. I'm telling you all this because I've been doing it – sticking pins in a map. And from what I've seen in your work I just think you could have a knack for it, too. Speaking of tea, I am parched. Shall we take a libation?'

———

Aaron follows Hugh dutifully through the darkened door of a grimy, granite-faced pub on Guild Street, and accepts the offer of a half-pint of pale ale. The L-shaped bar where they stand is not busy, but the barman is in no hurry to serve Hugh, giving Aaron time to feel some hard stares coming his way from the dour clientele.

'What I was driving at, Aaron, my whole point – where risk is concerned, people can always find umpteen reasons not to bother. But sometimes a leap in the dark is what's needed. Like what Kennedy said about the US space programme? "We choose to go to the moon!" That's the spirit! You've got to *believe*!'

Munro rocks on his heels, feigning the strains of some American carnival evangelist; and Aaron for the first time wishes the great man might keep his voice down.

'For now we're a surprisingly small band of believers. But the data, dear fellow, is improving. So there's this little American oil company, Paxton Oil, they asked me for some research and they've paid me rather decently, and in this life we ought to pass on a favour . . . So! Here is my advice, Aaron. Petroleum geology ought to be your thing. A coming area for a coming man . . .'

Aaron looks into the rim of his glass and smiles abashedly. Hugh then claps his shoulder, causing his teeth to rattle. Nothing Munro has said is without interest; quite the opposite. It is simply that he cannot see his meagre self, the Aaron Strang he sees in the mirror, signing up to this heroic endeavour in all its vertiginous risk. Suddenly he feels minded to a lie-down, in a room darker even than this dingy boozer. He glances to his watch, then sees that Hugh, with mild disappointment on his face, is doing the same.

As they head back to the spot on Market Street where Hugh left his little red Imp, Aaron feels it incumbent on him to revive the discussion somehow, to give his professor something to prove he paid attention through the lesson.

'Hugh, you say it's a small band of believers, but . . . if there really is so much oil to be had, well . . . aren't the government interested?

Why aren't they out there hunting, too?'

'A valid question. There have been debates in the House, committees picking it over in their usual inexpert way. Ach, I say that, they're not all bad. Don is sharp enough. Don Cowan?'

'Our MP?'

'Yes! He's a doctor – medical doctor, not some mediocre PhD. And he's on that committee. I keep meaning to call him up and bend his ear.' Munro bites his lip and kicks his driver-side front tyre. 'You know what, as a matter of fact . . .'

Moments later Hugh is leaning into a nearby telephone box, asking Aaron to feed him the change from their halves of ale, addressing this 'Don' in a manner that seems cheerily to brook no argument. Then he slams the receiver back into its cradle. 'Okay, let's pay the man a visit. You fine with that? No other plans?'

None indeed. It seems to Aaron that Munro has placed some kind of faith in him. So he decides, heart over head, that if the purpose of today's lesson from the master was to lay oneself open to change then, however dizzying the ride, Aaron must stay on it, see where it leads. Maybe that was what the fates intended today.

'No, fine by me, Hugh. Anything new is fun.'

At first Aaron assumed they were headed to the MP's office somewhere in town; but soon Hugh is motoring south across the river bridge, and they enter a spick-and-span suburb where Hugh turns into the driveway of a detached, double-fronted granite house with broad bay windows and a neatly tended garden. The door is opened by a stocky, fleshy-faced fiftyish fellow wearing thick black-framed spectacles, cardigan and carpet slippers.

'Come through to the sun lounge,' he bids them.

There, once settled a mite warily in the comfiest seating of the day, Aaron sees that the corn-yellow walls are decorated with coalmining ephemera: faded prints of pit tools, an arrangement of painted plates commemorating scenes from Auchengeich Colliery, plus a pensive portrait of the former Labour leader Gaitskell.

Once Cowan has lowered himself into the largest chair, Hugh leans forward. 'Don, my research student and I were just down at the harbour reviewing the data from the seismic boats. And some of it is really quite striking.'

'Pray tell,' says Cowan, affably enough, prising open a small box of tobacco on the side table.

'What I want to stress, Don, is the huge potential value for this country. A sedimentary basin of the size I expect . . . you only need a fraction of that to be productive and you've in clover. So I have to ask, are we really acting fast enough to grasp the opportunity of something that could be so . . . what's the word I'm looking for, Aaron?'

'Transformative,' tries Aaron.

'Hugh,' Cowan begins patiently, filling his pipe. 'I well understand the hope we have for natural gas, and how valuable to—'

'Don, I have been certain there's oil there since Groningen.'

Cowan lowers the pipe, affable still. 'Well then, Paxton should be paying you more, Hugh. Lead them to it, my friend.'

'Don, there are very experienced operators here standing ready to drill, at their own expense. But they're waiting on licences to make it worth their while. You have a voice on that committee and you should push—'

Cowan looks suddenly less agreeable to the game. 'Hugh, it's not in my grant to make international agreements with neighbours over the boundaries of the continental shelf.'

'Why is that not getting done? Two ticks of a day's business.'

'I know you're confident of many things, Hugh, but national sovereignty over miles of water and seabed is a matter that needs careful consideration . . . and we don't let ourselves be rushed by any old freebooter wanting to prospect.'

'The point is what the oil could do in the right hands with the right forward thinking. Labour needs to grasp that and do something right for bloody once.'

'The electorate will decide that, Hugh. We await our opportunity. Now would either of you like a cup of tea?'

'Oh, I'll make it.' Hugh is fast to his feet. 'Somebody has to.'

Aaron is discomfited to sit in silence, nothing of his own to offer; more so as Cowan has fixed him with rather a knowing, mischievous look.

'So, you're the sorcerer's apprentice? What's your opinion of all this? I'm keen to know what the young folks are thinking.'

'Mr Cowan, in my opinion . . .' Aaron knits his fingers together, wracks his brain – and lines materialise to him as on a page. 'I'd say, there's a perfectly decent bet to be made on drilling under the Jurassic rock. It could amount to millions of barrels of oil. A risk, yes, but then, so is keeping quiet and never taking a chance on something that could be, as we say . . . transformative.'

Cowan purses his lips amusedly – contentedly? And Aaron has the strange but pleasing sense of inhabiting a role successfully – of having expanded himself in a small but important way so as to play a part that, maybe, initial wariness aside, he was made for?

'A diverting afternoon, wouldn't you say?' says Hugh once they are back on the road.

'Hugh, just to say – I'm really interested, in your advice, all that you've suggested. I'd like to have a think, maybe talk some more, about petroleum geology as my field of study?'

'Good man. Possibly it sounds a little crazy. But that's part of the allure.'

'If it didn't work, if I didn't take to it – what would that mean to my career?'

'At this stage in life you can never be quite sure how long something will take. But, look, I'll see you get your degrees, you'll always have those. If we could nab you a bit of work with Paxton, that could be your doctorate there, frankly.' Aaron can see Hugh studying him now with a sort of delight, as if he were a magazine puzzle newly solved. 'You know, Aaron, I owe you more than a lift home. You need feeding, there's no flesh on you, man!'

As he crosses the threshold of another solid bourgeois home, Aaron can hear piano playing from another room. While Hugh hangs his coat on a hook and pats his pockets, Aaron stands in the plush-carpeted hall, inspecting a row of musical certificates and a wall-mounted glass frame: a fossil more than a foot long, grey like a tank and menacingly arachnid, six-legged with the suggestion of jaws and claws.

It's the music, though, that is really beguiling Aaron: its gentleness, married to a force and fluency of expression. He cranes his neck a little to see round the door into the sitting room. The piece has some strange serenity to it, a repeated melody that is pensive and a little bit 'off' the time signatures Aaron is used to from his limited acquaintance with good music. This sounds to him both sad and tender. Until a little jarring sound makes him wince – and he imagines the pianist wincing also.

Hugh comes to his shoulder. 'Admiring my sea scorpion? The pianist is my daughter. She studies at the Royal Academy in Glasgow.'

Hugh leads Aaron into the rear reception room, where Aaron is shy of following – in case the spell is broken. The melody has turned graver, darker, the rhythm unsettled. He wants that sad romantic melody back. But through he goes, to see this daughter seated at a parlour grand piano, her father standing nearby perusing some correspondence. And now the melody Aaron so loved returns – briefly, quietly, until a lingering reverberation of the last note.

Hugh glances up. 'Heather, say hello to Aaron.'

She rises from her bench, removing her round-rimmed spectacles. She is pale, with long black tresses, and she wears a black muslin dress with thin straps. She reminds Aaron of the Roman women in his history books – maybe because of that dress, which accentuates her slight girlish frame, the boniness of her shoulders and wrists. She has the same black eyebrows and broad pursed lips as her father.

'I'd better see what's in the larder,' Hugh mutters. 'My wife's a consultant, the cooking so often falls on me . . . Perhaps the two of you can play a duet.'

'You play?' The warm, husky voice that emerges from this wan girl is momentarily disarming to Aaron.

'Oh, no, not a note.'

Her smile seems to forgive. Already she has returned to the piano to collect her sheet music. But he feels he must make a different display of how to be with Munro's daughter: his usual self will not do, that has been the lesson of the day.

'I'm just an admirer. But I must say you play beautifully.'

'You're kind, but it's not true. I'm still such a duffer, really. I try with all my might but . . .' – and abruptly she looks downcast, as if painted that way – 'I never quite achieve what I really felt I had in mind.'

Her candour touches something in him. 'May I ask what was the piece?'

'It's by Robert Schumann. He wrote it for his wife.' Now she is looking at him very directly. 'Have you been gallivanting all day with my father?'

'Research, really. But it did take us all over town.'

He describes a little of their odyssey that day, trying to make it sound as if he had more agency in it than was truly the case. She looks at him with what appears to be genuine interest. He can tell that without her spectacles she is prone to a slight myopic squint; and he hopes that perhaps her first impression of him has been favourably blurred.

Then she comes closer, as to confide. 'I imagine my father seems awfully impulsive. But he doesn't do anything lightly. He must think well of you.'

What response will sound right? Aaron thinks fast. His usual self-deprecation?

'Oh I don't know. He's a great scholar, he sees an awful lot of students . . .'

No! Steelier! Something calls to him from the recesses of his father's bookshelves.

'But I, ah, hope I shall study deserving.'

In the merest movement of the corners of Heather's mouth, Aaron draws encouragement for his performance. As this long day seems at last near an end, he is buoyed by the belief that he has taken its lesson.

September 1963
New Starts

Aaron is going up, up, up – albeit warily. New shoes nip his toes and his fastened collar pinches his throat; but he mounts steps to a portico, into the granite quayside building, thence up three flights of creaking stairs to an office door on the top floor. A plain sign has been affixed there: PAXTON OIL & GAS. What kind of occultism lies within?

'Aaron? Charlie McGinn.'

A sharp-eyed man in shirtsleeves and tie, fuming cigarette in hand, admits Aaron to a scarcely inhabited office space. Mr McGinn's sandy hair is thinning, his American accent is soft and mild. Yet from behind another closed door and some lowered Venetian blinds a voice much more bumptious is speaking at high volume.

'Aw, Harry, I wish the government had the sense to leave it be. But they're sticking their damn noses into this, and it's not their bailiwick!'

Aaron's assessing gaze takes in mounds of paper on assorted desks, a sparseness of plain hired-in furnishings, a slight fly-by-night feel.

'Have a seat, Aaron.'

After a moment, Aaron identifies a stool he might sit upon. 'It seems quite quiet here,' he offers.

McGinn smiles slightly. 'Our business is kind of a skeletal operation. Makes for less trouble if we find there's no dice and we gotta up sticks.'

Mr McGinn is pretending to peruse some paper, among which Aaron recognises his own curriculum vitae. He takes a lasting draw on that cigarette, then crushes it into a crowded glass ashtray with a look of regret.

'So we have great regard for Professor Munro, and he's spoken highly of you.'

Behind the closed door the phone-caller is signing off with stormy flourishes: *'That's right! Goddamn that's right! You got it!'*

'Let me take you to meet Mr Paxton.'

Inside that private office, over a polished walnut table serving as a desk, stands a masculine specimen of six feet four, packing every inch of his tan suit, with a jutting jaw and sky-blue eyes perhaps a tad rheumy. His high, brushed crop of russet hair has a bristling look that belies the lines on his face; also the liver spots Aaron can't but notice on the hand that shakes his firmly.

'Charlie, hey' – Paxton gestures as McGinn withdraws – 'can you see about getting me a steak medium rare? And coffee.' Then, to Aaron: 'So you're the boll weevil, kid?'

Aaron isn't sure he heard correctly.

'The new guy on the team? Aaron, yeah? You gotta let my people go, Aaron!'

Still stumped for a reply, Aaron just blinks and grins – fearing he must look like a loon.

'They tell me you're quite something at passing exams. Never got past prep school myself – they kicked me out. But hey, you make your own way, whatever it takes. This is a business for that. So we're looking to start you out on the seismic boats, right? You're dependable on water?'

'I'm a qualified diver, sir.' Aaron has found it increasingly easy to dispense half-truths for the sake of progressing a conversation.

'You don't say? Well, money and tools we already got, but what we need is some hard-working guys, plus a whole bunch of luck.'

'I can promise you my best efforts, Mr Paxton.'

'I'll accept nothing less, Israelite.'

Aaron has but an instant to puzzle over this odd exchange when the phone rings and Paxton lifts it at once. So Aaron glances aside, to framed photographs propped up haphazardly atop a filing cabinet: Paxton and family at home by a gaudy Christmas tree; Paxton gladhanding a candidate at some packed rally (GOLDWATER

FOR SENATE!); and a younger Paxton in monochrome, naked to the waist, hard-hatted and oil-stained, stood with another man in a similar state beneath the stark frame of a derrick.

'That's me and Magruder bringing up pipe like we did it in the old days. Dirty and all-hell dangerous, but worth it, by God. A big old thrill when you smell oil that no one's ever found before. Been there millions of years . . .'

Aaron is rather transfixed by the photo, with its silvery look of being centuries old itself, a relic of a world far stranger and darker than the scant, anonymous office in which he is sitting.

'But that's all the past. Tomorrow's what we're looking at, young Aaron. We ain't hunting for gushers no more. We gotta go deeper – however damned hard that is. And, believe me, I don't want to be sat here with a tie on behind a load of paper. I want us to be spudding in and drilling and goddamn *doing* something.'

'Me, too, Mr Paxton. I really look forward to this work and I really thank you for giving me the opportunity.'

'Well, we can't say yet what it'll add up to. We're having a helluva time getting the permits we need for acreage. If you happen to know some politician you can call?'

'I might do,' Aaron dares.

'Oh yeah? You got a lot more politics here than I'm used to. Can't buy nothing with cash. I mean, jeez . . . We've come all this way to help the British people. They get oil and that's a helluva thing for a nation.'

Aaron is feeling that Paxton sounds not unlike a politician himself, a man on the stump, a confidence-seller. Despite the small size of the crowd he is on a roll.

'I'm an independent, see, a maverick. But my money's as good as anybody's, and so is the money I bring to a place if I find—'

Then a rap on the door, and the hawkish man from the photograph strides in directly, wearing denim jeans and jacket.

'Clay, this ain't gonna wait.'

'Yeah, we better get goin'. Give the glad hand to the Israelite here. Aaron, meet my old associate Hal Magruder.'

Abruptly left alone in the care of Charlie McGinn, Aaron notes again this man's soft smile, and wonders if it is genuine.

'Don't look too shot up. Mr Paxton gives everyone nicknames, it's his thing – you're the this or the that. You got yourself not too bad of a one there, Israelite.'

The following afternoon Aaron takes a train north to Tarnwick for a long-promised call upon his father and his best friend. As familiar and dull is the journey, within he is brim-full of new assurance and purpose.

Outside Tain station David Strang awaits at the wheel of his Morris Minor. Straight away Aaron can see that no fuss is going to be made over Aaron's new job, the news of which his father had received equably over the telephone. Instead – after their customary handshake, and Aaron having to shift from the passenger seat some hefty book titled *The Humanity of God* – David proposes that this evening they look into the regular meeting of the council at the Carnegie Hall, where a report on the local economy is due for consideration.

'It might be of some interest to you, Aaron. They've been putting their minds to how we help our young people find meaningful work in these parts. So that not so many leave. Mrs Juliet Gallagher has been very influential in it.'

'Her own daughter hasn't got so far away, has she?'

'Mrs Gallagher might look to the example she set – the child left to herself brings shame.' David looks like he would rather think no more of it. 'You have your plan with Robbie for the morrow?'

'Yes, will you mind if I borrow your car?'

'I will have to trust you in that, Aaron.'

Aaron, mildly irritated, knows nonetheless that despite his newly acquired licence he is not yet such a confident driver. But he has promised that come the morning he will drive out to visit Robbie

Vallance at his workplace, the sawmill owned and run by the Laird of Blaikdoon on the Laird's own estate; and make himself useful by bringing Robbie some lunch.

At the Strang cottage, while David fills the kettle and cuts hunks of bread and cheese, Aaron steps idly from the crowded, undusted bookshelves to his father's desk under the light shed from a window by the kitchen table. A typewriter sits squarely amid piles of papers, and a freshly signed letter dries on a blotting pad.

Curious, Aaron reads enough to glean that his father is supporting an application by Torrance McVey for church ministry. Accepting a mug of tea, he finds he cannot let this turn of events pass without comment.

'It was a surprise to me also, Aaron. But Torrance came and asked to see me, and to do this for him, and when we spoke . . .'

'You didn't doubt he was sincere?'

In an instant, by those veins on the forehead, Aaron sees he has offended his father. 'He's seen some trouble, the dogs in the street all know that. But there came a day when he walked into a church and heard God, and he was changed. We all know what it means to bear regret. If a man admits he did wrong but has changed we should believe until he shows us any different. Thus went Paul down the Damascus road. If folk can't understand forgiveness they will never understand grace.'

Aaron wishes that his father, while extolling this forgiving marvel of grace, might try to sound a mite less crabby. 'I wonder what the Reverend thinks to this?'

'Oh, Torrance's father is very much gladdened.'

'Dad, you've said nothing to me regarding my own news.'

'I'm glad also of your news, Aaron. A good report maketh the bones fat.'

'It's quite a change for me. But I really look forward to it.'

'I'm sure you will apply yourself, son. A man whose drive in life is for the hope of material reward, well . . . that man like as not will get what he deserves.'

74

Recognising this sermonising manner, Aaron weighs what is unspoken in the room and decides, regretfully, that some sharper words must be said.

'Would you be more pleased if I applied for ministry, Dad?'

'Each is called to their own, Aaron. Whether you would preach or teach or dig ditches, or work for the Laird in the sawmill . . . my only wish is that you work hard and do well in it.'

'I thought you set more store by books and learning, Dad. There's plenty of that in the path I've chosen.'

'No doubt, Aaron, and I—'

'Just, for example, the fossil record? Our proof of the order of life on earth, over millions of years. First single-cell creatures then invertebrates, fish, dinosaurs, mammals . . . I know that doesn't support all the things you treasure in the Book of Genesis. But I don't believe in miracles.'

Aaron can feel himself twitching in pique. His father, though, is calm. 'You're sure about that, Aaron?'

'I don't know what you mean.'

'I mean the evidence of things not seen – there were, as you say, no human eyes present when creation occurred.'

'All done in six days, I hear.'

'Aaron – I have never questioned that in certain places the Bible shows us not literal truth but allegory. There are fine scientists, I'm sure, who are also men of faith and can reconcile such things in their minds. But perhaps not you and I. At any rate, son, please believe I will always hope for your happiness. Now please have the tea I made you.'

Aaron is minded to let his father attend his bloody council meeting solo; but having nothing better to occupy his evening, come six o'clock he duly climbs back into the passenger seat of the Morris Minor.

By the time they enter the Carnegie Hall the chilly venue is decently full and proceedings underway, Juliet Gallagher giving an echoey verbal report on the progress of an aluminium smelter at Invergordon and its prospects for jobs. Taking a folding seat alongside his father at the back, Aaron spies the local eminence conspicuously right up front – Robbie's employer, the Laird of Blaikdoon, distinguished in his fifties, erect and tall even when seated. As the Laird turns to speak to his wife, the size of his forehead and aquiline nose are made pronounced.

Now Councilwoman Gallagher invites questions from the floor. A more than usually spectral Reverend McVey is first to his feet. 'It is clear enough to me at least that another factory built here will be a brutal-looking scar on our landscape. We should mind what we do to the good earth for the sake of a petty wage.'

Aaron can feel his father by his side, stiffening all sinews in approval of the Reverend's point. Then David, too, is upstanding, and Aaron realises how serious he was about his attendance tonight.

'I would like to say, also, that we mustn't neglect all the practical difficulties that will come along with the factory – you must expect incomers as well, bodies seeking work who will also need housing, perhaps bringing children who'll need schooling, too.'

But Mrs Gallagher only smiles, seeming to look toward the Laird. 'Mr Strang, I do believe economic growth will make possible those other necessary developments, at the same time as we improve the prospects of our young people.'

'I do wonder at times' – the Reverend McVey interjects, clearing his throat with audible difficulty – 'I wonder, Mrs Gallagher, who is this "we" you always talk about?'

Juliet Gallagher seems suddenly to stand a little taller on the small stage: the imperious mother of Marilyn, no question. 'Reverend, I have lived here long enough, and frankly I do resent it when I am not counted among the folk who are judged to have the honest welfare of this place at heart.' Aaron sees her scan the room as if seeking any other dissenters, before moving on with the agenda.

Later, while folk put on their coats and hats, the Laird is sweeping out down the central aisle, but he pauses by the Strangs and places a hand on the shoulder of Aaron's father.

'Mr Strang. I hear your concern about an enlargement of our population because of the smelter. Were that to occur, be assured, we would certainly want to see a further expansion of your fine school. The resources would be found for it – you have my word.'

Aaron's father only cocks his head, unhappily, unpersuaded. 'You remember my son, sir, you've perhaps not seen him in a while?'

'That I've not. What are you doing with yourself, young man?'

Conscious of another pair of judgemental eyes on him, Aaron tries to rise to the query. 'I'm about to take up a junior position in petroleum geology, sir. With an American oil company.'

For a fleet moment the Laird looks very perplexed, as one who likes never to see a prejudice overturned. But then a grin spreads over his features and he nods vigorously. 'Well, may you prosper, laddie, may you prosper.'

Come the morning, with great caution but deep determination, Aaron drives his father's Morris Minor out into the wooded regions, down roads lined with larch and pine, beech and Douglas fir, to the sawmill on the Laird's forestry estate – two hundred acres of timber on the slopes above Blaikdoon Manor. Reaching the narrowest, most rugged roads, he slows to a wary fifteen miles per hour, tooting each time he nears a sharp turn. On one such, certain in the advance notice given, he rounds the corner only to confront a big lorry blaring its way toward him. He swings the wheel, then recovers his breath while watching the lorry rumble off in the rear-view, stacked high and wide with sawn and bound lengths of clean timber.

Soon he is approaching the sawmill gates and the busy yard beyond, BLAIKDOON spelled out in big carved wooden letters fixed to the crest of the main building's roof. Aaron parks on a mound of earth opposite, grabs from the passenger seat the satchel holding his and Robbie's lunch, and strides out toward the log yard.

A sour-looking foreman trudges in his direction as if to seize him by the ear. But glancing across the yard Aaron's eye is caught by a figure in an iron faceguard holding a welding torch to the drawbar hold of a tractor, amid a spectacular fusillade of sparks. Now this man stands up and unmasks: Robbie Vallance, darkly tanned and grinning broadly.

As Robbie lopes in Aaron's direction, slapping his gloves against his palms, Aaron is sure his own grin is as big, and then the two friends are beating one another keenly about the shoulders.

'So you managed not to crash your da's motor, eh?'

'Someone had to fetch you your flask and piece, didn't they?'

'I don't starve, Aaron, never you fear . . . Wait on, I've to tell the gaffer I'm taking my break.'

While Robbie confers with that grumpy foreman, Aaron has to step aside smartly as a dogsbody wheelbarrows some waste wood from out of the long main shed. All the real action of the yard seems to be emanating from within – a racket of motors and attendant vibrations, the nerve-straining shriek of the bandsaw, in the air a remarkable aroma of resin and sawdust, new-cut beech and fir, with a slight harsh undercurrent of hydraulic oil.

Then Robbie returns. 'Let's walk a bit, eh? We can chip out the back of the fence yonder. There's a cabin up in the woods, the Laird gives use of it for them who've got far to come.' Robbie throws a knowing sort of a grin over his shoulder as they stride out. 'We might even see a pal of mine.' Aaron absorbs this, not especially wanting other company for the afternoon.

So they walk, passing from under the hazy cloud cover to beneath the dappling canopy of the woods, where they make their way with crunching tread through clusters of aged firs and fallen cones, mingled odours of freshness and decay. Now and then in the thicket

Aaron hears birdsong, and the beating of wings. Robbie has picked up a slender snapped branch, and he whips cheerily at the legs of his overalls as he walks.

'What all have they got you doing here, Robbie?'

'Aw, just now? I told them I can weld a bit from being raised on a farm, so if there's a job like that they'll have me welding. Usually, but, I'm in the big shed, working the bark stripper.'

'Rather you than me.'

'Aye it'd no' be your thing. Not with the fancy work you do. I'm careful, but, Aaron, bet on that. I plan on keeping all of my fingers, pal. There's plenty things I like doing with them.'

'How's the money?'

'Fine. There's bonuses and all. I'll not be striking oil but it'll do me.' He gives Aaron a friendly shove, and Aaron rolls with it. He knows he is going places, while Robbie sticks with the familiar. Still, he looks well enough on it.

They emerge from the woods to a coppiced expanse, and now Aaron sees the cabin of which Robbie spoke, part-sheltered by overhang of the canopy. Its walls are stone and mortar, its roof corrugated iron, and it has one greyed wooden door and one darkened, grubby windowpane. Aaron expects Robbie will bid them enter; instead he indicates the fallen trunk of a tree over which they have just stepped, and they settle down upon its gnarly length. As Aaron unpacks his satchel, Robbie lights a cigarette.

'Will you not have your piece first?'

'Don't be nagging, mother.' He grins as he exhales. 'So what else ye bin up to in Aberdeen?'

'Well . . . I've met a girl. Heather's her name . . .'

The grin that breaks over Robbie's face is as bright as Aaron ever saw. 'Ye dog, ye! Quiet man . . . Fantastic, Aaron! So who's this lucky wee lassie?'

Touched by the response, Aaron struggles to describe the relationship in a way he thinks Robbie will understand and approve of. He dares not confide that for quite some time he and Heather Munro did no more than write each other letters. But, since her graduation from the Academy he has taken her out once a week.

'How well you got to know her then . . . ?'

Aaron is fairly sure Robbie is asking about sex. That has not happened. One time they sat together listening to a record, pieces by Liszt that she called 'sonnets', the bittersweet flow of which sounded to Aaron rather like feelings coming alive in a person. 'You're sweet,' she said, and then she had looked into his eyes so long that finally he pressed his lips to hers.

'I'm not sure she likes me that way.' In truth, he wonders if their respective wants have been only a minor factor in this; that they have been somehow pressed together by the force of Heather's redoubtable father taking such a guiding hand on Aaron's fortunes.

'Oh I'll bet she does, Aaron. Fine man as yourself.'

But Aaron doesn't feel quite fine. As a lover, he feels miscast. His regard for her musical gift was real – *is* real. But he has struggled to impress on her the charms he finds in carbonate rocks. She is less keen on geology than he first imagined; though he made her a gift of an amethyst on a silver chain, by which she seemed so touched that he wondered if it was the first such gift she had received.

'I swear, Aaron. You put a hand on her and she'd not push it away. She'd take it and she'd put it right there . . .'

The sky has become a shade darker. Aaron falls to studying a tiny insect on the hairs of his thin wrist. Then he realises Robbie is not staring at him – rather, past him. And he can hear the nearing sound, unmistakeable, of hoofbeats. He looks to Robbie, concerned.

'Told you we might get company, aye?'

By moments Aaron sees, first, that the horse rider drawing near is a female; then that it is, incredibly, Marilyn Gallagher – boldly astride, a foot in each stirrup, wearing a shirt and breeches and her hair tied up. Robbie rises to his feet, and Aaron follows suit, feeling as if some dignitary is entering a drawing room.

She trots the horse to a halt ten paces from them, slips to the ground like some elegant hoyden, and ties the reins to a tree. The horse, for all its rider's insouciance, looks to Aaron a little over-heated. It whinnies and nickers, inclines its head to Marilyn as to nuzzle her. *As well it might*, Aaron imagines. But then by her fond ministrations the animal is becalmed, and Marilyn approaches.

Robbie has wedged a fresh cigarette between his lips. 'Eh, sweetheart . . . you remember Aaron, aye? Come up from Aberdeen to see me.'

'All that way?' she bats back coolly. 'Heavens. I wish I had a friend like you.'

Now Aaron gets a straight look at the face he has fought shy of. A little harder in definition, a little flushed by exertion – but the same sloping cheekbones and arching eyebrows, the dark-lashed eyes and red-budded lips of a beauty. Aaron can sense Robbie's pride in his triumph.

'But, Robbie, now you've got this poor man . . .' – Marilyn sighs – 'all tangled up in our web.'

There is a fancy in those eyes and Aaron gets a sharp sense of what is its object. He feels very much that he is obstructing, very sure that otherwise Robbie would already have taken hold of her.

'Look, I, uh . . . I'd best be on my way. It's nice to see you again, Marilyn.'

She nods and smiles very cheerily.

Robbie, grinning, follows Aaron aside. 'Surprise, eh?'

'You said it.' Aaron has begun to feel almost clumsily light-headed. 'I'll leave you with your queen. Take care with that one.'

'Aw, Aaron' – he speaks low – 'I've got her where I want her.'

Trudging back into the woods without a glance back, Aaron allows himself a laugh he rates as rueful. Robbie might not have very much; and yet he maybe has all he could wish for – and without exerting himself so greatly. It is good, Aaron believes, to be happy for a friend. Better still not to dwell on why one isn't happier in oneself.

Then he pulls up, chagrined, realising he has left his satchel on the fallen trunk where they sat and ate.

On his return, the clearing is deserted save for Marilyn's tethered horse, its nose in a bag of feed. As Aaron steps nearer, the horse raises its handsome head as if sentinel; and for a moment Aaron fears he might have to deal with the animal – pet it somehow? But the horse only idles away by a few steps, as if dismissive of him. Aaron looks all about him one more time before deciding that Robbie and Marilyn must have entered the cottage. Really, he should head off.

Instead, stealthily, he approaches the greying door, but he does not make a sound or turn the aged doorknob; moves instead to the window, intensely conscious that he cannot resist this trespass.

Through the cobwebbed, murky pane he glimpses two standing figures, bare-chested, entwined.

He flinches, steps aside and out of sight, away from reprisal. For some moments he is motionless, tensed. Then he hazards a second look.

They are no longer in sight, and all is silent, and so he raises his head stealthily over the edge of the frame.

He hears a full-throated sound of female longing so plangent – one could say distressed – that he has to peer closer still.

And now he sees them, undressed on the dismal floor, but as if mindless of these mean surroundings, Robbie cupping Marilyn's breast and kissing her mouth, she spreading herself as Robbie undulates over her. Her arms encircle his shoulders, her fingers clasp around his neck.

Their seeming languor is in sharp contrast to the erratic, lurching blood in Aaron's veins, the uneven thump of his heart. It feels like he is seeing a proof forbidden to him of what it really means to be alive in a body – by way of what these lovers seem to possess, all of their own, given freely to one another. *Eden*, he thinks. From which he is excluded.

In the next instant he knows he can't endure it any longer. Bad enough to be looking; infinitely more abject to be caught. He turns heel and hastens away – into the safe shade of the firs, ground crunching accusingly under his boots.

February 1964
Power Revisited

The Secretary of State has been in post only a few months, but likes to believe he commands authority by his presence: a seasoned politician, a trained engineer, with a voice that fills a room and physical stature to go with it. From the start he has felt, in truth, a shade too big for the job he was given.

Thus he is unenthused by the prospect of this afternoon's meeting about *alleged* oil in the North Sea, and sits glumly watching a number of departmental minions shifting armchairs and preparing a display board for Mr Kynaston's presentation. With legal barriers to exploration now lifted, drilling licences are to be allocated – but in some mathematical manner best known to Kynaston, whose fingerprints have been typically and obdurately all over the whole rigmarole.

At last the board displays a tacked chart depicting the continental shelf area of the North Sea, divided into blocks by criss-cross lines. The Secretary of State is briefly put in mind of old maps illustrating the carve-up of Africa.

His thoughts shift rapidly to the glum question of how much longer his party has in office. An election come the autumn . . . A sense of all governing now done in a rush, the chief motive to spoil and poison as much as possible before it is handed over to Labour. He decides that a decent show of his surviving authority before Whitehall underlings today is of the absolute essence.

Kynaston enters, pensive, and the Secretary of State, not wanting to give him the chance to compose himself, launches into the preliminaries from seated.

'Good afternoon, everyone. Our purpose is to take a first look at a proposed system for licensing in the North Sea. Soon enough the

Crown will have proven rights over designated areas where prospects of oil are rated noteworthy, and so we will be at liberty to oblige parties wishing to drill. Many an explorer must fancy their chances. They have for some time been parading in and out of this office telling me all they would do in return for a block – 'blocks' as indicated on this chart. These blocks, then, are the spoils. But we will not look to hand them out to just anyone. Applicants must be resident here, paying our taxes. British Petroleum we might well expect to be licensee number one. However – all oil that is found will be vested in the Crown, per the national interest. Mr Kynaston, then, would you?'

Kynaston, with a short bow, moves from where he had been leaning against the wainscoted wall to a spot in front of his display chart. His observation of politeness is always impeccable; yet to the Secretary of State it always seems more a tethering of internal displeasure, performed in a spirit of forbearance.

'I ought perhaps to make clear that the national interest as defined in this matter is the most rapid exploration of these blocks. Things simply must proceed as urgently as possible – we must have drilling as of the summer, and by any parties who are competent, experienced and committed.'

'Is that not what I said, Kynaston?' The Secretary of State is already riled.

'Sir, of the many who have petitioned this office, I have asked them all the same questions. We will award licences only to consortia that can demonstrate access to a drill rig, and who undertake, moreover, to begin within six months of the award.'

'My point, Kynaston, concerns ownership of any oil these drillers find. It is our oil, and any benefit from it must first go to improving the national economy.'

'With respect – oil's effect on our economy will be zero if the oil stays under the seabed. But regarding it as some national treasure to be hugged close is . . . counterproductive. We need the oil, and quickly. As such, it is essential to attract the maximum possible exploration. The competence and experience required for that – the capital required – will inevitably come from abroad, and we must look to encourage such interests. They will likely present in combinations – the major firms partnering with each other, but also with some of the so-called independent or junior explorers. We can, for instance, expect BP to seek some arrangement with potential North American partners, as will Royal Dutch Shell and others.'

'Didn't I hear' – a minion pipes up – 'that the best geologist at Shell said they don't expect to find a single barrel of oil in the North Sea?'

Kynaston smiles into his chest. 'As a lady lately remarked, he would say that, wouldn't he?'

Laughter in the room, a little uneasy, but the Secretary of State considers all of it to be in poor taste; nor does he care for Kynaston standing there in tight-faced relish of how his little show is going down, and evidently judging the moment right to resume it.

'This exploration will cost the earth. It will be highly dangerous – it will cost lives, of that you can be sure. It will require extraordinary skill, in conditions where the old tools simply will not cut, so that will call for innovation, too – and we should expect the more experienced Americans to show us the lead.'

The Secretary of State finds himself profoundly out of patience. He has long suspected Kynaston, with his much-vaunted Washington experience, of being a Yank by proxy. And yet Kynaston, infuriatingly, seems to be not quite finished.

'The oil companies are not neophytes, and they will not be our lackeys. They are powerful trans-national entities, for whom many of the usual rules do not apply. They deal with organised labour and governments only where they absolutely must. That is their world, and we should not imagine we hold the whip hand.'

The Secretary of State gets to his feet with a grunt by way of cancelling the performance. He has tried to formulate something properly acidulous in response; but he has not managed.

'Well, thank you, Kynaston, for educating us all so ably.'

Kynaston has removed and is polishing his spectacles, seeming to invest more of his attention in the task than in his boss. At last, he glances up. 'Sir, in this great matter I do believe all of us will find we have an awful lot yet to learn.'

July 1964
Pirates

The trawlers of first light are basking two and three deep by Blaikies Quay, waiting a turn to dock and have their hauls unloaded. But the *Reaper* of Killday Fishing Limited is already in pole position. To the eye of Joe Killday, watching from the quay, it is much the same vessel on which he suffered his first teenaged venture to the Faroe Islands – only yet more beaten-up and baleful-looking.

'They don't die, these bloody boats, do they?' he murmurs to no one in particular.

But his brother Walter at his side is certainly listening. 'A hundred thousand pounds for a new one, Joe.' He smiles apologetically. 'They just have to endure.'

At their back is the great canopy of the harbour fish market, as long and high and cantilevered as a railway station's platform, already clamorous with folk awaiting the auction of the catches now being offloaded. Wicker creels seething with wet-slapping fish are winched up and swung out of the *Reaper*'s hold, then deposited onto the quay, their contents immediately sorted and boxed for sale by busy hands. Walter, as chief financial officer – incongruous in three-piece pin-stripe, owlishly intent behind his spectacles – tallies the boxes as each is filled. Joe knows that, for all Walter's meekness, there is little that escapes that eye of his.

Joe for his part avoids catching any eyes among the *Reaper* crewmen who are doing the hard lumping. He doesn't doubt that a certain few remember the stripling version of him. *Aw aye . . .* Instead, detachedly, he observes the queasy slop of fish on concrete, the odour of scales and guts, and the dirty seagulls lurking nearby. Mindful of the smart threads he has on, he eyes the market's standing taps, fancying that the whole place could do with a hose-down. A neglected conger eel has slipped from a creel to land by his feet, and with the toe of a polished Oxford he pokes it in the direction of the packers – only to see it thrash alarmingly as if somehow stirred back to life.

From under the shade of the market awning emerges the baw-faced, pie-fed, white-coated Malky McGraw, Killday's chief salesman. Joining Joe and Walter, he casts his eye over all that is getting done – the mounting crates, the sheen of large cod – and he sees that it is good. 'Plenty good green,' he declares.

Walter inclines to Joe to translate. 'The high-margin stuff for us, Joe. It'll sell in a flash next door, then off down to Billingsgate by dawn tomorrow.' Joe nods, finding the promise of London and good money to be of more interest than the muck in which they are presently kicking their heels.

Garth Killday, now ship's mate, has clambered off the *Reaper* and onto the quay; he confers with skipper John Cutter, who wears the troubled brow of a man preoccupied by bigger matters. Together this pair approach Joe and Walter, and Garth spits tobacco before thrusting a battered logbook at Joe.

'There you go, brother Knox, you be the judge of how the boys have behaved.'

Joe recognises the discharge book: a ragbag of scribbles on the ability and conduct of trawlermen during the voyage. He won't scrutinise it too closely; he would not have cared to be judged so himself. He sees John Cutter regarding him distrustfully.

'Has your da roped you into the fishing at last then, Joseph?'

'No, no, John. I've a new job starting September, as a management trainee with Dunlop down in Birmingham.'

'The tyre boys, aye?' Cutter grunts.

'Tyres and other things,' Joe corrects. 'Being as I'm at a loose end for the summer, Da asked if I might lend a hand in the office, have a look at the business on the management side.'

'Aye, there's a fair bit could do wi' looking at.'

Joe decides that any response on his part would be inappropriate.

'Right.' Garth rubs his hands. 'I've to see these lads are fed and watered.' *The pub*, Joe assumes.

'John' – Walter offers, manners ever impeccable – 'you'll come back with me and Joe by the office so we can arrange your breakfast and taxi?'

'Aye, but I'll be wanting a word with your father and all.'

The trio move off under the awning to shortcut through the fish market. Porters in metal-studded clogs clack across the slimy screed concrete, dragging the boxes of fresh catch by steel hooks and steering them into tight rows, there to be inspected by shuffling gaggles of punters. The tannoy system blares a garbled call to order and then Malky McGraw is clambering atop an upturned crate to auction off the Killday share of cod and haddock. Joe pauses to watch as Malky, keen-eyed, orchestrates bids that seem to be lodged by the merest of nods or raised eyebrows.

'It's a gift,' Joe remarks.

'It is that,' Walter responds. 'I had a try at it once. But you need a big voice. I wasn't a natural, as with many things.'

Joe always feels an awkward fondness in his eldest brother's unflagging modesty. He has never seen Walter truly laugh from his gut – only ever these mild smiles in the act of self-deprecation.

'Well, you've got other skills, Walter.'

'Joe.' Walter pats his shoulder kindly. 'I know that.'

Cutter seems keen to get moving and they exit the market on the landward side to the public road, where vans have drawn up to bays to load fresh purchase.

'Another winning mission then, John?' Joe ventures to see if Cutter can be flattered into better humour. 'Good catch?'

'Could have been more if it wasn't for the damn pirates. Them eejits out there hunting oil. The flotillas . . .'

'What, there's really so many of them?'

'Too many. Lethal to our business they are, too. An awful lot of good fish they're killing, and not the decency to bring them to market, neither.'

A hundred miles out at sea – gloomily grey and turbulent even in early summer – Aaron Strang is among the pirates aboard the seismic research vessel *Jaybird* chartered by Paxton Oil & Gas.

He grips the starboard rail, keeping his eye on the dreary horizon in the way he has schooled himself to combat nausea. But he keeps an eye, too, on what is close by his side, under the wheelhouse – the stacks of silvery cans each loaded with fifty pounds of dynamite, this cache of ordnance stored almost casually on deck, tons of compressed violence out in the elements, albeit lashed in place by thick ropes. Yet Aaron is not afeared, for he has confidence in his captain Hal Magruder – whom he can see now at the stern of the boat, in a moment of uncommon contemplation, staring out at the unlovely waters in his faded cowboy clobber and Stetson.

At last Magruder turns Aaron's way, shaking his head. 'Well, it ain't the worst morning ever. Just hope to hell we are where we think we are . . .'

Magruder has a sanguinity that Aaron admires. He is meant to keep to his station in the geologists' cabin; but he has come to prefer hanging round Magruder on the main deck. Certainly he covets this man's approval more than that of Erwin Shields, Paxton's chief geologist – an Ulsterman, yeasty of breath, oddly prissy and bullying by turns, the kind of pedant Hugh Munro had assured him he would avoid if he chose industry over academe.

'Okay, Israelite, you gonna lend a hand to get them magic ears in the water?'

Aaron nods, and joins his shipmates beside the mighty cable-winding drum at the stern. The job is to crank the geophone cable out into the sea, checking its integrity as it unwinds, tweaking in places so it pays out straight. Aaron enjoys this manual labour: a small facet of a larger project to prove to himself he is a more robust character than he formerly imagined. In his rented room in Aberdeen – a cramped, barely furnished space – he has taken to hefting a pair of dumb-bells bought by mail order, despite the landlady's tuts about the clanking thud on her ceiling.

'Keep it steady, you bastards!' Magruder chides the other deckhands, Texans in the main, hard-wearing as himself. 'Don't be going no faster than the goddamn ship!'

Aaron watches the cable snaking out into the churn of the water, like a wedding train in the wake of the ship, until its weighted length slowly slips under.

'Okay,' Magruder barks. 'Let's get that dynamite over the side. Israelite, time you got back in your cage, son. See if Miss Lady Luck is ridin' with us.'

Reluctantly Aaron retreats down starboard and into the confined cabin he shares with Tim Wyndham, an Oxonian Englishman with cheeks pink as lean ham, who scarcely acknowledges his entrance, absorbed as he is in the outputs of the sound-level meters and amplifier system that dominates his share of the space.

'*Shotpoint!*' comes the cry from out of doors, followed by the *whumph* of underwater detonation. Through the cabin's poky port-hole Aaron can see a white column of plume thrown into the air by the dynamite.

'How's it looking, Wyndham?'

He scowls. 'Tidy up the paper, would you, Strang?'

Aaron shuffles to where the seismograph machine is steadily churning out printed shockwaves on a long spool, six or so feet of paper already ballooning onto the damp floor. His main work on the *Jaybird* – as Wyndham by force of silent irritation never lets him forget – is to collate these records and keep them dry and under padlock overnight, as if they were precious jewels, for all that they make an inauspicious sight currently.

'*Shotpoint!*'

Aaron straightens up the pile, sits, hunts for a pencil, then peers at the printouts to see what sort of profile is emerging: coarse parallel lines, punctuated by the wavelets of the dynamite blasts, and the arrival times of the reflections coming back from the depths. He is looking to spot abrupt changes, unusual patterns – anomalies of any sort in the otherwise monotonous lines. And he is quietly desperate to spot these before Wyndham does, thus to gain some advantage in the contest for favour from the Paxton office – a contest he is sure Wyndham feels just as intensely despite his mask of boredom.

Wyndham has risen and breathes hotly over Aaron's shoulder. 'My God, this is such meagre stuff. So much reverb, it might just be showing us the waves hitting the damn hull. What I'd give for a few more channels on this tinker-toy . . .'

To Aaron the shallow levels are fairly readable, suggesting a familiar structure: base Zechstein anhydrite, a dependable Upper Permian salt cap. Grounds for a guess at what might lie beneath, but no more. He longs for some visionary force to help him penetrate deeper, perceive a suggestive pattern. Onshore, he knows, better machines will construct better read-outs from audiotapes. But in his daydreams he imagines himself achieving some breakthrough divination – a magician's reading of the runes – from the confines of this cabin. *That* would show them, no two ways.

Wyndham has called it correctly, though. There is just so damn little before him on which to base a decision. Aaron sighs, feeling acutely the limitations – those of the equipment, also his own. Miss Lady Luck is certainly needed. Hal Magruder is not wrong.

Joe sits in the Killday office at the desk temporarily his, wiping fish guts from his brogues with toilet tissue, pondering the digest of company finances that Walter has diligently handwritten for him.

Facing him, behind Walter's desk, there is a chalkboard with markings recording the tallies of skippers' catches this month: John

93

Cutter firmly at the top, as usual. This is what the business has been for as long as Joe has known it. Cutter is now ensconced in Andrew's office, Walter in there, too. According to Sheila's prim account, Cutter pitched up from the Crown Hotel with drink taken, which strikes Joe as unbusinesslike, whatever the man's prowess at sea.

Joe believes that his father has of late taken to looking at him a little differently – reconsidering him, as though he now stands a little taller, sometimes seeking moments to quiz him keenly about the Dunlop way of doing things. Joe has become, after all, not only the first in the family to garner a first-class honours degree but the first also to secure employment outside the family business, and with such a reputable firm. Andrew has never uttered a word of outright praise; and yet more than one of his father's old mates have muttered the same thing to Joe: *'Your da tells me it's a braw thing you're doin' now.'*

With his new expertise Joe doesn't find it hard to evaluate the Killday figures with a cold eye: just another case study to which he can apply principles, questions he has been taught to ask. *If you're a business, what sort of business are you in?*

He is aware, though, of carrying some bias derived from all the diligent research into the Dunlop way that he conducted in advance of his interview there. That business is increasingly more than meeting the needs of motorists: it has turned its vision to sportswear and sports kit, footwear of all sorts, umpteen applications of industrial rubber. *Diversification.* Killday is a far more modest enterprise, but decently sized: a fleet of twenty vessels, a hundred men on the payroll, various services done for money aside from catching fish – the repair, rigging and marine stores. Does it do enough, though? *Does the business do all that it could?* This reflection Joe adds – blue-inked, in precise characters – to the foot of Walter's page of figures.

Now John Cutter emerges from his conference with Andrew, looking a tad truculent, hat already on his head, if askew. Walter shows him to the door in silence. Andrew, smiling tightly, frowns as soon as the door closes.

'Joseph, a moment? I'd be glad of your judgement.'

Joe caps his pen and joins his father for this private consultation. 'Has John Cutter been bending your ear about the oil boys dynamiting his fish?'

'Ach. That and many a grumble besides. John's a big thinker. It's part of what makes him such a braw skipper.'

'Was there anything he said that made you think?'

'What I think is that a half-dozen glasses of malt will drive any man to a bit of fighting talk. But then he'll have a good sleep and think better when he wakens. Joseph, there's not another company will treat that man kinder or pay him better than Killday Fishing.'

'Does Walter think the same?' Joe asks with real curiosity, itching to uncap his pen again and append some notes to his Killday case study.

'Walter's head is all numbers, he's no judge of a skipper. Listen, this is what I want to know from you. What's your opinion of this sleekit fellow we have bidding to be your brother-in-law? What do you reckon to this Mr Raymond Bodie who's courting your sister?'

Joe has yet to meet the gentleman. He has thought only that for Angela – always so subdued and unforthcoming a lass – getting the attentions of some lively gentleman must surely be an encouraging development.

'I understand he's a car salesman . . . ?'

'He runs the showroom at Kaminsky Motors on Justice Mill Lane. Flashy place, flashy cars. I've a concern this Mr Bodie is a bit of a Flash Harry and all.'

'How so?'

Andrew leans forward as to share a scurrility. 'My pal Tam Drury was after this particular motorcar, and Mr Bodie tells him they have the very thing in the showroom. Tam makes clear he doesn't want the vehicle they have in the showroom. To which Mr Bodie takes great umbrage. "Our showroom cars are in mint condition," he says to Tam. Giving it laldy, y'know? So Tam pays the deposit, the motorcar is delivered – and, wouldn't you know, the bumper's scratched, the paint's got flakes, there's a wee ding on the side. Well, Tam is straight onto the telephone but this man Bodie tells him most adamantly that the deal is done. Quite a row. Now, is that any way to do business, Joseph?'

'I've heard worse,' Joe murmurs, mildly tickled.

'Would you buy a motorcar from such a fellow?'

'Maybe not. But I might not mind if he was on my team selling whatever I was selling . . .'

'You might not want him for a son-in-law.'

'Oh well, if things are heading in that direction then I daresay it's Angela's feelings are what matters.'

'No, son, it's my feelings that matter.' Andrew chuckles at himself. But Joe can see his father's disquiet, and the place from which it emanates.

Walter knocks and enters. 'Da, I'm done balancing the cashbook for the day. I'd like to get on my way to Mo Seiche now, if you don't mind?'

Andrew nods assent. The Killdays' quaintly-named weekend cottage, two hours' drive north in Pennan Bay, has been rarely frequented by the younger ones since they were bairns – save for Walter, who takes regular sojourns, a lonely soul, Joe never sure as to what can occupy his brother up there beyond Mo Seiche's modest garden and beds.

Now Andrew studies the clock. 'Joseph, we need to get Garth out of the pub. Would you do a good turn and go retrieve your brother?'

Joe winces. He has a date, a bonny Margaret whom he met at the Abergeldie jazz club – not in the Belinda Morland league, nothing serious for either of them, he feels sure. But they have arranged to take in the new Hitchcock picture at the Capitol tonight.

'Shouldn't Bryony be out with a rolling pin? I've plans for this evening, Da.'

'You're a busy man, son, I understand. Will you do this for your da? I've a sore need of men I can count on.'

96

Joe scrutinises his father's face, certain that some irony must be intended. To his surprise he realises that Andrew is in earnest.

As he strides forth Joe rehearses a number of affable hail-fellow greetings such that Garth might not curse him, nor the crew sneer, when he descends on them with the clear intent to break up the party. Yet on pushing through the pub doors he finds his presence is scarcely noted. There is a wildcard element to the gathering: the crewmen of the *Reaper* have made a new friend.

They are sitting in the manner of an audience around a voluble American, all in denims topped by a cowboy hat swooping up at the edges. And it looks to Joe that this big Mr Stetson is holding court, entertaining the lads. He has one boot up on a chair, and takes occasional slaps at the back of a pale, youthful sidekick sat next to him, who looks swamped inside a needlessly thick Aran sweater.

'Eh, Joe!' Garth gets up to greet his brother.

'Garth, it's maybe time to call quits?'

'Naw, one more. You gotta have a listen to this boy, get yourself one in, I'll have a malt and fetch another for Mr Magruder.'

Joe reluctantly buys this small round, then pulls up a chair beside Garth and tunes back in to Mr Stetson.

'... tough at sea, sure, big guy. But you best believe it weren't pretty for them prospectors in the Klondike neither! No sir. Your dick got froze! But, God willing, you got rich – *you* got rich, not some other bastard. So that's why we come a-huntin' here, boys. Though, I gotta tell ya, your government down there in London could be a whole lot friendlier about it ...'

This sentiment stirs a few grumpy noises among the company. Magruder flashes what looks to Joe like a pretend *Aw-shucks* grin. 'What? Am I out of line?'

'Is it California you're from, Mr Magruder?' Joe merely guesses, but it is the part of America most vivid to him: golden sun and sand, Beach Boys, beach girls.

'You got that right, bud. Bakersfield. Kern County. South San Joaquin Valley.' He knocks up the brim of his hat and reaches for his whisky. Joe senses that the trawlermen think this the stuff of legend.

'Bakersfield's godawful pretty. I mean, it's got oil, but the place ain't all pump jacks and derricks, no sir. We got apple orchards and vineyards. We crown us an Oil Queen every year. You got a Miss Aberdeen? You got her phone number?' He cackles. 'But that's what oil does to towns, see. Turns 'em upside down and shakes 'em. Makes work for all hands. Money, too. If you find the Lord's buried his blessing in your little acre of Eden . . . I mean, Aberdeen could be the California of Scotland. It just wants to rain a little fucken less, but . . .'

'I hear it's a fair lot of explosive you use out there?' Joe takes care to put his enquiry in an even tone, aware that he is feeling oddly proprietorial about the Killday fishing business, and a bit like the new marshal in a western movie.

Magruder regards Joe with a slightly harder look than previous, as if his whisky buzz were abruptly worn off.

'Dynamite seem a little rowdy to you, son? Well, see, what we're huntin' for, it's lying deep out there . . .' He flares up a cigarette with some ostentation. 'Yeah, it ain't like there's gold under your feet no more. This oil is hiding some. And the Israelite here, we gotta give him something he can use.'

Another slap on the shoulder is suffered by the pale young Scot, who looks to Joe – with his button eyes and mop haircut his mother might have given him – as the least likely candidate for rugged outdoorsman he could imagine. Magruder, though, appears fond of his sidekick.

'Yeah, young Aaron Strang here, he caught a break when he joined this circus. Thanks us for it every day! You boys, too, you could be oil men someday. Soon as we strike lucky out there we're gonna need bodies out on rigs. And a roustabout can come from anywhere, son. No diploma needed. So long as you're a hard-workin' sonuvabitch.'

Joe is beginning to think he is hearing a recruiting sergeant; and that is concerning. Only now does he sense the figure newly arrived behind his chair, but Magruder and Strang surely have, for they are both looking abashed and getting to their feet.

'Hal, you wanna flap your gums some more or were you and the Israelite planning on giving me a report anytime?'

And the show is over, for the pair are trooping out behind their boss-man, another big ageing Yank, redheaded and packed into his dun-coloured suit. Joe notes that Magruder has a distinct swagger to his gait, as if he were gripping a pencil between the cheeks of his backside.

Garth bashes Joe's arm, chuckling. 'Some boy, eh? He knew a thing or two.'

'Aw he was a flash cunt,' mutters a younger deckhand, rising with his empty pint glass and heading for the bar. It occurs to Joe, though, that the young trawlerman is walking a bit funny, as if affecting just a bit of the swank displayed by Hal Magruder as he vacated his stage.

September 1964
Mark and Ally in Edinburgh Society

'Do you *want* to be a reporter, Rutherford?'

Tuesday afternoon in the Edinburgh offices of the *Scottish Daily Express*. In this newsgathering machine it is not easy for young reporters to get noticed, but Mark is drawing attention for the wrong reasons. He is a writer of sorts now, true, but a long way still from the writer he has hoped to become. And presently the newsroom has no sound of industry, no chatter of typewriters or linotype – just the obtrusive noise of Mark getting bawled out by his superior, 'Big' Archie Buchan.

'The hell you doing, son, sitting there blethering on the phone to the Labour Party?'

Mark gestures as to say it was hardly the craziest notion. 'Because there's an election on, Archie.'

'Whass that got to do wi' you?'

'Because it's news, because there's a good chance Scottish voters will decide who wins, so I think—'

'You're a junior here, son, do as you're fucken told. The job is to scoop the *Record*, so get you on that phone to the polis and the emergency services, not the bloody Labour Party.'

Archie waddles off. Mark notes that the neighbouring workmates who had earwigged this exchange have turned somewhat smugly back to their work. He suspects a fair few around here rather relish 'Rutherford' having a strip torn off him. He has been clued-up enough to glean from certain looks and edged remarks that he is a suspect figure round these parts: viewed as some flaxen-haired, self-impressed product of Kilmuir School, one who doesn't know he's bloody born. Mark knows fine well that to protest he was only a scholarship pupil, and was and remains a staunch socialist, would be humiliating as well as doing not a whit of good.

Mark wishes there were more women around the office: maybe a few more opportunities for sympathy. But there's really only Shona McCall, who pays him no attention whatever. Worse, Shona is finishing today – off to better things. Not for the first time Mark is feeling left behind, not quite cut out for the career he chose.

His desk phone rings. He allows himself a vicarious *Who cares?* pause before lifting the receiver. 'Mark Rutherford, *Express*.'

'*Good day, sir, are you the man at the* Express *who does all the scandal? Well, have I got a story for you. As I speak, there is a man screwing a cow in Charlotte Square. I am watching this appalling spectacle from behind my twitching curtains and I feel that the Scottish public ought to know.*'

'That's interesting.'

'*Do I detect it's not an ideal time for you, tovarich? Listen, then, tonight – our usual drinks before the Spec? Meet me at the bar of the Balmoral at six. Toodle-pip.*'

'I will do that, thank you for calling, madam.'

Replacing the receiver, Mark is glad of the relief offered by his great friend Ally Drummond. Only as a plus-one to Ally does Mark gain admission to the exclusive gatherings of Edinburgh's Speculative Society, a cultural-intellectual soiree that Mark feels to be his natural habitat, though he lacks Ally's means. But he knows he will feel a damn sight better in such company than he does right now.

Always on these nights he and Ally have a good drink beforehand, and a good dinner after: a tradition ever since they made their postgraduate ways into the world of work. Ally, graduate in law, is now an advocate with Sinclair & Pirie, specialising in company law. Their elegant offices do indeed overlook Charlotte Square, and Mark supposes that Ally must at times want to break out from his own daily grind. Between the two of them, though, Mark is disconsolately conscious that Ally is outshining him.

101

An hour later the contents of a big bottle of Johnnie Walker are being splashed into a cluster of proffered coffee mugs so that the newsroom can toast Shona McCall's leaving. Mark takes just a trickle, saving himself, and sidles up beside the paper's industrial correspondent Bill Middleton, whose job and its terrain – the factory floors of Linwood, Bathgate, Ravenscraig and Upper Clyde – Mark rather covets.

Archie tugs Shona a little importunately to his side and gestures to the small gathering to shut up. 'So then, this is just us wishing the best of luck to our Shona who's off to the *Scotsman*, don't you know. I've telt her she's mad to leave, and not to come greetin' about it to me when it all goes wrang.'

Amid compulsory chuckles Shona, who is not drinking, merely smiles and waves a hand without malice.

'Naw but, she's a great wee girl, Shona, always went along to the Women's Institute and the flower shows when I asked her. Isn't that right, hen? Mind there's a lesson there for all you young 'uns. Well done, Shona, good luck to ye . . .'

'Thanks, Archie, thank you, everyone. I've had the most tremendous time here . . .' Mark, irritated as he is by Shona's irresistible rise and her ignorance of his very existence, cannot hide the admiration he feels for her – her imperturbable poise and seriousness, but also the personal flair apparent in her office outfits and elegant updo haircut. And he wishes she could see the flair in him, too.

Bill Middleton has bent near to Mark's ear. 'I asked her to the pub once. You ken what she says to me? "I don't really see any mileage in that, Bill . . ."'

Mark grins to show solidarity.

'Are you recovered from getting your arse bitten? What were you on to Labour about?'

Mark shrugs and drains his thimble's worth of whisky. 'Oil in the North Sea.'

'What of it?'

'I just think it's interesting what Labour's saying – that if they win the election then all the licences the Tories gave out to explore might get reconsidered.'

'What do you take from that, then?'

'That Labour must be up for a fight. I reckon those companies who've sunk a load of money into buying the licences might not be best pleased to see them cancelled. So when Archie wasn't about I made a few more calls . . .'

Middleton cocks an eyebrow. 'That so? How's about you and me adjourn, laddie?'

At the crushed bar of a busy boozer Mark is sandwiched with Bill against the pie heater and the peanut vendor, pints of eighty shilling before them. Bill lights an Embassy Regal and offers Mark, who refuses.

'You gotta smoke, son. Any reporter knows that. It's the easiest trick you've got to start a conversation with a stranger.'

'I don't find that too hard so long as something has my interest.'

'What did you learn about them oil licences, then?'

'Oh, I just called up one or two licensed explorers in Aberdeen. Got through to quite an amusing American, name of Paxton? Said he'd spent three years in Scotland "working his ass off". And if "Her Majesty's Government" wanted to take his deeds off him now then he'd be talking to friends of his in Washington.'

'Did he now?'

'Yep. Said it might be time to reopen the Treaty of Paris. Something about Cornwallis handing over his sword?'

Middleton seems to enjoy this yarn almost as much as his cigarette. 'Bigshot Yank, eh? He'll only have got that bloody licence cos he crawled into bed with a partner over here, like the foreigners are meant to.'

Mark nods, comfortable of his advantage in this conversation. 'Oh yeah, he owns a third of his consortium but Texaco and Rio Tinto have a quarter each. Associated Newspapers are in on it, too. And some merchant bank in London has a wee stake.'

'Associated Newspapers, eh? You and me are in the wrong game, boy.' Middleton grinds out his Regal. 'Some good digging you done there, but. Can I stand ye a pie?'

Mark makes haste to drain his pint. 'Cheers, Bill, but I've a date. And it could mean a lot.' He winks heavily, eliciting a grunt of amusement from the older man; and then he is out into the alley, pacing his way through the Old Town.

In the comfort of the smart bar of the Balmoral, his tie knotted nicely, Mark feels not so far off the mark in the little white lie to Bill. A night out with Ally is a date of sorts, with certain equivalent excitements: there is little he finds more agreeable, even when – as now – his pal is running late, hardly an uncommon experience when dating. The red-jacketed bartender is making rather a palaver of serving his vodka tonic with a doily and a stirring stick. Mark is a mite abashed by the bourgeois manners, while reminding himself that redistribution ought to mean tall drinks for everyone.

And now, lounging into the place as if it were his living room, is Ally Drummond, wearing his dapper three-piece as easily as pyjamas, his inimitable shaggy black fringe tidier these days. 'Apologies, comrade, I come to you more or less directly from nine holes at Muirfield, and the A1 was indecently crowded.'

'Don't be comrading me when you're off playing that rich man's game with your posh friends.'

'Don't be throwing revolutionary gestures at me, comrade, when you were once a single-figure handicap yourself.'

'It's a great game,' Mark concedes, 'only spoiled by them that play it.'

'I actually find it infuriating' – Ally appeals to the bartender – 'but only like life is. My game is still second-rate, if that consoles you? I spend an awful lot of time hunting in the heather, and congratulating my opponent, very insincerely. But that's also just life. And in business these things count a fair bit, Mark.'

The sophistication of Ally's professional milieu is something Mark feels as nearly a reproof in comparison to his minion status at the dowdy *Express*. Their birthdays are but months apart, and yet Mark increasingly feels he is speaking to his senior.

'So did you follow up on that incident of bestiality in Charlotte Square? It would have made a change from your usual cat-up-a-tree rubbish.'

'Today we were mainly concerned with seeing a colleague off on her way to the *Scotsman*.'

'Oh, Mark. Shouldn't that have been you?'

'They seem to think I've still a fair bit to learn.'

Ally rattles the ice in his gin-and-tonic, contemplatively. 'The *Scotsman* would be right for you. It has a civility . . . an outward look you struggle to find elsewhere in this bloody country. Perhaps you should be aiming at Fleet Street.'

'I've never cared much for London.'

'Well then, maybe Glesga, not Embra?'

'I'd not see you nearly so much then, Al, you're okay with that?'

'There's no prize higher than true friendship, Mark. But I rate personal ambition a close second, and the two things shouldn't clash. Shall we drink up and toddle?'

The civility of Edinburgh, or Embra . . . Mark resists the overvaluing of it, and yet he surely feels it as he and Ally give up their coats to be taken by a smart attendant before passing through the lobby into the meeting room of the Speculative Society. There, civility bespeaks itself: in the gleaming white woodwork and hessian walls hung with august portraits, the marble fireplace and shimmering chandelier, the lectern awaiting the speaker and the red baize banquettes set for his audience.

It is Ally who is hailed by others and performs introductions – to the proprietor of a leading auction house, and a senior lawyer with whom Ally has recently been teamed. Mark is courteous, quiet, slightly inhibited. Then he stiffens at the approach of a familiar face atop a banker's grey suit: smarter than he was at Kilmuir School, for sure, but the same bustling frame, the same bullish forehead and implacable gingery parting.

'Well, if it isn't Ally the Cat and Rutherford . . .'

'Gordon Fyfe, as I live and breathe,' exclaims Ally.

Ally lets his hand be pumped furiously – 'Good to see Kilmuir men!' – everything inside Mark is bent upward and bristling. In an instant he has been borne back to the memory of Fyfe's grip on his collar, incensed breath on his face. They are not in a locker room now: this is Edinburgh society. And yet Mark, smiling tightly, feels ready for a ruck.

Instead he lets clubbable Al do all the talking and listening, while retaining the vague resentful feeling that an interloper is shining on his pal. Fyfe exhibits not a flicker of interest in the *Express*, but seems fascinated by news of Sinclair & Pirie and conditions at Muirfield – if keener still to get to the topic of himself, how he had been an insurance broker for a while after Oxford, until lured back home with a post worthy of his stature at the Scottish Council for Development and Industry.

By the time they take seats on the banquettes for the evening's presentation, Mark's feet are sore from shifting on the spot, and he is seething inside. He knows he should not be so; yet he finds himself mentally rehearsing the grounds for his vexation instead of concentrating on the speaker from Strathclyde, who has come to expound on the prospects for an electronics industry in Scotland. By a little, though, Mark tunes in to the fellow's rather involving theme of 'education, salvation and damnation' – that Scotland must now train up new men for new skilled callings, that an electronics industry above all might redeem the whole national economy, so long as it is not left to 'the multinational men' to 'move in, deplete our resources and move out again, leaving behind them desolation' – the speaker shifting to a tone darker still – 'as plenty have visited on Scotland before'. Mark feels himself nodding along at this Marxian turn, toward history and prophecy combined.

'What did you men think to that?'

Afterward, as Mark and Ally collect their coats, Mark anxious for supper and the night air, he curses that Ally has dallied such as to allow Fyfe to resume their conversation. Ally's reply is noncommittal, which Fyfe seems to take as an invitation to a lecture of his own.

'This is my area, in a sense, the council puts a certain amount of taxpayers' money into these efforts, and I agree there is a perfectly sound basis for a respectable industry here, it simply needs to be – as the speaker implied – about more than turning out cash registers and time clocks. We need more market entrants, it calls for a bit of pioneering spirit. Scotland doesn't have the strength in depth that a great team needs, but we *do* have promising players.'

What a surprise, thinks Mark, moved to rebut. 'I expect as an industry it will need to promise a few more jobs than it does right now if it's going to get people excited.'

'Electronics wallahs are not going to be shipbuilders, Rutherford – it's not the same work. And if Scotland actually wants to attract more employers then its workplaces will need to be a bit more conducive to modern management than, say, how they run things on the Clyde.'

'Well, Fyfe,' says Mark, fixing his muffler determinedly for the door, 'good luck on persuading more Scots to mind their bloody manners with the boss. I thought our speaker's whole point was that Scotland needs a homegrown industry, not just to take what it's given by blow-ins.'

'Oh God, if someone wants to start a business and hire and train men then I really don't give a damn if he's a Scotsman. That's the road to Scots Nattery. But maybe, Rutherford, you're a bit of a Scots Nat?'

Mark breathes deep. *Why should I be damn this, that or whatever just because you say?* 'I think in a lot of ways that we know very well, Scotland has been disadvantaged and deserves better. But, no, Fyfe, I'm a Labour supporter, and I trust them to do something about the mess we're in as soon as they're back in power.'

'You don't change, Rutherford.'

Still a commie pig, Mark supposes.

'It's worse than you think, Gordon.' Ally smiles indulgently. 'Mark has aspirations to be a Labour MP.'

This is, to Mark's ear, a fresh outrage: something said in confidence once or twice over a companionable drink should not be handed as ammunition to the enemy under very cursory interrogation.

'It sounds to me, Rutherford,' says Fyfe, tilting his disagreeable forehead, 'that you're perhaps not the most objective newspaperman.'

'I'm a professional, Fyfe, what I write and report is absolutely objective.' Pleased with how this sounds, Mark nonetheless knows all too well just how little he has written at the *Express* of which he is remotely proud.

'What's your position then, Alastair?' trumpets Fyfe as if it is his role to settle things. 'Still a Unionist man, no?'

Mark sees Ally throw him a practised glance of a *soigné* sort that he treasures, before making his reply. 'Gordon, my chief allegiance in life is to the Drummond Party. And it's a party of one, but I very much welcome new applicants.'

Mark's relish is killed by Ally's next words: 'Now, Mark and I are for a bite of supper, care to join us, Gordon?'

The infidelity makes Mark livid, even as it becomes clear that Fyfe has other, better plans for the evening. He has noticed anew in Ally something he has always contrived to ignore: a kind of instinctual status-based rubbing-along with people and things otherwise objectionable. Yes, they are three Kilmuir men, but not at all cut from the same cloth. The unthinking Unionism, the deferential bow to bloody London, the stolid bourgeois view on all things – that much is Fyfe, for sure. But it is not his friend Ally. He wonders how easily Ally's head can be turned – wonders if in fact it has been turned for a while.

February 1965
Tests of Mettle

A big day for Aaron Strang, and a big night yet ahead. Set against the many that drift by, this one has been marked in red and dreaded, its significance enormous for the chance to change all that follows. Now he sits and waits his allotted turn among the junior geologists, each to be summoned into Paxton's office, there to present their best guess at a site out at sea where oil might be found.

The office blinds are down, the current victim doubtless sweating his cross-examination. Aaron holds a bundle of rolled maps awkwardly across his knees. His wallet, in which he keeps a hitherto ceremonial prophylactic, weighs heavy in his pocket; but then that will be tonight's test.

The time is now to impress or fall short, to show oneself as a spark or a dud. He is well aware he was handed his opportunity on the basis of a strong recommendation, the writ of which has run so far but no further. It is graduation time, and the stakes are high now, like the stack of cash Paxton has paid out already for the right to explore; the research he has bankrolled, Aaron's included.

Aaron's preference would have been to sit some written exam. Hal Magruder, though, has advised him that Mr Paxton relishes a live brawl. '*Clay likes to see a man come in and fight for his share. If you go in there like a straight talker, you'll get through. But see if you get asked something you don't know? You ain't gonna make it no better by pullin' something outta your ass. Say, "Mr Paxton, sir, I'm sorry, I do not know the answer but I will sure go find it . . ."*'

Now Wyndham is emerging from the office, his own papers ungainly underarm as he fumbles the door, looking a little less pink than usual – blanched, even. Aaron is pleased to think that session might have just gone rather poorly. For his own part, he has done time with the seismic data – the mad search for meaningful undulations on paper under lamplight. He has integrated his data with care. He has looked at so many samples, drawn so many sketches. He knows he has come up with a choice that is rational, not deranged. He understands the source rock. He believes he understands the migration path. In short, he hopes devoutly that he has answers to most all they will ask.

In the lion's den he sits and waits for the jaws to open, glancing around the familiar decor – Paxton's photographic record of his adventures in oil. Across the walnut table Paxton, Charlie McGinn and Erwin Shields are flicking through his report and recommendations. Between them are the bloody remains of Paxton's lunch. But Aaron knows the Ulsterman Shields to be his chief adversary: rotund, bespectacled, thinning hair swept across his broad forehead, the pallor of one who shuns the sun.

At last Paxton throws his ring-bound pages onto the tabletop. 'So, Israelite, you're putting your chips on block four-eight-six?'

Aaron nods, tensely.

'Exactly where,' asks Shields, frowning, 'do you get your confidence about these depth profiles?'

'I can only say it's a hunch, sir, based on the considerable variations we've all seen across the Mesozoic reflections every time we've shot seismic.'

'A hunch? You don't feel like trying a better pitch on us than that, Aaron?' McGinn's usual mildness strikes Aaron now as a note of disappointment.

'I believe the general shape of the structure I'm envisaging down there has a very good chance of proving to be valid.'

'Because of what? What's clinching it for you?'

Aaron flaps open the report to the right seismic graph and jabs a finger. 'I'd argue – where it's brightening there? – that seems to me a decent marker of a possible structural anomaly. We could be talking about reservoir rocks in situations with cover and trap elements – a fault acting as a structural trap.'

At this, Shields's jaws seem to snap. 'Oh, that is highly speculative. And I notice you extrapolate a straight line in all directions, as so often doesn't happen . . . This is really your best effort?'

Aaron is lost for a robust response, as he was sure Shields hoped.

'Speak up, Aaron,' McGinn exhales. 'If you think so then you'd best get used to saying so.'

'My settled recommendation is that we should test there. Of course, I appreciate the top Zechstein salt is nothing, but at the depth we're after I rate it a very decent bet. If we drill and that's not what we find, I'm certain we'll still learn something vital about the sub-surface.'

'For a million dollars,' McGinn chuckles, 'we had better.'

'A million if the weather plays fair,' Shields mutters. Aaron feels himself sitting on a powder-keg as fire is exchanged around his ears.

Now Paxton sits forward, removes his hands from where they cushioned the back of his head, and joins them before him on the tabletop. 'C'mon. We don't ask the Israelite to master the winds. Wait 'til you're out on a drilling rig, kid, maybe you can part the seas for us. So we're good with this, Erwin?'

It takes Aaron a stricken, silent moment to realise that, as if from nowhere, he has received the blessing of Moses. Shields has, less happily, realised the same.

'I suppose this is just about adequately documented. We might do worse.'

McGinn lights a cigarette and smiles as he shakes the flaring match. 'Thank you, Aaron. Now the drill bit will test your reading. And you're quite right, we're all a little old to be fighting shy of it.'

As night comes down Aaron goes to meet Heather Munro per The Plan, for dinner at the Victoria restaurant: an occasion meal. The approval of his report has buoyed him with a sense of validation, of having impressed a few people. And yet the morning's work has already begun to seem to him like it was meant to be, only the most basic measure of his competence. Tonight is a subtly different challenge.

The Plan is that he and Heather will dine and then attend a recital at the concert hall where she works an occasional stint as an usher. Heather, still living at home with her parents, has told them that she will stay overnight in town with an old schoolfriend. In fact, she will, for the first time, spend the night in Aaron's flat.

Aaron has prepped his bedroom as far as he is capable, though as a site for romance – with its brown wallpaper, cracked ceiling and moth-ridden wardrobe – it feels to him forlornly lacking. He fears, though, that the deeper lack is in himself. Ever since endorsing The Plan he has felt oppressed by its import – the ridding of shared virginity. Their chaste courtship has been heading to this moment, the two of them seemingly locked together by an unfeigned mutual fondness that has, nonetheless, lacked a certain passion. He has grown used to Heather peering at him as if with an unspoken query. He has kidded himself to wonder how much she truly sees without her sheet music reading specs? But he suspects she can see his limitations.

Aaron feels sure that for his to pass muster as an object of desire would require him to be in some skin other than the one he is in. As for his own desires, and his struggle to summon them – surely Heather sees this, too, and ought then to do something about it, to save herself, if nothing else? Could it be sufficient for Heather that he love and cherish only her mind? No, clearly not; absurd to think so.

Arriving at the Victoria he is nearly relieved to find that Hugh has joined them, just for a glass of wine; and Hugh greets Aaron like one of the family, as he has been doing for some time. Heather smiles at Aaron from seated. Her glasses must be in her purse, and her dark and deep-set eyes seem to glimmer with the covertness of The Plan. She wears a blue velvet minidress, an Alice band in her hair, at the throat the amethyst he gave her. She might have succeeded in making

Aaron forget she is Hugh Munro's daughter were it not for his sitting opposite – the same strong nose and long mouth, the same heavy eyebrows and clever high forehead that the Alice band emphasises. Heather is sipping white wine that Hugh has ordered, and already a second bottle appears needful if Aaron is to get a decent glass. Indeed, Aaron's report of the day moves Hugh to a toast.

'I never doubted you, Aaron. And "hunch" is a perfectly good expression. For now it's all about throwing darts, and you have done a fine job of straightening the dartboard for them. McGinn is quite right, only the drill can tell you what's what.'

'But your passion was the key, Aaron,' Heather exclaims, with her usual huskiness but a bit more exuberance than Aaron is used to. He senses she is making a special effort on his behalf, which he finds both touching and slightly worrying.

Hugh is on his hobbyhorse. 'I find few things are more dispiriting than clever people faced by problems deciding that a thing can't be done and shouldn't ever be attempted. You hear such pitiful reasons. Anything new is hard. But fear of risk is a disease. Of course, yes, performance will count in the end, but you have to try things first. You learn by first failing – it's true, Aaron.' Deftly he pats Aaron's hand where it rests on the tabletop. 'You've done well, I'm proud of you.'

And Hugh could have stayed longer and said more, as far as Aaron is concerned, but now the busy professor is excusing himself and wishing the young ones a pleasant evening – 'Have fun, you two!' – and Aaron feels nothing but his mentor's entire blessing. He pats Aaron's shoulder and murmurs, 'Don't drink too much.' To Aaron this seems peculiar; then, a moment later, somehow pointed.

They walk to the concert hall arm in arm, silent, Heather's smile still so sphinx-like that Aaron decides they simply must speak. They could converse forever, a clever young man and a clever young woman; but always, it seems, of the same topics, and somehow not of the essence. And yet, what he asks her is to say a little of the string quartet they are shortly to hear, certain at least of how eloquently she can do so.

'Well, it's a little unique in being inspired by a book which was inspired by a sonata? The book is by the Russian, Tolstoy. The sonata's by a chap you might have heard of, name of Beethoven?'

'There's a story to it, then? To the music?'

'There is. It's about a jealous husband who suspects that his wife, who's only a poor pianist, is having a wild affair with a dashing violinist. When in fact the two of them are just regular music lovers. But the husband won't be told, and he kills her.'

'Kills *her*? Not the violinist?'

'Well, quite.'

They process up the steps and under the Ionic portico, into the handsome foyer, where Aaron feels his familiar unease of being among connoisseurs more cultivated than himself. Before they take their seats, though, Heather requests another glass of wine; and Aaron, slightly thrown, orders for them both.

Then they are up in their gallery seats gazing down upon a stage set with four stands before a gargantuan organ. To generous applause the quartet appear and assume positions, tuning up while Aaron summons his own powers of concentration. At last, an anticipatory hush; then the music starts.

And very soon Aaron can believe he is hearing some sort of dispute transformed into music – first sonorous loveliness, then a violent, agitated, rhythmic scraping. The tempo, the dynamics are jagged that way. He glances about him as to gauge how others might be feeling; and then he looks to Heather. Her heavy-lidded eyes are closed, her lips slightly parted.

Something is going on inside her that seems to him highly complicated. She has gone somewhere, albeit not so far-distant as suggested by her bearing whenever he watches her play – that sense of her being both composedly present yet transported by the emotion of what she is producing, like she has become an instrument of a higher authority, one to which Aaron has no access, that sense of exclusion making him feel lumpen and graceless.

He puts his hand on top of hers. She looks at him, at first sharply – until that slight smile returns. The music is gradually turning to a kind of autumnal, regretful lugubriousness. Aaron wonders suddenly if this is the theme of the murderer, the imagined cuckold, now guilty and penitent.

Then the hall is filled with stormy applause. Heather puts her mouth to his ear. 'Did you appreciate that?'

'Of course! Absolutely . . . I don't really have the words.'

'But you *felt* it, yes?'

He follows her into the bright-lit foyer. The night's great business is near at hand. To his surprise, though, Heather wants another glass of wine, and wants him to have one also. He is suddenly confused: does she want to be drunk? And him, too?

Returning with the drinks to where he left her, he sees she has been joined by a neat, bespectacled, rather birdlike young man with the air of an overgrown if undernourished schoolboy. No obvious threat, then. And yet Heather is conversing with him very easily, smiling now more than slightly, touching this fellow's arm in syncopation with his remarks. His name is Paul Burns, and he is a cellist – a fellow graduate of Glasgow Academy.

'Oh but didn't you love the third movement, Heather?'

'I adored it, Paul!'

'The third bit sounded to me like a fight,' Aaron offers.

'You might well say that.' Paul pushes his metal spectacles up his nose, so roughly Aaron imagines it must have hurt. 'I always feel as if cello and violin are soulmates, playing that lovely theme? Which Janáček takes from Beethoven, of course. Then the viola and second violin come crashing in with the bitter ponticello.'

'That what, sorry?' Aaron frowns.

'They were playing ponticello?' Heather mimes, with a vigour maybe unneeded. 'You put the bow right up next to the bridge? Very particular sound.'

'Eerie, I thought,' says Aaron.

'You were scared?' Paul asks, avian eyebrows raised, seemingly sincere. Heather laughs, and Aaron finds he has no better response.

In the taxi to Aaron's flat he is torn between rehearsing for the romantic manner he has supposed he must summon from somewhere within; and ensuring that Heather does not get sick in the backseat. For a while her speech has been a little slurred. While he pays the driver she exits the cab abruptly, and he sees her swaying *en route* to the pavement.

'We must be quiet,' he chides her gently as they climb the stairs to the top floor, and she presses herself into his side, but less for intimacy, he feels, than to have the help in remaining upright.

'You are kind to me, Aaron, you are,' she slurs, and Aaron senses some sort of penitence in her voice that makes him uneasier still.

The room is chilly, as always. Heat seems needed: he hastens to switch on three bars of electric heat. Moonlight falls from the skylight window, and Aaron feels he wants no other light. What is there worth seeing other than his bookshelves, his wall-mounted geological map of Scotland, the drooping fronds of his spider plant?

There is, of course, his sagging bed, onto the edge of which Heather now plumps – or, rather, slumps, drowsily, turning to the unbuckling of her shoes, the rolling off of her black tights. He goes directly to the bathroom to fetch her water.

On his return she is fully recumbent. He can hear her breathing. Her blue velvet dress has ridden up, her underwear a shadowy white triangle in the dark. Rain has begun to fall like a clatter on the skylight.

Aaron sets down the glass on the bedside.

He stands there and thinks that he must act. Nothing can be worse than not to. He must make something happen.

117

He steps near, then sits still on the brink of the bed.

His eyes watch his hand move – trailing up her inner thigh and between, until the fingertips reach the white lace trim of her underwear; then further, beneath.

Now she is breathing faster: small, tight noises escaping her. The tendrils of her hair spread wide across his pillow.

He retreats. 'Do you want me to . . . ?'

She reaches for his hand and – just as his friend once said – she 'puts it there'.

And with this intimacy – in a trice – the tenderness required of the lover becomes just as vivid and palpable to Aaron as it was baffling before. Now he slides himself down beside her, seeing better the flush of her face, the bite on her lower lip. Something raw and unforced in her arousal is stirring in him, too. Glad of the dark still, he gropes with his one free hand for the wallet in his pocket and removes it to within reach on the bedside.

'Love Is Strange' is the song in his head as he lies there in early light, aware of every inch of his prickling skin against sheets he knows now he must change; conscious, too, of some transfigured relationship to his own flesh, and to hers. Dreary traffic hubbub filters up from the street below. The room has not lost a stroke of its dismalness and he avoids glancing at the pale rubber pouch deposited on the bedside.

Instead, he turns over to face her recumbence, and he looks at her and tries to read her look as returned. Is it fond, or somehow rueful? Pleased, or embarrassed? He understands she might be waiting for him to say something – a fuller consummation? Or perhaps she just needs her glasses. *Anyhow*, he resolves – it can wait. Her lips are very dry, clearly she needs more water; and so he draws back the sheets to go fetch, gratified inside by the sense of a trial run done with promising results, albeit room for improvement.

June 1965
Angela's Wedding

'Are you awake?'

Joe Killday hears his lover's question clearly from behind his closed lids but decides, for the moment, not to stir from supine. He can feel her mouth near his ear, but he is leery of the nocturnal conversation he expects her to pursue. Yes, he, too, has not slept for thinking; and he suspects she has a reasonable idea why. Janet is nobody's fool.

His sister Angela is due to be wed in seven hours, two hundred miles north of their hotel bed for the night; but Joe has given the marriage little thought. He does wonder, though, what his family will make of the date he is bringing up to Scotland for the occasion.

And then, of course, there is the job offer, and what to be done there.

The two of them began the long drive the previous afternoon, after finishing their respective duties for the week at Fort Dunlop in Birmingham. The decision to break the journey in Gretna Green was born of necessity, and Joe hadn't minded the nervy laugh of it, or signing into the guestbook as 'Mr and Mrs Killday'. First a meal and then intercourse, in the vigorous, unfussy manner to which they have become accustomed. It is all going much as Joe thought it would; yet he remains unsure if he should be doing it at all.

Janet McCreadie is four years older than him, senior in Accounts and administratively adept. One day, after voicing admiration for a set of costings he had drawn up, she made her deeper interest in him clear, in a very grown-up and gratifying way; and so they began to see each other after work under a certain veil of secrecy. That was seven weeks ago. Soon enough he understood she would be very pleased to

119

accompany him to his sister's wedding – just as soon, in fact, as he had inadvertently mentioned the date.

And Joe cannot discount such steadfastness, so very deficient in she whom he considers still the principal girl in his romantic history. Janet is a woman; and all ways round she makes him feel like a man. But she hasn't affected him nearly as seriously as Belinda Morland once did. He finds it foolish, unmanning, even, that the notion of his heart's desire still takes such a specific shape as one he hasn't seen or heard of in years. And yet, there it is – a haunting glamour he cannot deny.

And still, the job offer, and what to be done about that.

The post is in Malacca, with Dunlop Malayan Estates Limited. He is to be a plantation manager, running an estate, in charge of tree-tapping operations and the yield of rubber for latex production. He applied for the position keenly enough, managed the interview capably, and wanted very much to beat the rival candidates to it. Taking it up, though, is another matter.

He is to live in a modern Corbusier-style house, well connected by company-made roads to company-owned amenities. While his workforce in the main will be Malay, Indian, Chinese, his direct reports will be as British as himself. And he will have permanent protection from less amenable locals close at hand in the form of armed guards driving armoured vehicles. A handy job for a handy wage. They told him when he was just a graduate hire that he was 'joining a family', a big and big-hearted firm whose elders want the best for those who follow; and this family have now picked him for this progression from the West Midlands to warmer climes.

And so, he asked Dunlop for the weekend to think about it.

For so long Joe has wanted to break out and away, to fly into a future of his own making. When he called his parents to tell them of the offer, he could feel a solemnity in his father's response that was difficult to bear. *'That is quite some achievement of yours, Joseph. My congratulations to you . . .'* Malaysia, though, suddenly feels like an awfully long way to go for all that. It carries the shades of some kind of confinement, of inherited burden. He can picture himself cutting a modern figure in that fancy house, for sure; but can see himself stuck in it also – caged, encumbered. A colonial administrator of a sort, and maybe – who knows? – marooned there at the very moment the colonies revolt, like that famous old painting of Gordon of Khartoum, one limp pistol facing a sea of bristling spears.

'Can you hear me, Joe?'

Now Janet's hand is on his arm, gentle pressure, but insistent. Nothing else for it. He feigns to stir.

'I'm sorry, Joe. I can't help thinking.'

Joe is torn, wanting to do whatever might look nearest to the gallant thing.

'Janet, I know. And I don't want you to feel just . . . bound into decisions that I've got to make for myself. On their own merits. I can't ask that of you.'

'I just want you to understand . . . it would be my wish. To go with you. There's work for me in Malacca, too, we both know that. You'd only have to ask them. If you wanted.'

Three hours later it is rosily light even through the drawn curtains, though Joe is no better rested; but there is no time to lose since they have miles yet to cover. And yet, Joe can see Janet is just a mite bemused by his clouded, over-deliberate manners. She chivvies him by the clock, presses his shirt, and he begins to suspect she might try to tuck him into his suit. But he tends to himself; and while buttoning up and bending to lace his smart boots he studies her while she brushes volume into her hair, draws her eyebrows to a peak, paints her lips purplish and inserts herself with a degree of wriggling effort into her olive-green dress with full skirt and modest neckline.

Checked out and back on the road, they are soon in some confusion over the best route. Joe has no map and wonders if he should be

121

heading in the direction of Glasgow or Edinburgh. Janet is calm but resolute, even a little chiding. 'You just have to make a decision, Joe.'

They reach the door of Queen's Cross Church with two minutes to spare, and within they trot directly to the front pews. But Joe doesn't mind standing out; he only hopes to be cutting a decent figure as he does so. To have made his own sister's wedding by the skin of his teeth calls for quite some tale about traffic conditions, but he has that ready, too. He notes the Bodies to the right and Killdays to the left, and so turns left. The Killday turnout is a little shorter of bodies than he had expected.

In the low murmur of the high space, Ma leans across Janet to tell Joe: 'Your da was so worried. "Where's Joseph?" he was saying. "We'll not start until he's here."'

Eyes front, Joe sees that Mr Raymond Bodie is smiling at him quite directly from where he stands at the altar – smiling a little oddly, even; but no reprimand there, anyway. Joseph remains unsure what to make of Angela's beau. His view is that people normally pair off at approximately their level of attractiveness – as fair or unfair as that, part of what concerns him with regard to the woman now seated by him. Bodie is no matinee idol, either, but he is assured and well-presented where Angela is somehow apologetic for the space she takes up. Why did he set his cap at Angela? Romantic feeling can't be made out of air. Of that, at least, Joe is sure.

And now here comes the bride, in a long pearly gown suited to her modesty, patriarch Andrew gravely at her side.

Upstairs at Netherdown, facing the old familiar bathroom mirror, Joe dampens his brow and once again confronts his perplexing reflection. Arrayed above the sink are his father's trusty shaving materials; they look older now, careworn. Through the open window comes the sounds of reasonable gaiety spilling out from the marquee tent in the garden, a ceilidh band playing eightsome-reels for the guests out on the lawn, the reception perhaps nearing its knees-up stage.

Sober but unsettled, Joe considers what is wrong with the picture – the reflection of the man he has become. He has added strings to his bow, gestured in the direction of dancing to his own tune, not the one set by others. Down there at Dunlop they rate him well enough, for sure. But the picture of the man he wishes to be remains undeveloped.

He is wondering if what he wants is really in Malacca. Or if the game has been more about being *seen* to get away. His appetite for the posting – and all else that might be coming with – is not as it should be. There is no move that is not a losing move.

The open window gives Joe a decent vantage of the eightsome dancing below it, chief among these the newlyweds, also Garth and Bryony, and their married cousins. Angela has gamely picked up the hem of her dress so as to join her husband; and Joe is struck by the spritely way in which the two of them dance, doing their part in fluid motion for the shape of the formation, fitting snugly amid the other couples – just as snug as Bodie's arm round Angela's waist. When he spins her, there is delight on her flushed face – a sudden flag to Joe of something notably vigorous between them, a measure of sap he hadn't hitherto considered.

When Angela takes her turn as 'lady in the middle' her movements are deft with a charm she more often conceals. Joe sees now that his father – never much of a dancer – is watching on just as intently, perhaps amazedly, as himself. And the sight of Garth and Bryony clapping and cheering on the newlyweds, too, reminds Joe, rather piercingly, of the importance of pairing off in this life. Perhaps Angela has done rather well. Maybe she sized up Mr Ray Bodie better than anyone knew?

Abruptly conscious that to fritter much more time alone in this manner could look unseemly, Joe turns, unlocks the bathroom door and heads back downstairs to the garden.

There from a distance he spies Janet stood in what appears to be a very cordial conversation with his parents. She has that capable way with others – a way he might do well to acquire more of. Ma is watching Janet closely, craning her neck, since Janet is a foot taller. Da is smiling, nodding, nursing a dram. Janet told Joe how much she admired Andrew's speech, but Joe had heard its main notes too many times: 'When Da bangs on about having the sea in his blood it sounds to me like a disease.' 'You're a little bit hard on your family,' Janet had responded, and Joe hadn't liked that, but let it pass. Rather than join the mutual appreciation society now, he scans the gathering to see if he can spot one or other of his brothers.

'You can stop with that, big lad.'

Joe sees that his new brother-in-law has materialised at his side.

'Hullo, Ray, I'm sorry?'

'Quit the staring into space when there's a party on. Don't be the Lone Ranger, Joe. I'll keep you company, if you've no pals.'

Joe stiffens a little. 'It's your wedding, Ray. Shouldn't you get back to the dancing?'

'Aw, I'd a wee bit of business.' He produces from within his morning suit an item that Joe recognises as a remarkably small transistor radio, likely of Asian origin. 'I've a bet on the Kilmarnock game. And I'm pleased to say it's come good.' Now Bodie looks left and right, almost comically, before putting his lips close to Joe's ear. 'What do you make of the heft? The talent?'

Joe keeps his voice low as he can. 'I brought someone, Ray.'

'Of course you did.' Bodie's mien remains a good bit more sleekit than Joe would like. 'As I see it, kemosabe, there are the women you can get, and the ones who are out of reach. But when you're stuck in the moment you don't always know how far you can stretch. You might need to chance your arm.'

Joe looks to Bodie with a flicker of irritation only to see the man's expression has changed in a flash, his hands clasped before him as if in deference.

'Listen, Joe, I may not have a chance to say this later, but I really appreciate what your family's done here. What they've spent on this occasion, the conduct of it. It's all true, all I ever heard about how the Killdays do things?' He nods sagely. 'Pure class.'

'You can tell my da yourself,' Joe murmurs, bemused, watching Andrew and Winnifred and Janet now approaching. But Bodie only pats his arm, grins and slips off toward the dancing.

'Joseph' – Andrew indicates the door back into the Netherdown house – 'may I have a word with you indoors just a while?'

Janet leads him a few steps aside as Andrew heads on in. 'I'm going to the Station Hotel? I'll take a room, join me once you can get away? I love your family, they're good people.' She kisses him softly on the cheek.

In Andrew's study the blinds are closed but the last of the light through the louvres throws patterned shadows onto the walls. Andrew pours two generous Glenlivets into crystal tumblers and proffers one to Joe.

'Well, Joseph, a fine and fitting turnout for your sister as she embarks on her new life, and may she have all she hopes for.'

'Amen to that,' Joe murmurs and takes a sip, wondering – as he sometimes does these days – whether his father sees further than the end of his nose.

'We should drink to you and all, Joseph. To all your accomplishments, and those you have ahead of you. You're doing things in your life beyond my ken, son. You make me very proud.'

Andrew's unvarnished approval still feels so relatively novel to Joe that he takes a big throat-burning swallow of the malt. 'Thank you, Da,' he responds at last, somewhat raspingly.

'That woman of yours is handsome. Your mother and I were pleased you could bring her.'

In response Joe merely smiles, not in the mood for any parental blessing of that sort, then hastens to change the subject. 'Da, I noticed Uncle Allan and Grace didn't come? Are they well enough, or . . . ?'

Andrew sets down his glass, and sighs heavily.

'I'm sorry, if that's—'

'No, Joseph, it is quite right you ask me why my sole surviving brother didn't see fit to attend the wedding of his niece.'

In the silence that follows, Joe wonders if he has ever before seen his father seem so much at a loss.

'Allan was certainly invited. I thought that was right, in spite of things between us. But the fact of it is that he wrote to me in refusal. And he had some other things to say. That he'd decided we should not pretend to be friendly. Nor see one another ever again.'

Now Joe, too, puts down his glass. 'How has that happened?'

'It happened a long time ago, Joseph, and there's no fixing it. He's right – we've pretended friendship of a kind for years, or you might call it tolerance of one another, maybe. But, the fact of it is, all of twenty years ago we had a rift over the business, me and him. I took a certain view which he took to be to his detriment, and he went his own way, and has done ever since. And it will be that way now until he passes, I expect.'

Andrew has taken a few steps as to slump into the chair behind his expansive desktop. Joe also lowers himself into the visitor's seat.

'What was the cause of it, Da?'

'Just one of those things that happen in business that you have to cope with. Harder, for sure, when there's blood involved. Ach it's such a long bloody tale, Joseph, but . . . when I took on the business from your granddad it was with Allan, the intention that we manage it jointly. But it was desperate times, son. We needed steam ships and we didn't have them . . . We needed new fishing grounds, we'd to look to Iceland . . . There were big challenges, and it was clear to me we had to do things different, take a risk or two, go to the bank, if we were to keep our heads above water. But your Uncle Allan . . . he just dug in his heels and said we'd to keep doing what we were doing. Which to me meant ruin, and I told him so, and in the end I said it so strongly that he took great umbrage and said some things in turn, and . . .'

Joe recognises well the shake of Andrew's head, done so sharply as if it could dispel a bad memory.

'But this is how people fall out, Joseph. And I regret the way of it, but I'm telling you now, I was right on this matter, hard as it was, and Allan knows that fine well but he will never, ever say it. And it is a simple fact that every business must decide how it's run, by who. I'm sure you've understood this yourself in your working life – I know you've a keen eye on the management side of things. But with my own brother I learned a great lesson.'

'What was the lesson?' Joe is leaning forward in his chair, very engrossed in this case study, the most absorbing conversation he has ever had with Andrew.

'Ach, it's that there come times, son, when you've to part company and go different ways with a person . . . but then you've to take care you make peace. You can't fall out and have it fester. And maybe I've been fooling myself.'

Joe stands to retrieve his glass, suddenly surer of his assessment of the matter. 'It's like you say, Da. You were right. You made the big decision for the business, the family. And you made it well.'

Andrew, too, has regained his feet, and rejoins Joe by the sideboard with the decanter. 'It's right enough that if I had feared the hard thing, the new thing, then I wouldn't be here now. And perhaps my brother and I would still be fast friends. Or maybe today would not have come to pass because we'd all have perished. If not in the bloody nineteen-thirties then in the bloody war or thereafter.'

Joe watches Andrew take a solid swig from his tumbler, an action that seems to stiffen his purpose, for now he looks keenly.

'Fishing has been the North Sea way for one or two centuries, and I reckon it will do another century yet, no fear. I'll not see the end of that, nor will you, or your children, or theirs. In due course, this business will need new leadership.'

In the silence Joe feels the force of his father's stare, and a growing sense of what Andrew has wanted from this word indoors.

'I know you have other ambitions – better offers, even. As befits the fine young man you have become. But before you take the next step . . . I would feel I had made a great error if I didn't make you an offer of my own. I would like for you to join the Killday Fishing Company, in a senior post befitting your qualifications. As Director of Services, initially. Whatever others might pay you, I know I can better it. And in time, it would be my wish . . . I would want you to run this business, Joseph. You would have your head in that matter, of course, I could not hold you to it if you decided otherwise. But – that is what I hope for.'

For a moment or two Joe is fixed on the pattern of the rug beneath their feet: the ground is not as familiar as it was a few moments previous.

Finally he says: 'What about my brothers?'

Andrew sets down his tumbler again, decisively. 'Garth's a skipper, that's after my own heart, but he's no head for business. Walter, he'll always have his place with us but he's not a leader, he's not got that stuff. My faith is in you, Joseph. I look to you for what you've got that I know my older sons don't have the same way. And that is ambition.'

Caught so unawares, Joe struggles in his head, between the convictions of most of a lifetime, and a sudden stirring that is altogether new.

'Know that you'd have my blessing to make decisions as you judge them. New approaches if they're required. In this game you can't stand back admiring the view of what you've done in the past and think that's forever dandy. You have to anticipate what's round the bend and be ready for it. That's why I look at you and I wish for what I'm offering you.'

Joe is not wholly persuaded, not on the strength of his acquaintance to date with the subtle art of recruitment, the ways one might haul a new hire aboard. But could his father be merely fishing, tempting, to see if he will bite?

At the same time, as ever, he is getting certain images in his head. If he were to do such a thing, how impressive or not would it appear to others? And then how might it feel to him inside? Like a leap into liberty, or another kind of confinement? Better or worse than the company home plus helpmeet awaiting him in Malacca?

In another instant he sees the efficacy of the solution to his most immediate dilemmas. *It's not forever. I can walk away. I heard him say it, that is the bargain.*

'I don't need your answer now, Joseph, I'd ask only that you think and decide as soon as you're able.'

'Thank you, Da, I appreciate it, and that's what I will do.'

But Joe has the shape of a decision before him: he will go to the Station Hotel, explain the whole situation to Janet, with the care that he owes to her. He has a fair idea how she will respond to the news – dog's abuse, most like, but he will deserve it, no doubt, so he had better put his paws up and take the shaming. Then he will go and take another room elsewhere: he will have the night alone, to ponder what such a late and large change of tack will mean.

Exiting into the hallway, headed to the front door, Joe hopes to slip away off to town unnoticed. But there, standing framed in the bright doorway to the garden as if awaiting him, is Raymond Bodie, the newest member of the Killday family, who grins to see his brother-in-law, and raises his glass.

PART III
COVENANTS

January 1967
Dirty Work

The hour is late, near on ten, and Dougie Stewart hastens up the stairwell of the Station Hotel with his basic plumbing kit in his big jangling kitbag. He is impeded still by the slight limp he's carried for two years since coming off the back of his pal Ricky's motorcycle. But the Station's lift is broken; and Dougie has made it his business to answer late calls that others might disdain. This one is a problem in a bathroom suite, and the guest in question seems to have some clout at reception, where they had on hand one of the business cards Dougie recently printed and distributed. The power of advertising! So then, to the fifth floor, Room 57, there to ask for an American gentleman, name of Paxton.

What Dougie's heard is a toilet blockage. Well . . . he doesn't love the plumbing game, but folk need these jobs done in a spot, and he can hack them. Dirty work at times, but nothing much repels him: he grew up in an overpopulated household, and Grandpa Stewart had mucky habits. He has been learning the ways of new appliances, he can mend most things, and is at ease with water systems – at least, since one early-days calamity where he stood amid a wifey's bathroom in great perplexity, getting pissed on by pure malicious jets of water.

Being a lone wolf, Dougie works into the nights, and his office is his car, most often parked opposite Ricky's chipper since Ricky being a pal is agreeable to a share of the phone number. And Dougie quite likes a mercy mission; likes being dependably useful, likes people being awfy pleased to see him. He doesn't mind the chat, either. No two days are ever the same. You do meet some people.

The door to Room 57 is opened by a tall sixtyish man biting on an unlit cigar, with the look of being rather hastily dressed, albeit in a fancy untucked shirt, and slacks that must have cost a few bob, too.

'Good to see you, friend. Clay Paxton. What do I call you?'

'The name's Dougie, sir.'

'Dougie? You got it. Come on in here.'

The bedsheets have been hastily smoothed, the *Woman's Mirror* magazine is on the nightstand beneath a bottle of some clear firewater. Dougie is conscious of Mr Paxton staring fixedly at his gait as he comes past.

'You okay there, fella?'

'Aw, ready for action, sir.'

'Attaboy. Listen, Doug, beyond that bathroom door there is water, water everywhere and not a drop to drink. Now I'm a capable kind of a guy, you understand?'

'I don't doubt that, sir.'

'Yeah but I had me a root round there and I thought, "The hell with this."'

'We cannae do everything ourselves, sir.'

'You just said it right there. And, Dougie, when a man can't shit in peace and comfort, that's a big chunk of his happiness in life gone clean out the window.'

'Shall I have a look at the damage, sir?'

'Through there. And let me tell ya, I respect you answering the call. This time of night some guys would be yellowin' out.'

Dougie ventures alone into the bathroom. Significant water, yes, is pooled on the floor; the toilet seat is down; carefully Dougie lifts it. It is not at all the horror he feared. He pushes his heavy black specs up to his forehead so he might peer closer.

Re-entering the bedroom he sees that Mr Paxton has poured himself a tumbler from that bottle of spirit. 'There's a shot of this for you when you're done, friend.'

'Looks like a strong drop of drink, sir.'

'Tequila. That it is, Doug, but – I'm full grown, you know? So I can stomach it. Here's to the Queen!' Paxton knocks it back.

Dougie drops to his knees to rummage in the bag for his trusty plumber's snake.

'Looks like you got all the tools, Dougie.'

'Adequate to the job, sir. What line of work are you in yourself, may I ask?'

'Only one I ever known, son. I'm over here hunting for oil in that damn North Sea of yours.'

'Wow. So do I understand right you'll be out there drilling on the seabed?'

'Hundred per cent. Got me a rig two hundred miles off the coast, towed all the way from the Gulf of Mexico. I got fifteen rooms in this hotel just for my guys. Food and lodging. But no liquor, you get me? I was born at night but it wasn't last night.'

'I hear there's tremendous money in the oil business?'

'Well, there's usually a little truth in anything you hear. But your damn North Sea has yet to turn me one red cent. And I've been here a while . . .'

To Dougie's eyes Mr Paxton looks suddenly a little moody. Snake in hand, he gets to his feet. 'Well, shall I see if we're lucky, sir?'

'You said it . . .'

Dougie returns to the job site; delicately, probingly, he threads the head into the bowl, then begins to uncoil the snake by a purposeful hand-cranking. Shortly he feels pressure, the encountering of the obstruction, and he moves to rotate the head, careful just as promised not to mark the bowl. He chances a hard pull – and the obstruction comes away. On inspection, he determines that it is a sanitary towel; and he returns to the bedroom to report his success to the client.

'Well, don't that beat the band! Goddamn it, Sheryl, come on out here, can't have Dougie here thinking I'm on the rag.'

For a moment Dougie rather worries how much of that tequila Mr Paxton has put away. Then from underneath the bed a young woman slides forth and gets sheepishly to her feet: long-legged and clad in a short towelling robe, her appealing oval face framed by deep blonde bangs.

Paxton refills his glass and pours another. 'No need to be shy, Sheryl, honey. I'm trusting a guy like Dougie here is no kind of a bluenose. We just about done, fella?'

'I'll just, uh, check the obstruction's gone, sir. Maybe check your flush, have a wee look at the flapper and the fill valve.'

'You do that, son. You're the do-it guy. Hey, you're Do-It Stewart. You're Dougie Do-It!' Paxton is nodding to himself as if he has made an important discovery. Dougie repairs to the bathroom, and there fiddles meaninglessly with the pull-chain until his embarrassment has receded.

Five minutes later he finds Mr Paxton stretched out and perusing a book with a samurai sword on its cover. The girl is stretched out by his side albeit looking as comfy as if she were lying on planks laid over bricks. Paxton sets down his book, swings his legs over the side of the bed and offers Dougie a tumbler, then clinks it firmly with his own.

'Here's to you, Dougie Do-It. You handled the situation with dispatch, and I respect that.'

'Thank you, sir. Might we drink to the President of the United States?'

'Screw that fucken guy. Just about the one Texan I met that I can't abide. What I owe you?'

'It will come to two pounds and six shillings, sir.'

'That is nuthin' for a job done well. Listen, Doug, you want work regular that pays you what you ought to be paid, then you should come work out on my rig.'

Mr Paxton goes hunting for something in his bedside drawer. It seems to Dougie that the client is surprisingly keen to have him stick around, maybe a mite discourteous to the girl, whose green-eyed gaze has put in him just a wee bit of a haunt. But then, he reasons, the girl has maybe a tariff of her own.

136

'Ring this number, okay? Talk to Charlie McGinn. Whatever you make in a week you'll make tenfold offshore.' He pumps Dougie's hand, and Dougie finds the oil man's grip a little clammy; but he's handled worse, and the offer has an undeniable appeal.

March 1967
Married Couples

'You enjoy that, darling?' Robbie asks his wife as he flares up both his cigarette and hers.

'God, yes,' Marilyn responds loudly, before drawing on the Rothmans with avidity. 'God, we lead boring lives.' A plume of restless smoke leaves her red mouth.

Two young married couples linger amid the throng in front of the Tain Picture House that has just turned its evening audience out into a cold and starry night. Marilyn, in a cape-coat with slashes for her arms, is stamping her feet and gazing intensely at the framed poster for the entertainment they have just consumed: SEAN CONNERY IS JAMES BOND! *YOU ONLY LIVE TWICE!* The artwork depicts Mr Bond in a tuxedo, suavely piloting a sleek little yellow helicopter without use of his hands, while raining down gunfire upon villainous neighbouring helicopters.

Robbie puts an arm round Marilyn, though she doesn't quite ease into it – at least not as Aaron reads. Aaron takes hold of Heather's hand, feeling a chill drop of rain on his neck.

'Shall we head on back to the house?' Robbie frets.

'Spoilsport,' cries Marilyn. 'Let's stop off for a nightcap at my hotel.'

Only Marilyn, thinks Aaron, would describe her place of work as 'her' hotel. His own preference is indeed to go home to Robbie and Marilyn's little house where he and Heather are being accommodated for the weekend; it is a nicer place than most newlyweds of their age acquire, if only to the standard a Gallagher would expect. Aaron isn't so sure what Heather makes of it, but then the same goes for a lot of things. First, though, that nightcap, since it seems – and Aaron

138

glances at the silent Robbie just to check – that Marilyn must have her way.

Soon enough they are seated in dry and cosy comfort in the dated saloon bar of the Lockdare Hotel. Only a couple of other guests – two older golfing males, one morose businessman – are cluttering the place. *Not the tourist season*, Aaron supposes. Their drinks are carried to table and Marilyn exchanges murmurs with the waitress – as though she were the owner of the establishment rather than its off-duty receptionist.

'Maybes not Aaron's kind of a film, that,' Robbie offers.

'Oh, it was perfectly entertaining.' To the limited degree that Aaron likes films, *You Only Live Twice* was – yes – not his preference: far-fetched, its depiction of 'science' just lab-coat boffins and shiny gadgets, all second fiddle to a big brawny hero punching bad guys and preventing a nuclear war.

'The music' – Heather ventures – 'struck me as much the most distinguished thing about it. Rather an elegant use of motif.'

'You really didn't like it, Heather?'

Aaron is aware Heather could have said more about the score and orchestration, perhaps of interest to the table, had Marilyn not interrupted her, as she seems to have been doing throughout their evening. Heather reconsiders, running a straw around her Campari. 'I thought it was maybe not the most authentic portrait of Japan and its culture. I could have wished that all the girls weren't just flapping about in next-to-nothing.'

'Oh but that's kinda sexy, isn't it?' Marilyn cuts in, breathing smoke declaratively. 'Not as sexy as Big Sean, mind.'

'That big helicopter fight, though.' Robbie grins, thrusting out his straight glass of beer as for emphasis. 'Brilliant.'

'Well, Aaron's the man for the helicopters, isn't that so? Takes one to his work, doesn't he? Beat that, Mr Bond.'

139

Not for the first time on this outing, Aaron is conscious of Marilyn paying him an uncommon number of compliments – in particular with regard to his work for Paxton Oil, his status there, the remarkable nature of the job et cetera. However sincere is her interest, he has already fielded questions about Paxton's drilling rig: how on earth it stands up in deep water, how it is powered, how deep the drill goes and how it's made to turn; and, in essence, how come they don't all drown out there under great columns of violently gushing seawater?

Aaron feels bound to stress the derring-do of others. He skirts any reference to his essentially lowly rank of junior geologist, or his loathing of the stomach-lurching journeys to sea by chopper, or how his principal task is to sift mud and gravel and peer at unpromising rocks under a microscope. Were he to start showing off, Heather would hear and know better. Anyhow, he frets inwardly, why should he be playing up to his best friend's wife, enviably lovely as she remains?

'Heavens,' Marilyn continues. 'That's a way to make a wage. Spare a thought for the rest of us, Aaron, while we grind it out? Six a.m. tomorrow I'll be back at the desk out there. Robbie will be down to the sawmill to tug his forelock at the Laird.'

'The Laird minds well enough who I am.' Robbie scowls. 'He pays me decent, he's given me a hand and all that.'

'Oh, Robbie, what he pays . . . twenty pound a week, it's clear enough how a man like the Laird keeps himself in splendour, forever short-changing others.'

'You do alright, Mrs Vallance. That's more than what you're paid here. You know where you can take your complaints.'

Aaron hopes Robbie is only acting riled. He does wonder, though, about Marilyn's high-handed manners. Their wedding party was quite swanky in comparison to Aaron and Heather's collegiate occasion; but Aaron will never say to Robbie that the great Juliet Gallagher seemed scarcely best pleased by the match her daughter made. And now he feels torn, wanting his friend to be robust and blithe as ever was, not some put-upon hubby; while not entirely minding the good favour shone on his own person by the former Marilyn Gallagher.

'Luck,' Aaron now offers to the table, 'is a big part of how people get on. Who you meet, what others see in you, whether you can pass a certain test when it comes.'

Marilyn nods vigorously. Aaron supposes, with a touch of guilt, that people are looking at Marilyn all the time and making up their minds about her pretty quick.

Heather raises both hands over her mouth to stifle a yawn. 'Gosh, I would say I'm about ready for bed.'

Robbie rises off his stool. 'I'll get Aitken's taxi out.'

'Yes, but Heather' – Marilyn, with her usual sweetly veiled imperative – 'shall you and I take the taxi and let the boys have a dram and a blather?'

'I don't think Marilyn much cares for Heather.' Aaron feels brave enough to lead on this topic, they having become two married fellows, now in conference over whisky.

Robbie looks perplexed. 'You say so? She's always said Heather's exactly the girl she thought you would marry.'

Aaron suspects Robbie does not interpret his wife's tone as closely as he might. And yet he isn't feeling slighted. He does believe there is something in his and Heather's union that is a little more elevated than the bond between Robbie and Marilyn: one he knows by his own eyes to be intensely physical, but which seems, of late, to have suffered some loosening.

'At the sawmill – is it going alright? What Marilyn said?'

'Aw . . .' Robbie waves a bothered hand as to say such talk is beneath them. 'We've to keep an eye on the purse-strings just like anyone.'

'I've wondered, Robbie, would you ever consider a job out on the rigs?'

Robbie eyes him a mite warily. 'Aw, I know nothing about that, Aaron. What sort of a thing would it be?'

'There's nothing you can't do, Robbie.'

'No' what I've been telt lately.'

'The work would be simple at first, but for money as good as the sawmill. And if you show you're handy, like with tools the way you are, then you can progress pretty quick. They start you as a roustabout—'

'Like Elvis!'

'That's right. And it's a lot of humping gear, taking it off of boats, shifting pipe – just cos the drill's always wanting a new length of steel. But then you're a roughneck on the drill floor where it all really happens.'

Robbie is gazing at the bottom of his glass, listening, but frowning.

'You could do awful well, Robbie. You'd be in on the start of something big, too. It's hard enough, two shifts a day, twelve hours, seven days a week. But you do a fortnight on the rig then a fortnight off?'

'And it'll pay what?' Robbie looks up. 'What they paying you . . . ?'

Aaron doesn't want that to cloud the matter. 'My work's something else, in the lab with my rocks all day. But if you move up like I say, you could soon be seeing a hundred quid a week?'

At this, having reached for his cigarettes, Robbie stops and seems very struck. 'That much? Dear God. Eh but I appreciate it, Aaron, you looking out for me. I might talk to some of the lads at the mill. And Marilyn.'

It doesn't sit right with Aaron that Robbie should weigh what these others thought of something about which they, unlike his best mate, know nothing.

'They aren't you, Robbie. And Marilyn's a Gallagher, they like a bit of money.'

'She's a Vallance, Aaron.' Robbie is looking at him a bit harder, and Aaron wonders again what is and what isn't putting on. But then the flare is out, and it is plain that Robbie is not seeking a scrap on the matter. Rather, he looks to Aaron as if caught up in some kind of inner roil.

142

'Naw you're right, but. We're in need of a change. We can't just be . . . havin' it the way things have gotten to be.'

'Things how, Robbie? With your work?'

'Me and her and everything.' He puts a hand to his brow and rubs hard. 'There I go, see, don't want to be talking about this.'

'Robbie, what is it?'

Robbie's head stays low but his eyes, very melancholy, find Aaron's.

'It looks like, me and her, we might have a struggle for to have kiddies. We'd thought it would take no time, but . . . she wasnae feeling so great recent . . . and we got her in for some tests and all. They reckon there might be some problem.'

'Aw, Robbie. I'm sorry . . .'

'We should have looked to it sooner. She blames herself – I blame *my*self, Aaron.' Robbie's mien is a mite harder again. 'We're enough for each other, people shouldn't think nothin' but. It's just what it is, y'know? That part of a marriage? I'd never even thought that much about it, but . . . we're maybe not to have it, me and her.'

'There's a chance, but? It's not ruled out?'

'Aye, a chance.' But in Robbie's mouth the word sounds forlorn.

Aaron stares up at the darkened ceiling in the guest room of what he can only think of as the Gallagher residence. The oak beams supporting that cciling, the separate lounge and dining rooms below, the big bay windows – all are more in the Gallagher manner than the crofter's cottage in which Robbie grew up.

Heather enters on tiptoe, in her nightdress, teeth cleaned; she lowers herself to the edge of the mattress and takes up her hairbrush. Aaron, already warmed under the covers, feels the new relative ease of their domesticity even in this unfamiliar bedchamber.

'You know what Charlie McGinn told me the other day?'

She doesn't turn, and so he addresses the lace at her shoulder blade.

'He said that if a geologist identifies the site where oil is struck, if it's really found because of his estimates, then the geologist gets to put his name on it – on that oilfield? Like a proper scientific discovery, y'know?'

Now she swivels to him, looking quite diverted. 'Like a star? Or a comet?'

'Yes. Or a disease.'

'Such a romantic, Aaron.' With a slight smile she resumes her brushing. *Unfair*, thinks Aaron. No great romancer, he, true enough. But something in his chest does rise at the dream of a *Eureka!* moment, at its prospect of glory: that a stretch of sea and a black bounty many leagues below might be a kind of posterity to which he – and only he – might stake a claim.

'I feel that Marilyn finds me very dull,' Heather says, calmly.

'I don't think you should give a thought to anything she thinks. You've little or nothing in common.' Aaron can see, though, that this has not mollified her.

'I'd rather we got along, since she's married to your very best friend in all the world. For the moment, at any rate.'

'What do you mean by that? Heather?'

'I think she looks at men the same way you see men looking at women.'

Aaron half rises, puts a hand to the lace, keeps it there. 'What, how I look at women?'

'Not you, Aaron, no. Though, she gave you a good enough look this evening.'

'Don't say she made you a little jealous?'

'No, no. I just think she enjoys having men around. Robbie should watch she doesn't find a ticket out of town.'

'Robbie might be on his way first. I said he should look at taking a job out on the rig. I think he might. I said he could stay with us on odd nights, before he flies out.'

'Very convenient.'

'What's that tone?'

'Nothing. You and your friend . . .' She sighs. 'Yes, of course he can stay.'

Aaron is sensing indulgence. He had been considering whether to draw her close to him. Now he decides otherwise, slumps into the mattress, waits for her to turn off the light.

In the dark his thoughts stray back to the film. Diverting silliness, really. And yet, despite himself, he had been drawn to something of the Japanese setting – to the ninja allies of James Bond, silent, proud, swift. And he is still hearing the swelling, melancholy theme song, the female voice singing of one life for yourself and one for your dreams. Perhaps that wasn't so silly.

The following morning Aaron drives Heather back to their Aberdeen semi, largely in a not quite companionable silence. As he pulls into their driveway he wonders, not for the first time, about the integrity of the home they have made – front garden patch, blue front door, mod cons neat and tidy, and possibly no more than a facade.

Heather, having immediately picked up the phone to her parents, now comes to find Aaron in the white-tiled kitchen.

'My father wants to see you.'

'Shall we get ourselves together and go? Do you need—?'

'No, just you, Aaron.'

The door is open and Aaron finds Hugh in his study, its disarray so different to the rest of the house, with overflowing shelves, all surfaces repurposed for piles of books and pieces of scribbled paper.

Today Hugh appears to have cleared space on his desk, to make a curious montage of newsprint cut out from multiple papers, the perusing of which he looks up from in order to beckon Aaron into a seat. It's all redolent of schoolboy hobbies: Aaron recalls his boyhood rock collection. Yet he has never seen Hugh looking quite so burdened by gloom – as if encased in the stuff. Nor has he ever known his mentor to be so quiet.

The swiftest scan of those cut-out headlines, though, is sufficient to apprise Aaron of what Hugh is brooding over, a headline story of the week just gone: OIL FLOODS FROM BROKEN TANKER; RACE TO KEEP OIL OFF CORNISH BEACHES; NAPALM MAY BE USED ON TORREY CANYON.

'Have you been paying attention, Aaron, to this absolute debacle?'

'God, yes.' Aaron sighs. 'Foul. What a disaster.' Aaron can think of no other sentiment. He has heard Paxton's phlegmatic views on the matter – *'The damn newspapers love an oil spill. Won't stop folks needing to fill their damn tanks'* – but then that is Paxton all over.

'I struggle to conceive, really, of anything fouler than an oil slick. Hundred thousand tonnes of crude in the water. The sludge it makes of the sea for miles. Seabirds poisoned, needing this filth cleaned off them feather by feather . . .'

'It looks that you've been following it closely,' Aaron murmurs.

'Every day a fresh horror. So, now they're sending in the army.'

'To do what?'

'Bomb the wreckage. Burn that scum of oil off the water.'

'That seems . . . drastic.'

'You see, Aaron, how great minds arrive at solutions. For days now they've had women with watering cans, plodding up and down the shore, sprinkling some sort of Unilever detergent on the sand. At sea, too, pouring it over the sides of boats.'

'I suppose that's not a half-bad idea – the emulsifier will break up the slick?'

'It's more poison, Aaron. Already we're getting foam in canals, rivers like some claggy kitchen sink . . . Honestly, how can you look at this bloody mayhem and not feel sickened?'

Hugh with his old fire . . . Aaron hears it clearly; but his own dismay is more benumbed. 'It's, like I say, a disaster. I mean, by definition, that's a rare misfortune. This was a navigation error, wasn't it? The ship hit a rock. I'd have thought there'll be great cares not to repeat that. Lessons learned.'

'By who? You think these pigs ever . . . ?' The room suddenly feels to Aaron far more fraught. 'No, no, the one thing you can be sure of, Aaron, is that this will happen again, sooner or later. Another disaster, another so-called clean-up. The price paid by the marine environment.'

'That's . . . a very pessimistic reading, Hugh. Not your usual way.'

'Well, it comes to something – it's a pessimistic sort of a day, Aaron? – when you're made to realise you've been bought and paid for by the business that causes this filth, then tries to buy everyone off so they forget until next time.'

Aaron feels as if he is watching himself from the corner of the room – a dispassionate version of himself whose instinct is not to defer to a former mentor now cutting such a contrary and obdurate figure.

'I suppose,' he tries, 'my view is that certain things are worth doing, and they come at a cost, as you say. But that we take a risk, learn the lessons, and not be deterred. I thought that was your credo, Hugh.'

'Yes, I took money from people who seemed decent, who I reckoned I would learn from. The challenge excited me – I did believe in the possibilities. And I've learned plenty, God, yes. Now I've seen enough. I'm no longer a believer, Aaron.'

'But the possibilities are still to be explored, Hugh, there's so much opportunity for so many—'

'Don't say *this*' – Hugh slaps this newsprint – 'can be justified for *jobs*. There are always other jobs.'

'Well, for a lot of people a job's not a small thing.'

'No? Well, I've told myself you weigh the scales and there are some things you live with for the general good. I couldn't live with myself if I kept on at this.'

'If it's not us, Hugh, someone else will do it.'

'I see that, Aaron. Myself, from here on I'll have nothing more to do with oil.'

'You're serious?'

'Believe me. A fellow I've known since college, works for the World Wildlife Fund, he's given me a thought about what I might do. There are things you might yet consider, too, Aaron.'

There is an angry buzz in Aaron's head to which he dares not give full vent. It is saying, *You got me into this!*

'Hugh, I've gone so far down a road now, made commitments. The further you go with something . . . it gets a lot harder to turn around.'

Aaron makes out a flinty affront in Hugh's eyes. 'You still have the perfectly good option of an academic career, I've helped keep that road open to you.'

'Right now it's not an option I feel I can afford.'

'Really?'

'No. Please don't think I'm blind to your concerns. I just wonder if, in the round, they could prove to be a luxury. In a society where decisions about how we get the things we need will always be complicated.'

'Aaron . . .' Hugh is shaking his head with a little incredulity. 'I really don't think it's as complicated as all that.'

Alright for you, Aaron thinks, and realises at once that there is nothing more he wants to say – that to follow Hugh's tutelage any further will no longer be the making of him, only the undoing of all his own hard work invested in these difficult past few years. He only wishes now to settle up politely and be gone from the room.

Descending the stairs, glumly, he feels the scale of the rift – its aftershock – in his bones. How could it have come to this? A separation is not going to be simple in any sense; there is more than one party involved. Feeling just as morose in his own way as Hugh, Aaron closes the front door and heads home to his wife.

June 1967
Roustabouts

On time, as instructed, feeling all the bleary bone-weariness of being up with the dawn, Robbie Vallance sits and waits for his summons on a plastic chair in a Portakabin by Aberdeen harbour. There's a round ginger girl with a logbook at a collapsible table, processing the new starts, and a fair few in front of Robbie are still to have their turn.

Robbie steals the odd glance at those other men seated near him – the uniformity of their working breeks and boots, their weathered hands and scanty scalps. The working life, it leaves a mark. Robbie wonders if the mark is on him: he can count so many different things he's done for a wage. Today, he will start doing one more. Before that, just to get to the workplace, he must take to the air – another first, causing him a bit of worry.

Fourteen days at sea. Already he feels the missing of Marilyn – the warmth of her body, their bed. In a way, he has been missing her for a while. Their farewell was not the fondest. *You know I'm doing this for us* was what he'd been minded to say; until he imagined her sceptical face.

Last night, he had bedded at Aaron's in Aberdeen: Aaron was already out on the rig, so Heather gave him his tea and a little chat – as much as she could manage, god love her. Then in the early hours Robbie ghosted out, closing the latch lightly behind him. He remains unsure what he will find at sea, for all Aaron's advice. At least Aaron will be there, looking out for him – as much as that one is capable, too. In any event, Robbie has resolved: the money promised had bloody better show up.

Now he's called forward by the girl and he rises and states his name. 'Aaron Strang sent me,' he adds for effect.

'You're for Pecos rig, aye?'

Robbie is briefly flummoxed. 'This is Paxton Oil, right?'

'Pecos is the rig, Paxton's the contractor. We've had your forms, no bother. On the rig you'll be checked in by the drill rep, and the tool-pusher, that's Mr Hood, he'll assign you your work. What size overalls you take?'

'There's a thing . . . I dinnae know.'

She ticks a box. 'What size boots?'

That Robbie knows.

'Bide over there a bit, would ye? I'll send ye's as a group in a wee moment so's to get your gear and a taxi to the airport.'

Robbie gives way to the lad behind – lean with a pointed face, heavy black glasses, moving a little awkwardly.

'Hullo, Miss, the name's Dougie Stewart, I've a letter.'

'Okay. You're a plumber?'

'That's me, m'dear . . .'

Robbie slumps into the spare seat next to a solidly built and baw-faced fellow, ten years his senior at least. They exchange nods.

'How do. D'yuh smirk?'

Robbie can't quite pick the accent, but he sees the packet of Bensons thrust at him: he gratefully accepts, and together they puff up a pensive little fug. The fellow's name is Stan Robson.

'Have you flown before, Stan?'

'In a plane, like? Aye. Took wor lass to Majorca last summer. The whirlybirds, but? Naw man. You'll not have, neither?'

Robbie shakes his head.

Stan nudges him hard. 'Never worry, kidder, you can hold wor hand.'

As Robbie's feet carry him unsurely across the tarmac, just one in a pack of ten lads – all now in rig boots and hard hats and orange overalls like spacesuits, each clutching their gear bundled up in a big poly

150

bag – he gets a closer look at the helicopter branded WESTLAND WESSEX; and he wonders if there's really no way back; because this big metal bug with its long, drooping blades looks as if it might carry them into a theatre of war. They chuck their bags into the hold, then form a line before a man with a clipboard who takes names as they mount short metal steps. Once seated and strapped in as instructed, Stan next to him, Robbie peers out of a porthole window at the gull-grey skies and the small glint of light off the runway. He takes another cigarette from Stan, wishing he'd done as others have and brought a pack of cards. Now he sees – feels – the chopper rotors beginning to life and turn, the whole craft shuddering throughout, an odour of paraffin suffusing the cabin. Then the loathsome sensation of being plucked vertically up into the air, the taste of sizing in his mouth. He shuts his eyes tightly and keeps them clamped a while, resisting Stan's recurrent nudges and cries of 'Whirlybirds, man!'

The journey doesn't lend itself to chat – rather, to hand gestures and shouts over the din of engines and rotors. A dour bloke opposite Robbie seems affixed behind his copy of the *Express* proclaiming CELTIC CHAMPIONS OF EUROPE! By observation, though, Robbie gathers that the roustabout way is to act like these flights are no bother.

Then Stan elbows him, shouting, 'What wuz y'deein' before, like? For work?'

'Sawmill.'

'Woodcutter, aye? I was at the iron works in Consett. County Durham. Like every other bugger in Consett, y'knaa? Tapping off molten iron, hellish, man.'

'So you're in for this instead?'

'It's dyin' in Consett, man. I thought, I'm not waitin' for them to close us down so we's canna pay the mortgage. I've a mate fuels planes at Newcastle Airport. He was talkin' to a mate of his in Aberdeen, says you want to get yerself oot on the rigs, bonny lad, fortnight's work, two hundred quid.'

'I heard that.' Robbie chews his cheek. 'That sort of money, aye.'

The newspaper opposite has inched down to expose a dourly lined face. 'See these rigs, boy? Money's alright, for whit they get out of you. But they make sure and they get it, aye?'

'I'm not bothered by hard work,' Stan retorts.

'That's what they all say when they start. Hiring a desperate man's easy. So's firing 'em, if they cannae keep up. See how you like it, right enough.'

'What'd *you* do before this?'

'I wis guttin' fish.'

'Bet your fingers stank, aye?'

The dour eyes narrow. 'I was paid near as well for guttin' fish, boy.'

'Well then you want to gan back to it, bonny lad, cos I'm sick o'you already.'

Robbie is moved to put a hand on his new pal's arm; and Stan, after one more hard look, lets the matter lie. Robbie can see, though, why Stan might have wished to stick one on the surly bastard.

He turns to contemplate the view out the porthole. Far below, the murky surface of the sea is being streaked white by the winds; raked, as if by claws.

As their final destination emerges on the horizon line, then steadily enlarges, it is by a stretch the weirdest sight Robbie has ever beheld – at first like some ancient skeletal sea-creature protruding from the waters as though shackled there; then, closer, like a grim, enmisted island of metal, its derrick tower rising maybe a hundred feet in the air. It doesn't look to him at all fit for human habitation.

But the Westland chopper circles in around the tower toward its landing on the top deck of the structure, and what Robbie sees closer yet has the look of a building site where everything built is

152

already weathered, rusting, veteran. He can see Stan, too, is looking concerned.

'What's that little boat doing moored a way off?'

'In case you fall overboard, pal,' the *Express* reader sneers. 'Or somebody pushes ye.'

Touchdown; and the door is flung open. Robbie unstraps and hastens down into a gale, the terra firma under his feet a vulnerable blessing. He stoops and collects his bag from the hold. Then, straightening and glancing about, he feels the colossal strangeness of his new situation, surrounded by darkly inhospitable sea under leaden sky – the epic and uniform horizon inducing in him a sudden vertigo. A man in overalls, hard-hatted and half-bent, is coming at them from an open doorway. 'Duck yer heids, lads!' Then they are waddling after this man, clanking down a flight of steel steps as if into the innards of a ship, all long corridors and tight corners.

After a hasty check-in at a hatch in a wall, Robbie and Stan are hustled down one such corridor to their quarters: two double-decker bunks with reading light, four lockers, two chairs, one table, all in a sickly youth-hostel yellow.

'Four of wuh in there?' Stan asks, disbelieving.

'There's only ever two of you's at a time. Get settled, five minutes, then you've to meet the tool-pusher on the drill floor.'

As Robbie and Stan consider their cupboard space, a fellow they can recall from the journey out as 'Irish Pat' fills the doorway, an oddly musical voice emanating from this overfed redheaded unit.

'Eh, Geordie, listen, you give me a laugh on the chopper, how you gave out to that old cunt, y'know?'

'He was asking for it,' Stan grunts modestly.

'Good lad. Now listen, the tool-pusher, Randy Hood, he's a good lad, too. When you meet him be sure and give him the crack about where you're from, now? The Yanks, they love all that, man, y'know?'

———

Waiting with Stan amid the hurly-burly of the drill floor, Robbie is silently intent on a mental inventory of his new workplace, complicated by the sheer barrage of sensory data coming at him: the overpowering stink of diesel, the monstrous roar and vibration, men in fire-engine-red overalls yelling at each other over the shearing, scraping metal-on-metal of the drill's rotary table as it turns the great shaft of pipe running down from the derrick and driving through the deck.

The floor is walled, but above the shaft the space opens up to the sky; and when Robbie lifts his eyes to the derrickman's crow's nest a hundred feet above he feels dizziness anew. He looks aside only to see – unmistakeable, coming directly at them – the tool-pusher Hood: sinewy and hard-worn, with his army buzzcut and cowboy boots, parting the air as he ploughs forward.

And yet Stan steps up to him, hand extended. 'How do, Randy? Stan Robson from Consett, County Durham, reporting for work.'

Hood scowls at Stan's hand as if he might hit it with a machete, had he one at his disposal. 'You shittin' me? The fuck I care where you're from? Sweet mother of Christ.'

Robbie hears sniggers at their back; Hood rubs his face. 'Okay, *greenhorns*, you made it out here. The job is to make hole. All we do is make hole, meaning we keep that drill biting down, seventy god-damn feet an hour 'til we hit target depth. Okay? This is my fucken floor, I run the show, what I say goes. Every second you're on my floor you're on the job. Watch out, listen, do like you're told and see you learn fast. You help me make hole or you ship the fuck out.'

Robbie nods cheerlessly, feeling as if Hood's hard directives are being slapped into him, one skelp after another. Stan just looks sick.

'No whiners here, no pussies. If you screw up and get a boot in your ass, take it and say you won't screw up again. You think you got it tough? It's nothing to the boot I got on my neck, and you won't hear me cryin'. You got that good? Okay, so go shift me some fucken pipe.'

As they troop after their foreman to the next deck down, Robbie thinks that Aaron must surely be somewhere near, that it would be handy about now to see a friendlier face. He can see Stan is seething.

'If I get my hands on that Irish Pat . . .'

'Easy, pal. You'll no' fall for that again.'

'Bliddy right I'll not.'

The lower deck is a long, stark, water-slicked storage floor, like an exposed warehouse with its roof torn off – great lengths of steel pipe stacked high, crates and containers of all sizes, surrounded by rumbling, crashing sea at all sides.

Get your head on straight, Robbie warns himself.

At the foreman's command he and Stan together start teaming up on a chain pulley so as to lump clusters of banded pipe from the stacks across to the foot of a steep ramp ascending to the drill floor where they are wanted. Quickly he can feel a decent rapport with his workmate. What is new is the sickly sense of heave under Robbie's boots, and he fights down a lurch in his stomach.

'Get your back into it!' jeers a roughneck from on high.

'I'll have that fucker's job if it's going,' Stan mutters.

The treacherousness of the floor, the brute weight involved, the sting in his fingers even wearing heavy gloves – all these factors have Robbie on alert. Stan breaks first, striding determinedly to the rails and vomiting into the sea, leaning far so as to clear the steel toes of his boots. Robbie averts his gaze until Stan returns, red-eyed, wiping his mouth with this sleeve. 'Bugger it, I've done dortier work than this.'

The foreman shouts to say the supply boat is coming in at midday and they'd best be ready, 'take the chance while the weather's decent'. Robbie stares down at the ten-foot swells now thumping into the columns of the rig. *This is decent?*

He closes his eyes and swears forbearance. If he can make it to the bottom of this day, it will be a day worth several of what he got paid at the sawmill. More than halfway to the mortgage payment. Pure spending money to bear home to his queen.

When the din from the drill floor suddenly subsides, Robbie hears the silence loud and clear. The pipe deck is in a relative lull, a supply boat now unloaded of pipe, sacks and drums, all logged and stacked, lashed with ropes or stashed away. Robbie decides to trek back up the stairwell. Stan doesn't want to join him – not ready, Robbie suspects, for another run-in with Randall Hood.

Up there the drill shaft is stilled, the red-overalled roughnecks milling. Hood is in repose, leaning on a wall, paring at his thumbnail with a cruelly sharp-looking pocketknife.

'What we stopped for?' Robbie speaks low to the closest hard hat.

'The geologist boy said so.'

Clanking footfalls resound from stairs to a little suite of elevated cabins next to the derrick. And now descending is Aaron Strang, swamped in rollneck sweater and oilskin breeks, batting a metal tray against his leg, a very harried look about his gaunt features. He is cutting as improbable a figure as Robbie could imagine at this godforsaken outpost; but Robbie has rarely felt such gladness in seeing someone.

Aaron, though, has yet to see him back, headed directly to Hood. From across the floor Robbie watches Aaron murmur and gesticulate, then nod gravely, eyes fixed on the floor, while Hood responds, jabbing shortly at the air with his knife for emphasis. Then Hood is abroad and hollering, and the roughnecks are in motion. Aaron heads chastenedly for the stairs and Robbie half wants to shout – but then Aaron looks up and sees him, and there is half a smile, a sheepish wave, and he changes direction, venturing a pat of Robbie's overalled shoulder.

'Good to see you, pal.'

'Eh, it's good to see *you*.'

Now the derrick is raising the shaft of drill string steadily up from its former depths, and the roughnecks wrangle and haul over to it what looks to Robbie like a giant's spanner wrench, chain-suspended, which they steady and then shove into place with a vicious clamping of steel jaws around the shaft. Robbie watches so as to study the roughneck way. Already he knows he won't hack it here too long as a dogsbody: he will need to prove himself fit for that promotion, for that extra fifty quid a fortnight. Aaron, he notes, is looking on, too, rather tensely.

'You runnin' things here now, eh, boy?'

'Ah, this is just my bit of it. They're taking a core for me. They swap the drill bit for a barrel that'll carve out a dirty great plug of rock, so I can get a closer look – at all the strata and the holes in it and stuff?'

'Interesting rocks, eh?'

'That's it.' Aaron musters a smile. 'Interesting rocks . . .'

The foreman has resurfaced at the top of the stairs down to the pipe deck, and he gestures irately to Robbie, who starts – only for Aaron to lay a hand on his arm.

'Hold on! I need a hand from this man on the mud-shakers!'

Aaron beckons Robbie to follow him, Robbie momentarily discomposed by his pal's new air of seniority. Round the floor's encased engine works they go, down a half-stair to where a fearsome system of pumping tanks and stacked trays stand, temporarily quiet. It's instantly clear to Robbie what is this function of this heavyweight kit – a 'shaker', just like Aaron said, of a kind he has seen on big arable farms, a stacked system of screens and sieves for sifting crops – the lowest tray over which Aaron is now kneeling. The difference is that the tray is not corn-grain and husk but rank mud and gravel, a slop into which Aaron is now immersing his tin tray. It looks to Robbie like the sorry stuff of a wet winter garden, only worse smelling. Aaron, though, is chittering away keenly.

'This is the heart of it, Robbie. This is the mud that goes down the drill pipe, to keep the bit cool. But it's pumped back up here, just full of rock cuttings that the drill has cut up. I have a rummage, take the good bits up to my lab, dry them out and inspect them. See if there's any magic in it . . .'

His pal has got his nose near enough into the stuff, snuffing it. When he looks up again his cheeks are soiled with muck, and to Robbie's eyes – he hates to think such – but it all feels just a little bit pitiful.

Aaron sets down his sample tray, shuts the door of his cabin behind him, and takes a moment before flipping on the light. Gloom better suits his mood; and the effort of showing his pal a cheery face has strained him. He is due to report progress to Paxton, and there has been no progress to report for ten days gone. No review of the current status will make it sound any better.

The core is being taken dutifully, arguably a last hope to redeem this drilling location. The mood in the rig's main 'doghouse' cabin is unhappy, and Aaron relishes facing Charlie McGinn and Erwin Shields no more than he likes chatting with Randall Hood. How much longer before it's given up as a 'dry hole'? That would seem imminent – time to mark up the next location, pull anchors and move, chalk up one more failure on Aaron Strang's forecasting record. There has been quite a succession of duds since his first estimates earned Paxton's blessing, and he knows that, had he anticipated such routine inadequacy in the role, he might never have dared to stick a pin on a board.

He switches on the light, and his microscope, and his fluoroscope, takes down his well logbook, hunkers at this desk and hunts for a sharp pencil. Rock fragments must be cleaned, inspected, identified, labelled according to depth, sorted into foolscap envelopes, filed in a cabinet . . . He wipes and dries a small handful of sandstone then sets it on a glass slide under a UV light lamp, and peers closely, the fantasy always that he will spy the dull yellow fluorescence of oil. *No chance.*

There are moments, in the short-lived silence and solitude of the cabin, when Aaron feels as though he is some hermit ascetic, his days consecrated to weird Christian devotion. But it can feel, too, more primitive, pagan. He could fancy himself an Egyptian high priest, venerating mystical balls of dung rolled up by scarab beetles. Or an alchemist toiling to turn excreta into gold . . . He wonders if this process is making him incidentally mad. He wants to laugh aloud, if only to relieve the tension in his chest – but he fears someone might hear. *Is this cabin fever?*

When the core is brought up to him, it will need to be cleaned and packaged for transport to the lab onshore. Aaron has begun to think it should have an escort.

Stripped out of working gear, Robbie and Stan follow the herd into the canteen for feeding time, forming a line under the strip lights, shuffling down the lino to get their plates piled with hot food. Robbie's focus on his order is disturbed by Stan exchanging a volley of insults across the floor with 'Irish Pat', seated among a gaggle of mates. Again, Robbie has to advise his combustible new friend to take it easy. Then together they find a lonesome table.

After a short while their silent chewing is disturbed by the shadow of a rotund man, currant-eyed and fleshy-featured, his cropped hair and beard all grey.

'New aboard, eh, lads? Mind if an old one joins you? Kenny Cooper's the name, I'd be father of chapel if that were tolerated out here.'

Neither Robbie nor Stan have any objection to the amiable request. They trade names and how-dos, and their new pal starts to tuck into his minute steak with dedication. Moments later, though, he sets down his cutlery thoughtfully.

'I noticed, Stan, you'd a wee bit of a set-to with Irish Pat?'

'It's nowt.'

'Can I give you a tip from one who's seen it? You'll get people raggin' on you, but dinnae take it personal, eh? You can't be startin' nothing out here – you've nowhere tee go. Fighting, it's like the booze, gets you the sack straight off – and it's you what gets it, not the bastard was raggin' you.'

Robbie can detect that Stan might be feeling the slight resentment of a parental tell-off, but he is nodding nonetheless.

'Eh, hope you'll not mind me saying so, you're working men, you'll have seen plenty. But see this place? It's no' like any other shop floor. You've to look after yourself, y'know?'

Another figure has sidled up to their table and Robbie glances up to see an awkward-seeming Aaron with a long metal container under his arm.

'Robbie, I was looking for you. Settling in okay?'

'Aye, alright. Getting by.' He points to Kenny Cooper with his fork.

'Listen, I'm away back to the beach on the chopper. I've some tests to do I can only do there. I'll see you soon, but. Look after yourself, eh?'

As Aaron strides off to the door, Robbie takes care not to show his shipmates any of the odd, unsettled, schoolboy feeling of abandonment just arisen inside him.

Kenny Cooper offers to show Robbie the fixed telephone stand on the platform where crewmen can queue to make a call home. 'You get six minutes then they'll cut you off, so be sharpish, eh?' Stan seems less desirous of contacting his missus; but Robbie feels he needs a break from holing up with Stan in their cabin.

On the deck Kenny points the way, outside a cabin that is given over to recreation. Through a Perspex window Robbie can see a card game going on with some seriousness.

'The usual reprobates,' tuts Kenny. 'There'll be one or two losing all the money they're meant to bring home to their wives.'

Left to his devices, Robbie ventures a look across the threshold of the rec cabin. Aside from the card school, there's a dart board on the wall, next to a pinboard studded with handwritten notices, and a rickety pool table. A television set is pushed up against a wall, and a few men are seated with their feet up, studying a silently flickering projector image on a pinned white sheet. It takes Robbie a moment to register fully that the pictures are of some mature woman, dark-haired and bare-chested, sprawled atop a bed and now peeling off her sensible black underpants.

'Eh look at the fanny,' jeers one in the audience. 'Like the dog's been at it.'

Robbie decides he must step outside again, directly. He's no puritan, but the sordidness in that room, the smell of it, is plain rank to him. He's thinking about the unfortunate woman whose fanny it was – some father's daughter. The indignity of it. She must have needed the money.

He crosses to the railing. Nothing but miles of sea all around this weird marooned structure. Staring down into the waters below he feels he is contemplating some essence of darkness. He has to remind himself why he has put himself here.

He needs to speak to his wife.

There is a queue of men at the telephone, not too scary, and he joins it now, and turns to the question of what can be done with these six minutes – what he can tell her without sounding false, and what she might say to comfort him.

June 1967
Pieces of Silver

Joe Killday is driving to work, perky at the wheel of his snappy red roadster – a smart choice for a young executive. His brother-in-law Bodie got him a fair price with a tune-up of the V8 engine, and Joe loves the throb and rasp of it each time he fires the Sunbeam Tiger to life. His father rated it a flashy buy; and Joe has half wanted to tell Andrew it has already paid for itself in terms of the number of young women he has taken out for a spin. But he has held his tongue, for fear Andrew might observe that none of these women seem to have found much else in Joe to be impressed by subsequently.

As he nears the harbour, car radio tuned to Tony Blackburn playing The Who, he's detecting through his windscreen that buoying feel of newness all around: in the morning sun even Aberdeen can glimmer, and with passing days it seems to glimmer on the surfaces of new buildings round the harbour: crane towers, depots and huts arising everywhere, big tracts of quayside put behind wire fences. Walter is wont to comment on how jam-packed and understaffed is their local branch of the Clydesdale Bank. Garth – now a skipper, with the skipper's air of perpetual discontent – will grouch about how the harbour is crowded by boats ferrying supplies out to the oil rigs, or even lurking offshore at anchor to the dodge the docking fee. Joe, though, is sanguine: all this industry feels meaningful to him, all these signs are pointing some place. The trick might be to anticipate where.

Parked up next to his father's brake, Joe takes his carefully folded jacket from the passenger seat and smartens himself in the window's reflection: the suit, too, is a recent acquisition, pale blue polyester, lean and sharp, though it nags at Joe that, really, he needs new boots to sign off the look he has in mind.

Through the office door, and Joe is intercepted by Sheila Balfour, her high-collar dress and high manners always giving the impression she is on her way to church or else just returned from it. 'A gentleman from the harbour authority is in with Mr Killday.'

Joe nods, a little irked by her ageless insistence that there is only one true 'Mr Killday' on the premises. Joe hankers after a secretary of his own, but the office is already a little more crowded with bodies than he would prefer.

He is hardly settled in his own office chair before his father charges in without knocking, beating the air with a rolled newspaper. 'Joseph, I wish you'd been here a little sooner, I've just had the most diabolical proposition put to me – I say proposition, these rascals are presuming to give me an *order*.'

'Da . . . what?'

'This whole damn stretch of street, from the chandler's down to Davidson's? They're handing over the lease, lock, stock and barrel, all because the oil boys want it. This numptie's just after telling me we've six months to vacate. Twenty years we've been here . . .'

Joe blows out his cheeks. Hard news. Maybe not the worst he has heard. He casts a sidelong eye round his office, its aged hearth, the shabby dado rail and faded wallpaper, the history of tread across the carpet. He could see a case for new digs, new decor, new start.

'. . . the hell's going on in this world? Them oil boys have been fooling about in our waters for years. Where's this bloody oil then? But the damn cowboys get every courtesy, and a real business with years of good standing gets pushed aside in an instant. Encroachment, I call it. *This* is the same bloody thing.'

Andrew thrusts the front page of his paper before Joe: DE GAULLE TELLS WILSON 'NOT YET'.

'Do you not think, Joseph? Bloody Harold Wilson going cap in hand to this Common Market. It's clear enough what they've in mind

– taking our best fishing grounds for themselves. If they asked my view they'd soon enough know I'm not for a Frenchman telling me what fish I can catch and where.'

Joe wishes his father would cease the tirade: its bitterness he finds unproductive, unprofessional, even. He can feel the angry, offended force in Andrew's distrust of the oil business; and yet to Joe that young business has a certain momentum, a tide that no lone opponent could hope to hold back. And ever since joining the firm he has been awaiting an ideal moment to talk to Andrew seriously about strategic choices, 'changing headwinds', the notion of perhaps 'fishing in other waters'. But a certain delicacy is called for, since little of what Joe has in mind has very much to do with catching fish.

'We have to contest this, rebut them,' Andrew is insisting still. 'You'll help me do that, Joseph?'

Thinking it a more proper matter for a qualified lawyer, Joe nonetheless nods firmly, putting off 'the talk' for yet another day.

During the morning Joe can make out the sound of Andrew on the phone to Netherdown. That seems to him a waste of words: Ma will not console much and have nothing to offer strategically. On that score, he believes his father should keep conferring with him. In offering a job to Joe Andrew had held out a certain licence – that Joe might take the company forward in his own direction, even if Andrew were to feel differently. He broods on the thought of when will be the right moment to claim on what he is owed.

Sheila Balfour interrupts to say that John Cutter is off ship and wishes to see Mr Killday and Joseph. In short order they are congregated in Andrew's office, Cutter removing his cap to sit.

'Gentlemen, it's only right that when a crucial matter comes up we should speak straight.'

'Quite so, John.' Andrew nods.

164

'I have received an offer of permanent employment from a company exploring for oil out at sea.'

'As a skipper, John?'

'Aye so, to skipper a vessel ferrying supplies out to a drilling rig.'

Andrew wears a wry face. 'The sort that's been the bane of your life for a year or two now, eh, John? Well, that's a job well within your great capabilities. I know a few of the younger trawlermen have been enticed onto those bloody rigs, though it doesn't look to me to have done them any favours.'

Joe puzzles his father's response: he doesn't believe Andrew is seeing what is in front of him.

'The oil boys, the cowboys, handing out crumbs from the table to locals here for decades . . . Eh, I'm not surprised they came for you, John, and I appreciate you're telling me. I realise, too, it's a chance to restate how highly you are valued—'

'You must understand, I'll be accepting this offer. Things are what they are. It's too valuable to refuse. Not at my time of life, seeing how the wind's blowing.'

Now the blow landed is clear on Andrew's face, uncomfortably so to Joe. 'John, I'm not sure I believe my ears . . .'

'Andrew, we've done much together and I've valued that. I've given a lot to Killday. Thinking it over, I have wondered whether I've had fully the same in return.'

'You think you'd have got better elsewhere?' Andrew is sharper now.

'Well, the question is just that. I might have found just such the place. The offer is good money, and I need to see the future. To know what I'm worth. Now, unless you can see your way—'

'Can I improve on thirty pieces of silver, John? Is that what you ask?'

Joe, who had been already calculating the counter-offer, stops short at the balefulness in Andrew's words, in his eyes.

'Why do you suppose Judas Iscariot did as he did, John? Was it more than just a handful of coin? Was it maybe a grudge he'd stored away awhile, without saying? Would you not say when you betray a man, you can injure near enough as to kill them? Might be it's as bad as that. Though in the act, I reckon you kill a bit of yourself and all. But maybe that's overdue, too.'

'Da' – Joe feels he should have intervened sooner – 'we should try to—'

'Your father should speak as he means,' Cutter snaps, unblinking.

'Oh I will do so, never fear. When I insult a man I want him to know it and hear it. From now on I'll not want to be seeing you again, John Cutter. If you see me coming, cross the street, you hear?'

Joe has never seen his father so incensed. Nor, he assumes, has Cutter, who lifts his cap from his lap and stands. 'I'm sorry that's your feeling. Plain enough there's no more to be said. I will put this in writing for you, Andrew. Goodbye.'

Hours later, Andrew having left early for the day, unmanageably out of sorts, Joe sits alone at his desk picking over the damage.

He thinks above all about the admirable rationality of Cutter's decision; also its calm delivery, by contrast with his father's temper – as weak in its own way as was the company's negotiating position.

Joe knows that Cutter only did what Joe would have done had he been in that man's boots. He has been troubled of late by the marks of age on his father – in his mother, too – their physical vulnerabilities, his bentness, her gauntness. He can easily recall the younger versions he knew; but here they are now, made out of their years with nothing else spare, weathered like the company boats.

When his telephone rings he expects it is his father, or else Walter. In fact, it is his brother-in-law, asking if Joe might meet with him to discuss an urgent matter, in an hour or so at the private Club Bar of the Gardner Hotel.

———

Joe has not been inside the Gardner before, though he's heard it's a favoured spot for wheeler-dealer types. After a brisk stride through the town he finds the hotel facade down a cobbled alleyway and he pushes through double doors to ascend steep carpeted stairs. The Club Bar is elegantly sedate – crimson walls, walnut in its woodwork and all furnishings – and it is quietly deserted save for Bodie by the window, at ease in a chair. As Bodie rises to shake hands, Joe notes that he sports a single-breasted suit much like Joe's own, only in a fawn check. On his table are a bottle of burgundy, a glass half-full and a plate licked clean but for the fat of a steak.

'Have a seat, please, Joe. Will you take a glass of wine?'

'Nothing for me, Ray, thank you.'

'Joe, I won't dress it up, I hear the business has a problem?'

'Which one are you referring to?'

Bodie frowns. 'I heard from Angela you're in line to get turfed out of your offices?'

'True. But we've also just managed to lose the services of our senior skipper.'

'Ah. Blast. But your brother's a fine skipper, isn't he?'

'He is. It doesn't change the fact we have a significant vacancy.'

'Right. I can see that's a bit of a poser. But the matter of the offices? I wonder if I might be helpful?'

'If you could, Ray, I'd be delighted. What's on your mind?'

Bodie shifts forward in his seat, with a quick glance from side to side. 'Joe, I happen to know of a lease coming up on a warehouse premises very handily placed right near to you by the harbour? It's changed hands a bit down the years. But a terrific spot, I'd say. Especially with the fight for floorage we're got in the city just now. And I could help you get in first on this one.'

'How's that information come your way, Ray?'

'Well, I did sell the freeholder a rather spiffy Alfa Romeo the other week.'

Joe rubs his chin, amused. 'That's a useful coincidence.'

167

'Is there such a thing, though?' The sudden brightness of Bodie's smile disconcerts Joe slightly. 'I really think you should get in on this. Start by a look inside? You'd refurbish, of course. But you'd have plenty room to put your name above the door – a big timber hoist door. The minute I heard from Angela I was sure about this. Sure you'd see it, too? Though, you're being rather stubbornly silent . . .'

Joe wonders if he's being ungracious. 'Listen, Ray, I do appreciate your thinking of this—'

'Think nothing of it. Obviously I want to get you out of a scrape, brother. For a while I've wanted us to be better pals. You can imagine how much I've heard about you now. And one thing that always grabs my interest is an opportunity.'

Bodie's peculiar manner again . . . in the teeth of which Joe reverts to his preferred circumspection. 'I have to say some old bonded warehouse is maybe more space than we need.'

'A-ha, but let me ask you this, Joe. Exactly what is it you think the Killday business really needs? Today, tomorrow? You already have those different operations in other places. This is a chance to bring them under one roof. But then, think what additional space might help you do fresh? To expand?'

The sense that Bodie is driving at something, has been so since they sat down, is becoming more palpable to Joe, inclining him to keep his own counsel. Bodie, though, seems in no way deterred.

'Anyhow, I can set this up, put you in touch with my contact right away. Be assured of my help here—'

'Please, Ray. Don't do anything until I've had a think about it and asked you to . . . The real trouble is that I can't think it will sit right with my father's idea of what Killday offices ought to be.'

'He's had to change before, hasn't he? Thirty-odd years of business? Some changes you don't get any choice about. It's how you navigate change – that's what decides if you will survive.'

'Oh, this company will survive, Ray.'

'Of course! I was thinking more of others. Take Mr Cutter. There's more than a few will feel the wind blowing right now and try to shift out of fishing. That doesn't mean they'll flourish in the new conditions.' Bodie pauses, smiling almost shyly. 'And on that score, there's something else I've meant to say a while. I don't want to seem forward . . .'

'Go on.'

'I've expressed to you that new premises could be a time for new thinking. Think about this. Why doesn't a business of your size have a board?'

'It does, Ray.'

'Oh, Andrew's the chairman and you and a few others have senior titles. I'm talking about the sort of board that gives a company strategy and direction? That can bring in people from outside, other sorts of talent. Not just one boss-man calling the shots.'

Joe responds with a tight smile. 'My father's never wanted that kind of outside interference. He's wanted to keep it in the family, what you're talking about just isn't for him.'

'Not for him, you say. How about you, Joe? Has Killday got all the expertise it might need for its future? I'm thinking about investment, access to the sorts of funds that make real growth possible. A proper board can be a big step to that.'

'We've never struggled for financing.'

'What, an overdraft from the Clydesdale Bank for a new trawler every ten years? Fine up to a point. But anyone who's in business has to ask themselves what business they're in. The answer doesn't always stay the same.'

Hearing his own thoughts voiced back at him from another's mouth is disconcerting to Joe; at least for a moment. Then he is struck by what it means to have a co-thinker so suddenly close at hand. New ballast for 'the talk' he has for so long meant to have with his father?

'Joe, I feel sure you see this just as I do. Especially on a day like you've just—'

'Suppose we did look outside the firm for expertise? Where would that be?'

'You might not need to look that far. I wondered for starters if I could offer something to the company?'

A-ha, Joe thinks. *Now the cat peeps out of the bag.*

'Hear me out. You maybe have too fixed an idea about me.'

'I hadn't seen you as an enthusiast for trawlers, Ray.'

'Nor I you, Joe. It's true a fishing boat is nothing to me next to a fast car. But I'm not really talking so much about fishing, Joe. I think you know. I'm talking about the oil. Don't tell me you haven't been thinking similar?'

Bodie is looking at him most intently, and Joe allows himself a smile, a nod. *Affirmative. Carry on.*

'The oil and all what comes with it, Joe – the whole reason why everything that's happening now is happening, the opportunity for smart people to exploit. A person like yourself.'

'And *your*self, Ray. For that, you see a role for yourself at Killday?'

'Only if you did, Joe. Obviously I'd have to have your support. Let's not kid about, you're going to be the boss-man soon enough. It's not just that, though. I do believe that you and me, we have . . . well, a certain shared outlook? I sort of felt it from the moment I clapped eyes on you. "Here's a boy after my heart." I think I've guessed your secret.'

Joe stiffens. 'What secret?'

'What you would like to do with the company, given half the chance? You know as well as I do, a business can't stand still. That's not leadership.'

'As it stands, I am not the leader.'

'Understood. But with a proper board the old guard could still play a role. The older man as chairman, the younger as managing director – with more power to act, lead, make decisions. And in that situation, you'd have an ally in me. If it was your show I'd be backing you to the hilt.'

'You've given this an awful lot of thought, Ray.'

'If I hadn't, Joe, then I wouldn't dream of taking up your time.'

Despite himself, Joe has fallen to imagining a new version of 'the talk' with his father, in which he is assured and compelling, armed with Bodie's rather ingenious suggestions. *We just separate the powers, Da* . . . Still, he shakes his head. 'Ray, forgive me, I appreciate this but I would have to have a long think of my own. About all of your proposals.'

'Joe, they would have to be *your* proposals. We both know they could only pass muster with your father if they came from you. They can't have my fingerprints on them – indeed they shouldn't. Only those of the chief.'

Feeling a thorough invasion of his headspace, Joe is momentarily lost.

'Forgive me, have I said too much? In one bite?'

Joe gestures to the contrary. He knows fine well he is being worked upon; he tells himself he is not easily fooled. This man has all the guile of a serpent; and maybe as much trustworthiness, too.

And yet . . . Bodie's candour and directness, his strange energy and mirthfulness, they all add up somehow to someone who wants to make things happen. Albeit a potentially disruptive force. He is thinking once again that his sister Angela was not so naïve in her choice of spouse – Bodie is a man you don't meet every day.

He knows where his real disquiet lies – in a sense of conspiracy, disloyalty, even. He can hear his father's fury at John Cutter: he wouldn't care to be seen as that kind of traitor in Andrew's eyes. And yet, he has to admit, Bodie has read him rather well; maybe as well as anyone ever did. Such a man might be a major ally.

'You know, Ray, I will have a glass of that red, thank you.'

November 1967

South Lanarkshire Decides

'Two more pints of McEwan's eighty please, barman.' Ally Drummond waves a five-shilling note airily.

'Mebbe fuckin' try suppin' them ones in front of you first.'

'Is my money no good?' cries Ally Drummond. 'We might even risk a pie if my friend here fancies.'

But the barman has already turned his back, unimpressed by 'The Cat'. It is after-work standing room only, Mark and Ally sandwiched at the bar between the pie heater and a few heavy-bellied regulars. Mark appreciates that, while this is not really Ally's kind of place, he is making a game go of tolerating the old waterhole that is closest to Mark's office.

And for once it seems to Mark that between the two of them he is nearly the busier. He has wangled a proper assignment for the *Express*, to cover a Westminster by-election in Hamilton, Lanarkshire, which he knows to be a few miles south of Glasgow and a few miles north of Ally's hometown. And Ally alone seems to appreciate the size of this coup.

'A feather in your cap, tovarich. Grown-up reporting at last.'

'There'll likely not be too much to report. Just about the safest Labour seat in Scotland. But, it's politics . . .'

'Not even a chance for the Unionist man, whoe'er he be?'

'They're only voting because the incumbent is retiring, and he was pretty popular. The new man might be less so.'

'Oh, if they can pin a red rosette on someone they needn't even be a warm body. Maybe there's an amusing weirdo you can cover among the no-hopers?'

'The Scottish Nationalists are putting up someone. A woman, in fact.'

'Ah! Some noble Flora, some bonny flower of Scotland . . . Anyway, look – giving a decent account of yourself on this is the kind of thing that could get you out of that bloody *Express* and on your way up to the *Scotsman*.'

'For what? So I can address the *Scotsman*'s princely eighty thousand readers?'

'That number includes everyone important round these parts.'

'The good bourgeoisie of Edinburgh . . .'

'It's where you belong, Mark.'

'Your view, not mine, Al,' scoffs Mark into the rim of his pint. He is, however, lying. A more prestigious platform for his writing is certainly what he wants; but the idea of abandoning the basically proletarian readership of the *Express* has for Mark a troubling smack of betrayal.

Ally has been staring down with distaste at his own pint of heavy, as if something were floating on its surface. Now he snaps back. 'Don't be cutting your nose off over this, comrade. At least the *Scotsman* understands we're part of a wider world here, it's not just finding stories they can stick a kilt on. A man like you ought to be writing on the big issues of the day.'

'And what are they?'

'Well, I mean!' He gestures impatiently. 'The price of oil, Mark. The league of nations now gathered at Aberdeen harbour.'

'That story's been running a while, Al. There's never anything to report. It's the story that never happens.'

'Perhaps it doesn't move at the speed you lot would like. But if you're smart you'll keep watch on all the bets that have been placed. The oil is one pie I wouldn't mind a piece of.'

'How would you ever go about that?'

'How else do you suppose I earn my wage, tovarich?'

Seeing the wry look in Ally's eye Mark is momentarily abashed. Since Ally's 'big change' a year previous, from law to investment banking, Mark is a lot less certain of what his great friend actually does in an office every day. He rates it a good thing that friendship doesn't depend on such trifles.

'Mark' – Ally's tone, at least, is indulgent – 'the work I do now is all about commission on the financing that gets companies off the ground. We can get in on it ourselves, with the right company, if we see a notable opportunity. And right now, I tell you, there are an awful lot of notable opportunities. All the big boys are nosing around like North Sea oil might be their fortune. So, here's my argument to you. If Cazenove and Kleinwort and Rothschild are going to do well out of this, why not a homegrown Scottish financier? We need our own merchant banks up here – I'm sick of the bloody bowler-hat brigade in London shouting the odds.'

Surprised and rather pleased by this vehement turn in Ally's voice, Mark nods vigorously, fetching his pack of Embassy Regal from his pocket and sparking up, before noticing Ally's distaste.

'When in hell did you start smoking?'

'Oh, I find it comes in handy.'

At nine the next morning Mark's train carries him past open fields and a great pithead wheel looming over rows of terraced housing, before wheezing to a halt such that he can step down onto the platform at Hamilton in front of a grassy embankment dotted with dandelions. A light drizzle settling on his hair, he shoulders his kitbag and heads out into the streets, on the hunt for real voters.

He elects to head to the Social and Welfare Club, a long cinderblock shed set behind gates. There, as he expects, the off-shift or retired workforce of the town are drinking pints and playing games. In this milieu he is comfortable, as soon as he puts his shilling down for a turn at the snooker table. Soon enough he is shaking the calloused hands of new acquaintances, making free with his Regals.

None of the men to whom he chats are bothered by questions

about the election. All sound a bit sceptical, though, about the new Labour candidate: a 'blow-in', since the man they knew is away off 'for a money-job'. But then these men seem sceptical of nearly everyone. *Votes in the bag for Labour just like Ally said,* Mark thinks as he adjourns to the toilet to urinate and scribble some quotes in his notebook. After consideration, he chooses to discount some grating remarks he heard in respect of Labour's man being a 'Fenian', and the SNP's Mrs Winifred Ewing bearing some blood relation to an ex-player for Glasgow Rangers.

Leaving the club in possession of some handy names and addresses of others who might talk ('My Jean'll bend your ear.'), Mark picks a row of spruce miners' cottages for door-knocking. Several women are willing to step out onto their well-tended doorsteps, in aprons and carpet slippers. Jean sports her morning curlers.

'Do you know who you'll vote for today?' Mark smiles, the column in his notepad already ticked mentally for Labour.

'I'm after voting already. For yon SNP woman.'

'Can I ask why you voted Nationalist?'

'Aw she sounds honest, like she's for us. What she'd to say about the schools, getting shot of the eleven-plus? Gi'ing a chance to them 'uns as don't get it.'

'Right. Of course, that's a Labour policy, you know?'

'Aw Labour . . .' She shrugs that away like old hat.

'May I ask if you'd have voted Labour previously?'

'Aw you're fine to ask, love.' She smiled. 'I did so, aye. But sure they're in power and what are they doing for us? The cost of the gas and that. It's criminal.'

'Your husband mentioned you have a son who works for the council?'

'Aye. He wisnae gunna follow his faither doon the pit.'

'How do you think your son will vote?'

'Och I know cos he telt me. He's for the SNP woman an' all.'

'Do you think I could possibly speak to him?'

'You'd have to get to the new estate, other side of town. Have you a motorcar . . . ?'

Trudging back to the main road Mark is a little perturbed, shaken from that state only by a hooting car horn and a blaring loudhailer. He looks up to see a very incongruous vehicle coming his way down the left lane – an open-top jeep truck, with the hailer fixed to its windscreen bar next to a saltire flag. Half a dozen young people are aboard, exuberant, near enough hanging out the sides.

The jeep slows and pulls up – Mark feels *spotted*, somehow. A grinning girl in a plastic mac and miniskirt scampers up to him and presses a leaflet in his hand. 'SNP' is writ large upon it, though hardly more prominent than the debonair portrait of the film actor Sean Connery, together with some lines credited to James Bond himself about the party offering Scots a 'modern, prosperous, self-governing nation'.

Good grief . . . Mark looks closely at the grinning girl. She doesn't look away.

'Listen, you wouldn't happen to be going my way, would you?'

It's later than intended that Mark finally presents himself at the Angara Hotel, a functional sort of a lodging with off-street parking, where the SNP were due to hold a final pre-poll press conference – a briefing that Mark immediately learns he has missed.

Unable to spot any obliging hack with whom he might share a cigarette and some quotes, Mark hunts down the narrow hotel corridors to find the bustling, over-occupied room where the SNP has made a temporary office. An unshaven young man in shirtsleeves breaks off an intense exchange with a colleague to greet Mark, presenting an open posture but an obstructive smile.

'I'm sorry. Mr Rutherford, but you're not the only one who's got on this story a bit late. We've been fighting our campaign a while.'

'I've noticed, your operation, I was surprised, pleasantly, I mean—'

'Aye, something's happening. And you don't know what it is,

176

do you, Mr Rutherford? Never fear, if you rush you might get to Ladbrokes.'

'Could I not grab just a minute with the candidate?'

This student-age fellow pats Mark's shoulder indulgently, with an insouciance worthy of Ally Drummond. 'Come back and see us after she's won.'

Back in the foyer, rattled, dissatisfied, and looking about for a chair where he might sit and start to bang some copy into shape, Mark spies the very spot he would have chosen – a chaise longue by a low table, made for two were it not that the occupant has stuck an overflowing handbag and a pile of newsprint in the second berth.

That occupant, plain as day, is Shona McCall, once his fellow galley-slave at the *Express*. But some bloke bulging out of his polyester suit is standing over her as if petitioning the seat; Mark's feet start to draw him in their direction, and soon he is hearing the exchange.

'C'mon, let me take the weight off, Shona. We'd be close enough to cuddle.'

Mark is working fast in his head, some variation on *Is this creep bothering you, doll?* Then Shona is looking right at him with the air of one who thinks faster.

'Mark! Is that you?'

'Shona!' Mark tries a line he thinks workable. 'Should I look if I can get us a pot of tea?'

'Oh you're a doll. Bob here was just about to fuck off, weren't you, Bob? Milk and sugar if you can!'

While Mark pours and they lightly discuss the local climate, he sees, protruding from that handbag, a novel: *The Ravishing of Lol Stein* by Marguerite Duras. Mark wishes he had read it; but its cover art – a cool graphic rendering of a black-haired woman with a challenging look about her – feels like a mirror of what is before him in the flesh. He musters a few remarks from what he can recall of earlier Duras, and Shona seems to coolly approve of his having seen *Hiroshima Mon Amour* at the Cameo when it came out. To his delight, while she refuses a Regal, she produces her own packet of Bensons.

'So do you think the Scots Nats really have a shot here?' he ventures.

'Oh it's going to happen, I'd say. Everything I've seen and heard in this charming corner points to that.'

'What do you think to them? To the candidate?'

'Mrs Ewing? Winnie the Woo?'

'Sorry?'

'No, *I'm* sorry, I shouldn't, that's what the bloody men are calling her. No, she's very clever, very canny. Articulate. Stands on her own two feet. She won't be pushed around. I can't tell you' – her eyes close painedly for an instant – 'how much I respect that.'

'What about the politics?'

She shrugs, makes a moue. 'What is nationalism, anywhere you see it? A romantic notion. She makes it sound not too unpalatable. I wish she was a bit keener on the Common Market.'

'But they want us in, don't they? The SNP?'

This earns him a stern, teacherly look. 'They want us in once we're out of the UK. So that the Europeans can have a full undiluted dose of Scots. So that we can give them what for, instead of the English. And that's not really the spirit of the thing, I don't think.'

'You're really keener on Europe?'

She exhales thoughtfully. 'I don't care for what I hear from the SNP about the great, unique Scottish character – like we have so much to teach the world that we've never had the chance to, under the English boot? I think we could do with a bit of civilising here – Europe might rub off on us. On the English, too, to be fair.'

'You saw this?' Mark fishes the crumpled Sean Connery leaflet from his coat pocket.

'Ah yes. Well, wouldn't you, if you had James Bond onside? Even though Sean's a Londoner now. Myself, I set more store by the views of people actually living here.'

'But that's a problem with the Common Market, too. No?'

'Touché,' says Shona, and with a smile – after an instant that felt to Mark a little worrisomely chilly. 'What do *you* think then? To the Scots Nats? Shall we let them have their moment?'

'It's down to the people.' He thinks hard, wanting to do well here, to impress upon her the cast of his mind, since she doesn't seem enthralled by the look of him. 'I don't believe Scotland gets the best deal from Whitehall. And I think nationalism can be unfairly maligned sometimes? Socialism tends to treat it as a problem.'

'As well they might.'

'I understand that. But it seems to me that nationalism can express real discontents. And if it expresses a desire for change, and it has proper roots—'

'Ein Volk, ein Reich . . .'

Mark winces, abruptly more assured. 'Come on, Shona, that's not fair. What bothers me in politics is how working people are forced to live, what could make their lives better. Anything that means decisions taken about what happens to their lives get a bit closer to them? That mightn't be a bad thing.'

'Oh you're right . . .' She sighs as if conceding. 'I suppose I just find it a wee bit parochial? But I agree, Scotland's a bit loveless, trapped in an unhappy marriage. And marriages should be happy. Made of equals.'

She is looking at him so intently that he begins to feel he is regarding the red mouth on the cover of the Duras novel. Then she has reached for her cooling teacup. 'Well, here's to Winnie the Woo. It'll be worth it for the mayhem. For sure it'll annoy all the right people if she wins.'

'*When* she wins, said the woman from the *Scotsman*.'

'When she wins' – she smilingly self-corrects – 'does that tell you the Scottish people are wanting self-government?'

'Crivvens . . .' He smiles. 'I'd worry more it's that they think Labour is busted. I wish my lot had a response to the Nats that wasn't just to pour scorn. The right wing of Labour is very conservative.'

He is hearing himself sounding worriedly a wee bit parochial; and yet she seems to be favouring him with an approving smile. 'Maybe you ought to be in politics, Mark.'

'People have said that, Shona.' He wants to return the approval he is feeling, its promise. 'No, but I'm a writer, really. I need to try to make a better job of that. If I'd done as well as you in that line I'd be a lot prouder of myself.'

'That's really nice of you to say.' She touches his arm.

'No, you deserve it. I really admire you – your progress. It's an example.'

'I've done my best. It was a help that my father wanted it for me. Maybe you're not so different? Good at school, best at writing? It's just there's so much more you have to be good at. I'm not sure you boys appreciate that so much.' She lights another cigarette, keeping her gaze on him, as if awaiting a worthy response.

'I suppose the papers must seem a bit of a boys' club.'

'I'm not the only woman at the *Scotsman*. It's not as bad as the *Express*. But there are no *married* women at the *Scotsman*. You see the size of the problem? What's to be done about that, Mark?'

Then she bursts out laughing, so he laughs, too – a little bemused, but wishing wholeheartedly to join her in more or less anything she might be up for.

They agree a plan to a quick bite of dinner, thence to trip down the road together to the count at the local grammar school. Mark is careful to secure from the hotel the loan of a golfing umbrella, and she slips her arm easily into his. The rain is fairly pelting down soon and yet they find a lively crowd of a hundred or more gathered outside the school, sufficient as to have summoned a watchful police presence. Saltires are being waved, a piper is pacing about as if in readiness: the rain is deterring no one from what suddenly feels like an occasion.

Within the school hall where the count is located, Mark can instantly read the looks on party workers' faces, foretelling a simple story, the same one Shona had told over tea. He spots the girl in the plastic mac from the jeep truck earlier – she appears gleeful. Mark begins in earnest to mentally rehearse a lede: *SNP sensation! Winifred Ewing this morning became MP for Hamilton as Labour lost a seat they had held for fifty years . . .*

He turns to Shona and sees the shine in her hazel eyes.

'It's exhilarating, no?' she says.

'A lot to take in. Maybe we'd be as well to get back to the hotel? Start trying to file copy to our newsrooms?'

'No, let's stay to see it happen. The hotel will be rammed anyhow. You might have to sit on my knee . . .'

The moment is broken by a man Mark recognises as news reporter of the local *Advertiser* pushing through the throng and past them to get out. Shona is thrust toward Mark and stumbles against his chest. Her hand stays there, though – lightly, but with an impress, he feels sure.

He looks at her, she looks straight back, and he reaches to stroke her hair, feeling the soft strands pour over his fingers.

November 1967
Shore Leave

Nine at night and Robbie Vallance lies on his yellow cabin bed, fully dressed with lifejacket handy, staring at the ghastly yellow curtains and the bare bulb on the ceiling. Being as there's nothing better, he looks aside to the pin-up Stan cheerily taped onto the wall – at the fullness of her hair, the sheen of her lips and eyes and teeth, the whorls of her nipples. Such abundance is a cruel provocation, and he feels he mustn't rise to it.

'Bonny, in't she?' Stan will declare at intervals, with a little whistle through his teeth. 'How'd you reckon I could meet that lass?' And him a married man. Robbie wearies of it, but he has come to accept the burden of shared digs, the small habits of a person – their humming and sighing, their talking utter shite – and how it's better to resist telling them they should pipe down.

Just two more nights, though, and one more day in Stalag 58, before the fortnightly redemption of being lifted off this prison. Still, Robbie feels it will be too long: it will never come.

Never any peace here, no true quiet. Only in truly foul weather does the rig rock so badly as to disrupt sleep; and this is foul. The sea was surging over the deck when they were ordered to take to their beds but remain ready for action. And Robbie felt real apprehension inside – fear of the steadily mounting immensity, surge upon surge of these marbled walls of waters, the white spray against the bulk, its searing sting and hiss. It felt to him like the vast open waters were taking some spearheaded shape to launch a surprise assault on the rig – as if their work had finally stirred up and riled a giant into reprisal.

Home soon. Real night's sleep. Hot bath. No more showers in the bilge water reeking of diesel. Proper bed. Proper bedmate.

Robbie thinks now of the last communication he had with his dear wife: a letter of surprising flatness, mainly concerned with household purchases. Marilyn is on the beach, just like Aaron, and he is lying on top of a lonely bunk wearing a lifejacket.

Stan clatters back into the cabin from his piss. 'Eh, nee wanking,' he cracks to Robbie – another of Stan's worn lines – before collapsing heavily onto his bunk.

No chance is what Robbie thinks at a snap. His Marilyn is at home, only a day away, and whatever the fluctuating state of their relations, his desire for her stands tall, never falters. For forty-eight more hours, though, he must pen it away. His surroundings are certainly helpful to the discipline – being the negation of romance, the bully of intimacy, the dead opposite of all in a woman's touch.

The gales subside before dawn, the 7 a.m. shift is back on schedule, and so Robbie waits outside the shitter for his turn to sit alongside three others, bent over his own stink and forced to mind theirs. This morning, though, there's no movement of the line, only jostling discontent.

Dougie the Plumber comes limping out of those bogs, shaking his head, a bad sign from a generally good-natured guy who has somehow persuaded all the lads to call him 'Dougie Do-It'.

'It's no' happening, boys, it's a bigger job than I can fix.'

'Son, I've a bigger job brewin' in ma guts here, where'm I gunna drop it off?'

Amid the laughs and jeers, Robbie groans. He will just have to manage. Already, at his back, the war stories have begun among his international workmates, led by the roughneck they call 'Klondike' who claims to have helped drill holes in Nevada for the tests of the atomic bomb. Now he's sharing how a rig he was on out in the Gulf of Mexico got 'down-manned', near enough evacuated, all because of fully blocked shitters. But Robbie doesn't believe that even such a calamity here would bring his redemption any closer.

———

The drill floor has barely resumed operations before they stop again. After twelve hours' service the drill bit is knackered, its teethed cutting cones worn to stumps. And so Robbie and his fellow roughnecks set to the laborious grind of changing it – 'tripping' – and that is going to take the full shift. The whole string is hoisted upward, several thousand feet's worth, to be broken down into stackable lengths.

Waiting his turn to apply the clamping tongs, slapping his thickest pair of gloves between his palms, Robbie sees Randall Hood pacing toward him and knows he must brace himself for the tool-pusher's version of chitchat.

'Jesus H, Vallance, this fucken boulder clay you got.'

'Sir?'

'This fucken North Sea boulder clay, under the sand bars? Your buddy the mud chemist – he not tell you all 'bout that?'

'"No" in so many words, sir.'

'Well I'll tell ya . . .'

Robbie is aware some of the lads have a notion that Hood has taken a bit of a shine to him; they josh him, wearyingly. In fact, Hood has begun to strike Robbie as not the absolute worst human being. Clearly, he has gone round the world for God knows how many oil explorers: there seems no situation that truly rattles him. Now he leans on a riser and goes about his own irritating habit, using his knife to pare crusts of mud from his bootheels.

'. . . yeah but out in the Gulf of Mexico we never heard of no boulder clay. Just nice, good, soft stuff and you'd drive until you get tired of driving or run out of piling . . .'

No, having heard out this man's version of wistfulness Robbie feels sure some of Hood's teak-like hardness is a front, a necessary ingredient of the job now sun-baked into him.

'Boy, it's been a life,' Hood man mutters, suddenly looking almost melancholy. 'I could never tell no woman all the things I seen drillin' hole.'

This Robbie finds less explicable. He is thinking of his own Marilyn, to whom he will usually recount as much of his workdays as she is willing to listen to. Hood, though, must be made of lonelier stuff, so much of his life spent drilling for black gold. Maybe that's where his passion tends? *If that's the way he likes it*, thinks Robbie.

As often when downtime comes, Robbie takes a wander and a look-see to what the divers are up to, on their cellar deck lying just below the drill floor. He feels alone in this interest: 'Divers, fucking skivers' is the common roughneck sentiment. But Robbie feels a good deal of affinity with their processes and practices.

And now he observes a man in wetsuit and scuba gear, standing by a metal cage, oxy-arc cutting tools at his feet. He is audibly ex-army and is being given pointed directions by Randall Hood about inspecting a length of broken drill string somewhere near the blowout preventer on the seabed.

The diver seems not to fancy it. 'Sir, with respect, I worry about our positioning. The thrusters could be a hazard when I'm a hundred feet down.'

'Son, you're already costing me time. This is my show, you need to get in that goddamn water.'

Robbie is seeing it the diver's way. What about this cold, these depths? What about the decompression stops coming up?

'Can you wait at least for me to get some assistance with my prep?'

Robbie feels his usual urge to make himself useful; he ventures a few steps down the stairway. 'Mr Hood, sir, I can gi' this man a hand, I know diving.'

Hood's scowl is transformed – if not quite into a smile then at least to a flash of teeth. 'Attaboy, kid. You're a beaut!'

Robbie goes to join the diver, who is not overjoyed to see him. Conversant with all of the gear the diver has at hand, Robbie feels nevertheless – as he glances down the moonpool through which the cage will be lowered – that it is an awfully long way to the water.

Dinnertime under the strip lights. Robbie and Stan share their table with Kenny Cooper and Klondike, ever sure that the boys look to him to fill the air with blether.

'Guys, I tell ya, right about now I've got me a raging thirst for a beer. A whole quart of cold beer in a long glass.'

'Tell you what, Klondike, we'll sink one for you on the beach the morra.' Stan looks uncommonly narked.

Robbie, having bolted down his haddock in parsley sauce, is now considering sponge and custard. Klondike, polishing off his second plate of pork in Marsala wine, makes a show of lip-smacking. 'Aw this is the good stuff, friends. Serious. I've been around, seen my share of canteens. And I tell ya, this is good cooking. I enjoy my food, I really do, I enjoy—'

'We all fucken do, man, shut up about it,' barks Stan.

'Hey, what's your problem, buddy?'

'I mean give over gannin' on about it! Just shut your hole for a change.'

Klondike has a mean grip on his fork and Robbie wonders if he will have to intervene. But Kenny does so, wearily, without raising his voice. 'Quit it, lads. Okay? Get your heads on and quit it.'

Robbie slumps back in his seat. So nearly done now, again. He's dreaming of departure time, the fug and low light and refugee air in the cabin where you wait for the chopper and play table football. Whirlybirds for a few hours, then down them steps, down to the office, wage packet in your hand, money and freedom, *dead on.*

—

They've made it – Robbie, Stan and Kenny – to the tidy snug at the corner of Mearns Street and Regent Quay, where the landlord has installed bat-wing doors at the entrance and the lads can bash their way in like John Wayne. Robbie stares at his pint, the froth and suds, and feels himself begin to relax, the overpowering weirdness and tension of the rig left miles behind. His oppos are a funny pair, but he doesn't much care. He intends only a couple of pints tops before beginning the wend home to Marilyn.

Stan is drinking quick, but he's not so obviously happy. A Texan clatters through the bat-wings and shouts to ask if any man had a Second Engineer ticket. 'Away and shite!' Stan blares, careless. Soon he has started a domestic tirade, over-familiar to Robbie and Kenny alike, such that they could nearly miss Klondike.

'Everything she sees in the adverts, she wants it, man – record player, hoover, new bathroom suite. What do you actually *need* in your life, man? But they want you to think like you've never enough.'

'The capitalist system,' Kenny intones, then belches.

'Eh, now.' Stan rubs his hands. 'Shall we's gan on the pull? Pull us a couple of tarts?' He tugs at Robbie's arm even as Robbie tries to drink. 'We've got this lad, wor secret weapon with the blart. He's a shagger! This lad drills hole, he's a beaut!'

Stan is gazing at him, grinning, bleary-eyed. But Robbie has zero interest in a bender. He knows Stan will shortly be after a shag off a hooker, smuggling the lucky lady into his guesthouse room on Crown Street. This pub is often awash with pleasant girls, some with kids at home, some up from London, a number from Newcastle, albeit of lesser novelty to Stan.

The landlord barrels over with a pencil and a pad and tells them it's a lock-in while he drives to the cash-and-carry. Stan, elated, shuffles off for a piss. Robbie can feel Kenny, himself a mite redder in the face than normal, looking closely at him.

'We're a bunch, aren't we? What's it all for, eh?'

'You tell me, Kenny,' Robbie stonewalls.

'I tell you, this life – it's no bloody good for family. Not if you want your own bairns to like you. Cos you get used to not seeing 'em, and they get wise, see. Get wary of you? You miss one birthday, oh no. Then you miss another, cos you've done that now, right? Soon enough they've lost interest in you just the same. They've managed without ye, grown up without ye. Made pals they actually like . . .'

These maunderings are paining to Robbie. He has been holding on to say cheerio to Stan; now he is desperate to be gone.

'. . . and in the end you see them look at you like, "You still here?" Eh, and one day you head home for your warm bed, and your woman's warm tail, and there's another geezer there already . . .'

Oh fuck, Kenny, don't be saying that. Robbie scrapes his chair on the sticky floor in getting to his feet.

At their house he finds his wife alone but – and he can guess even at the doorway – feeling not free-spending with her sympathies.

'Enjoyed yourself, did you?'

'Got here as quick as I could, sweetheart. I'd one pint, that was it, then straight in the motor.'

He is not drunk, or even tipsy. And he is sore from the drive, in his neck and back and legs. But now he just wants to get a good solid hold on those soft curves of hers, find the purchase he's been waiting for, the pull and the push and the release.

Marilyn, though, doesn't yield to his embrace. She has something on her mind, clearly.

'I'm tired, too, Robbie, if you care to ask.'

'Sweetheart, am I s'posed to beg you for a kiss?'

She sighs, in a manner he thinks overdone. 'Can you not at least be nice about it? Robbie, I'm not going to become fisherman's wifey . . . I know on that rig it's all the nudie mags and stag films. But could you maybe try a bit of conversation before you go ramming your hand in my undies?'

188

Through the fatigue he stares at her, stung. She only bobs her chin at him as to say *You heard me.*

Robbie kicks his kitbag aside and plonks down heavily on the sofa. It seems there could be no rescuing the night. Finally, he tries: 'Listen. I work hard, for money.'

'You were nicer when you were paid less.'

He looks up to see her contemplating him with a coolness he can't recognise from any past set-to.

'Rob, you know, you're beginning to get the look of your pal Aaron. Like you carry the weight of the world, you and you alone.'

Getting a smile out of this one now seems to Robbie like a distant memory – not to speak of other things that used to flow so free and easy between them, which felt at the time like the finest stuff in life. She seems weary of him, as if he were not the husband in this marriage but its offspring – a child unwanted, tolerated at best. He feels an injustice there, and an urge to give her a piece of his mind. But he's sure this would only worsen a poor state. She is judging him, yes. Maybe correctly? He has given her what he would call his honest best but has failed to give her happiness; and that failure weighs hard.

Later in bed, her warm tail turned coolly to him, he finds his hand straying down to his groin. Glumly, grudgingly, he decides that he will just have to be a comfort to himself.

189

November 1967
Industrial Action

Joe is at his desk early, as now his custom – charged by the purpose he has found in the role of MD, and by the pot of coffee he likes to brew for himself in a French press. Sheila Balfour is the sole other presence at this hour but Joe keeps his door firmly shut to her, and she has learned not to bother offering him stewed tea from the office's antique pot.

The head-start on the day feels essential, today especially: Killday Fishing will soon have new offices, with carpenters and plasterers engaged in renovation of their warehouse space down the street, as arranged so ably by Ray Bodie. Already this morning he has looked in on the site, and if much reupholstering remains to be done – to the barracks-like walls and the cracked screed floor and the aged, murky windows – still, he can see what it will be and he believes in it. Midday, though, will see the real marker of change: a meeting to approve the new structure of the business. And so Joe reviews the relevant papers one more time, his eye straying only slightly to the brochure he has ordered for selection of new office chairs, open at his preferred model – Corbusier-style, tubular steel and black leather.

Andrew won't adore those, but Joe is content to take frowning silence as a form of consent, an honouring of the agreement they struck on Angela's wedding day – the succession plan, as it were. 'The talk' with his father for which Joe felt such foreboding has never really happened – not as such. In fact, Bodie talked him out of the idea of one decisive, air-clearing conference with Andrew. 'The trick,' Bodie told him, 'is to keep making the patient feel things aren't so very different, and the whole time they're just getting more and more pregnant . . .' Joe didn't much care for the connotations of 'trick' nor

190

for the image of his aged father as child-bearer – stranger still coming from Bodie who appears in no hurry to start a brood of his own with Joe's sister. But Joe has reasoned that Bodie's indelicate utterances seem to be a part of him; and you have to take the whole of the man or nothing at all.

And so, for the time being, little is substantively different. If Walter is now called Finance Director and Credit Controller, this is merely a new billing for the son who has trained in accountancy. Walter has seemed lukewarm about the whole thing, but then Walter is keen on so little. That said, Joe has seen him stiffen visibly before Bodie's manners and proposals; and so the approval of Bodie as Director of New Business presents the main wrangle, maybe. But, as Joe had said to Andrew from the start, this is only to keep things in the family.

Of course, there is disingenuousness – Joe knows fine well as he swallows the bitterish dregs of his coffee. Today's agenda bears Bodie's fingerprints as well as his own: one could say these are becoming indistinguishable. So the meeting will review the company's financial performance, current market conditions, foreseeable threats, future opportunities ... Privately Bodie has floated to Joe the idea of buying another company so as to expand. They are also supposed to approve the recruitment of non-executive directors: the new investors Bodie has in mind, the part of the plan Andrew disliked above all.

'*Answer me why, Joseph, after all this time, we should invite out-siders into our company? Throw open to them all our business, how we make decisions?*'

'*Because there are things we could do better that we maybe aren't seeing, Da. If it doesn't work as we want then it can be changed back to how it was.*'

That, at least, was how Joe sold it. Privately, he is steering by that principle that, once conception has occurred, no one can be half-pregnant.

A rap on the door breaks his contemplation.

'Joseph, may I show in Raymond Bodie?'

191

'Oh for sure, Sheila, no question.' Bodie moves cheerily and smoothly past her, shuts the door behind, and relaxes into the chair opposite Joe.

'Any more of that coffee going? I refused Sheila's claggy tea, of course. She's done well to keep her job all these years. The faithful servant, your father's spare pair of eyes . . . Neither bright nor competent, but cunning – that's my view. She passes herself off.'

Joe winces: this is surely a fight to have some other day. 'Is that why you wanted to see me, Ray?'

'God, no. Something eminently more important. I've had an approach from Paxton Oil. They need the hire of a support vessel for their rig, just temporary. And they asked if we have a trawler boat going spare – plus skipper and crew, of course? I said that was entirely possible – particularly if they would pay three hundred pounds a day. And they agreed with nary a beat, and I'd just pulled that figure out of my backside, Joe. Damn, I wonder now if I could have doubled it?'

'Hold on. We've never done this, our boats are trawler boats, not for oil rigs.'

'The make of the boat is no matter, Joe, it doesn't have to do a thing other than be there, floating – just in the event of some poor bugger falling in the sea.'

'But have we even got the right safety equipment? Legally, I mean? To send our men out with that responsibility?'

'Really, Joe? I'd say Killday crews have coped with a lot worse out in the Faroes. There's nothing they won't have seen. And there'd be a big drink in it for them at the end, the money we're talking.'

Joe, having run out of meaningful objections, decides he must buy time. 'I should talk to Walter.'

'Should you? Not just to me? We need to move quick. This is new business, Joe. The definition of it. It's exactly what you've tasked me to do.'

'It's not quite as clear-cut as that, Ray.'

Bodie sits back with a slight shake of the head, as a teacher disappointed in a pupil. 'Joe, we have a spare boat sitting there, men to crew it, excellent money on the table. Even Walter would see that. But my sense is, you're more concerned about offending your father?'

Bodie's face suggests only concern, no taunt about it, but Joe feels his middle stump has been knocked clean out. Now Bodie leans forward, hands pressed together for emphasis as if in prayer.

'I understand, believe me. But haven't we got to start somewhere with the strategy we've discussed? Good God, if your old man was so opposed to one simple job of this kind, how on earth will we ever—'

The door swings open without warning and Joe braces to give Sheila a rocket. But the alarm on her face is so plangent that he holds his tongue.

'I've had a call from the harbour, there's an awful situation with Garth and his crew, talk of getting the police.'

Joe shoots Bodie the briefest look. 'My God. We'd best get down there.'

From fifty yards Joe can see the gloomy bulk of the *Reaper* at berth, seemingly ready to sail, were it not for a cluster of bodies standing as if fixed in antagonism on the quayside. As Joe and Bodie approach at pace, Joe can read the tension in his brother Garth's frame, evidently inspired by the young deckhand – ragged-trousered, ragged-haired – who stands at arm's length between Garth and the ship's mate.

His brother spits before speaking. 'Well – Mr Lawrence here's after refusing to sail this morning.'

Lawrence the deckhand bursts forth: 'It's not just that—'

'Shut your yap, boy, I'm speaking.'

Oh no, thinks Joe. He has long observed how physically alike Garth and Andrew are, compact and whiskery, though Garth can be very cool where their father would be volatile. Not today, though.

'What's the reason, then, for this man refusing work?'

Garth has produced his tobacco pouch. 'I'd to put two men on short pay for lateness, that means docking the whole lot o' them in the way of things. Well, this one here starts running his mouth off about it, "all for one", isn't that right?'

'Something like that,' mutters Mr Lawrence.

'And, hear this, Joe, he can't be following a skipper's orders if the skipper is the boss's son cos that's . . . What's the word you said, wee man?'

'Nepotism,' says Mr Lawrence, looking boldly from face to face. Joe looks to Bodie and Bodie is looking right back, as if distinctly interested. While wanting to project authority, and seeing the slight implied, Joe is rather envious of someone having given out to Garth in a way Joe himself has never managed.

'Aye, see, he's swallowed a dictionary, this eejit.' Garth licks a cigarette paper sharply, then pauses. 'I should put your teeth down your throat to follow.'

'Okay.' Joe raises peacemaker's palms. 'Let's see if we can't calm this down. We don't want to get the law involved.'

'There's more, but, Joe.' Garth takes from his pocket some scraggy-looking pages, folded and stapled like a pamphlet. 'See this man has been handing out his words for the men to read? Follow me, he says, and I'll make ye's fishers of men. Eh? Is that it, wee man?'

'Let me see that.' Bodie frowns, and Joe can make out its stencilled cover: 'Concord. A Newsletter for the Left. Sept/Oct 1967'.

But Joe can also see two young deckies drawing near, reinforcements to get this ship out to sea. So much for the immediate problem. He considers the troublemaker. 'What's your Christian name, Mr Lawrence?'

'It's Callum, Mr Killday.'

'Callum, this is a serious matter.'

'I'll be glad of a chance to explain if you'll hear me out. I'm a good worker, we's all are. But there's a feeling on the ships about fairness, that things aren't right.'

'What's right starts with our boats going out to sea by nine in the morning with everyone aboard and ready for work.'

'You know we never sail on the dot, Mr Killday. I say that, you've maybe not been to sea yourself?'

The implied slight nettles Joe – not least in front of his brother Garth, who has gone along with Joe's elevation to boss-man without fuss but no special marks of respect neither.

'Well, I don't see anyone else out here complaining, son,' Joe ripostes at last.

'Oh the other lads feel it just like me, be sure of that. Only they're more afeart. They don't want to speak up in case it comes back on them.'

Joe frowns. Bodie raises a hand. 'May I propose we walk over to the new premises? Close at hand, and we'll not be disturbed.'

'Christ alive,' Bodie utters, head shaking as he sips a Bloody Mary. They have adjourned at his insistence, to the calm of the upstairs Club Bar of the Gardner Hotel.

'Maybe the thing is to see what we learn from this?' Joe proposes, turning a tumbler of water reflectively in his hand.

'From that little squirt and his commie propaganda? We're not running a co-operative here.'

'No, but he's maybe not wrong on everything. He's bright, forward-thinking, give him that. He might have done as a favour.'

'Eh? Which bit did I miss?'

Joe weighs his response, aware that his brother-in-law is much more an ideas man than a man-manager. True, in the echoey chill of their warehouse, perched on crates over a pasting and decorating table, they had listened in disbelief to Callum Lawrence very earnestly putting forth a list of workers' demands: no more docking pay for lateness; new and better safety gear; a guaranteed weekly wage for every man, mandatory union membership . . . But what struck

195

Joe most amid young Callum's critique of working conditions and practices was his clear distaste for the macho manners of some of his fellows. *'The older ones, they act so bloody proud of how mad dangerous their work is, so they just keep at it – soaking wet, bashed up, bloody freezing like it's a badge of courage. And slagging anyone who says different. But that's a backward attitude.'* And 'backward' is the very word, to Joe's mind.

Now he leans in. 'Listen, it's a fact that for a while now on the hiring front we've been short of able new men for the boats. Maybe it's the pay. Maybe the work itself. Any road, we've taken on some who we might have turned away before.'

'Like Callum the commie.'

Joe waves a hand. 'Be that as it may. I don't see lads as smart as him wanting to rush out on the trawlers. Not when we've the competition from the rigs.'

'You think the rigs are a holiday camp, Joe?'

'Of course not. But the money's so much better. We just get outbid. So where's our new blood going to come from? Obviously we're not giving in to all those bloody demands. But we might pinch an idea or two.'

'What have you got in mind?'

'I was thinking like a proper recruitment scheme? Every year, where we take a certain number and make them certain pledges – that we'll train them, not just for the boats but other skills. For the office, even? But so's they can see a real career path, that they can earn better pay and promotion, if they show us good work and the right attitude.'

Bodie glances to his near-empty glass as though in need of another stiffener. 'Joe, this isn't Dunlop Rubber. As long as Killday is in the fishing business you're gonna need big brutes of men. Not a load of wee Walters to sit behind desks.'

'That's short-sighted, Ray. Do you not see a day when we might need as many clerks as we do trawlermen?'

And at last it seems to Joe that Bodie is looking past his glass, such as to comprehend the shape of the boss-man's strategic thinking. 'Well, okay. I get you. I hear you, Joe, I do.'

Joe drains his water. 'Like I say. He gave us something to think about, young Callum. It's a shame we've to send him down the road.'

Bodie grins. 'Eh, you had me worried you'd taken a shine to him. Yes, he gets his bloody cards handed him. We can't let that sort of behaviour pass. He'll have to sell his labour elsewhere. I don't expect they'd care much for his manners out on the oil rigs neither . . . Now, speaking of which – I need to call Paxton Oil. Remember? About their wanting the boat off us? What do I tell them?'

'Tell them they can have it. Make the contract and I'll sound out a skipper and square it with Andrew.'

Bodie's grin is wider still. 'Alright, boss. You know, we say we can't pay the trawlermen better money, but if we can invoice the oil boys three hundred quid a day then things might start to look different.'

Joe nods at this, feeling better by the moment about his decision, wondering indeed why he ever hesitated.

May 1968

The Hospitality Business

Marilyn Vallance is painting her nails, laughing a little at herself in the act. *Lady Muck*. This because she is allegedly at work, manning the front desk of the Lockdare Hotel; but so little, really, is there to be administered. The clock ticks past ten thirty, the lobby is deserted. Occupancy rate is low, and there are no guest issues of note, save for some gossip in the stairs about 'The American'. While Marilyn arrived at reception defiantly unmade-up, the barest eyeliner and lippy, she feels no shame now about her collection of balled-up crimson tissues, the pear-and-acetate scent of lacquer.

Always she has felt conscious of – nettled by – being seen as 'spoilt'. *How spoilt can you be in Tarnwick?* But Marilyn is conscious, too, of being taken for a little too happy-go-lucky; and it irks her, like the irritant fly in the kitchen. She has always worked for money, just like her mother. And she feels sure she can graft with the best of them when the work means something; it just, to date, has never seemed to mean all that much. She has a keen sense of her own appetite, taste, opinions; and they are quite particular. Perhaps by now, twenty-six and wed, she should have done more with these distinctive preferences, settled rather less for simpler options?

It had seemed to her highly distinctive to be coupled up with such a beautiful boy, the thrill of their covert trysts – the raw pleasure of them, too. By consenting at last to Robbie's pursuit of her, and his passion – she had been affected, no question. And when eventually she led him by the hand to the Gallagher homestead, after strenuous intercourse down by the rocks only an hour before – well, it had been worth a fair bit to survey the confused vexation that her parents couldn't quite mask by their good manners.

That was then. Now she fears a little that the parade has gone by. She just cannot abide that her mother's faint and chilly smile all through the wedding ceremonials should be proven correct.

Hearing a tread, she swiftly straightens up, stashes the nail kit, and sees Mr Farquhar in cap and tweeds marching out of the lounge bar – only to pause for a squint at the lobby pinboard with its tacky inked notices about catering for birthdays, weddings and anniversaries. He murmurs as to himself, but loud enough for Marilyn's ear. 'Warm, friendly place . . . Good home cooking . . . Well, I don't know about that breakfast. Don't know at all.' Then, resolved, he strides to the desk. 'Now, would you be a local lassie?'

'Oh, very much so.' *Regrettably.*

'I'm after a round of golf at your local links, can you assist me in arranging that?'

'Certainly, Mr Farquhar. Shall I ring them for you . . . ?'

As Marilyn cradles the receiver, she notes the entrance to the lobby of The American, Mr Mount, in his rollneck, slacks and blazer, leather bag over one shoulder – rather a short-arse, in her view, but with a restless, pacing air about him. He pokes a suntanned nose into the breakfast room, gives the pinboard the briefest glance, projects a sense of intent.

Mr Farquhar is frowning, his eyes straying to the front of Marilyn's own white rollneck sweater. She smiles at him as for a trying child. Quite often when men study her too long she wants to say *Oh look at yourself. So boring.*

Hand on receiver. 'Mr Farquhar, what time would be ideal?'

Mr Mount has produced from his bag a portable cassette deck and is holding a small microphone attachment to his lips. As Marilyn jots down the details from her opposite number at the club, she half hears Mount's mutterings: 'Two-storey stone property. Single-storey extensions to front and rear. Three miles off the highway south to Inverness. Views across country to the ocean . . .'

'That's you all set for one thirty, Mr Farquhar.' Marilyn smiles, glad to be of service. The efficient moment, though, is instantly wrecked by Gregory the ginger bellhop stomping out of the stairwell in a massive strop.

'Fucken Cuthbert, fuck this place!'

Marilyn, aghast – 'Gregory, please . . .'

'What? I get my pay, it's wrong, just like my fucken holidays is wrong. I go tell him and he tells me to pack my bags. So fuck this place. Fuck Cuthbert, that cunt.'

Helplessly stuck in her spot, Marilyn fears the worst as Mr Mount now approaches them both, inscrutable. 'My friend, I see that you're occupied, but might I ask you to do me one small service before you go?' He plucks car keys from his bag, and a ten-pound-note from his pocket. 'A set of clubs in the trunk of my vehicle – would you take them up to room seven?'

Gregory's clouded expression is suddenly filled with light. 'Aye, you're on!' And he is away as if fearing Mount might change his mind. Instead, Mount turns his gaze on Marilyn.

'Marilyn Vallance – good to know you.'

'I'm awfully sorry for the disturbance, Mr Mount.'

'High turnover you got here, huh? Only the chef is indispensable? This great home cooking I've been reading about?' Mount drums his fingers thoughtfully on his side of the desk, then points to space as if remembering. 'You know, it's akin to what we've been hearing from Paris? General disorder in the streets there, of course. But some hotel staff, as I understand, have upped and rebelled against the management – banded together to actually take over their establishments, run the places themselves. You read any of that, Marilyn?'

'Something of it, I think . . .'

'Listen, Paris aside, I am in need of some advice – local intelligence, yes?'

Marilyn quite likes the bite in his diction. He has good thick hair, too, and a prominent nose that she thinks a bit sexy. Hooded eyes, too, as if wanting his bed.

'Certainly, sir. Is your stay with us for business or leisure?'

'Do I have to give a reason?'

'We find no one comes here entirely by accident.'

'Well now, I daresay they don't. As a matter of fact, I am myself in the hotel business.'

'Oh, I did sort of wonder. Your name seemed familiar. But perhaps it's Mr Cuthbert you should speak to.'

'Ha. Based on the intelligence I've already had? I think not. Now, you were just speaking to the gentleman about golf? How much to play the links at day-rate?'

'Three pounds and eight shillings, Mr Mount.'

'Richard. Call me Dick. And you have eight bedrooms here. Any staff living on site?'

'There are two rooms at the top of the property for overnight staff on call.'

'And tell me this, Marilyn – ordinarily, say the average day this season – how many covers will you take in the bar and the restaurant?'

'The restaurant seats thirty-two, we can fit another thirty in the lounge.'

He wags a finger, but jokily. 'That's not what I asked you, Marilyn. What kind of turnover are you actually getting?'

'I'm not sure what's appropriate for me to say.'

'Quite right. Now, what I know very well by my own God-given eyes is that out back there you have a tennis court.'

'Yes, the gravel court in the back area. We can hire racquets and balls.'

'Balls I have. Racquet also. What I do not have is a partner. Might I ask, would you be so kind as to play a little with me today? Whenever I travel I find it so important to stay in condition.'

Marilyn knows very well she is going to do this. As of now she wants this man to admire her. She can play. But she will have to put together an appropriate outfit. She can already see her tennis dress in the wardrobe at home, unworn since last August. Thirty minutes to drive there and back?

'Dick, I can meet you on court at midday?'

Within minutes she realises she has overrated her prowess on court, and underestimated his. Titchy as he is, he winds up his body to serve in the manner of an uncoiling king snake, and then the yellow ball whizzes by her. She further realises she had discounted the chill, palpable on her bare legs; also the cruelty of the gravel, clear to her when she slips and falls in a failed lunge at a return.

Mount jogs to the net, hurdles it, and helps her to her feet.

'Forgive me, Marilyn, I was quite inside my own head. Perhaps let's just hit up a little across the net?'

She concentrates now, he relents; and a rhythm is established between them, an easy banging back and forth. She feels his control of the pace, the pleasing stretch of her thighs now as she plays her strokes. She starts to perspire. If he still appears distracted at times, he favours her with regular smiles. Her height advantage had put her off him slightly. *But height's not the whole of the thing.*

When they are done, he wraps a towel round his neck but stays on his feet. 'Marilyn, I have just a little more business in mind. I would be so glad of your input. If I could borrow you just a while longer today?'

So she tours him through the small, simple garden at the west side, with its beds and wooden benches. Then she takes him to the outbuildings used for storage; unlocks the doors and turns on the lights so that he might walk from end to end. Intermittently he speaks into his tape machine, making guesses at dimensions that Marilyn reckons to be not so far off.

'Dick, may I ask what this is in aid of?'

He wags that cod-admonishing finger. 'Opportunities, Marilyn! Opportunities not being taken . . . No, hey, listen. You got me. I'm scouting, my dear. For my business? I was in Aberdeen just the other day and I have a site there looking pretty much tied up. And now, I am going to buy this place.'

'You want to buy the Lockdare . . .'

'Oh yes. There is gold here – a little deep beneath our feet just now, you follow me. But with a little digging . . . ?'

She believes she does indeed follow him. 'Dick, is this to do with oil?'

'Marilyn, I formed a high opinion of your acumen when first we met. I have not yet been disappointed.'

'My husband works on a rig out in the North Sea.'

Now he eyes her very thoughtfully. 'Is that so? You must be left to your own devices quite a lot.'

Now, for the first time, she's less keen to meet his eye.

'Hey. To be apart a lot is tough on a marriage. My ex-wife could never really make peace with all the time I took away. She liked the money pretty good. But the things one must do to make it? Not so much. And I learned, Marilyn, that marriage has to be a partnership that way. Two people have to be in on the same deal.'

La-la-la! she thinks. *Not appropriate!* 'Can I ask what you'd have in mind for the Lockdare?'

'Oh! Refurbishment, wholesale – of course. But I see terrific potential to extend. I would expect planning permission for that garden area to be a simple matter. Your storage buildings really should be extra bedrooms—'

Glancing aside Marilyn sees Mr Cuthbert framed in the door of the outbuilding, tall and suited, coot-bald and bespectacled; and now he is coming at them, irately, his steps slapping on concrete.

'Marilyn, a word with you please.'

'Mr Cuthbert, I've just been—'

'Privately, Marilyn.'

'Mr Cuthbert?' Mount steps forward. 'I was so hoping to speak with you. But it so happened I was fortunate to find Mrs Vallance first. Less fortunate for her, perhaps! But lucky for you.'

'Sir, if there's any—'

'Because this morning when the water in my shower was stone-cold, and when my breakfast eggs were sloppy with grease, my thoughts really were that this was not the "Highland hospitality" your literature promised.'

'Sir, we always make time for a guest who has any kind of a complaint but—'

'Well, that could take a while. And, trust me, this is the start and the end of my interest in you. As of now, consider me an ex-guest? My name is Richard Mount of the Mount Hotel Group, California. Has that name ever reached you at this dump?' He has produced another tenner from his pocket, and now he flicks it at Cuthbert's face. 'Have a drink on me, you cheap son of a bitch. You're gonna need it.'

He takes her to his room, and she stands and watches from across the width of the bed – which, clearly, he has made up himself – while he packs a pair of canvas-and-leather cases bearing the monogram of Gucci. As he folds and presses, he expounds.

'Marilyn, wherever I go for my work, and most especially when I am visiting hospitality businesses, I keep my father's great rule in mind. At all our hotels, in the quarters reserved for staff – where no guest ever came – he hung a sign that said, simply – "My family's name is in your hands". That was what he asked of his people. And in return, he took care of them. That ethos is also mine. I want to know my staff, what their problems are. If their kids are sick, I want to know. First, though, I have to feel an employee is deserving of such cares on my part. You get me?'

'I think I do, Dick.'

'Sure you do. Now, before I'm set up to get this place running again I'll need a full review of staffing. We need a real chief porter, a real head waiter – a real head chef, for crying out loud. A housekeeper, concierge . . . And I'm going to need a real manager, who can converse easily with guests, in the style appropriate. That is your gift, my dear, I see it in you. Are you happy that we keep talking?'

'Absolutely, Dick.'

'That is fantastic. I'll be on my way now, but I'll be back. If I need to bring you out to Los Angeles first, I will, and I hope you'd be amenable . . . ?'

Marilyn, most uncharacteristically, feels a little breathless, giddy even. It's turning into a version of a day she has dreamed of – doubly surprising since its particulars are so far removed from any fantasy she ever entertained hitherto.

'In terms of those other impending vacancies, perhaps you might even know the names of a few good people?'

Mentally Marilyn runs the quickest of fingers over various possibilities. This is certainly big news to tell her husband on their next phone call. There might even be something for him in this – to get him, at least, off that rig which has made him such a misery.

And then she thinks again.

No, this is not for Robbie. It feels quite distinctively like something just for her.

October 1968
Mutiny

From a smeared window in the exploration office of the Pecos rig, Aaron Strang surveys the North Sea and sees the dull glare of a now familiar adversary, one that seems forever to have the beating of him. The usual forbidding bloody day, conditions torrid: lumps of ten feet, wind at twenty knots. The drilling location might change, but the Paxton operation's luck stays roughly the same.

Seated with his loafers up on the desk, Charlie McGinn tosses aside *The Times* in disgust and looks about him momentarily with what strikes Aaron as a dog-like longing for his forbidden Marlboros.

'Price of crude's down to three dollars a barrel. Whoopie-doo. If the day ever comes we produce out of this hellhole, we'll all be rich as, oh, the fucking guy packed our groceries at Walmart . . .'

'We'll be moving again soon enough,' says Erwin Shields curtly, arms folded, his eyes on Aaron. 'You'll recall I never had the confidence that others expressed about this location.'

It feels shameful to Aaron, having such an odd fish as his antagonist. Shields is as well-travelled as all these oil veterans who have become Aaron's associates; and yet the Ulsterman strikes him as being made from the same petty stuff as certain Scots he has known, always implacably sure of their own rectitude. Per the hierarchy of this rig, though, Shields's boot is on his neck.

One more dry hole, then. Aaron wonders what will be the last? The point of cut-and-run? It seems to be examination season, and he is not excelling. An oilfield named 'Aaron' now seems a far-fetched prospect, a bad joke, even. And he feels the pressure of scrutiny acutely: all through his vitals, the drain of Paxton losing faith after nearly three years of no joy. The weighty company presence on the rig has the feel of a try at expediting the process by magic, but to Aaron it has a terminal kind of grimness. McGinn, previously the cool customer in the Paxton operation, now appears permanently aggravated.

With silence becoming oppressive, Aaron elects to speak. 'I should say, as I've said before, while I accept that we move, I don't believe we should be moving so far.'

'As *I* said' – Shields at his most prim – 'there was never anything in the Paleocene here. Nothing showed in the Zechstein interval. So who was right? No, Strang, it's time to plug and move.'

Aaron finds he cannot let that swipe go by, not from the Ulsterman. 'This is a complicated field, three horizons. Nothing above the Zechstein conforms to expectations. We could still just be looking at a really complex reservoir architecture. There's a horst block just a few clicks north, tilted, an odd one but it still looks to me like a decent shot.'

'Another one?' McGinn is sour. 'You're too decent, Israelite.'

Shields removes his glasses, rubs his boiled-egg eyes, muttering, 'How in God's name do these nicknames stick . . . ?'

'Erwin,' says McGinn, stretching his stiff arms, 'you ought to hear what Paxton calls you.'

Suddenly the room vibrates to the blare of the klaxon that signals a cessation of drilling. McGinn bangs the desk. 'Aw Jesus, what now?'

Aaron heads directly out the door to see what's the story on the drill floor. Immediately he can hear Randall Hood. *'Goddamn it to hell!'* But McGinn overtakes Aaron at the top of the steps, and down on the floor he goes to join a vexed group of head-shakers. Aaron can see the diving supervisor is in attendance. Hood steps aside to kick out at a riser with a booted heel.

The roughnecks, meantime, look raggedly bemused. Aaron sees that Robbie, having retreated to the distance of the railings, is absorbed in the perusal of some scrap of paper. But then McGinn is stomping back in his direction.

'What's our problem, Charlie?'

'One of the damn anchors. Looks like a pennant wire to one of the buoys has come off. From which end, fuck knows.'

'Is it bad?'

'We won't be moving from this spot until we can get the anchors up, and that ain't gonna happen if we don't know where to find them on the seabed, Aaron.'

'So what do we do?'

'I, Aaron, will send Mr Dean the diver down, see if he can find the broken end and reconnect.' McGinn clanks back up the steel steps.

Aaron wanders over to join Robbie at the railing, glad at least that he is not that diver. The winds are worsening. Under the rig the pontoons are awash, the lumps high. *The sea doesn't care.*

Half-heartedly he claps his friend on the back. 'Not so long of your shift left now, Robbie. Home soon to Marilyn.'

'That's if there is a Marilyn . . .' Robbie smacks the gusting paper in his hand, despondently.

'Robbie, what . . . ?'

A tale comes forth, in a halting, desultory manner, of what Marilyn has told Robbie in the letter he's holding: of how well things are going in her new role at the Lockdare, the building works that have begun, her improved salary.

'That's all . . . pretty good, but, is it not?'

'You say that. I dunno, Aaron. I daresay soon enough she'll be earning better than me. So what'd be the point of me then? The point of this?'

At Robbie's gesture round their desolate home, Aaron begins again to feel himself uneasily a part of what oppresses his friend. 'Eh, look, you could be a kept man and her the big breadwinner, how would that be?'

Robbie shoots Aaron a sore aggrieved look, shakes his head, stares back at the water. Aaron knows the emptiness of his marital advice. There is no danger of Heather out-earning him, not by piano lessons given patiently to small schoolgirls plus the very occasional recital.

But such chores are barely the half of her, if that. At home she has been trying to compose, making a mess around the piano akin to Aaron's own in the child-size room he calls his office. Whenever his ear is caught by passages of her own music, he stops to listen, caught up in its drama. It hints at something taut and charged inside, with its unusual rhythms and surprising, lilting, stirring melodies. It reminds him, yes, of recitals he has heard, sitting dumbly by her side; but it is always also inimitably her. She has been shy about pursuing it. On an occasion when he sought to encourage her, she said something that has rather haunted Aaron since. *'What I'm most capable of, inside me, I fear I just enjoy it too much.'*

Thus at Robbie's side, both of them disconsolate, Aaron watches the diver preparing on the deck below, in his wetsuit and scuba, getting tethered to a signal line as his supervisor instructs him with animated hands. Aaron watches Robbie watching, and knows that Robbie, always the superior diver, would relish this assignment hardly more than he – to be lowered by crane into the freezing waters in a steel basket already rattled by the wind. Finally, with a shudder, Aaron again drops a lame hand on Robbie's shoulder, and returns, clanking up the steps, to the exploration office.

The mood is torpid. The senior men have taken up newspapers and are idly discussing reports of the Apollo 7 rocket launch from Cape Kennedy, the NASA mission to orbit the earth in readiness for landing and walking on the moon. Aaron has thought this rather a crazy quest – though if it could succeed then he would pay dearly to examine a sample of moon rocks. Erwin Shields observes that the Apollo crew seem a curious set of talents – the veteran commander, Schirra, and two rookies; also that wind conditions in Florida were not thought ideal for the launch.

Charlie McGinn shrugs. 'There comes a day when, based on all that's riding on it, you just gotta suit up and go.'

To Aaron's mind the astronauts are heroic, no question. But from the pictures he has seen of the launch he would not have been in their boots for the world. Perched on top of that erupting volcano, waiting to be fired out of that cannon . . . and then ten days in a can, with the perilous return still to come. In those conditions Aaron feels sure, even the smartest person must believe they are lucky.

Shouts are emanating from out of doors, and the room has begun to pay a disgruntled, reluctant attention.

Then Aaron is startled to see Robbie burst through the door. 'Sorry, gentlemen – Aaron, please, there's an emergency.'

This time McGinn is faster from his chair than Aaron.

Aaron looks down, helpless, aghast.

The diver is in serious trouble. He has surfaced under the anchor bolster that juts out from the rig's titanic leg, and he is trying in desperation to cling to the pontoon, to haul himself up. But it is hellishly slippery and turbulent – again, and again, he is washed off the pontoon like marine debris, battered by the waves.

Aaron feels this high vantage on the man's plight to be hideous, impotent. It seems insane that no one else is doing anything. The rig's leg has a fixed ladder, agonisingly close from where they watch. Surely he can get to it somehow?

But now the diver is seized by another lump, and for a moment he disappears from view altogether beneath the rig. In the next his head is back above water, but a terribly vulnerable sight.

Aaron feels Robbie seize his arm. 'They've gotta get him the basket. Tell 'em to drop the basket!'

But this is already happening: the main rig crane is groaning into life. Of course, it is the sensible thing. As Robbie paces the spot, clenching and unclenching his hands, Aaron believes the solution has been found.

Now the basket is dropping steadily down to the waterline, and the diver is thrashing toward it, fighting the tide – having to kick madly just to try to keep where he's at. He lunges toward the basket as it rears close to the pitching sea. But the waves throw him aside again, and he flails.

Again Aaron has Robbie grasping and imploring at him. 'It's gotta go down, under the waterline, you've got to tell them, somebody tell the crane op!'

'I don't understand,' Aaron mutters. Paralysed by indecision, he urges himself to move, do *something* – but just as he turns, Charlie McGinn is at their back.

'The crane op's doing all he can. We don't lose our heads here. We can't risk the crane block going in the water.'

'Mr McGinn, there's a bigger risk down there, I'll tell you that.' Robbie's eyes are wild and his voice has a force about it Aaron can't muster.

In the next instant the diver has got a hold on the basket. He has made it, Aaron is sure; he will clamber to safety at last.

Then another violent surge crashes into him, tossing him aside, fully ten feet away. Another shoves him away further still.

'Fuck!' McGinn at last is shouting as to call out reinforcements. 'Okay, radio the support vessel to get in close, now!'

The last daylight is fading and to Aaron, already, the diver's bobbing figure – arms fighting upward, straining to show his position – is becoming less clear from where they all stand, helpless. Aaron catches a dark look in McGinn's eye.

'Okay, everybody inside! Off the drill floor now!'

Randall Hood, his voice unheard for some time, now snaps, 'You fucken heard the man!'

The crew keep vigil in the canteen, hot tea dispensed, talk unusually low – mere mutters, a crushed and hollow atmosphere. Aaron sits with Robbie. He is sure they are thinking the same thing – of that man, alone and scared, waves slapping his face. The memory of Robbie's cousin Sandy has crossed Aaron's mind. *Lost at sea. Jesus.* There are no words, and so, silent, they hold on to the dull warmth of their mugs. Kenny comes in the door, carrying a cardboard box in his burly arms, and seeing all eyes upon him he shakes his head slow and sets the box upon a table.

'Lads, I, uh . . . with regret I've to tell you we've lost our colleague Peter Dean.'

Groans and curses go round the bleak room.

'By the time the standby boat got out he was gone. They have him now, but . . . he's been pronounced dead. The company asked and so I've been to Peter's cabin and looked out his things, for his family.'

Aaron looks to Robbie, his pursed lips and creased brow, and realises abruptly that, while he feels as desperate as anyone over this terrible thing, he is quite likely to be seen differently – not so much colleague as company.

Then the klaxon calling the men back to shift resounds through the room. It occasions an immediate commotion.

'Aw for Jesus' sake,' Kenny shouts. 'That's it, I'm having a word.'

Robbie, too, is off and following Kenny, and Aaron feels that in all conscience he must follow.

'I don't like it any more than you do. It's just a fact, tragic as it is, and I wish there were a better way to say it – but an accident, even a fatality, we can't let it shut down the rig.'

On the drill floor it is Charlie McGinn who stands with his palms aloft, seeking to calm the dissent coming at him. Randall Hood, at some remove behind McGinn's back, wears a skulking look. Aaron wants to maintain a distance of his own, between dissenting parties, but it is Kenny Cooper, clearly, who has stepped forward to speak for the Pecos workforce.

'Mr McGinn, I dinnae believe in accidents. Things happen for reasons. So when a so-called accident happens, we want to be asking why, and that means stopping to think.'

'You're right, Cooper, there's an inspectorate that watches what we do according to our licence, and there will be an inquiry into this accident, as is right, and we'll comply. None of that changes what I just said, where we are right now.'

'Aye, and I'm saying it deserves some recognition now, what's just happened! What we've all seen. It's not on, Mr McGinn. A man's after dying at work on this rig. That means a problem with safety, it applies to every one of us. But here's you letting me and everyone else know that the policy on safety is made by the same folks as are cracking the whip to get us all back to work.'

To Aaron's eyes McGinn is having unusual trouble bearing up in front of Kenny's anger. It makes sense to him when Randall Hood steps forward at last.

'Listen, Cooper, I hear you, we're all just men, and that man's gone and God rest him. But the rest of us are still here, and there's no other goddamn reason but to make hole. That's what we're paid for, me and him and you and all the rest – and if we don't, then there's no excuse for us.'

'Mr Hood, I don't do this job for the money.'

'The fuck *do* you do it for then?'

'I mean it's not just the money. There's a right way to go about things.'

Aaron has had one eye on Robbie throughout the dispute. As Robbie now steps up beside Kenny, Aaron realises he had known it would come to this.

'Kenny's dead right.' Robbie sounds tightly wound. 'A man dies on the job? You're done for work that day. You try and remember you're a man yourself. You show some bloody respect. It's a disgrace, this is. Why are we even talkin'?'

Hood, in no way shamed, moves up to get his face squarely before Robbie's. 'Boy, I guess you need to hear this again. If you're on this rig you're on my time, and if there's breath in you then you work. You say you ain't working? Then I send for a chopper, get me some other men.'

Kenny rejoins, 'Eh well, you wait and see what sort of men are happy taking a job where their fellows downed tools. You might get a surprise, Mr Hood.'

Hood turns to train his wrath on Kenny. 'You talk that shit about downing tools, Cooper, and you'll see a chopper bringing law enforcement out here. How'd you like that?'

'What you talkin' about?' Kenny grimaces.

'Mutiny, son. Meaning rank refusal to follow an order and stirring up others to do same. Sounds to me just like what you got in mind.'

Charlie McGinn has put a hand to his face, maybe now regretting the decision to let Hood off the leash. It is McGinn to whom Kenny now appeals, bulking a path past Hood. 'You're hearing this? This is Scotland. Mr Hood's a long way from Texas if he thinks Aberdeen polis will fly out here to clap handcuffs on me or anyone else.'

Hood pushes his way back in front of Kenny's face, and to Aaron's horror he has produced his lock-knife, jabbing it for emphasis. 'That right, you son of a bitch? Tell me, then, who you think *is* in fucken charge out here? You?'

'Eh, man, watch where you're waving the fuckin' knife.'

Hood throws the blade aside and it skitters away over the deck.

'Screw that, I don't need nothin' in my hand to take you, boy.'

'You mad bastard.' Kenny turns away. In that instant Aaron is horribly sure that Hood will lunge at his retreating back. A moment more and he knows he was not alone, for Robbie has sprung in between them and shoved Hood down onto his backside, the tool-pusher slip-sliding several feet across the slick floor.

For a second or so the floor holds its breath. Aaron can feel calamity coming down from on high.

Then Hood has scrambled back to his feet, apoplectic. 'Okay, fucko, you're out! Charlie, call a chopper for this motherfucker, he don't work a minute more.'

'Naw, naw.' Kenny comes forward, arms wide as if to make all his weight count. 'This man doesn't leave. He did nothing wrong.'

McGinn has his palms up again. 'Okay! Listen—'

'Look at these witnesses. I'm telling you, you send Robbie down the road and there'll be others go with him, starting with me. See how you fare replacing the lot of us after folk find out what's gone on today.'

'Listen!' McGinn implores. 'Please. Okay? Let's agree – it's been a terrible day. Some hard things got said. Why don't we . . . take time out? Call it an hour. To take a walk. Have a think. See if some . . . cooler heads can't prevail?'

With a start Aaron wakes himself from a bad dream. In seconds he has remembered who he is and where he is – under scratchy sheets in his cell on the Pecos.

He lies there dismayed in the dark, staring up at the low ceiling. In the dream, some shadowy creature had crawled up onto his chest, was squatting there, and despite his panic he could not move a muscle to throw the thing off.

He resorts now to his regimen for dropping off to sleep: counting in his head while tensing each muscle of his body in turn, top to toe. The drill, though, is not sufficient to stop all the grimness of yesterday seeping back into his consciousness, immovably true.

He is thinking of the extraordinary demeanour into which his senior colleagues immediately fell, as if in lock-step – as if everyone had agreed by telepathy to say only the shortest, most banal things with regard to the death of a man on their watch. He tries to think of an excuse; comes up short. *Because what we do is so much more important . . . ?* Maybe they were all trying to manage the shock. More likely, he feels, they had been practising just how much they are prepared to overlook; how large the devil's share of creation.

Aaron knows fine well that he had hardly behaved any better. *We're all in it together.* He knows, too, that he was shaken by the antipathies laid bare on the drill floor – by how Robbie stood up to be counted. Before retiring to his cell he contemplated a phone call to Heather, then decided against. That had felt to him too much like seeking a comfort he didn't deserve.

Sleep won't come. Really, he wants to be gone from here. He knows, though, there is no real option for him but to keep on. His stake in the game feels meagre indeed, set against a man losing everything. Aaron is certain, though, that some further punishment for all of this must surely follow. Someone will have to pay.

Forty-eight hours after the incident, Aaron boards the regular chopper for return to the beach together with a full contingent of mutineers, their heads a good bit cooler, among them Robbie, Kenny and Stan.

Hard as it was to imagine that work could resume with any kind of normality after the fracas: still, by the next morning's klaxon, Randall Hood was back, with a black and self-contained look about him, but shouting the usual orders and no more. Some muttered that he must have had a proper talking-to. The crew went with it, as if in shared readiness to leave the wreckage behind, feeling maybe that some negotiated position had been reached, wordlessly. The only chopper that had left the Pecos in the preceding hours was the one that bore away Peter Dean's body.

Charlie McGinn has said nothing more in the exploration office. Kenny Cooper has only mentioned in his tersest manner, that he will be making a petition to the Ministry of Power. And it looks to Aaron, at least by surveying his travelling companions, that they have been knitted more closely in some way by a consoling experience of solidarity. He offered to take Robbie for a pint in Aberdeen, and Robbie, nodding, said that would be good.

Off onto the tarmac at Dyce, then, and into taxis to the Paxton Portakabin at the harbour to get their pay packets. Aaron lingers outside, as the sole one among them who gets his pay direct through the Clydesdale. His mates take a while longer than usual, though. Once they emerge it is all scowls and curses and thrusting torn envelopes forward for Aaron to see what's only gone and been done now.

He looks at Robbie's enclosures. Some scant lines on Paxton letter-head state that he is *'summarily dismissed with immediate effect for gross misconduct as witnessed by senior managerial staff'*. His work card has been stamped with red letters: NRB.

'Not required back,' says Kenny, grimly. 'The bastards only played along as far as they had to.'

Stan is aghast. 'It's like you said, but, Ken. Who'll they find to take wor jobs?'

'I think, wi' that one, they mebbe knew better than us,' responds Kenny quietly, lifting his eyes to the grey sky.

Stan scrunches up his letter and card. 'If I get my hands on that bliddy Hood.'

'Forget that, son, waste of time. I've a mind to go now to Paxton head office, but.'

Aaron opens his mouth to tell Kenny that will be just another waste. He thinks better of it; but the others are staring at him, with a sourness in their looks he can nearly taste. Robbie is silent but evidently full of feeling. Aaron wants to put a hand on his friend's shoulder, some gesture of consolation; but in this moment it seems clear no such gesture will be accepted.

PART IV

FORTUNES

August 1969
Choosing the Moon

A sunlit Friday morning: Aaron in his tidy Volvo leaves behind the flat pastures that have bored him since Invergordon, entering the home stretch marked by the obelisk on the green at the head of the meandering main drag into Tarnwick. Now the village shows him its familiar, sedate skirts: the crescent of sandy beach hemmed by sea defences, bungalows and fishermen's cottages gazing out blankly onto the Firth for a stretch of half a mile to the harbour.

These return visits Aaron always finds onerous – this one especially. For a while he has needed to call on Robbie: they have seen little of each other this year, and nothing at all since Robbie's and Marilyn's separation. First, more taxing still, he must pay his respects to his father.

As Aaron opens the cottage door he can hear low murmurs: David must have other company already. Entering the ill-lit kitchen he sees his father sat rather amicably at table with a visitor, and a pot of tea between them. Glancing up he seems oddly caught short, as if Aaron were the unbidden guest.

'Aaron, you remember Torrance, of course.'

The visitor stands and steps forward from the shadowed nook, long and lean, all dressed in black. 'It's good to see you, Aaron!' And though it's been more than ten years, the brooding youth all grown, Aaron knows Torrance McVey at once. As he shakes Aaron's hand he smiles broadly, disarmingly, the stretch of his lips revealing that top row of big tombstone teeth.

Thus Aaron sits and is poured fresh tea and subjected to a different

221

conversation than that he had anticipated. He learns, for a start, that Torrance's father is not much longer for this world; and Torrance, lately ordained, is in discussions to succeed the Tarnwick ministry.

Over these mixed fortunes Aaron makes what he hopes to be appropriate sounds of condolence and congratulation, accepted by Torrance McVey with a smile now turned rueful.

'Your own work is in the oil business, Aaron?'

Realising that his father must have explained little of such to Torrance, Aaron swiftly if sketchily details what he does for his living.

'It sounds like you've found a fit place for your talents.'

David nods. 'That's why our young people leave.'

'Some come back,' Aaron offers politely. 'There's a good chance, too, that the oil will bring plenty more work here, in time – here and all over the north-east.'

This opinion is chewed over in silence for some moments. Then Torrance resumes. 'Aberdeen's a handsome place. I found a loneliness about it, though. A hard place to make friends.'

'I find it alright.' Aaron shrugs, wondering at the roads Torrance must have taken in his wilderness years such as to arrive at these strange new sober manners.

'I gather you and Robbie Vallance are still great pals.'

Aaron nods, smiles – unsure, though, if Robbie would agree.

'Your father told me that his marriage is over. A shame.'

'It is that . . .' Aaron is frankly loath to speak of Robbie's and Marilyn's private matters before 'Torry', as if he could be some priestly judge of them, and not one who ran around with Marilyn in his youth. Aaron can only imagine how much worse such a discussion would be for Robbie; and for a moment he fears Torrance might enquire about Aaron's own marriage, too.

But his father is getting to his feet. 'I will go fetch down that book of theology I promised you, Torrance.' And so Aaron is treated to some moments alone with McVey, whose grey eyes disconcert him.

'Aaron, I just want to say – I owe your father a big debt of gratitude, one I doubt I'll ever repay. For the kindness he showed me, when others mightn't? There'd have been not a chance of my being ordained – useless even trying – if it wasn't for the testimony he put in for me. I don't pretend I ever gave anyone reason to think me better but . . . your father did, and I will never, ever forget that.'

Aaron, abashed by the earnestness surging across the table at him, unsure of a fit response, nods as keenly as he can. Then David returns with a book he now places in Torrance's hands, received gratefully. Torrance studies its backboard, smiling, and murmurs a few words aloud. '*The courage to be is the courage to accept oneself as accepted in spite of being unacceptable . . .*'

Aaron drains his tea, stands, says he must be on his way. Not the visit he intended, then, but he needs the air, free of this solemn atmosphere.

Striding out to his car, he feels irked by how irked he feels – God again, all that nonsense, those past disputes. Has his father now landed on a way to revive them? Worse, has he chosen to settle the score by the election of an alternative son? No question, watching the two of them so companionable, Aaron felt a touch supplanted.

He is only a shade late to the harbour where Robbie awaits him as agreed. They are going fishing: at least, Robbie will fish, diving for scallops that he sells to a few local restaurants. But they are going out together, for sure. When Aaron clocks Robbie's bobbing, weathered skiff-boat, though – maybe eighteen feet long, with its beaten-up outboard motor – he realises he hadn't fully reckoned with how they would do this.

'Old times, eh? Geez'a hand with the gear? I've spare if you fancy a dive . . .'

The good sport of their shared boyhood – Aaron remembers it fondly, but only as part of a past now long lost. 'Naw, thanks.'

'You'll be my tender, then. Good man.'

Robbie strips from his jeans and shirt; Aaron helps him into his dry-suit, before humping the air tank and a wooden crate of gear onto the unsteady skiff. Then they push out into the bay. The sun, a little hazy behind clouds, nonetheless lends a deceptive glint to the surface of the murky waters as the pair of them plough their way in silence.

A mile or so from shore Robbie kills the motor. Aaron assists in fixing his tank to his back while Robbie finicks with his weight belt.

'How deep will you go?'

'Maybe seventy, eighty foot? I've about a half-hour of air so I've to be mindful. You remember, Aaron . . . ?'

Aaron accepts the small jibe.

'Pass us them mesh bags?'

Robbie adjusts his mask, lowers himself to the boat's side – and with a wriggle he is off and away, backward over the edge. Aaron feels a slight, irrational clutch in his chest. Soon enough, though, he is seeing air bubbles rising to the surface in bursts. Robbie can handle himself.

Aaron looks up to the blue yonder, the sun on his face. He is thinking of the television pictures everywhere through the week – the Apollo moonshot, at which he had stared in fascination just like millions the world over. Saturn V on the launch-pad, in all its smoke and fire . . . Aaron imagined dials flickering on those miraculous controls, before the lift-off of the beautiful torch, briefly lost into mephitic clouds, before rising imperious, flame at its tail . . . *We choose to go to the moon.*

Robbie resurfaces and bobs up toward the waterline. Aaron makes busy, relieving him of the mesh bags and helping him clamber aboard.

'What was it like down there?'

'Aw, nice and easy. Peaceful. They're no hard to spot on the bed. Like wee fans, they are. You've to dig a bit sometimes, but you'll turn a rock over and see all sorts.'

224

Robbie shakes out the bags in turn and their bounty rattles wetly onto the floor of the skiff: clusters of hinged shells with blackened crenelations. Then he rummages in his crate, comes up with a pair of short, sharp blades, and proffers one handle-first to Aaron.

'Geez'a hand with this and all, aye? You'll see the wee white of the meat clear enough when you crack the shell. You carve that out clean. The rest of it you chuck. See if you get a shell no bigger than your hand? Chuck that and all.'

They set to it, Robbie dripping wet but vigorously paring and tossing the meat into a tin bucket which is quickly all a-quiver with its pearly load. He takes an occasional bite of the flesh he has cut; but Aaron is not tempted. They work in their familiar companionable silence.

'What'll a bucket like this fetch you from a restaurant?' Aaron has begun to wonder. The work, while bracing, seems to him a low-prospect situation.

'It's fine for what it is. For the season. I've gotta earn my keep, Aaron. I didn't bring much to my marriage, I've not come out of it with any more.'

Aaron, having waited in wariness for this matter to be raised, finds himself at a loss now for how best to address it. Mercifully, after a pause, Robbie continues.

'Listen, the other day I went to see the Laird. Cap in my hand, you know? He said there's work at the sawmill. You know me, Aaron. I'll take what's going spare if I can do it.'

'There's a fair bit you can do.'

Robbie hurls a shell back into the water with a bit of force, then chuckles, but sourly. 'You should've heard Marilyn after Paxton sent me down the road. "Why've you got to be picking fights with people? Can you never keep your head?"'

'That wasn't very kind of her.'

Robbie snorts. 'Aw I heard worse. But what's a man if he doesn't stand by his pals? She said I was a loser. Daresay I don't measure up to that wee American that's her hero now.'

Aaron winces, wanting to say he is certain Robbie is worth ten of the man in question. But he isn't convinced he can lift Robbie's mood – not on the evidence of the dejected face Robbie is now showing him.

'What d'you think, Aaron? Do you think the less of me?'

Aaron is appalled. 'Robbie, my God, I could never—'

'What, you couldnae think less that you do already?' Robbie guffaws.

'No! I mean, my opinion of you, that'll never change. Never . . . Marilyn, she just wasn't good enough for you.'

'You're good to say that, pal.' Robbie's eyes, though, are fixed low. 'How d'you ever know, but? What anybody's good for?'

Aaron is suddenly desperate to lift his friend out of this dolour, and for both their sakes. 'Robbie, you know . . . I felt so bad for how things finished on the Pecos.'

'Aw I know that, Aaron. I've seen it times past, that poor look you get on your face, like you could away and cut your own throat? I saw it clear enough that day. So don't be thinking no more of it, eh?'

Aaron nods into his chest. The sentiment, while welcome, has given him something else to consider. When he looks up, Robbie's eyes are very intently upon him.

'That rig, Aaron. That lot, that world. Watch yourself, eh? It's not good . . .'

'I know. I'm maybe not much longer for it myself – if we can't find oil soon, if I can't make anything happen.'

'Aye, but – see if you do that? That's your fortune, eh?'

'Somebody's fortune . . . Will you believe me if I tell you that's not the motivation for me? I mean, not to sound like Kenny Cooper . . .'

'No chance. What is it, pal?'

'Well, you know . . .' Aaron struggles with a near-culpable sense of shyness. 'An exploration manager who makes a discovery, gets credited for it – if he's the one who picked the spot that turns out to be a real oilfield – then he gets to give it a name. Like a star or a comet, y'know?'

Robbie nods keenly, appreciative. 'Eh, fair enough. That's a big thing. So what'll you call your one? "The Robbie Vallance"?'

They crack up together for a moment, the boat shaking amiably.

'Naw, look, you've gotta be calling it "Heather". Best get that right, boy.'

That is a proper notion, Aaron realises: one that simply never occurred to him. Instead he has begun to toy with a very different and personal selection of possible names: *Proteus*, *Hydra*. *Cetus*. Would it bring Heather any happiness? He cannot deny the marriage is otherwise making her unhappy. He has heard her crying, alone – a terrible, wrenching sound, to which he has had no response. The naming would be a token: something, perhaps, in place of children, the possibility of which he and she have ceased to discuss. Aaron is unsure if he is denying her on this score, or if she has no wish for it. Perhaps no faith in it.

Robbie has taken up his knife again. 'Eh well . . . I don't like to say it but, you must have wondered – maybes there's nothing down there.'

'No, don't be saying that. I hear it enough from Paxton and McGinn. I can't afford to believe that.'

'You do still believe?'

'Robbie, I've no choice . . . I mean, it's mad. You want and want a thing, and it never comes, and you ask yourself why you wanted it. And the way it's got for me now – I don't know any more if it's finding the oil, or just wanting to shove it down the bastards' throats for doubting me.'

Aaron feels a little poor in himself for confessing the ugly sentiment; but it seems to have delighted his friend.

'Aye, that'd be it. That'd be more than worth it!' And Robbie clambers to his feet, for all that the boat shakes, causing Aaron to grip the sides. Dripping still, he shakes a fist at the sky and shouts, '*You'd tell 'em "Fuck off ye bastards!"*'

He laughs with a glee so infectious that Aaron has to join in. 'That's it!' And Aaron gets to his own feet, for the pure sport of mimicking his pal. '*Fuckin' fuck away off, the lot of ye!*'

'*Aye! Eh? Y'hear me, Paxton? Get – away – to fuccccck!*'

And together they stand laughing and cursing to the heavens like loons, until their sides are as thoroughly shaken as the skiff.

September 1969
New Premises

Awaiting his appointment within the thirteen-storey pile of the *Scotsman* office, gazing across a marbled floor, past a polished banister and through a picture window onto the castellated splendour of north Edinburgh – Mark has come round at last to Ally's view that this is a heady place to be a newspaperman. From the moment he passed through the mahogany-panelled entrance, he has felt an annoying uptick in his heart rate. But he anticipated as much in the morning while about the uncharacteristic acts of ironing a shirt and shining his Oxfords, donning his one suit and putting a brush through his hair. Now he waits, armpits prickling, outside a rank of forbidding doors, the largest of these into the lair of the managing director. This is a moment: he must give a good account of himself, no messing.

A young woman in a chequered minidress approaches, smiling. 'Mr Rintoul will see you now.'

'It's a lively time for us. The company's expanding – you might have noticed.' Rintoul gives off a frank, pugnacious air, rolled shirtsleeves and spectacles gleaming atop a fleshy nose.

'Well, I saw your proprietor just bought the London *Times*.'

'Indeed. In terms of our news coverage, generally we're after more of a shape to it. Snappier headlines. More to get conversations started. People can get very settled in their thinking, our reporting wants to stay fresh.'

'I couldn't agree more.'

'So, look – if you could be anywhere this morning reporting on a story, where would you be?'

Mark leans in, rating this a good one, indeed the kind of question that preoccupies him often. 'I reckon I'd want to be in Londonderry? When you have such a size of a community aggrieved within a country, and the army sent in, and the PM in the north of Ireland saying "neighbourly relations" with the south are over? That's definitely a moment you'd want to witness.'

'Huh. Interesting. You fancy a bit of that action?'

'A good reporter should be getting their hands dirty.'

'Just from your cuttings, I see . . . well, you've done a fair bit on the industrial side, depressing as that is . . . but you've been pretty good on the Scots Nats. Ever since Hamilton, aye?'

'That felt like a moment, too.'

'Has that one maybe rolled back a bit?'

'I wouldn't write off the SNP. They've made things happen – made Labour change their tune, and the Tories, too. Swung them both round to backing some kind of self-governance for Scotland . . . That's huge.'

'What do you make to the new leader? Mr Wolfe?'

'Staunch Scot, quite a liberal bent . . . Pro-CND. I hear he's a poetry lover? I'd expect he might take the SNP a bit more to the left, relatively.'

'You expect that or you fancy it?'

Mark decides to let that sortie go by. 'I should say, I've assumed this paper is broadly receptive to the SNP's case for independence? You've published a fair bit of opinion on those lines.'

'Well, I suppose we all wonder about it. Is independence doable? Or do you put your money on devolution? It's a question for Labour, Tory – you, me and oor Wullie. For a'body!' He smiles and rubs his big hands. 'You got any more ideas for me, then? Stuff I might steal?'

'The North Sea, of course. No one should be taking their eye off that.'

'You think? Awful lot of wells been drilled, not one drop of oil. Has a look of doom to me. You sure we should care?'

'I do. For what it would mean. For a'body, really.'

230

—

As agreed he meets Shona for debriefing at midday, in the Halfway House pub favoured by railwaymen, rather than the Jinglin' Geordie where her *Scotsman* colleagues might notice and pass comment on some conspiracy. Upon seeing her, chic in her tweedy skirt suit cinched with a leather belt, he feels the usual surge in his chest. He leans down to kiss her and she lifts her lips. Then he allows himself half a bitter while she sips water.

After he has described all the splendour that he observed at the *Scotsman*'s offices, Shona smiles wryly. 'Wait 'til you start. The poor workers have to go in by a dirty doorway on Fleshmarket Close.'

'Well, I don't want you to think my head was turned. I saw the newsroom . . .' And that had seemed to Mark as drear and airless as a school common room, desks crammed into every nook, books, papers and newsprint piled on every surface.

'I like that guff about new ideas. Really, what you get are orders handed down from the bridge where the editors sit.'

Shona's self-assurance continues to stun Mark. His impending adventure is only to a place she has already traversed. And soon she will be off on her travels again, now the paper's Eastern Europe correspondent, armed with her fluent German and her history degree. First stop Berlin, thence to Prague via the Bavarian border, visa permitting. For Mark this is a relatively rare audience with his live-in girlfriend.

They have taken one holiday together, to the Greek island of Spetses, where by day they hiked its full diameter and swam its blue waters, then by night talked politics and books, candle-lit over grilled meats and retsina. Every day, too, involved lovemaking, with lots of seeming mutuality. Even a sore bit of sunburn hadn't stopped Mark's ardour; Shona had only touched him more tenderly. In all, the excursion had felt to him like a highly satisfying experience to be one half of; and yet he couldn't shake the sensation that Shona had done it before – and might do it again, perhaps a richer version of it, without him, somewhere further flung and more fascinating still. *Sophisticated* – that is how he rather helplessly sees her.

'You'll keep the flat in good order while I'm gone?' she says, with more query in her tone than he would like.

'I might even look into the flea market I passed the other day, see about a couple of armchairs.'

The flat they share in Leith is more than pleasant for a fiver a week, white walls and stripped floors; but it was rented as unfurnished and largely remains so – the tell-tale sign of the lair of two writers, busy with duties more pressing than the domestic. Still, it is their place together, the mark of a commitment.

He touches her face. 'Promise me you'll look out for yourself?'

'I won't be all alone. I know a good few people in Prague now.'

'That's what worries me . . .'

Now she bats him away, but fondly. 'And, I know I'll be watched and tapped everywhere I go, so you can trust me to be as cautious as a Scot.'

He feels and respects her contained excitement, as much as he resents it being attached to a mission that takes her away from him. Forlornly monolingual himself, he just hasn't got the same feeling for Europe. But Prague has magnetism for her: she had been deeply engrossed in reports of the reformist Dubček, then downcast and incensed by the Soviet tanks rolling in last summer.

'I'm hoping, by the way, to get a meeting with a college friend of Jan Palach.'

This pleases Mark even less – another fixation of Shona's, the student martyr who burned himself to death in Wenceslas Square, protesting the regime. 'God, you know I hate to think of that. It's so drastic. Hopeless. It's the opposite of politics.'

'Well, you have to try to imagine powerlessness of that order. From all I hear, he was a rational young man. He thought long and hard about what it meant to live under all that oppression, the lies

232

all the time. And it did mean something. Here we are talking about him.'

'Yeah but, Shona, we follow this stuff.'

'Not just us, Mark. The world is watching.'

Again, just a twinge within; but with Shona, Mark does at times feel himself that little bit parochial, somehow cast as the dumb blonde in this relationship. Wanting to counter that feeling, he leans in again and kisses her.

'Sorry. I'm going to miss you. And it's been a big day.'

'It has. What'll you do with the rest of it?'

'I'm going to pop in on Ally at his new office.'

'Ah, you've an appointment at the palace? A big year for your friend, this. New company, new office. New Mrs Drummond . . .'

Just a trace of smirk on that mouth, Mark sees. He is quite sure Shona rates Ally highly, just as Ally has shown her every courtesy befitting. Any other outcome would have been inconceivable. But Mark is fairly convinced, too, that Shona has decided Ally is a bit of an operator, however affably so; and that she may feel similar about Mrs Drummond.

Up the stone steps to the door of the Charlotte Square townhouse: a certain Georgian regality appropriate to Ally, though the name on the brass plate mounted to the ashlar gives him a small affront.

DRUMMOND FYFE LIMITED

Mark, though, has made reluctant peace with the fact that his friend brings different standards to life and work, and that the latter includes this partnering with the obnoxious Gordon Fyfe – so obnoxious that Mark feels sure Fyfe will have argued for his surname to get first billing.

When the big black door swings open, Mark is somewhat surprised to be greeted not by some penguin-suited Jeeves but by Ally Drummond himself, in shirtsleeves, removing a small cigar from his mouth.

'Well?'

'I'm hired.'

Another surprise for Mark, as he is silently enfolded in Ally's firm embrace. Then Ally bids him enter, across polished parquet and a succession of Persian runners: so surely the domain of a merchant bank, though Mark sniffs wet paint, and sees cardboard boxes lined end to end along the skirting.

'You still have the decorators in?'

'Yes, I've roped Belinda into overseeing a bit of that. She has an eye. And it keeps her out of mischief. She'll maybe come say hello. Gordon's about, too – busy, but if you want to put your head round the door for auld lang syne?'

Mark shoots a reproving look. Ally throws open a door painted gleaming gloss white. 'Let's take the rear drawing room, shall we? This will be our space for proper fraternising once it's done. Cigars and so forth.'

'I see. So you're smoking now?'

'I find it handy.'

This rear drawing room enjoys a plasterwork ceiling and a sumptuous white marble fireplace. Under dust sheets a number of evidently enormous canvases await hanging. Ally tugs another such cover from a powder-blue damask sofa, such they can sit, and Mark tells the tale of his interview with Mr Rintoul.

'It's the perfect time for you to get aboard there, tovarich.'

'I was struck that he went on about how they're getting their hands into businesses other than newspapers.'

'Oh, everyone's up to a bit of that. The more Thomson makes from other ventures, the more they can pay you and fellow oarsmen to carry the news to the people.'

'I'm afraid I'll be writing a fair bit on the independence question.'

'Just try not to be a bore. I've no doubt at all that the *Scotsman* would love a Scottish parliament – right here in Embra, of course, perfectly placed for the *Scotsman* to rub shoulders and write up

234

proceedings. For all the interest that will hold for those elderly readers out in the provinces.'

'Or for you, Al?'

'Or for me, Mark.'

'Of course I told them I wanted to cover the North Sea, too.'

'Very wise. In fact, I have some news on that score – we now
officially share the interest. This company will be getting its feet wet
in the North Sea – I hope we don't bloody drown.'

'What's that about?'

'We've decided to take over a stake in one of the firms that are
drilling right now. One of the consortia, I should say. Quite a measly
stake, just one-fortieth of the whole. The main player is Paxton Oil,
they're an independent from Texas—'

'I know them! Know *of* them.' Mark is pleased to have an informed
role in this exchange. 'Yeah, I looked into them way back, I even
spoke to Paxton.'

'Very good. Well, one of the London banks had a nibble originally
but they've lost their appetite. So Gordon and I took a look and we
reckon it's worth the bet.'

'You make it sound simple, it must be a lot of money.'

'Not mine, as such. There's a slew of older investment trusts that
are backing this ship you're sitting in. But I always take care with
what I spend. Unlike the Contessa here . . .'

Belinda Drummond, née Morland, has swished into the room, in a
blouse and laced waistcoat, floral skirt and leather boots – a look that
Mark guesses the Sunday supplements might describe as fit both for
town and country.

Mark rises in greeting. 'He's put you to work, Belinda?'

'With the decors? Oh, it's just a lark.' She is florally scented as she
kisses him on each cheek. 'My own fault for marrying into this fly-
by-night scheme.'

Ally tilts his brow at her. 'Darling, you were welcome to stick with
that rugger-bugger stockbroker you were with when we met.'

'*Il n'y a pas d'amour sans jalousie.*'

'Oh ferme ta bouche.'

Husband and wife have a short exchange about curtain fabrics before Belinda breezes out again. Ally's marriage had first seemed to Mark somewhat mercurial – but, after inspection, built on shrewd calculations. Ally has surely needed a woman of this sort, as pin-sharp as he in her own way, if perhaps just a mite more offish in her manners.

'It's such a big year for you, Ally.'

'For us both, comrade.'

'It feels as if things are moving awfully fast.'

'Are they, though? Isn't this what hard work is supposed to yield? For me, Mark, getting this thing off the ground has felt like aeons – I'd like to put my foot down on the accelerator, frankly. For instance, what are the odds of you ever making an honest woman out of the fabulous Shona?'

Now Mark feels a mental wall going up. *We don't all need to be the same, do the same bourgeois stuff.*

'I know her parents think we ought to. Mine aren't so bothered. Nor is she. It's boring to say it, but if we were to take that plunge – we'd need to buy a house, I think, a good one. Somewhere proper. And I just feel I ought to bring the deposit for that, and I just haven't got it. Penniless hack, you know . . .'

'Oh God, Mark, of all the things – don't let that be an obstacle. I mean to say . . . if you ever needed any help, I'd happily step in. The two of you should have a decent place as befitting.'

Mark considers this, bemused. 'Al, are you saying you'd help me buy a house?'

'Why, yes! I'd loan you for the deposit, certainly. As long as you'd need to settle up, no interest or any nonsense.'

'That's terrifically good of you, but . . . I couldn't accept. You understand, I couldn't have Shona thinking . . .'

'Why tell her? Just say it's your rainy-day money. Your maiden aunt Jemima's bequest.'

It feels to Mark a slightly risky, rather strange proposition: one that would make his friend like a kindly father to him. Disreputable, too, smacking of hypocrisy. But he can't deny the temptation. And a favour of such size, if not exactly socialist, would be undeniably comradely.

January 1970
At the Òrach Hotel

No connoisseur of neckties, Aaron holds before him the two that he owns, and considers: the blue one with brown dots, or the brown one with blue stripes? He is dressing for an after-work occasion he doesn't want to attend. Heather, persuaded to accompany him, does the same before their bedroom's long mirror.

The venue is to be the newly opened Òrach, 'Aberdeen's first modern luxury hotel', according to its brochure – uneasy browsing for Aaron inasmuch as it bore the signature of Richard Mount, the man who has seemed to play some significant part in the break-up of Aaron's best friend's marriage. But the evening is vaunted as a meet-and-mingle for businesspeople in the locality: those already in the oil business, and those who might like to be. The latter category has grown sizeably and suddenly since Christmas, when the American major Amoco confirmed it had made an oil-strike in the North Sea of real commercial potential.

Lucky bastards was Aaron's first, gut reaction to Amoco's find; and yet he knew a certain pulse-racing moment long awaited by many had arrived at long last. And he has been hoping just like all those others that Amoco's luck might soon be shared more widely. With another licensing round at hand, he is certain a lot of bets are about to be piled onto blocks.

But Aaron is asking himself, morosely: who would place a bet on his acumen now? His zero success rate he cannot hide from. He has sensed, too, a limit to the depth of Paxton's pockets, four years into an adventure that has not repaid its first promise.

He turns to regard Heather before the mirror, watches her fix her earrings and her amethyst necklace. 'You look bonny,' he murmurs.

'I do appreciate you doing this for me.' She hardly smiles; it's clear she no longer believes his compliments. The ritual politeness, the pretence when feeling is absent – is it not so bad as outright antipathy, at least? Or is it perhaps worse?

In this way they are limping on. Aaron wonders if it is a simple, mutual failure of imagination? Of what would be their lives without one another, of how lost time could possibly be recouped? Or failure of courage, a reluctance to disappoint Hugh Munro or any other concerned onlookers?

He wishes dearly that, even just once, he could speak to her again of his real regard for her – speak well, and have her hear it, so that relations might be repaired even a little. And then perhaps, too, she might speak to him and look at him more in the way she did before the fall.

The Òrach looms out of the night lit up rather as Aaron imagines they do things in California, showing off its whitewashed wings and colonnaded entrance. He parks in a generous landscaped enclosure adjacent; and then in go the Strangs, through a foyer with tropically patterned wallpaper and carpet, up to a greeting table where a suited lady offers them name-badges and directions to 'the ballroom'. Aaron can see Heather gazing bemusedly about her – at the incongruous Versailles furnishings, the bordello-like globe lights, the trailing pot-plants on plinths, and – set back in a nook, proud but neglected – a baby grand piano.

As they approach the ballroom entrance there is an audible buzz – lively, grumbling, expectant. Within are perhaps a hundred smart guests, milling. The couple accept glasses of wine from a tray. Two lines of Doric columns designate a polished dancefloor space, a generous buffet set up at its centre, the sides flanked by seating at tables covered in clean white linen. Aaron scans the room nervily for anyone he might know. To his surprise the one onto whom his gaze latches is now tapping his glass with a breadknife as to say a few words from the dancefloor.

'*Good evening ladies and gents, my name is Donald Cowan and it's my honour to represent North Aberdeen down there at Westminster.*'

Aaron is gladdened that Cowan – stout, nursing a whisky, in a politician's navy suit-for-all-seasons – is clearly no more a necktie man than himself.

'*It's my further honour to welcome you to this sodality on behalf of the council and my fellow MPs of the region, with thanks to Richard Mount of the Òrach as our kind host.*'

Aaron glances to where Cowan is directing polite applause; and there, by the side of a short, spiffy, suntanned man with luxurious hair, he sees Marilyn Gallagher, svelte in a sleeveless jade-coloured dress, light in her eyes, a smile on her lips. He glances to Heather, whose dark eyebrows move slightly, reprovingly.

'*I will be brief. And I'm not kidding. Trust me on that, try to forget I'm a politician . . . It was my great friend Professor Hugh Munro who first enthused to me about the hope of oil in the North Sea. Now it's a dream we can all believe in and hope to be a part of.*'

For these generous words – Cowan is a pro, no doubt – Aaron wonders if Heather might feel it was worth her while coming, for all that he knows Hugh would not have been caught dead here.

'*At this exciting time, what can Aberdeen do for you? Be it said, the city welcomes you here – welcomes your interest in oil exploration. In return we offer you resources, services and skilled working people. Aberdeen is open for business – oil business! So let's work together.*' Cowan lifts his glass. '*Sláinte!*'

Aaron takes Heather's arm gently to go say hello to Cowan. But Clay Paxton is moving forcibly to get there first, and as he and Aaron make eye contact Paxton gestures sharply as to say that they, too, should have a word. Instead Aaron makes a show of letting his boss go first, and steers Heather toward the food, hearing over his shoulder that Paxton has begun to weigh in: 'Fine talk there, Mr Cowan, but—'

The buffet is largely fish-based – trays of whitebait, rollmops and smoked kippers, arrayed around bowls of boiled eggs and sliced tomatoes. Aaron offers Heather a plate, though she looks no more enticed than he. But they are geed into it – 'We eatin' here or what, guys?' – by a tall American at their back, clad like a rancher in a plaid shirt and blazer, denims and boots, his hair brushed off his temples. Unbidden, he tells them that his name is Sam Lietzske and he runs a plant for Baker Oil Tools of Los Angeles, five miles out of town.

'Yeah I used to work for Standard Oil in Taft, California. Nice company house there, real pretty. But it came the time to hitch wagons, y'know? Taft got to be kind of a ghost town.'

'Isn't oil supposed to make places rich?' Heather asks, arch-sounding to Aaron.

'For a little season, ma'am. But over time, the oil just flows out.'

'And nothing comes in? Were you near that awful Californian oil spill last year?' His wife's interest is news to Aaron, but Lietzske is slow-shaking his head.

'That was down in Santa Barbara, ma'am. Big shame. Union Oil, they just had some bad advice from geologists on how to case the well. Damn thing blew up. Gallons of oil in the ocean, just awful.'

'Yes, we've seen the like of that here.'

'Well, drilling is never foolproof. And they just didn't get the damn thing done right – not the oil men nor the scientists.'

'My husband is both. One part of himself might need to have a word with the other.' With that, Heather waltzes off the way they came in, to Aaron's chagrin. For a panicky moment he wonders if her surprise acceptance to join him tonight had in fact concealed an intention to cause him some awkwardness.

'Boy.' Lietzske chuckles. 'That's a forthright one you got there.'

Desperate to change the subject, Aaron enquires after Mr Lietzske's tool business. To his surprise he is soon engrossed by the man's voluble holding forth on all the state-of-the-art wares he keeps in stock. Baker is, it turns out, chief local supplier of drilling equipment from the renowned firm of Schlumberger. When Aaron attempts to relate a little of the importance to his job of cutting cores out of rock intervals in wells, he is rather pleased to receive a very animated sales pitch from Mr Lietzske for a 'just fabulous new tool' he calls the Tri-Corer.

'Aaron, I will bet you've had that moment where you thought, "Damn, I should've took a core, and now we've drilled through and it's too late!" Well, this beauty, you can send in after the fact. You shoot it down a well to the depth you want, and this corer, see, it swivels, and a couple of diamond blades come out and dig into the side of the rock to cut you out a nice slice. Is that not cute as all hell?'

'Oh, that's brilliant . . .'

'It's James Bond, my friend. The thing is, it gives you that second chance. And there's times when you really need one of those.'

Amen, thinks Aaron. It is a wrench to remove himself from the conversation with his new friend; but he must check on his wife. He finds her back out in the foyer, reclined on a Louis Quatorze arm-chair, perusing the hotel brochure.

'I've learned so much,' she says with a put-on gaiety that pains him a little. 'It has a pool, they do weddings. Every room *en suite* . . . No, really, Aaron, I'm happier here.' She gestures to the nearby piano. 'Just let me know when you're done.'

Aaron sidles back into the ballroom, wondering if maybe Sam Lietzske could effect an introduction for him to someone big at BP or Shell – some party that might be hiring, and ready, against the odds, to overlook his unprepossessing appearance and track record . . . Instead, worse luck, he bumps up against a table where Paxton is seated with a younger man who exudes a languid, *soigné* air. Aaron is beckoned by index and forefinger.

'Aaron, pull up a chair and give the glad hand to Lord Al – this is Alastair Drummond of Drummond Fyfe, our new investor in the consortium. Al made the drive from Edinburgh to join us tonight.'

'Staying over, too. My wife was keen to try out a suite in this place. Kick the tyres of the thing, as you might say, Clay.'

'We gonna meet your good lady anytime?'

'I'm afraid I rather struggled earlier to get Mrs Drummond out of the bathtub. She's been told, is all I can say . . .'

Aaron can't tell if it's a good or bad omen that Paxton has taken some fledgeling Edinburgh financier as a partner. And yet Drummond, with his drawling tone and ironical pockets under his eyes, seems wholly comfortable in the company.

'We were discussing prospects, Israelite. Drilling locations. Your expertise.'

'I suppose,' asks Drummond, 'we can guess where everybody will be looking this year, based on that discovery by Amoco?'

'Yeah, plumb luck.' Paxton looks about him and lowers his voice. 'Those bastards were near clean out of time and money, just seeing out their licence . . . No, we're still focused on the blocks we already got, half of which we're running out of time on ourselves. We gotta be realistic about any new bets. BP and Shell, they're in deep over-budget, too – bet your life their top guys are feeling just as tight-assed about things as me.'

Drummond looks quizzical. 'You're not saying they're about to give up on the North Sea? Clay, I only just got to the party . . .'

'No, I'm saying round about now they might be looking pretty hard at Alaska, you get me? I mean, they can do that – cash out, if they want to. We can't afford to. So we keep up the hunt.' Paxton claps Aaron's arm, a little roughly. 'And for that, we look to Aaron here.'

For a dread moment Aaron fears he will be called on before this Mr Drummond to account for his prediction record to date.

'Speaking of which, Israelite, I do believe you're being looked at by others. Friends of yours . . . ?'

Joe Killday and Ray Bodie have arrived to proceedings a little later than planned. First came a stiffening drink at the Gardner; and Joe had wondered if for once Bodie might be feeling the same slight inhibition by which he knows himself to be haunted. But now they are here, and Ray, clearly, has read the room with speed, for he smacks Joe's shoulder.

'Ten o'clock. That table, see? We're going over there.'

'Why?'

'That's Paxton. And he's sitting with a guy I was at school with . . .'

Despite such promise, Joe sees Bodie's eager introductions fall rather flat. His old schoolmate is polite, but hardly overjoyed to remake the acquaintance. And in the next instant Mr Paxton is hustling this 'Israelite' away, apparently for some private piece of business. Thus Joe and Bodie have to settle for a sit-down with 'Lord Al', an Edinburgh banker who looks a bit too pleased with himself.

'Call me Alastair, eh? Ignore Paxton, he gives people names, it's a quirk. What business are you gentlemen in, may I ask?'

Joe leads with the story he has rehearsed: a renowned North Sea fishing firm, now diversifying to meet new opportunities in support boats for oil rigs.

'How do your trawler skippers find it, just bobbing around at sea all day twiddling their thumbs?'

'It's a change for them,' Joe concedes.

'Bollocks is what they say in the boozer.' Bodie's candour, surprising to Joe, seems to go down well enough with this Alastair Drummond.

'But it's just part of the changes we have in mind,' Joe insists. 'Last year we moved into new, bigger premises—'

'Snap!' says Drummond. 'You and me both.'

'Right. The idea being to expand the business. With fishing at the heart of it, still, but a dual operation, a whole other side devoted to the oil industry.'

'Sounds less like a company, boys, more like a group. But, it's all about what's appropriate to your ambitions.' Drummond rubs his chin, amused. 'You know, when I was getting into this madness myself, a wise friend told me a story – how back in the Klondike days

244

the old prospectors learned to their cost that the most dependable business wasn't striking gold. It was selling food and board and dry clothes to all the fools who were out there with pickaxes, freezing their backsides off. The safest money, you see, is in supply, not exploration. Well, you can imagine, I heard that, and I straight away went out and bought a stake in an explorer.'

Joe and Bodie reach together for their drinks, beginning to find a certain entertainment in this droll company.

'I kid you, really. I'm hedging my bets. But services are a huge deal. I hear it clearly from Paxton, his business needs warehousing and dependable supply ships – for food and water and mud and cement and God knows what. Cargo is king. And of course, the rigs want everything delivered yesterday.'

'Alastair' – Joe is feeling expansive himself – 'I assure you for years now Killday has been taking prime cod out of the North Sea and getting it fresh onto plates in London restaurants. We know that time is money.'

'We have skills, expertise, resources in-house' – Bodie chimes in – 'that we really do feel could be adapted.'

'How about your fleet? Is it in the right shape for rig supply?'

'Perhaps . . . not ideally,' Joe hates to say, glancing at Bodie.

But their new acquaintance is smiling still. 'Well, listen, my partner Fyfe and I are looking around to take equity in businesses that see a growth area and can show us a business plan we find persuasive. We'll back a bold venture any time we see money in it.' He offers a hand, and Joe sees within it a business card. 'Perhaps we should talk again? Come see me in Auld Reekie.'

After initial doubts, Joe has been struck favourably by the manners and the nous of this gentleman, now getting to his feet.

'Forgive me but my wife has deigned at last to join us. Nothing better on the television, perhaps . . .'

Joe follows Drummond's eyeline; and as she sways across the floor – a dress of black velvet, clutch-bag in hand, thread of pearls at her throat – it is instantly and piercingly clear to Joe that he would have known Belinda Morland if her back been turned to him – just by the line of her, the eloquence of her movement. As she offers her cheek to Drummond to be kissed, Joe must avert his eyes, alarmed by the absurd thump inside his chest.

'Hello, boys' – she smiles, all vivacity – 'am I breaking up the party? Or would you like me to?'

And she looks now at Joe. But he has plastered a more assured look on his face as to meet her. By a slight twitch of her lips, he can see recognition falling at last upon her, too.

'Belinda, this is Joe Killday and Mr Bodie of Killday Fishing, Aberdeen.'

Joe rises to take her hand, seeing that her own face has taken on an intimation of warmth. 'Joe? Joe! How the devil have you been?'

'Walk me to my car, will you, Israelite?'

For a moment Aaron wonders if Paxton will ask additionally for a hand with shrugging on his camel-hair overcoat. But he tends to himself; while Aaron, hovering, hears piano chords pealing out into the foyer. Hardly more than finger exercises, and yet he cranes his neck to see if Heather might be about to favour the room with an impromptu recital. Paxton, though, is ready and goes forth, striding out under the illuminated colonnade, Aaron hastening to follow.

'So you're back out to the Pecos first thing Monday, right? We got a change of plan. I spoke to Shields, we're abandoning location. Wherever we go next, we got to make it count. The best shot. Cos, the way things are looking, it could be the last.' Aaron, already struggling to keep up, feels a sinking of spirits. 'So I need to hear from everybody who counts what they think that best shot is.'

'For me, Clay, I already know. I won't say different tomorrow or next week.'

'Oh yeah?'

'Yes. Block thirty-twenty-four. Southwestern edge of the Graben.'

Paxton digests this – then, in seconds, turns thunder-faced. 'Aaron, goddamn it, we've been there. And we got out. That fucken block is jinxed, we lost a diver.'

Aaron takes in a breath of cold night air. *Yes,* he thinks, *I haven't forgotten, it didn't stop you drilling, did it? That had to have been for something.*

'I was there, Clay. It's partly because of that I'm saying it's . . . unfinished business? I always advised we drill another well, close to the last.' Aaron hates the nerviness he hears in his voice, but a loss of hope is making him reckless; and clearly there is no other time but this one. 'There was a big high there that looked good to me, a real prospect, if we just moved on a few clicks. But we plugged and got out too soon.'

'Revisiting failure – that the best you got, Aaron?'

'If you say one more try, sir, I'm not going to pin a tail on a donkey. I'm going to tell you what I believe, based on the data.'

They have arrived at Paxton's big Oldsmobile, surely the toughest car in view, even a little menacing in its lustrous blackness and steel trim that gleams now in a patch of yellowy overhead lamplight – the same light in which Aaron now feels his face being studied closely.

'Look. You've given it a good shake, Aaron. It might be you just weren't meant to see the promised land . . .'

And Aaron supposes suddenly that the game might be over already.

'Thirty-twenty-four . . . Huh. It's far enough south, you ain't gonna cost me much insurance, anyhow. How you gonna make Shields buy it?'

'I'd have thought it's as much about you, Clay. I mean – you either have faith in my judgement or you don't.'

In the moment, Aaron has amazed himself. *Reckless!* And Paxton certainly has a new look on his face, though Aaron can't be sure if it spells respect or pity. He doubts that he sounds as forceful as he would wish, but he keeps trying. 'For what it's worth, I can write up a drilling recommendation tomorrow.'

'Sure. Write your letter and mail it.'

Paxton inserts himself into the bench seat of the Oldsmobile, fires it up and tears away, leaving Aaron behind.

He returns to the foyer, heading directly for the nook where the piano sits. He is following the music, for the instrument is being played, even though no one is paying attention. Still, to him the music sounds not so unalike how is feeling – heavy-hearted if not hopeless, something within that is yearning still. He has heard this piece before, with Heather – he hazards it might be Liszt. But now as he nears, the tempo is getting faster, more passionate, almost improperly for a public place.

Now he sees, unimpeded, that Heather is sharing the piano stool, her companion a bespectacled man in evening wear, reed-thin and wholly focused on her as she plays. Aaron observes how Heather, even in these incongruous surroundings – or maybe especially so? – seems transported.

She finishes, smiling, upon a little passage that is delicate as raindrops. Then she lifts her eyes and sees Aaron. There is a colour in her cheeks.

'Aaron, do you remember Paul Burns? We were at the Academy together a hundred years ago. He was hired to entertain the crowds tonight.' She gestures around the oblivious foyer.

Aaron steps closer and offers a hand that is taken a little diffidently, Paul Burns's slight smile directed only at his own armpit.

Back out in the cold, inky night air, Aaron chances a glance at Heather as they walk to the car. 'This wasn't too much of a bore?'

'It was fine. I was pleased to see Paul again. We had really a . . . a good conversation. He was encouraging me to think more about my composing.'

'Well, I agree with him, I've always said.'

Aaron feels unreasonably nettled. If her commitment were as total as his has been, if she really set herself to pursue the validation and vindication that her abilities deserved . . . What on earth had stopped her?

The party is over, but Joe and Ray have, as others, adjourned to the Òrach's handsome low-lit bar, served by staff in red fitted jackets and black waistcoats, further offering patrons the privacy of plush booths ranged around the walls. In one such booth, the Killday party bend their heads together over whiskies.

'That Drummond, he called it right.' Bodie remains super-animated even at evening's end. 'If we moved into supply boats we'd need the right boats. Purpose-built to carry all those different goods, on top of what you'd need for the crew. And they'll have to be registered differently, no doubt . . .'

Joe hears and agrees all that. His feelings, though, are mostly doleful, his head stuck doggedly on one slow-revolving bother. *Of course, Belinda saved herself for a man like that.* Of course, that was her proper ambition. Joe would have bet money on it. There is no shifting the self-reproach he feels – not when it was painfully clear that she remained, from where he sat tonight, more or less his ideal of how a woman might look.

'We've got to be more aggressive now, Joe, totally strategic. If we don't, you can bet our competitors will – the Woods and the Craigs and the Greigs. We can't be building any more trawlers. It's only buying your father off . . .'

Joe at last hears something to stir him from his fit of the glums. 'Ray, so much has to happen first. So much financing we need that's just fresh air for now.'

'Yes, but Joe, you heard that man. Nothing but encouraging, right? And you control who's coming on to the board. If I were you, I'd be wining and dining Alastair Drummond. You agree?'

Joe considers the gingery heel of malt in his tumbler. 'Agreed, Ray, agreed. Totally . . . What?' This because Bodie's face has suddenly acquired the slyness that heralds mischief.

'Don't think I didn't spot the look on your puss when his missus showed up. Just don't be letting your thoughts stray . . .'

Joe scowls at the very suggestion. 'Give over. Look, I know there's room on the board and, yes, with finance so vital . . .'

'Right. And, you know, if we're treating this as seriously as we should, without sentiment . . . you might need to think about your brother Walter.'

'Think what, Ray?'

'Well, in my view, from here – Walter should be frozen out of anything strategic. It's only what your father's done all along. It's a big role he's got, but he's a stick in the mud, he'll never take a risk, he needs to be—'

'Ray, stop asking me to do Walter down, he's my brother.' In the snap of temper, Joe feels relief – displacement of other galling things he is feeling.

But the show of it seems to work on Bodie, who now looks as if he would pour oil on stormy waters. 'Okay. Easy, Joe. I hear you. Let's not fall out.'

'That's exactly it, Ray. That's what you have to take care not to do. However hard and fast you want to be going. It's not so simple when it's family . . .'

And in saying this, with the bite in it, Joe realises he must back it up, must educate Bodie on a matter of which the man is ignorant. They are complicit in too much else for him not to be aware of the history of fallouts among the Killdays.

'Ray, listen – I've something to tell you. Get us in another couple for the road?'

He is going to relate the story of how Andrew fought with his late brother Allan, thirty years previous. It worries Joe just a little that Bodie might somehow relish the telling: it could easily confirm the view Joe knows him to hold of the world's secret badness, forever lurking at bay behind whatever vaunted propriety. And Joe hates, in a way, to betray a sort of family secret. But he knows that he and Bodie have too much between them now for this founding tale of the business to be kept hidden any longer.

September 1970
The Nonconformist

The first morning of autumn: the Pecos rig pummelled on all sides by high wind and crashing, sizzling lumps. *And who bloody well put us here?* thinks Aaron.

Hunched over logbooks and specimen trays at his desk in the geologists' cabin, he is contemplating total failure, fighting it down – hunting still for signs and portents that might justify the bet he put down with someone else's money. Running through the tickertape in his head, like music, is an invocative phrase – *Prayers to broken stone* – half recalled from a poem his father used to recite with reverence.

The evidence before him is bleak. Drilling has been slow, tight, with erratic breaks to clear a jammed barrel, Randall Hood shouting fiercely for more goddamn mud. The original objective – the supposed reservoir in Rotliegend sandstone, eight thousand feet down – showed at first a few little heart-lifting signs of hydrocarbons; but, on inspection, merely 'dead oil', viscous, non-volatile, unproduceable. In the judgement of Erwin Shields: 'It might do for the gearbox of your Volvo, Strang.'

Right now, with the mood of last chance palpably around, Hood has them drilling into a Zechstein interval, so slender on the evidence of the seismic data that even Aaron had judged it 'quite badly eroded'. 'Eroded entirely' was the verdict of Shields, seemingly bent on prolonging their vendetta.

And now the office's rickety door is opened and closed with solemnity, Shields stepping forward, bearing as ever the quietly self-important air of a senior cleric. He stands for a moment and surveys, silently, his favoured style of intimidation. Then he clucks his tongue lightly.

'Still dredging that Rotliegend, Strang? Looking for a miracle?

Has it occurred to you, maybe, that if all you do is blindly repeat an experiment that already failed – because you hope it still might give you the result you're after – then that's the exact opposite of good science?'

'It hasn't occurred to me here, Erwin, no. I still see a lot of things worth testing, things that don't conform to expectation.'

Shields lowers himself almost daintily into a moulded chair. 'Your undying attachment to this block . . . it's really rather queer, you know? Nobody else has fancied it, not across the whole span of the North Sea. Is that maybe its appeal? Because it's a wee bit different? Just like you, Strang?'

Realising he will be baited a fair bit longer, Aaron lifts his eyes from the microscope. 'My proposal was backed by the data we had that was—'

'Inherently unreliable.' Shields looks showily bored.

'I don't believe we're done here yet. The drilling's showing us a complex architecture, places where Rotliegend and Zechstein overlap, cross-flow between them. All because of the faults. We need to interpret those faults correctly.'

'I *know* that, Strang. Is that what you imagine you're doing?'

'I don't say I've called it all correctly. I do say it was a decent bet here, I—'

'Was, you say? The past tense. We agree on that, anyhow.'

At wits' end Aaron feels a sudden strong urge to ask Shields why on earth he does what he does, what animates him to get up in the morning?

'You sit there shaking your head, Strang. You think your hunches are so much better than mine? You'd have to have served a lot more time in proven oilfields for that, boy.' Shields gets to his feet, shuffles to the door and turns, his parting shot very clearly prepared. 'You're really a very foolish young man.'

I'm not done with you either is Aaron's hopeless feeling as the door clicks shut.

———

Not long afterward it is Randall Hood who raps on Aaron's door and jerks it aside. 'Strang, we got a funny kind of thing here. Makin' hole a lot faster than we figured all of a sudden.'

'Okay. I'll go take a look at the mud . . .'

He roots around dejectedly for his gloves and his tray, and troops down to the roar of the drill floor, round past the chunking engines and over to the drill pump and shakers where the wash of baryte mud and rock cuttings is coming up the conveyor ramp and then streaming and spattering filthily into the trough beneath.

Even before he stoops to get his face into the slop, his nose is sniffing something different, new. Not engine oil, not this time.

He slides his panning tray purposely into the trough, immerses it, then withdraws – gives it a shake – ponders and selects a fragment – a carbonate, dolomite. Then he brings it to his nose.

Easy now . . . He wonders, by the prickling of his nostrils, if he could be smelling pay in this well.

With the noise of machine-chuntering all around his head, he tries to fight his way toward one clear thought. Because suddenly, wildly, he has got himself to thinking of Apollo 11, dials flickering, smoke and fire . . . And surely after all this time the great prize couldn't present itself so simply, without warning? It has been so hard to sift the true from the false. He tells himself now that he must not fly too high; must not crash to earth.

He steels himself to work fast – but efficient, not so quick as his leaping pulse, more speed, less haste. He carries his tray back to the office as if he were bearing an infant down the aisle of a church to the font. He plucks out the most interesting little rock, sets it upon a glass slide, switches on the fluoroscope and observes.

What he beholds is yet another novelty: hardly blinding in its light, in truth rather dull. But undeniably yellow, fluorescent. Like gold.

I have come to worship thee . . .

In the next instant Aaron is out of his chair.

Bursting through the door of the exploration doghouse, his feet unsteady beneath him, Aaron is greeted by faces all solemn, perhaps guilty, too. Charlie McGinn looks to Shields before speaking.

'Aaron, hey. Look, we're thinking it's gotta be plug time. Paxton says we gotta be further north, so we might as well quit yellowin' — '

'Charlie, no, listen, we've got live oil shows on the shakers.'

McGinn cocks a head. 'What, "live" like test-worthy?'

Shields steps forward, frowning. 'Show me.'

Following his inspection in the lab cabin Shields says not a word to Aaron as they return to the doghouse. But Aaron knows what to expect and what he must do once they are reconvened through the door – where they find that Randall Hood has joined the gathering, the look of a hungry hound about his chops.

'Well, Erwin?' asks McGinn.

A rehearsed sigh. 'In my view, one can't say from this with any confidence whether it's a real petrophysical difference to that dead oil we got in the Rotliegend. Quite insufficient grounds to reverse the decision already taken.'

'I disagree, you're wrong,' Aaron bursts forth.

Shields's cheek twitches. 'Say that again, Strang?'

'We've got to test this. In any other context we would test this.'

'You're special-pleading, it's a waste of time.'

'No, it's what we came here for, that's the professional way we do it, and if you'd listened to me a year ago, Shields — '

'Don't you cross me, boy, I am the first here.'

McGinn intercedes sharply. 'Erwin, now you're out of line.'

In the hard silence that follows, Aaron can see Shields's mind at work, hunting for the way to get back on top. Finally: 'Well, we need at least a core. Don't we? A true core for the lab, from the interval just drilled. That's the real test of it, isn't it? The professional way, Strang?'

'We haven't got one,' Aaron snaps.

'Ah . . . Should have considered that sooner, while we were drilling. The moment's passed, hasn't it? No core . . . ?' He cuts the air with a hand as to say *Kaput*.

'Not true. We can still get one.'

'Say what, Aaron?' McGinn sounds baffled.

'We can still get a core. There's a tool, a Schlumberger, for cutting a core out of the sidewall *after* you drilled through.'

Hood weighs in. 'He's right. They do it, I've seen it. Diamond cutter, you drop it on a wire, it digs in the wall, then you fish it back out. We got a borehole good and clean, it'll get'cha somethin' for the lab boys, bet on it.'

McGinn, disbelieving, seems also disappointed. 'Sure, okay, so you gonna pull one of these diamonds out of your ass, Aaron?'

'No, from Baker Tools in Aberdeen. One phone call. I can get it here on a chopper by tonight.'

'Oh, but this is not serious!' cries Shields. 'All this for some broken-up, contaminated sample out of an interval that's barely there — ?'

Aaron looks levelly at McGinn. 'I take full responsibility for getting us a clean sample, packing and despatching it, whatever it takes.'

Shields has reddened again. 'Who says you do that? By what right?'

McGinn raises a warning hand. 'Erwin – can it, will ya? We gotta think straight here.'

Silence once again; and it lengthens. Aaron feels he can bear it no longer – just as Hood kicks the shaky cabin wall with a steel boot-cap. 'Well goddamn it, somebody gotta take a decision.'

Aaron's throat is drum-tight as McGinn stares at him, shaking his head.

'Get on the phone then, Aaron.'

The order is placed, a minimum six-hour wait. Aaron sequesters in his office while Hood's crew disassemble the drill string. It seems he will go this final stretch alone, with support given but sceptically, until such time as he is to be thrown overboard.

He sharpens a pencil and makes his calculations for where the corer might dig in, and he revises these several times over. He feels bone-weary, vaguely sick in his gut, and yet a powerful light-headedness – like some kind of self-elevating faith – spurs him on.

Come the dusk he is there among a small welcoming party, contemplating the night sky as the Wessex helicopter chunters nearer and descends to the landing pad bearing its prize cargo.

On the drill floor he watches the Tri-Corer being bolted into the wireline, cranked into the air and tested: a steel capsule chamber and, within that, a fitting like a lantern, whirring almost in the manner of music-box mechanics. The lantern rises, tilts upward and extends from out of the capsule, spinning still. The ingenuity of this toy is very evident. Now, though, Aaron wants nothing but the end-product and its verdict. He keeps his mind on just how little luck has attended all his efforts to date; how many imposters have presented themselves. He imagines only an outcome of failure, and what will follow if he has wasted his final bet. In that way, the floor beneath him stays solid.

He goes to gather up his tape measure, specimen bags, rags to wipe and paraffin to preserve, leaving Hood to send the device down to its designated depth.

McGinn, Shields and Hood have crowded absurdly around Aaron in the cramped laboratory cabin. In the pressurised atmosphere, though, Aaron is gripped by extreme self-possession. He feels weirdly ready for a lie-down, the mission of the faithful servant nearing an end.

He felt so from the moment the chamber was lifted from the Tri-Corer – 'Careful, you bastards!' he heard himself shout – and was laid out to be marked. Rag in hand, he knew better at once than to wipe the sample, seeing something in his prize that expanded his heart to extraordinary fullness.

Now the plug of core sits before them all in its trough, greyish-yellow, crystalline with grains of quartz, striated by fine layers and marked by the cracks and fissures known as vugs – but honeycombed, too, with big pores that could even be mistaken for emitting a honey of their own.

'Jesus H. Christ,' Hood exclaims slowly. 'Damn thing's *oozing*! Huh?' He slaps the lapel of the strangely subdued McGinn.

'He's right,' McGinn says finally.

Shields, quietened hitherto, mutters, 'Well, I'll be.'

Hood seizes Aaron's face, a startled cheek in each calloused hand, and for an instant Aaron fears he will be kissed. '"Lord, with honey of the rock will I satisfy thee . . . !" You did it, kid. You're a beaut.'

'Okay, Randy.' McGinn winces. 'We're gonna need a stronger identification.'

'Charlie, I got my nose, got my tongue, I'll drink this stuff if you want.'

Impulsively Aaron puts a finger to the rock and then to his lips, tasting the bitterness he should have expected.

'Come on, Charlie, we're lathered up, let's get shaving, see if we got pay.'

'An interval like this' – Shields still looks as if he has taken a bullet in his vitals – 'whether it's the hundred million barrels Clay expects, I don't know . . .'

'But we test, right?' McGinn presses. 'Appraisal time. Erwin?'

'Sure. Yes. Of course.'

'Okay. Randy, go tell the crew they've got a few extra days on board coming up. I know you'll be discreet.'

The room is in motion. Aaron, exultant, can see that exultance in his face reflected back at him in the polished case of the fluoroscope. He lifts an oily forefinger and anoints each of his cheekbones with the tip, a slash under each eye – then realises McGinn is watching.

'You want to call Clay, Aaron? Give him the codeword?'

'I'd love that, Charlie,' Aaron says calmly.

'I'd like to speak to Clay also,' says Shields, his voice unsteady.

'Later, Erwin? We got plenty to get on with. Aaron's owed this one.'

Don't let that bastard mess with my core is Aaron's driving thought as he gets up and goes to the door.

'Israelite. How goes the night?'

'It's, ah, been a long day, Clay.' Up on the darkened deck with the phone-cord swaying in the wind, Aaron feels not just the cold but his own nervousness now in delivering the prepared formula, the codeword, the signal meant to put off any unwanted eavesdroppers.

'A long one, yeah. Holy Moses . . .'

A short pause. *'Is that so . . . ?'* Then a short laugh. *'I'll await your report. Remind me next time you're onshore, I owe you a drink.'*

September 1970
Taking the Initiative

Joe's suit jacket, shirt and tie are laid across the passenger seat of his new Chrysler, parked handily in Edinburgh New Town. As is his habit, he completes his look for the meeting with the help of the car mirrors. He intends to arrive in mint condition – the sharpest version of himself. He has an appointment with Alastair Drummond to discuss an outline plan of partnership and financing, a plan so far shared with no other soul at Killday Fishing Limited other than – of course – Ray Bodie.

As much as Bodie midwifed this opportunity, Joe made clear he wished to take the meeting alone: top man to top man. There is another factor. He is meeting a man whom he can't but regard as a rival of sorts. He will be measuring himself like so. It thrums in the back of his mind that, should the two companies come to an arrangement, he might see Mrs Drummond more often in future. Another excellent reason to be at his smartest and best.

'Before we start, will I be forgiven' – Drummond smiles almost shyly – 'for bending your ear a little about all this art?'

'By all means,' Joe responds, following him into the rear reception of Drummond Fyfe. Drummond wears a banker's single-breasted navy three-piece, and Joe, quietly, feels he might cut the better figure. The man's workplace, though, has a dauntingly august splendour about it, paintings on every wall.

'We had to smarten up this old place,' Drummond explains, 'and we're very much a Scottish bank, so . . . we favour Scottish art.'

They step across the Persian rug from spot to spot, Drummond politely pointing out this or that feature; Joe feeling as if he ought perhaps to venture some anodyne remark about a use of colour; then thinking better. They study a mournful oil canvas of long-faced farmers being escorted off their land; then a portrait of some moody black-clad Enlightenment fellow, chin pensively in hand.

'I'm very sober-sided, my wife has the true eye. She was the advocate for this one here – one of the Scottish colourists?' It is a woman resplendent in black, enigmatically seated next to a mirror, her face elegantly blurry under a broad-brimmed white hat, a pink rose aglow at her breast.

'Beautiful,' Joe murmurs.

'Are you a married man, Joe?'

'Ah, I'm not sure I've met the right girl. Or one who'd have me.'

Drummond taps his nose. 'You know it when you know it.'

'So Belinda tells me she knew you a bit at university.' Drummond reclines behind his leather-topped desk in a first-floor office. 'And you were clever as blazes even then. Tell me what you did after.'

Joe recounts the version he has polished: first-class honours, fast-track at Dunlop Rubber, his move to the family firm in exchange for a leadership role and the opportunity to put his own ideas about diversification into practice, et cetera.

'Sounds like you don't look to play it safe.'

'Neither do you.' Joe gestures about the room.

'Oh, I didn't invent the merchant bank in Scotland, that was Noble Grossart. I just studied what they did and tried to do my version . . . So much for my dreams. Tell me yours.'

'To me our main business of the next five years is rig supply. But you'll have seen my prime objective for growth is to purchase the Devane shipyard – so that we move into a position to do not only our own shipbuilding and refitting but to do it for others, too.'

Drummond lifts and slaps down the bound documents Joe

brought for his perusal. 'Huge management decisions, Joe. Requiring sizeable financing. Get them wrong and it could mean curtains for your company.'

The assurance Joe has sought to project up to now, mirroring that of his host, falters in one vertiginous moment.

'But, I think you could be right, you know . . . I admire this. I see the shape of your thinking. The existing strength in the company, what it's been . . . But, more importantly, what it could be yet.' He opens his drawer and takes out, rather to Joe's surprise, a cigar and cutters. 'I happen to think that old arrangements must yield to new whenever it becomes clear they're past their moment. As Nietzsche tells us, whatsoever is falling – give it a push.'

The discussion of finer points that ensues is a source of both relief and satisfaction to Joe. He is sure now that a financing arrangement will be available, at the justifiable cost of a share for the bank in Killday's business. He floats the very informal suggestion that Drummond might consider a non-executive seat on Killday's board. Drummond nods slowly, in no way taken by surprise.

'I am open to that. And if you want my advice now, keep a seat warm on there for whoever's the top man at the Devane yard, too. When you come to offer to buy them it will sweeten the deal. Probably reduce your bill, too.'

It is nearly four thirty when Drummond suggests that they shut up shop for the day, since his wife will be awaiting him downstairs – and perhaps she should come up and say hello? Joe smiles, with the familiar quickening of his pulse.

Belinda appears, somewhat to Joe's surprise wearing a gingham frock in a green check, as if she might get her lift home in a spring-cart rather than her husband's Jaguar. The girlishness of its pleats and tied shoulder staps makes Joe wonder if she hasn't worn it as some sophisticated joke: he detects a little mirth in her eyes as she kisses each of his cheeks. He feels ruefulness, too, to be moving in the kind of company to which he always aspired, but in circumstances that propose a certain irony at his expense.

'Perhaps we might toast our arrangement, Joe?'

'I will if we all will.'

'Nothing for the lady, I'm afraid. Not ideal in her condition.'

Belinda nods, patting her stomach just under the shirred bodice of the dress. 'I can't be drinking for two.'

'My congratulations to you both,' says Joe.

'I'll fetch that bottle, you put your feet up, Contessa.'

Belinda smiles at Joe, and he wonders if the expression on his face might be so shellshocked as to warrant real amusement. Then she steps to a big arched window and gazes out onto Charlotte Square's fading sunlight. 'Gosh, Joe. It's been really so nice to see you again after all these years. I told Alastair, I never felt I saw enough of you when we were at university.'

For some moments Joe measures his response, trying to calibrate a suitably casual tone. 'Well, you maybe recall missing your chance to be launch mistress for me at Aberdeen harbour that time? A sad day, Belinda. I had to promise my father never to speak to you again.'

'Oh lord. And I'm not sure you ever did.' She puts her hands to her face, a shade too theatrically for his liking. 'Joe. I was so mortified.'

'I'm sure you'd other things to do. Better offers.'

'You know, I think I'd almost have felt better if you'd torn a real strip off me.'

'Yeah, I expect you would have. But I wouldn't. Same reason why you sent me a telegram that day. It's easier not to say things aloud.'

He realises that his mildly joshing facade has slipped; but he had been too easily irked by her own performance as some sort of penitent schoolgirl. Now, at least, they seem to recognise each other. Her coolness is reinstated.

'Well, forgive me, I hope it all seems like small potatoes now.'

'It does, Belinda.'

And then Drummond returns with a bottle of Chassagne-Montrachet and a couple of glasses which he fills carefreely, before passing one to his new partner and leaning unusually close to him, a heavily confiding look on his face.

'Let's drink to looking forward, Joe. Never look back.'

And for just an instant Joe thinks he maybe saw a flash of something steelier from behind Drummond's own customary mildness. But then it has passed, and they clink glasses.

October 1970

Surveyance

A draughty, crepuscular hangar in Aberdeen Airport on a dreich autumn night: a grim sort of spot for a press-call. But Mark has sworn he will go wherever he must for a genuine oil story. News of a commercial discovery in the North Sea by British Petroleum had a marquee feel to it. The show, though, was not compelling – some stiff exploration wallah holding aloft a jam-jar sample of murk, talking of tests underway with tentative hopes for production of oil in another three years or so.

Shuffling back into the terminal building amid the grumbling press corps, lighting up a smoke, Mark feels that the much-vaunted thrill of the gold rush is proving elusive. The eureka moment seems never quite to arrive; maybe it never will? Three years seems an awfully long time, though he could wish it just a bit longer, were there a chance of the bloody Tory government being kicked out by voters before they could claim any credit for getting the oil pumping.

Clearly he is far from the only fool chasing the tail of this story; but that's no consolation. Mark is gloomily sure that truly successful people never make such missteps or pursue so many dead-ended ventures. Shona, for one, gets things done wherever she goes – this week to Chemnitz, East Germany, with the aim of gauging local sentiments toward the USSR. At intervals over the last year Mark has knocked around the Bogside of Derry, another story he had promised the editor that he could bring home – civil rights, oppressed people, the fraying union, all that. But Mark learned slowly that certain situations were beyond his analysis, and the presiding threat of the IRA made him edgy. Even the regular folk of the Bogside seemed to judge him on sight: as an interloper, for sure; maybe even

265

as some agent of the oppressor? Mark worries there is some smack of privilege in his manners and speech that he cannot slough off – a 'natural aristocrat', as Ally once liked to style them both.

Heading toward the airport exit, he spots his old *Express* colleague Bill Middleton thumping the fag machine in anger, and reckons they might perhaps do one another a good turn.

'What did you make to that, Bill?' ventures Mark as he strikes a match.

Middleton leans in gratefully to the spark. 'Cagey, eh? They all play cute.'

'Three years?'

'You'll never get these boys to tell you anything straight. They're counting numbers while you and me are asleep. What it'll cost. What it'll be worth . . .'

'Still nothing to see, then.'

'Nothing any bugger's gonna be thrilled to read about. Tell you what, but, you'll see BP start hunting now for places to build. If they're thinking they've found proper oil they can pump, then they've to get going on building the big production platforms. Laying miles of pipe under the water and onto land – all of that.'

'Could be good news for the Clyde shipyards?'

Bill scoffs. 'They'll no' be at the head of the queue.'

'Have they not got a shout? All that experience, ready to go?'

'That's what the unions will say, son. But don't be surprised if BP get the whole kit built in Japan and shipped over.'

'Surely they'd want to look at doing it in Scotland?'

'Maybes. But no' Glasgow. That's two hundred miles south of where they say they've found the oil. What they'll fancy is wherever's the shortest line to landfall as the crow flies.'

Seated in his car a little later, still curious, Mark rummages his AA roadmap from the glovebox and hazards a play at the very game Bill proposed. His fingertip smudges a spot on Scotland's north-east coast, near the village and parish of Glinrock. He taps his teeth thoughtfully. With Shona in Chemnitz, he is not expected home tonight at the house in Leith. A road trip beckons.

Come the morning he is pushing on into the north-east of the country proper, with a blathering DJ and innocuous pop on the radio for company. Past Inverness the traffic is thinner, the ride more pleasant in pale autumn sun, the banked clouds almost picturesque within the canvas presented as he motors past crisp, neat fields and tame woodland, blue hills in the distance. It occurs to Mark just how little of Scotland he has truly bothered himself with outside of these research assignments – maybe too much a man of the central belt, in common with his tribe.

He turns off the main road and follows the taper of a peninsula round and down toward Glinrock, still charmed by the modest landscape while feeling increasingly less like he is traversing some future haven of industry. Scrappy grass and gorse flank the track as it gets progressively tougher but he follows it doggedly until he can park on a gravel patch before a pebbly shore, watched over by little more than a line of squat little whitewashed cottages, a number of upturned boats and some shrill, scavenging gulls.

He gazes out to the Firth where, a mile or so distant, two great headlands almost converge, the northern one with its fields dappled by sunlight, the southern so moodily shadowed as to appear heavily forested. Together they make a long channel of the calm waters.

Plenty land and sea, he thinks. *Maybe more sheep than people?* It strikes him as a place at slumber, perhaps not wishing to be wakened.

Then he hears the chunter of a helicopter overhead, small in the sky but – even from the shore where Mark stands – observably red, white and blue in its livery. It first looks to be tracing its way north across the sky in a serene line; but then it turns and swoops, and begins to loop back around those twin headlands, as if seeking a target. Mark watches it until his eyes are tired from squinting.

Having come so far and learned at least a little, Mark decides to treat himself to a plate of fish and a glass of beer in advance of the longish drive homeward. He tootles further north up the coast, toward Tarnwick, dreaming of a rural pub, but after a few miles of flat fields he fears he is to be thwarted. Then, a handsome new sign on the right beckons him into the long driveway of the Lockdare Hotel, and he decides this was to be his fate.

He is expecting traditional Highland accommodation, cosily awful. But round the bend the Lockdare reveals itself to him as a big Victorian property with conservatories grafted onto it, and a few stone cottages adjacent, embroidered by rosy landscaped gardens. Mark is yet more confident of securing his country lunch.

As he waits for a receptionist to finish her phone call, he notes that the decor is newly done, stylish even – thick carpet and fine wallpaper, bits of handcrafted woodwork in the nooks and corners. Glancing into the lounge, he notes a stag's head over a grand hearth – a nice touch for any tourist fancying themselves a laird for a night or two.

'Sir, how may I help?'

He turns to see that the hotel's manageress has stepped in to address him while her young colleague remains tied up. This manageress, Mark can't but note, is a knockout.

'I wondered if I could grab a bite of early lunch?'

The name-badged Miss Gallagher explains that the dining room is booked for a special function, but they would be delighted to serve Mr Rutherford in the lounge. She comes around the counter bearing a menu, and he follows.

'Is it a wedding you have on today?'

'You could say that.' She glances back over her shoulder. 'We're certainly trying to get some people hitched . . .'

She leads him to a comfy chair by a table under the beady-eyed stag. Presently, Mark looks up from the agreeable menu to see his dark-eyed hostess in hushed, urgent conference with an older lady in a skirt suit, elegant in her own way, who lays a hand on Miss Gallagher's arm in the way that perhaps only a mother would. Mark wonders if the Lockdare is a family business, run by a family made entirely out of clock-stopping women.

When, fed and watered, he trudges back to his vehicle, Mark is taken aback by the sudden grating of tyres on gravel and a convoy of Jaguars pulling into the carpark as if the Prime Minister and cabinet were stopping in for lunch. He sees now that both well-appointed Gallagher women have presented themselves beamingly in welcome at the hotel's portico; and he is tempted to loiter a little longer, find out precisely what sort of gathering he nearly gate-crashed. He cranes to catch the eye of Miss Gallagher; but she shoots him rather a stern look in return, while a cortège of suited men move with purpose inside the Lockdare. And then she pulls the big door shut. Knowing he has miles to go, Mark thinks better, and clambers back into the driver's seat to retrieve his roadmap.

November 1970

Aaron Strang is Busy

'We are pleased to welcome back to his alma mater Dr Aaron Strang, who is now . . .' – here the absent-minded professor must consult a scribbled card – 'senior wellsite geologist, at Paxton Oil and Gas Limited. And who has kindly agreed to share with us today some reflections on his research in petroleum geology out in the North Sea.'

Aaron gives the decent gathering his toothiest smile, for he is truly glad of the invite, and feels not unentitled to his moment in the sun.

'He joins us also, I should say, as the recent discoverer of an oilfield, which he has had the privilege of naming "Cetus" . . . and Dr Strang might perhaps explain that curious choice to us in the course of his presentation.'

Applauded, Aaron steps to the lectern, blinks past the slide-projector beam that is glaring at him, and surveys the long, tall rake of the lecture theatre under its forensic overhead lights: the banks of five or six dozen young and keen students facing him, interspersed with a smattering of staff.

'Thank you, Professor Knott. May I have the first slide please . . . ? So, here we have the North Sea, roughly divided into two basins by this ridge, the southern part relatively shallow but plenty rough, I can assure you. The north is deeper, more perilous, but also where most of the oil is hiding. Most inconvenient, no . . . ?'

Aaron is soon at ease, heartened by the low hum of attentiveness with which his presentation is received, beginning to feel rather gaily performative. There is a young woman at the front, one of few females in the room, who becomes a marker for him as he goes.

'The particular licensed block on which I became somewhat fixated – which is typical of me – was a rather unfashionable one. Also typical, I might add . . .'

He settles into an extended discourse on the complexity and characteristics of dolomite as it showed itself to him on the night he struck oil aboard the Pecos. As he moves to the peroration, though, he realises that the narrative of what has happened since – or rather, has not – could be as much of a let-down to his listeners as it has been for him.

'At Paxton we are now engaged in a very complex estimate of the extent of the Cetus field, and the challenges of bringing the proven oil onshore. This could well be the work of four or five years. Much can happen in that time. I wonder where might we all be then . . . ?'

The applause is robust, and Aaron indicates he will take questions. Moments of hesitancy before the hand of the young woman in the front row shoots up.

'Professor, I wonder—'

'You're kind to address me that way but I haven't earned it. "Doctor" is fine.'

The young woman blushes. 'Doctor Strang, from all that you've seen, would you actually recommend petroleum geology as a career for a qualified student?'

Tough one, he thinks. 'If it's exploration you mean . . . the work is undeniably interesting, but it maybe takes a certain sort of person? You have to be ready to take a risk, with a cost attached, which the higher-ups in an oil company probably won't want to spend. Let me say, though, one thing about this sort of work is that you meet some extraordinary people, highly skilled, totally committed to getting their heads round a problem and solving it, however hard it might appear. I find that inspiring.'

The young woman's hand is still apologetically half-raised. 'Also, Professor Knott said that you might tell us why you named your field "Cetus"?'

'Oh, that's Greek mythology. It's a sea monster, a creature of the deep. Also maybe better known in English as a kraken? I suppose after some years of hunting around I felt there was something down there in the water I had to find and slay. Also, I like the sound of it.'

As he gathers up his papers to join the students in exiting, he is not so very surprised to see the young woman lingering. There is something in her demeanour that he recognises – a desire to know, and to be noticed about that desire. Her name is Dorothy, or 'Dottie': pale and freckled, with bright eyes under a brownish fringe that she pushes aside repeatedly as they chat.

'I came here as a chemist, originally. Then one day we went on a field trip and I found my first fossil – a coral, three hundred million years old. And I just got utterly hooked.'

'I know the feeling.' He smiles.

'I'm hopeful of taking my PhD in micropalaeontology. Can I ask, do you ever supervise doctoral students?'

As he explains, regretfully, that he holds no academic post, Aaron is conscious of being watched from several paces by Professor Knott; and he takes care over the words with which he encourages young Dottie – urging her, nevertheless, to pursue her ambitions to the utmost.

'Ah, the hero of the hour!'

Aaron is greeted by Alastair Drummond at the reception of Edinburgh's members-only New Club. Again he feels the sin of pride at his ear; and yet he has to admit that his host has a real gift for friendliness.

The invitation to lunch was so finely tailored – the handwritten letter so affably admiring in tone, the Conqueror letterhead so crisp and substantial in his hand – that he knew at once he would get on a train. There was an additional enticement in the blithe reference to 'a possible collaboration of sorts?' Aaron has had older mentors; but is strongly drawn to the notion of a new kind of advocate. Heather has been away overnight, giving a recital in Glasgow as part of a quintet she's become passionately involved in, and he doesn't expect her home until evening.

'I give you my word' – Drummond begins, over a glass of wine that Aaron rates the silkiest he has tasted – 'not to address you as "The Israelite", if you can also forswear any reference to me as "Lord Al"? At school I was "The Cat" and I could live with that at a push, but really . . .'

Aaron smiles in accession. For all the trappings round the walls, with which he supposes Drummond likes to impress – the baroque wood panels, the noble portraiture – the man is clearly no stuffed shirt, and the liberty to poke fun at Paxton is welcome.

'Aaron, it's in large part due to yourself that my company's rather risky investment in Paxton has suddenly taken on a rosy look. Your instincts are really remarkable. Bravo.'

'Kind of you to say, Alastair.'

'Not a bit. That's why I'd like to discuss with you a very simple little remunerated position with Drummond Fyfe. A consultancy, you might say? In essence I'd just like to pay you for an occasional cup of tea and a chat? At very worst, an occasional day in the office?'

The offer of free money laden with praise Aaron finds so directly and agreeably put that very soon they are shaking hands, before turning to their broth and seabass.

'You can imagine your success has got me wondering what else Drummond Fyfe might get involved with . . . I have wondered about perhaps some kind of larger stake in the exploration game? Only the sort where we would be selling off a fair bit of our shareholding straight away.'

'For a quicker return on investment?'

'Aaron' – Drummond grins, pointing with his fish-knife – 'I see you are no slouch in finance, either.'

'I'm just assuming the obvious. I'd say there are more obvious and immediate opportunities than exploration – given, like you say, the time it all takes.' Aaron is thinking hard, wanting to get this right. 'You might want to consider BP's big find. I suppose they'll move to production now as fast as anyone. They're going to need an awful lot of real estate, to build platforms, lay pipe. Up in the north-east corner there's a fair bit of land that will be cheap enough, even today, but it will have quite a value on it soon enough.'

Aaron can see Drummond has taken this very seriously.

'To be clear, I know nothing whatsoever about land titles, or how you get a farmer to sell his farm. But I do know that corner of Scotland a bit. It's where I'm from.'

'Fascinating. Though, as you say, some people have a fair notion of what the ground beneath them could be worth. One might have to go about it with a certain degree of tact.'

For a moment Aaron fears his new patron has drifted off entirely into contemplation. Then the wry smile and the full, gratifying attentions are restored.

'Aaron, I'm so glad we have a chance to talk properly.'

The house is darkened and still when Aaron steps through the door. He is tired, and yet inside he feels invigorated. The passage of time since 'his' discovery has been peculiar – bringing him recognition of a kind for attaining the summit so long sought, and yet he has seen the same face in the mirror, the same hours on the clock. Just in these past days, though, he has begun to sense some sort of subterranean rise in his fortunes.

He hadn't thought he was hungry, what with the generous lunch, but he goes to the kitchen and contemplates the refrigerator, empty but for an egg and a suspicious bottle of milk.

He brews black tea and carries his mug into the rear reception room, blessed with the comfiest wingback armchair in the house, albeit dominated by Heather's parlour piano – antique and forbidding in Aaron's eyes, yet embodying some sort of promise that he struggles to put into words. It is about more, he knows, than his inability to get a sound out of the thing. But this room is Heather's demesne and in their differing ways of going about their shared home he has tended to leave her respectfully to it.

Now he steps over and sits down on Heather's stool, a little surprised by how unusual her usual vantage feels to him. At his feet he notices how the carpet bears dark scuffing from her restless feet while she has laboured with her practices and compositions. But then that carpet, respectably off-white when fitted, won't be saved now. The piano's wheels have dug indelible recesses, and dependably to his right is the historical sepia stain, octopus-shaped, left by a cup of tea he had brewed and carried to her and which, within seconds, in distraction, she had knocked over.

The sheet music spread open on the stand is hieroglyphic to him. This one is Brahms's *F-A-E Sonata* Scherzo, closed and standing cushioned upon pages of her handwritten annotations – a microscopic way of work, maybe not so removed from his own. With the thought that he might now steal some insight into hers, he tugs the pages free. A small cream notecard falls out onto the piano keys.

Retrieving it, Aaron sees that the spidery blue hand of the writing is not Heather's; also, printed atop the card is the name and address of Paul Burns.

'Darling Heather – I want you to know that I love you and feel now that I have been moving toward you despite all the trials, rehearsals, mishaps and missteps. I feel you and I both were believing wrongly that we had to renounce the hope of it. I can hardly begin to express the hope I feel now ...'

Reading on – and after moments in the cold grip of abjection – Aaron starts to experience another ill feeling creeping in, the worse for its absurdity: a sort of shame in knowing he has no share whatsoever in the extraordinary emotions upon which he has intruded.

Mortified, he tells himself: all the other stuff had simply been going too well. *Pride goeth before destruction.* He has underestimated her.

He sets the card back carefully centred and atop the Brahms music, then goes shakily to the corner of the room, into the grasp of the armchair – to await her return, to prepare some short words, to brace himself for the end.

PART V

AUCTIONS

September 1971
The Reverend McVey

Early risen as always, he goes to his table and writes in his journal: *'The enemy is apathy, the feeling you are going nowhere. There is evil in that. Each day we should strive to an accomplishment of some sort, with whatever tools we have to hand.'*

The journal is a daily task; and every day Torrance depends a great deal upon his rituals, their regularity and simplicity. Rituals remind him to strive for a sober life of work done with and on behalf of others.

Each morning in the bathroom of the manse where he was raised, he meets his reflection in the mirror and nods greeting to that old sinner with all his old flaws. Cold water on his face refreshes and renews. Then he takes his suit, shirt and clerical collar from the closet, and he assumes his uniform. The view of the Firth from the window brings him a sense of imminence on the horizon line.

At daybreak he heats water for tea and steel-cut oats, for himself and no other. Fortified, he goes to the chapel to absorb its peace, standing before the woven banner of the burning bush and the legend *Nec tamen consumebatur. And still it was not consumed.* His best reminder, every day, of the right spirit. Then a walk out to the coastal path, through the cemetery's weathered grey stones and rugged crosses, its overgrown grasses in need of the scythe.

This brisk walk is his means of concentrating thoughts for the day ahead. But he knows one matter outweighs all, and out in the air he lets it fall on him. In the days since he called a public meeting for discussion of the future of Tarnwick and Glinrock, a strange atmosphere seems to have arisen locally. He can sense afoot something he might call conspiratorial.

He pauses on the promontory and surveys the rocks below, the waters all around. He is drawn to step as near to the edge as feels solid beneath him. The precipice, he knows, is a kind of temptation – also a place on which a stand may be made. And it seems to him like he is being called upon right now to make that stand.

He catches himself before thoughts run away. *I hear myself, and I fear pride. Proud as Lucifer.* The consequences could be unfavourable for him. But he has known that a while. The prize of success is stronger incentive.

On his return to the manse, Mrs Tait the housekeeper is waiting at the doorway: she tells him that the Laird was only after telephoning, and would Torrance be so kind as to return the call?

'*Torrance, I would be most grateful for a conversation with you at your earliest convenience.*'

'It seems to be the way at present.'

'*I beg your pardon?*'

'I've had a few such callers lately. Some of them may be known to you.'

'*Well, I would never guess at all what a minister must deal with – I wonder, though, if I could trouble you to call on me?*'

'Is this a summons, sir?'

'*No, no, Torrance. But it's a matter of grave importance, as I think you know.*'

'I can come by you this afternoon.'

'*Ah yes. You were always a man for the bikes – even a bit before the age appropriate, as I recall. Thank you for that.*'

His past. Torrance sees in people's eyes, knows that folk do mutter about it privately, still. He would prefer – for himself, for everyone – that things got said to people's faces. And perhaps a time for that is approaching.

The disquiet began, perhaps three weeks previous, after the usual Sunday morning service. He had gone about his rounds, endeavouring to speak with everyone: such a signal effort of the job. Not the greatest talker himself, Torrance has had to come out of his shell somewhat so as to engage, as he must, with the crofters and the farmhands of Tarnwick. That day, though, a usually reticent congregant had sought him out – this being George Pease, council officer with special responsibility for land titles and applications for planning permissions.

'I'm seeing such an awful lot of paper now, Reverend, it's been mayhem.' He rubbed his scanty fringe worriedly. 'The last month alone? Nearly a hundred in for planning.'

Torrance looked about him, then lowered his voice. 'As many as that?'

'Aye. And the plots we're talking about, you look at what they got sold for, the size of them, where they're sitting. All relative to Glinrock . . . The Laird is in the thick of it, of course.'

'Is that so?'

'Oh aye. There's pieces of land bordering his own have been bought up, and it's nae his name in the papers, but I canna see how he'd let a chance like that pass. You expect the Laird to have his finger in the air looking how the wind's blowing. He's not the only one round these parts, I'll tell you that.' And George, too, had looked about him then a little furtively, as if malefactors might be in the very room.

And then came Friday 'Question Night', the open invitation to parishioners to the manse's parlour to reflect on a chosen scriptural text. On this night David Strang, Torrance's most dependable attendee, had in tow Robbie Vallance, much the liveliest body there among a half-dozen greying heads. Torrance didn't suppose Robbie had taken a sudden fancy to the scriptures; only that he was being his usual handy self in keeping Mr Strang company.

That night they had talked a while of the Parable of the Talents, a verse always troubling to Torrance: *For to everyone who has will more be given . . .'* They spoke of the virtue of hard work as its own reward, as opposed to work done for personal advancement; and they touched upon fairness, advantages enjoyed by some over others, sometimes having little to do with merit. But it seemed that a certain topic could not but obtrude.

For at that point, old Buchanan observed that a grand example of same might be Caldwell the farmer down the road in Glinrock having sold a stretch of rough grass and sand-dune abutting his pastures, for the sum of ten thousand pounds.

Torrance looked from face to face in the orange glow of the room's lamplight. 'It's the hope of the oil, isn't it?'

'Some hope,' said David Strang morosely. 'They say it'll be for the betterment of the young. But will it, now? What do you think, Robbie?'

Robbie Vallance considered the toe of his boot awhile. 'From what I've seen? I'd wonder. For some, maybe. More than others. And the work falls awful hard on some folk an' all.'

Torrance had then tried to draw Robbie out. 'The Laird might be another of those looking to profit?'

But Robbie had only shrugged. 'He's no fool, the Laird. You cannae blame him. Not just him, neither.'

'I don't understand' – David Strang interjected – 'how a farming man sells up so easily, stops doing something that is in his blood. Take a man like Hunter, you can't see him quitting the dairy farming like he and his family's done for decades just because a man knocks on his door.'

In fact, Torrance knew from George Pease that Hunter was well down the path of selling a great chunk of his farm to an American interest. And it seemed to him that David Strang was not seeing how the sureties he was raised with were vulnerable to this day and age – in much the way that he has sounded cut to the core still by his son Aaron's divorce, feeling the impropriety of it, failing to see it as a matter of a contract dissolved according to its own terms.

But from then it was sharply clear to Torrance that no one in Tarnwick nor Glinrock either could say for sure what was their neighbour's true view of this matter – quite a turnaround in a community so tight. The height of it would be akin to old Buchanan, secretary of the local Temperance Society, suddenly uncorking a good malt, enjoining toasts all round and glugging the bottle down to its heel. And thus Torrance decided to send out notice of his public meeting.

Why was he not surprised when, a couple of days after posting notices around the locality, he opened his door to Marilyn Gallagher, all kindly and asking him how he had been getting on? Looking more and more in the way of her mother, too, smartly turned out and formidable. Still, he had let Marilyn in and put on the kettle. She shrugged off a long suede coat to reveal a sweater dress with a slit, ever stylish; and it was a little strange to be seeing her so closely, so he looked away, until he understood that she was contemplating the monochrome photo of his father on the kitchen wall.

'Your old dad . . . These relics must be strange for you, Torry.'

'I'm glad he lived long enough that I could tell him I wanted to get right with God. Seeing him there every day reminds me of what needs doing still.'

'Used to be that you wanted him as far from your sight as you could manage.' She was sounding rueful. 'Remember that night we took a bottle up to the lighthouse? You, me and Bill Gow, I was on the back of your bike? You'd your lock-knife out, and when you talked about your father . . . God, I thought, someone had better get that knife off him.'

Torrance weighed this unwelcome reminiscence with tact. 'I didn't believe he cared for me. He was distant. His work was so much with others, I maybe resented that. My father only ever said that he loved me. Even after the accident, with Bill . . . I could see I wasn't a disgrace to him. Just a sorrow.'

'Oh, Torry . . .' The softening of her face, that apparent opening of herself was a style familiar to him of old. Now, he distrusted it.

'No, it was right that I'd to face my own shortcomings. But I realised the Lord suffered for people like me. And that way I could believe my sins were forgiven.'

'So simple?'

'No. Not at all, Marilyn. There are mistakes you can't atone for.'

He wanted her to leave right then, but the tea was made, and so they sat in the parlour and he saw her shift toward the business she clearly intended.

'Torry, why are you so set against all the development going on?'

'There's a bad odour about it, Marilyn. People are doing things for themselves, with no heed for what it could mean to others. The community.'

'It could be the making of this place and everyone in it. Is everyone meant to wear sackcloth and ashes? Just because of your past mistakes?'

'I don't know . . . what you mean by that, Marilyn?'

'Just that you seem bent on denying yourself. And maybe, in doing that, denying others, too. You can't tell me there's not things in your life that you miss because of that collar you've put on.'

He was tempted to outbid the innuendo, to tell her he was not yet defunct between his legs and knew fine well what was between hers, as if that slit up her dress didn't remind. But he wouldn't let himself go so low.

'I'm not the man I was, Marilyn.'

'I see that, Torry, I do.'

'Yes. Every day I try to shun things that are unclean.'

'Gosh, Torrance. Good for you.' The edge in her tone told him she would not be tarrying a moment longer.

That night he didn't sleep. The past blinked on and off in his mind, a shadow on his days, a restraining hand on his shoulder. He saw again the elevation of the obelisk, full tilt, as his hands groped upward

284

to it, the narrow slits in the rock etched in his vision against the black night sky, the shelf he was sure he could obtain. *Give up? Never!*

But then, the fatal glance aside, that gut-dropping dawning of just how scarily far he was from the ground. The pure madness of having invented this peril, for he and Bill both – and for nothing, out of witless high spirits. And the maddest feeling of all – that it might be simplest and most fitting to fall and plummet. Had Bill been touched – overpowered, even – by that same feeling?

Torrance sat up in his bedsheets and told himself, *You have to live with it.* No apology possible. Even though to be chastened so long was – in the end, being only human – to resent the stigma somehow, to want it gone.

And so he climbs onto his Triumph and rides out to the Laird's estate, conscious of the bizarre figure he cuts, haring down the rural roads. But the motorbike is a great aid to his making the rounds of the parish. He rides with excess caution, risking no harm to others, much less himself. On a decently clear stretch, though, he permits himself a little exhilaration and liberation, revving her up to feel the whip of the wind as he powers through it.

Nearing the gates of Blaikdoon Manor, he sees the Laird sauntering toward him down the white-pebbled drive, in a tweedy three-piece with tie and hat. There is a long-barrelled shotgun, breech open, over his arm. Torrance dismounts and wheels the Triumph inside the estate to rest it propped against a high perimeter wall.

'Will you walk with me, Torrance? Let's take the cut through the sawmill into the wood.'

Eyeing the gun, Torrance is not entirely happy to see shells slotted into the breech. 'You have plans to bag something today, your lordship?'

'Well, we do get the poachers. Twenty-five thousand acres gives them too much leeway. No, but I've got to pondering whether we might do more round the estate in the way of shooting and stalking? Very popular these days . . .'

They walk through the mill yard, the shrieking din of the big shed grating on Torrance's nerves. He spies Robbie Vallance in animated discussion with the driver of a flatbed truck, and exchanges with him the briefest wave.

Soon, he and the Laird are stepping together into the shade of the canopy, where Torrance feels the hush and the gloom, and an odour that heralds autumn.

'About this meeting you've called, Torrance. Is it for the best? If the development's to go ahead it will need council approval, and that only happens if people want it. Meantime you might stir up worry, resentment, even, for no reason.'

'I see no harm in the community having a reasonable discussion about something that will affect their lives.'

'But what is a community, Torrance? People sticking together, making decisions by majority on what is best for the greatest number. I'm saying to you that we have already a democratic process, you see?'

'All I know, sir, is that some folk are already worried about disruption that the development might cause. For sure I understand some others see great opportunities in it. Yourself included, maybe?'

'If it should turn out what's good for folk in these parts happens to coincide with what's good for me, I'll be delighted. But listen, Torrance, I've a suggestion. Your meeting – what say we cast it in the form of a debate proper? You and I putting forward our respective points of view. And let those who come along to make up their own minds from there.'

'I can't see why not.'

'Good, Torrance, thank you.'

Abruptly the Laird turns tail and begins to walk back the way they came. *You expect you've got your way, eh?* Torrance thinks. *We'll see about that.*

'I mean, that's sport, isn't it. Torry? We may as well speak our minds. I warn you now, though, my word has a bit of weight in these parts – forgive me if I presume to say.'

'I will do my best in turn, sir. There is but one judge.'

'Heh. We might all get our judgement a bit sooner than that, Torry.'

September 1971

A Sacrament

Mark Rutherford is the godfather; and now, with unusual care to place one foot before another, he performs his principal duty of bearing the infant – the soon-to-be-baptised Thomas Cameron Drummond – up the central aisle between the dark wooden pews of St Cuthbert's Parish Church, toward the grand arch of the apse and that focal place by the font where Ally and Belinda wait, beaming. He cradles the swaddled babe, supporting the neck as instructed, grateful that little Thomas seems not to divine any of the awkwardness Mark feels. Finally he hands the vital package to Ally, who receives with the assurance of a fly-half taking a pass from the number nine. Then he steps aside to his anointed spot, now appreciating properly the painted ceiling and the alabaster frieze of the Last Supper. Trust Ally to have done this thing with maximum finesse, the finest Edinburgh can offer.

He clasps his hands respectfully at his waist, aware that Shona will be watching him from the second row amid the Drummond and Morland clans. He can still feel the warm, vulnerable snugness of that babe in arms – delightful, of course. And even so, still, he doesn't 'want one'. Does Shona? He does wonder. She has expressed no strong opinion other than to observe that babies require a lot of one's time. And really there hasn't been much of that, with Mark neck-deep in politics at the *Scotsman*, Shona with her Iron Curtain specialism now practised for the London *Observer*. Still: four years together, unwed – mortgage, yes – but ought there to be a next step? It would, at least, stop people asking.

'Will you,' asks the minister, 'by prayer and example bring up this child in the life and worship of the Church?'

'We will,' intone the oh-so-serious parents together.

Mark suspects Ally will in fact pay someone to do that bit of the bringing up. He and Belinda, too, are busy people. Mark expects his own load to get heavier soon – but he relishes that, buoyed by a recent approach from the Scottish Nationalist Party. He was treated to tea off the Royal Mile by their head of research, Bryan Hubbard ('Call me Hubs') – young and intensely bearded like a college lecturer, who assured Mark that the party is now deadly serious about what North Sea oil revenues could do for an independent Scotland. Hubs wondered if Mark might lend them his expertise on a strategy for the press, maybe a larger PR campaign? And Mark had felt flattered, galvanised. A plan! And some action, so marked in contrast to his endlessly disappointing Labour Party, that lukewarm engine for change.

He knows that Shona still sees his dalliance with nationalism as a little bit backward. 'Trees have roots,' she is fond of saying. 'Human beings don't.' And when he explained to his new SNP pal how he had come to see Labour as insufficiently socialist, Hubs had not been hugely encouraging: *'Just for now, we prefer to focus on them as insufficiently Scottish.'* Mark, though, really wants Shona to appreciate that nationalism will be different in the way he does it.

'What does Ally think?' she had asked when he told her he had accepted.

'I haven't told him, it's all hush-hush for the moment.'

Mark knows very well what Ally will think; and he would fear a possible *froideur*. Ally, anyhow, has enough on his plate.

A screech now issues from the throat of the dauphin as the minister dabbles water on his crown; and Mark smiles at the inlaid floor, knowing how indulgent parents must be resigned to the ways that babies are onerous, annoying, that there's never any talking to them.

Afterwards, to the Drummond residence in Rubislaw: down a broad tree-lined street fit for lords, through the gate to the fine grey stone double-fronted property, its long stone-paved drive taking nearly all the cars. It is a relief to Mark that Shona, at least, seems so little wowed or made peevish by these trappings of Ally's success.

They take stairs down to a basement level of kitchen and generous through-space where mingling guests are being encouraged to take a glass of wine and a cucumber sandwich out to the pretty garden, hemmed by cherry trees still lightly in blossom. As Shona leaves his side to pay her respects to Belinda, Mark fears having to attach himself to a boring banker, maybe even Gordon Fyfe.

He is saved by Ally, ushering some other square-peg guest in his direction – a lean, chastened-looking soul, drowning a little in his suit. 'Tovarich, can I introduce you to Aaron Strang, the genius geologist at Paxton who struck oil for us?'

With Ally gone, Mark sees Strang squint. 'He called you . . . ?'

'Tovarich, yes. At school we were both history buffs, and some of our peer group reckoned I was a communist. They still do.'

As the geologist says a little of his own origins, Mark grasps keenly onto the name of the village he hails from. 'I know Tarnwick! I had a look around there last year.'

'I don't suppose you found much to look at.'

'Oh, it seemed like a sweet little place.' Naturally Mark refrains from reference to the beauteous dark lady who ran the Lockdare Hotel. 'Really, I was having a reconnoitre down the coast to Glinrock. I'd heard tell that BP fancied it for a building site. I gather that could still be the case?'

The geologist shrugs, takes a bite of sandwich and a sip of wine, appearing to Mark as though he has just remembered he is talking to a reporter.

'BP will want to build somewhere soon,' he says finally, chewing. 'I told Alastair, too, that he might look at the land out there by the sea. The deep-water anchorage is very promising.'

'For your company as well?'

The geologist looks pained. 'Our operation's a lot more modest.

And our field's more of an oddity.' He begins an explanation of his current work into how 'his' field could be made more promising than is feared, by special injections of gas or water to somehow drive out the oil . . . Mark has to lean close amid the garden hubbub, and certain technical terms are like voodoo to him. But he has warmed to the mild manners of this man, who puts him in mind just a little of those kindly chimpanzee scientists in the *Planet of the Apes* films.

'For a small outfit,' Mark offers, 'Paxton seems to punch above its weight.'

'Yes, it's voracious. A lot of us have been pulled in.'

'Feels a bit like goldrush time now, no?'

'Getting that way. Another round of drilling licences coming up . . . I mean, Paxton won't be getting involved, but this time the Department of Energy's going to sell the blocks at auction. Sealed bids. It's as mad as that.'

Here, too, Mark has a good yarn to relate, for it is known around the *Scotsman* that the Thomson Group has gone in for oil exploration with both feet. Only last month Mark happened to bump into the proprietor, jovially on his way out to lunch with a dapper, large-nosed old gent whom he introduced as 'Mr Getty', his hair of a surprisingly copperish hue, but suited, Mark supposed, to a man worth a billion dollars.

'That's been the way of the thing all along, hasn't it?' Mark concludes. 'Rich Americans partnering up with willing locals.'

'Yes,' the geologist murmurs. 'Marriages of convenience.'

They are both absently watching the proud parents receive their audience across the lawn – Ally, hand in pocket, recounting some story to his impassive elderly father and Mr Morland both; baby Thomas held aloft in Belinda's arms.

'Do you have children?' Strang asks; with what Mark feels to be a certain mournfulness.

'No, I, uh – I don't. Do you?'

'No. I'm divorced.'

Marks nods, in sympathy.

291

It's not until most of the guests have departed that Mark, helping to bear glasses and plates back into the kitchen, succeeds in flagging Ally down.

'Do I hear right from your geologist friend that you're trying to buy land out on the north-east coast?'

'You bet your sweet bippy. You've an interest?'

'Everything about the oil interests me now, you know that. Everybody wants to read about what's going to happen next.'

'And whether it meets with their approval . . . No, I understand, of course. I know you will do it wisely, seeing all sides.'

Mark is wondering how much money his friend really needs, and how much could be compulsion, or something altogether beyond his ken.

'Anyhow, well done, Al. You've a great place here for entertaining.'

'Well, I ought to clue you in – Belinda and I have our beady eyes on somewhere new. A little grander? This you should see . . .'

Mark struggles to compute the comedy of what Ally tells him next, about his newfound interest in a decrepit sixteenth-century castle set in grounds, equidistant between the southern banks of the Tay and St Andrews Links.

'The current owner's a Scot who got rich out in Canada from the silver mines. He bought this big pile thinking he'd retire back to the old country, but he's lost his taste for all the fixing-up that it needs. So, the mantle falls on me . . . The sale price isn't so terrifying, really, it's more the restoration.'

'And Belinda is game?'

'She says it will be a lark.'

'Ally, boy . . . you don't fear the bills, do you?'

Ally, busily rinsing a plate, only smiles with a crinkled brow as to say such thoughts never occur. Mark, though, is thinking very much about that no-strings loan of a thousand pounds that Ally made to him toward the deposit on his and Shona's house.

He had accepted with gladness for what then became attainable; but with a slight remorse nonetheless. *Not always easy to be a receiver . . .* and while Mark doesn't imagine Ally ever seeking a quiet word to call in the debt, he knows he ought to settle up soonest. It has bothered Mark, too, that he took the favour so as to get a hand-up in that bourgeois status game, the nice place in the nice neighbourhood. His gut tells him that such fixation on social standing – piled on top of the inequity of borrowing power – is a drag on the greater cause of fairness in the world: the cause he has always hoped to serve as a writer. Inwardly, though – and uneasily – he feels he can't do his work so well unless his own material status is decently assured. Otherwise, he fears he would be too anxious about money all the time to be of much use to all those folk in direr straits.

As embarrassing as Mark finds his own view on this matter, he is sure that if he ever confessed it out loud then Ally, at least, would understand. One who might not is his beloved Shona – now picking her way toward them from the garden. And since Shona blithely accepted back at the time that Mark had come into a bit of money via his maiden aunt – it seems as well to keep on keeping a harmless secret.

October 1971
Houston, Texas

Joe is stateside the first time ever, for the big oil services convention, and speed and size and superfluity are the themes he will take back home; consider just that hotel breakfast, so bountiful and delicious – bacon crisped on syrupy pancakes with fried potatoes and heaps of scrambled eggs, juice and coffee and cream – and it kept coming, until Joe had to loosen his belt, and contemplated a swift lie-down in his en suite room on the twentieth floor, but the shuttle from the Hyatt to the Astrodome was not going to wait. He is fast-tracked from the coach into a vast hall under shining lights, and the chill of air-con annihilates the heat off the street, and the stalls are as numerous as you'd get at a funfair, laid out in corridors with lively names, Petroleum Lane, Crude Boulevard, and it feels to Joe that he has left behind a spartan kirk and entered a sumptuous – if slightly gaudy – cathedral. He clocks the big men in big suits, ties and boots, but many, too, in denim and open-necked shirts that make him feel stuffy and fussy, but for sure everybody's real friendly, upbeat, entirely certain of themselves and each other, slapping his back and his shoulder and damn glad to meet him and to tell him of their needs and their services, to demonstrate some remarkable gadgets and explain some more about precisely what's really on offer, and very quickly he is filling his delegate satchel with free stuff, silver pens and a flashlight, candy bars and a calculator, not to speak of business cards like confetti. At a stand dressed like the inside of a log cabin he learns a whole lot more from a man named Dan about prefabricated site dwellings, and is happy just to listen but Dan wants him to speak some, too, just to hear him talk, *that accent, man*, and has he ever met Sean Connery? A bikini-clad model is reclining on a pretend beach but with

294

real truck-loaded sand, and her name is Sandy, *Can you believe that?* A trooper of a gal, but seeming to get gooseflesh under the air-con, and Joe offers his jacket and knows straight away that he has made a great impression.

He decides he should take in a presentation, so he sits in the enclosure for one that seems popular, a big guy who prowls the small stage and slaps his palm with a fist when he proclaims that the past sure don't point toward the future … and for all that American assurance Joe can't but be a little troubled in himself, having picked a way forward for his own business – bet the farm! – and left no real way back. So he tells himself, like the man says: *Change or perish, don't sit there waitin' for them to come roust ya!* which could only be frightening and yet still perhaps not so scary as the alternative.

He is feeling he might be done after a heck of an interesting day but then the hand of Dan the cabin man is on his shoulder and a few of the boys are heading for a big old steak and so the hell is Joe. 'Gotta get this boy some whiskey,' says one, and Joe goes along, and as they head out shoulder to shoulder they are pointing out women in short skirts like they knew them since forever, and to Joe's surprise Sandy is running after him to say that she will be in the Metropol Bar later, *just so you know*, and though these are grown men he's among it's as if he's back in school what with their talk of a great piece of tail and how he's a hell of a boy. Scotland now seems small and pinched to him, the company office back home feels like a dust-laden museum.

In the steakhouse the spirits are high and the talk is easy even if Joe feels hampered by the fact that he does not hunt or shoot in any fashion, nor can he comprehend what they call football so he can't discuss the Dolphins or the Steelers or the Raiders. 'It's a long way from Aberdeen fish market,' he says, and they seem to like that. They know this business, their business, talking so tough and expansive that he feels he must hold his own with some talk of the business he knows best, so he tells them how his company is wholly under his command, strategically top to bottom, and any staff who are not on board have to ship out, because the past don't point to the future. They drink to a real good time, to old friends and new, to coming back next year, to making the reservations just as soon as they get to the Hyatt, but first to the Metropol for happy hour, and by now Joe is flying.

At the bar it takes him a while to understand all these friendly women who can be also a little hard-eyed. But he sees Sandy approaching to save him. 'Can we be alone?' she asks. They find a spot. He kisses her and he can taste bubblegum, puts his hand into her sunny blonde hair, and she groans but he thinks, *No, I don't do this.* Still he wants to offer her something for her trouble, but she doesn't want another drink, and it seems to him her opinion of him has lowered somehow. Nonetheless, he feels better about himself, ready to turn in for the night, not notably drunk, and carrying some important small pieces of card.

Back at the Hyatt main desk the receptionist, desperately contrite, tells him that they have tried in vain for some hours to relay a message, and they will now arrange the trunk call at once, so in mere moments Joe is patched through to his sister Angela in Scotland who tells him that their mother has died.

November 1971
A Town Hall

In the quiet before folks are let in, Torrance prepares – on the dais, a chair for himself and for the Laird, a lectern between them. Out on the floor, chairs are set out and spaced neatly. The crimson curtains are drawn in the whitewashed hall.

The Reverend is turning notecards in his hand and considering his phrasing when the creak of the double doors alerts him and he observes a fellow of his own age sauntering down the aisle: jeans and a leather coat, satchel over his shoulder, flaxen hair about his ears – from the city, no question.

'Reverend McVey? My name's Mark Rutherford, I'm a journalist.'

Torrance is wary, but this Rutherford presents himself convincingly: polite, seriously interested in the business of the evening's gathering, and well-informed about it – above all, the issue of the buying-up of land, which emboldens Torrance to say a mite more than he intended about the sorts of parties he believes to have been doing the buying.

'Can you prove that?'

Rutherford's mild query unsettles Torrance. 'It's the sum of what I hear. But if you're around tonight then you might talk to my parishioner George Pease.'

By six thirty the chairs are filled and some are standing by the back wall, the chap from the *Scotsman* among them – as large a congregation as Torrance ever gets, and one or two still coming in. The Laird is seated at his side, dapper and peaceable, having asked for only a glass of water. Torrance can see George Pease, fretful at the end of a row; the Gallagher clan, upright and ready for business as ever; and

his Question Night group, including David Strang and Robbie Vallance. David had come to shake his hand on arrival and lamented the
absence of his son Aaron – 'the ghost at this feast'. The largest figure
in the room – a behemoth of a man in a donkey jacket – is totally
unknown to Torrance from his rounds of the parish, and he leans on
the far wall with his arms folded.

Now Torrance proceeds to the lectern and claps to hush the
murmurs.

'Friends, thank you for coming. We are gathered tonight chiefly
to discuss the planning application that has been lodged with
the council for a quite enormous building site to be made out of
Glinrock Bay.

'What we have in this town is a good communal spirit, where one
looks out for another. Local people must surely have a say in matters
that concern them so directly and drastically. I understand there is
both support and opposition for the plans. It is a struggle, always –
to decide on the right thing to do in life. But this oil . . . it was laid
down by God over millions of years, and we would be fools to make
overhasty decisions because of it. I have called this meeting so we
might discuss what we think will be best here, for all of us. I will say
a few words, as will the Laird, then your views are welcomed.

'First, I draw your attention to a remark made in the planning
application, where the applicants state that the bay is "the only
satisfactory location" for their plans. Why? There is nothing there
now but pasture and beach, but there are shipyards and men ready
for work not so far away in Scotland. If they stress convenience, it
is their own they have in mind, not that of folk in these parts. And
let's be clear, what they propose is a monumental upheaval of our
natural environment and amenity. The character of this place, its
simple beauty as God made it will be changed, severely. No doubt
you will hear tonight of the wonders of development, but I propose
that before these oil men have hired a single man or laid a single brick
we should not assume great things.'

He pauses, and behind his back the Laird speaks out. 'Nor assume the worst neither, perhaps . . .'

The Laird sets some notepaper down on the lectern but he does not look at it again.

'Great work is at hand. And it's proposed to happen right here. Oil does indeed offer Scotland extraordinary benefits – but only if the nettle is grasped. If you believe that should happen, that Scotland should get that oil with all its monetary benefits, and that this is the best way to get it – then why shouldn't our place seize its good fortune and start to reap those benefits at once?

'Understand that the oil will build us more than a yard at Glinrock. It will need new infrastructure by which we'll all benefit – new roads, new water supply, new amenities. This very hall, of which I am trustee? Fine for our purpose tonight. But we could have better, no? The oil will make that possible, too.

'I'm like any north-east man, I love our environment. I play my small part in maintaining it. But we can't claim to be a great beauty spot, the value of tourism goes only so far, we will not prosper on Harris tweed and whisky. Like many, I lament the drift of men from fishing, but such are the times. If we're to stand tall on our own feet and make good lives for ourselves and our children then Scotland needs new industry, private enterprise. If we're to have it, then some ground must be dug up – some sand-dunes, and some grass and gorse down at Glinrock. Some might say they'll take development, yes, only please not in their own small corner. Then there are lonely souls among us who prefer to subsist on locusts and wild honey, and might even like that. But self-mortification is not for everyone. Not when we can see and feel and appreciate material benefits and comforts that come to us all by hard work and bold enterprise.

'At any rate, those are my thoughts, so let's hear from your good selves.'

The Laird shuffles back to his seat with no motion in the room bar the sound of throats being cleared. And then a hand is raised tentatively. And then another.

The hour that follows becomes steadily more discomfiting and vexing for Torrance McVey, such that first he wonders whether his measure of the parish was wholly wrong; then, whether or not folk might have been somehow induced to speak.

Buchanan on the Temperance Society sounds the note that seems to get most fretful heads nodding along. 'I ken the Laird, and I worry now, about a chance we might miss. I do foresee a ruin of us. But not as you say, Reverend. It'd be *not* to do it that could finish us.'

Torrance is grateful, at least, for David Strang who gets to his feet with a capable air. 'I ken that a high value has been set on some things we never knew were there. But some parties might know better – might be conniving for their own benefit? I'm not sure of the value to us and our young people of outsiders coming in to make raids on us like this. I daresay the clearances should not be forgotten. We didn't resist then, and we might ask now if folk are to be driven off again.'

Hunter the dairy farmer – a goodly tract of his land already sold to the oil, as everyone knows – stands without ceremony, visibly truculent.

'I've farmed here long enough. If thon tells me I'm to be stopped from doing well, I need to be shown a damn good reason who it is I'm hurting. That it is not just jealousy, or folk so full of themselves they think they've the right to tell others how to behave. Reverend, your job of work you inherited from your faither, with a roof o'er your head in the bargain. And you'd a fair old black mark on you then that someone saw fit to wipe away. You've had every chance, and here you want to rob a chance from others?'

In his heart Torrance has known it would come to this. He stands and comes forward, with a tremor in his hand that he seeks to drive out by grasping the lectern.

'It was my honour to assume my late father's ministry. I have done so in humility – he was worth ten of me, no doubt, but still I want only to continue his work in my poor way by serving this community.'

He feels it now, irresistible, something else at hand that needs speaking – that he is not just going to stand and be nailed up.

'Luke tells us of the proud Pharisee at prayer who consoles himself in vanity with the thought he is so much better than lesser men. That is not me. But we might ask of any self-styled better man – are they as virtuous as they present themselves? So much of our coastal lands changing hands . . . You yourself might have made a sale to some party that came knocking. But could that party as well have been your neighbour in disguise? Seeing an advantage unknown to you? Is that fair? Does it benefit this community if some grab a big cut of land values improved by none of their own doing, thinking only to make a fat profit? That sort of behaviour is not communal – it is parasitical.'

Torrance has to wipe his lip for the vehemence that came out of him, evidently noticed by the room, which is murmuring anew.

The Laird has stepped up to his shoulder. 'If I may. The ownership and sale of land is a matter of public record anyone can consult. For some reason Mr Strang spoke of the clearances? Good lord, this area suffered by those. Here, though, no one is being coerced into anything. A man is responsible for any ground under his feet to which he has title, and if he is a grown man then he should know what it is worth to him, such that he enters into any bargain freely of his choosing.'

Hunter is back on his feet. 'Hear, hear. What you have is fine so long as you choose it. If it's my choice made with open eyes then don't be telling me I'm blind.'

Incredibly to Torrance, there is a solid wave of applause in the room, during which he feels compelled to study the floor. The Laird touches his arm, as if kindly.

'Torrance, is it time perhaps for a show of hands?'

The Laird offers his hand to Torrance but does not speak to him again as the congregants steadily process out of the hall into the night. He merely gathers his coat and steps down carefully from the dais. David Strang has come forward concernedly, Robbie Vallance at his side, clearly wanting a word, but the Laird simply raises a flat palm in their direction and presses on to the back of the hall, where he is greeted warmly by a waiting Juliet Gallagher, and that big man in the donkey jacket, his black curls bobbing as he grins and nods. Torrance feels a sudden pang at a thought he now reckons he should have had sooner – that he has lumbered David and Robbie with the same burden as himself by having wilfully incurred the Laird's disfavour.

Torrance is waited upon by Mr Rutherford from the *Scotsman*, rather grave and full of praise for his oratory, also very much hopeful of that word with Mr Pease. But Torrance sees that George Pease has long gone.

February 1972
A New Openness

'Really a remarkable headquarters you've got here, Joe,' says Alastair Drummond, gesturing from his seat in the reception area fringed by tall philodendrons in pots. 'Very forward-thinking. You know, of course, that my taste is back in the eighteen-hundreds.'

Joe Killday is pleased, wanting Drummond's approval. 'It's a style – a philosophy, almost – the Germans call it Bürolandschaft.'

Together the assembled non-executive directors of Killday Fishing gaze around politely at their surroundings, the whitewashed brick walls and far-stretching tile-carpet floor: desks for the workforce mazily spaced and divided by standing screens and steel support pillars, all evenly lit from above by suspended fluorescent strips.

Joe's pride in the arrangement is tempered slightly by the knowledge of how much Andrew and Garth both claim to hate it. *'Flashy,'* Andrew had said of the first blueprints. *'Are we all to sit in a bloody typing pool?'* But they have all had bigger things to brood over since.

They are all waiting for Andrew to appear; he will attend board for the first time in three months, thus emerging out of an effective sabbatical from company matters since Ma's sudden death. For some weeks after the funeral he cut a blank-eyed figure, a once-vital character apparently seeing only desolation all about him. But then it had been he who found his wife pulseless on the kitchen floor at Netherdown and had not been able to revive her; and for some time he had seemed to be reliving those awful moments interminably.

The business at hand today – the expensive acquisition of Devane the shipbuilder – ought to be a mere rubber-stamping; but Joe expects Andrew's mood will have to be watched like a barometer. Weeks before, he sat respectfully with his father at Netherdown, explaining the financing of the deal just as Alastair Drummond explained it to him, hopeful that Andrew's nostalgic reverence for the Devane business would seal his approval. His father's heart, though, hardly seemed to come into it: rather, he had wanted to speak of Winnifred. *'I just wish she was here, Joseph. It's that and only that. Thirty-four years of marriage, can't be otherwise.'*

In the face of his father's pain Joe had felt pity, but unease, too. At the funeral the minister spoke of a life of self-sacrifice; but to Joe it seemed this was done for one above all others. Her sons she had so rarely praised or shown pride in – more often mimicking the judgemental style of the prospering man she married. But it felt futile now to rue these shortcomings, whether they were truly hers or his. Whoever was the woman behind his mother, Joe knows he had failed to comprehend her.

He can see through the glass wall of the conference room that his new secretary, Isla, is busying about to make the place settings ready. He is conscious that Bodie is squatting next door in Andrew's office, forever on the phone to all sorts, and he trusts the cuckoo will vacate in good time before his father turns up. For weeks now Bodie has been bending Joe's ear about an engineering firm in Glasgow, Cassels; how they should be partnering up, thinking about all the money in repairing bits of sea-floor kit that the oil boys depend on – things of which Joe has scant knowledge. But Bodie's drive to keep getting the business *more and more pregnant* has a voracity Joe finds hard to oppose.

And now Isla is bearing a tray of coffee cups, gratefully received by Drummond and his fellow non-execs: Sam Lietzske of Baker Tools, Doug Stewart of Stewart Property Developments, and John Morland of Morland Shipping Lines Limited.

It was Bodie who lured Isla to work here, away from the reception at Kaminsky Motors, and she has, Joe feels, such a demurely assured warmth to her voice and manners, on top of her appreciable voguish slenderness, apparent today by a black jersey.

'Thank you kindly, ma'am,' says Sam Lietzske.

'You're welcome, gents. Glad we can offer you heat and light to go with.'

'Isla was our salvation these last three weeks,' Joe throws in cheerily. 'The moment the miners' strike was called she ran to the candlemaker and bought up the stock.'

'I was taken out to the Regal last Saturday,' says Isla, 'and would you believe the film stopped midway? So violent, mind, I was nearly glad of it.'

'What was the picture, ma'am?'

'*Dirty Harry*, I believe. And he was that, for sure.'

Joe wonders idly what sort of a man had the pleasure of squiring Isla. But now Andrew is entering, Sheila ever attentive at his side, having fetched him just now from Netherdown. His tie is knotted full Windsor, high shine on his shoes, though his white beard wants a trim. Angela has been on call for her father these past months, but Sheila, too, has seemed to want to extend her usual duties.

Now Sheila beckons Joe and Isla aside, worriedly. 'Joseph, will you see that your father has a cup of tea? Isla, be good and make a brew, would you?'

Isla heads off and Joe turns back, a little bewildered, to where Alastair Drummond has engaged Andrew. 'We were just chatting about the strike getting done with at long last, Mr Killday.'

'The miners' – says Andrew, thickly, as if chewing on baccy as is Garth's way – 'are no fools.'

As they all take their seats in the conference room Joe keeps his eye on Andrew above all, aware that Andrew's own gaze is trained sternly upon the non-execs – carefully selected and courted by Joe from their respective fields of expertise and high growth, but in his father's eyes perhaps still something of a rogue's gallery. Andrew seems subdued, yes, but in some way restored, as if armed with intent to show he is still chairman of the board. Joe decides to move proceedings forward.

'Gentlemen, we know what we've to do today. Our business has always been deep-water fishing, but for a while we have worked to a growth plan. To use our marine experience to diversify, so as not to be stuck in one shrinking market. We've sought to develop provision of support services to the oil industry – and the moment has come to put real muscle behind those efforts. So, we propose to acquire Devane, its yard and all its operations, and to integrate those into ours. At a stroke we'll have a full service offer – shipbuilding and ship repair, and a real engineering business with those skills and technologies, to which we add our strategic leadership.

'To be clear, this is not about getting bigger for the sake of it, but to capture that coming field where boats will be built for the North Sea. Devane are not flush with orders right now. But they very soon will be.'

'I would suggest' – interjects John Morland of the cruise ships, Alastair Drummond's father-in-law – 'you will want to take a very close look at Devane's audited statements these last years. Be sure their assets are what you think they are.'

'Walter will take care over all the due diligence.' Joe is sure of this. Walter in fact requested a quiet moment with Joe and offered special assurance on this very matter – *especially when Da is out of sorts*. Joe has feared that Walter was resistant to change, in Andrew's mould that way; so he was struck by Walter's desire to be trusted with something important, and wanted his unsung brother to feel the value of that trust.

'So,' says Morland, 'the offer you will make is . . .'

'A million pounds sterling. With a seat on this board for Mr Lennox Devane.'

'And will the name over the door stay Devane?'

'For a while,' says Ray Bodie, speaking out of turn in a way Joe can just about abide. 'It's a grand old name. But at the right time we will rename it Killday.'

'A grand old name indeed, for a great yard . . .'

Andrew's first intervention catches Joe off guard. He had just begun to feel that maybe the meeting and decision would go by without such.

'Devane have seen all the changes in Aberdeen. A great family business. Great maker of ships, including the one bearing my name. I'm humbled to think of my name over that yard. But let me say this. I want it on the record. The sheer level of capital expenditure this company has saddled itself with – that is a worry to me. For all our success we have never had bottomless coffers. We fish, we repair boats and we supply other fishers – that is the money in our pockets. Now we propose to spend it on something highly speculative. Here we sit in these fancy premises—'

'Let's remember' – Joe can hold back no longer – 'we had no choice about relocation, but Ray got us a great deal here and we did the refit under-budget.'

'My point, Joseph, is that we've spent big money. All these new hires for all this new business of Raymond's . . . I don't need reminding of what's needful for a company that wants success. But the time will surely come soon to strengthen our fishing fleet. We've not built a new stern trawler since the *Andrew Killday* was launched at Devane's, ten years gone.'

It is the topic Joe most feared – since the Devane yard is to be bought for its quayside facilities so as to build and repair offshore supply boats. Not to build trawlers anytime soon.

'Da, that moment must be judged with real care. The country is only just signed up to a Europe-wide policy on what we can fish and where.'

'Aye, and you notice how Norway backed out? Cos they're not fools. They no more want us in their waters than we want them here.'

'Yes, they backed out, but we went in.'

'Well, I tell you, I'm for any party that says we get out of Europe again before it's too late. It's the last fight worth a damn.'

Alastair Drummond breaks in. 'These are weighty matters, of course, beyond the remit of our business today. For the moment, though, I wonder if this meeting is satisfied that Joe ought to make a telephone call to Mr Devane?'

Joe surveys the room and sees in relief that the cause has been won. Andrew, clearly, did his own cause no favours by making it seem an obsession.

'Oh, Ray, come on, that's obscene.' Joe protests but Bodie persists, pouring Moët et Chandon into a tilted pint glass and topping with a head as if it were a bottle of McEwan's Export ale.

Most annoyingly Bodie has returned from the bar with a young woman in tow, too; and Joe shoots her a look of apology for these loutish manners. She smiles, as if at the novelty of an invite into the company of big-spending businessmen at the Òrach Hotel. But somehow Joe isn't fully convinced.

'Joe, this is what oil people do, I've been watching.' Bodie gestures back to the busy bar, where one gent is bullishly refusing to remove his Stetson hat. 'And we are oil people now, Joe. Now' – he refocuses on his glass-topping – 'smaller measures for me and Sheryl here, I'd say . . . But, here's to the grand plan, boss! *Sláinte!*'

Joe sees that Sheryl doesn't drink, instead slipping a packet of Silk Cut from her purse.

'So,' says Bodie cheerily, 'Sheryl and I just met, but we had the nicest chat, she's from Tyneside, and we love the Geordies.'

Joe nods but doesn't want to look too closely at Sheryl. Her prettiness has something gauche and duck-like about it; he feels oddly sorry for her. Salon-blonde, notably green-eyed, she has a scented, cosmetic sheen about her. She wears a black slip-dress glistening with sequin beads, a black flower sewn at its bustline; and she wears it well. That smile, though, strikes Joe as a wee bit performed, as if she has seen this set-up before.

'D'you've a light on you, pet?' she asks him.

'I'm sorry, I don't smoke. Fancied it sometimes, but—'

'Joe, if you want something but deny yourself then you have to ask yourself why?'

Bodie's bumptiousness has got to Joe such that he retorts through his teeth. 'Smoking's not for everyone, Ray. It can . . . irritate, you know? Can be unsocial. Speaking of which, I'm expecting the company secretary to join us any moment.'

'Really? Good God. Sheryl, my dear, I think my colleague and I have a bit of business still . . .'

'Oh I'm not bothered.' Sheryl, having lit her own cigarette, calmly exhales a bluish cloud. 'I went to secretarial school meself, I can keep up.'

'Maybe not tonight. Would you forgive us?'

Sheryl in fact looks a shade put out; but she slips her cigarettes back in her purse, stands, smooths her dress and sharply turns heel.

'Shame,' murmurs Bodie. 'Up close, though? You see her skin and teeth maybe aren't the best. That much make-up, that much perfume . . . I did ask myself why she was smoking and drinking alone. Then I asked myself, would she care for a glass of champagne . . . ?'

Irritation flares in Joe. 'Ray, I've said before, don't be talking like that round me, it's disrespectful to my sister.' In the nick of time, perhaps, he can see Isla is threading a path toward them, and he stands and performs a smile of his own, noticing that Bodie is showing him an insufferable look as to imply Joe is a sly one.

'Gentlemen,' she says coolly, sliding onto the stool vacated by Sheryl and slipping off her camel trench coat. 'Thanks for your hospitality.'

'Isla, how nice you could join us. We prepared a glass, and you're just in time for a toast. To the future Killday Oil and Gas! Sláinte!'

'Ray, please.' To Joe, this is telling tales out of school.

'Oh, our Isla knows what's what. You didn't join this company just to sell fish down the market, did you, my dear?'

Isla makes a carefree face, gesturing to the air with her champagne flute.

'Good, neither did I, and nor did Joe.'

The pint-pouring prank left only slivers of wine in the other glasses, and Bodie's is drained.

'Isla, would you slip across to that bar and ask for another bottle? They have my Barclaycard in that big tin of theirs.'

Joe watches her walk off, admiringly, until he sees Bodie looking hard at him.

'What?'

'You know what. The next phase.'

'Oh, Ray . . .'

'Straight after the meeting, Joe, I got on the phone to Cassels.'

'We're not going to buy them as well.'

'No we're not, but they are our right partners, I'm convinced, for this engineering service we want.'

'Can we do one thing at a time? I don't find it so easy getting my head in shape for all these battles.'

Joe is thinking of the flinty look Andrew seemed to shoot him as he clambered back into Sheila's car post-meeting. The bite in his father's words at the conference table had reminded Joe sufficiently of paternal disapprovals past such as to stiffen his resolve to keep going now.

Bodie leans in. 'You are doing Andrew a service, Joe. Doing what he asked of you. You are keeping the business, his name, alive. But, fine – what do you fancy tonight? We should celebrate, no?'

'After my pint of fizz, I think maybe a lie-down.'

'Great. Who with?'

Joe grimaces: Bodie in his rapacious moods can be a trial.

'Well, not with me in any case!' Bodie grins. 'Okay, then, I'll be heading home to Angela, brother. Consider me chastened.'

He pats Joe's shoulder, then slouches toward the exit, pausing only at the bar, where Sheryl is back on a barstool, recomposed, wreathed

310

in cigarette smoke. Bodie whispers something in Isla's ear, and she laughs, before wending her way back to their table with the new bottle and two glasses.

'I'm sorry, Isla, the party might be over.'

'Two's a party,' she says blithely. 'If we drink this together.'

'That might not be appropriate.'

'I so wish, Joe' – she looks at him levelly – 'you wouldn't see me that way.'

An hour or so later Joe has asked the hotel reception to call Isla a taxi. He stands with her outside, under the colonnade and the spectral yellow light of the lamps.

'Are you cold?' he asks.

She considers, then slips her hand into his. The taxi is coming onto the estate and Joe uses his free hand to wave it down, then turns to say goodbye, but Isla strokes his face and brings her lips to his cheek. This, coupled with the soft brush against his cheek of her fragrant hair, is suddenly and heavily arousing. He looks at her, and her look in return is resolute. They climb together into the backseat of the taxi, and Joe gives the driver the address of his apartment on Union Terrace.

June 1972

A Revenant

Back to the road, and Robbie rides pillion on Torrance McVey's Triumph, the two of them a unit bonded together for motion – Robbie's arm looped round Torry's waist and a hand on the grip rail at his back, his eyes on the road just like Torry's, his body leaning with Torry's as they take corners.

Robbie is glad they zip along at sixty miles per hour, halfway anonymised by helmets, for he imagines they strike any onlooker as a queer sight: the minister-biker held fast by some gadgie in working gear and boots, rucksack on his back. But Robbie knows Torry is able, not the hair-raiser he was when they were lads a million years ago. And if they are not exactly mates, Torry is doing him a decent turn.

The ribbon of the lately made one-track road carries them on, past quiet fields under afternoon sun; but soon, even above the gravelly burr and rasp of the bike, Robbie can make out a distant roar of heavy machinery. They climb a steady incline, and then a clunking dip down over the crest reveals to them a solid caravan of cars and loading trucks headed down to Glinrock Bay; and below and beyond them, in full aspect, is the wilderness transformed. Torry slows the Triumph to a standstill and Robbie peels himself off.

There, unmoved, are the bay's familiar sandflats, headland cliffs, the ten-fathom waters of the Firth – but all now made as to seem merely a frame around the stunning, brute augmentation of the coast that is the platform construction site – its sprawling work-yard and workshops within a perimeter-fenced encampment, and its deep, vast concrete basin, with a colossus of a dock gate to hold back the waters.

Robbie had heard tell of the work; but the scale of change is suddenly abundant, what was carved out of the landscape by the army that descended on the bay as if for war, men and machines, excavators and earthmovers to dig and blast and chew through rocks and dunes.

'Sure you got all you need?' Torry has his helmet off, blinking into the sun, and he is looking at Robbie's simple rucksack.

'I dinnae want any more baggage.'

'How you feeling, Robbie? You okay about this?'

'I'm fine, thanks, man. You?'

Torry shrugs. 'This is the work there is. We couldn't stop it. I guess we live with it.'

If ye cannae beat 'em . . . Robbie recognises the resenting flare he has felt toward Torrance at times ever since the Laird let him know there would be nothing else for him at the sawmill. Not Torrance's fault – each man his own and that. But now Torrance wears the same contrite look Aaron wore all those months after Robbie was 'Not Required Back' to the Pecos rig.

'Put the old things behind you, Rob,' says Torrance. 'Now you do a new thing. Good luck.'

'If I'd any luck I'd no' be here,' Robbie shoots back, glad enough of the favour but not wanting a sermon alongside. Torry wheels the Triumph back round and kick-starts it. Robbie shoulders his rucksack and, saddle-sore, starts the stride down past the line of cars to where men are queuing by an entrance hut to the yard. Din, vibrations and dust build about his ears, and as he nears his newest new start he thinks, dully, *I have done this before.*

He is processed by security and logged at the site office, handed a biro to complete a tick-box form and give a brief account of his intentions and relevant skills. He keeps his offshore experience to himself, hoping to ghost through any possible bar made by that 'Not Required Back'.

'You've done some welding?'

'Some. Not to your standard here, I'd reckon.'

'Eh well. I'd advise you think hard on it, son.'

'Labouring's fine by me, lift and shift, any o' that.'

'Two pound an hour. Get yerself to store for overalls and a hard hat. Report to shift seven in the morning, you'll bunk on the *Vergina*.'

'Eh?'

'I ken. It's the big ferry anchored in harbour, aye?'

Robbie picks a careful path across the site in the direction advised, steering clear of the heavy lifters and wheel-barrowers, past the shops from which a din of tools and raised voices emanates, and work spills out onto the yard, foremen bent over welders and grinders as sparks fly. The dry dock is huge, almost ominous, like a great corral for a monster gargantuan in size and weight.

Once he has turned the corner of a titanic scaffold, past the main melee, he can see stretching away to his far left a hillside dotted with small caravans and timber huts; and, looming before him, that hulking rust-bucket of an anchored passenger ferry, its gangway an unenticing invitation up to a gloomy interior.

With a key collected from a solemn Greek steward he enters a cramped cabin with a floor-to-ceiling crack in its wall, and a double-bunk. On its lower deck there sits a bleary, knackered-looking man in vest and y-fronts, the waistband of which he is scratching absently.

'Eh, bonny lad. I knew I'd not be on me own long. How do, welcome to the holiday camp. Stalag Luft Number Three. I'm Bob.' He extends a hand, and after a moment Robbie thinks better of telling the daft bastard to give it a wash first.

Come dinner-hour Bob is showing Robbie down to the ship's refectory, screwed-down seating around Formica tables, and instructing him in the drill of collecting a plate of grilled meat, chips and sauce from the service area minded by another swarthy, sad-eyed man in chef's whites. Once sat, they are joined by a tall, craggy Scot

314

introduced as Jack – possibly a looker when he was younger, but lividly scarred across his forehead and with a wolfish midlife mien that Robbie takes against.

'The scran's alright, eh?' Bob nudges him. 'They must think if we're tret better than dogs then we'll keep in the kennel.'

'Damn sight better off in here than the caravans,' Jack observes while munching. 'You're fucked for the electrics. The cludgies are a horror.'

Robbie soon gathers that Bob is from Sunderland, his ex-wife ('The bitch') was Scots, and his working life has been a meandering, sorry sort of a tale, a stint in a Wearside shipyard then some curtailed years as a panel beater in a car plant. Jack used to run a pub, drank much of its proceeds, and seems to want to leave his story there.

So the talk turns to recreation: it transpires there is a regular Saturday night minibus to the nearest dancehall. Jack asks Robbie if he knows of any livelier local options. 'Seems to me round these parts you're not encouraged to do a damn thing other than read the Bible. Not even love your neighbour. However pleasing she might be . . .'

A pale girl in a pinafore, surely no more than sixteen, is taking their plates. Robbie notes Jack's eye running down her and he doesn't like it.

The light is fading and his new associates suggest a stroll out round the pipe yard. Robbie has no better plan. There, huge steel lengths sit darkly stacked, each chalked with numbers in white. One has been graffitied VOTE SNP.

'These have all come o'wa from Japan.' Bob whistles. 'On geet big German freighters. That's Japs for you, filling orders for the whole bliddy world, we've seen it wi' ships, seen it wi' cars . . .' Just as Robbie is feeling the strangest playground urge to climb up and crawl inside one of these massive tubes, Bob offers him a foot-up. Getting comfortable within the echoey interior Robbie picks up a stray bit of stick and rattles it against the wall, only for Jack to snap at him – 'Security!' – before passing down a tin of Tartan Special.

Later in his top bunk under a thin sheet, nose close to the drop ceiling, gloom descends upon Robbie – the low feeling that he is returned to the world of the rigs, fallen among dubious company: a champion moaner and a sinister reprobate. Must he suffer it all again? If so, then to what end? It seems to him that he might have dreamed his marriage to Marilyn Gallagher, since not a trace of its promise remains. He turns his face and buries it in the pillow.

In the morning he heads out doggedly to shift, bearing a pledge newly made to himself. He can see how the mindlessness of shifting pipe will soon weigh heavy. And it's clear as day that the great business of this yard is welding – the volume of work is obvious, the pay miles better. The standard of work is far above what he has known; but he believes that, with dedication, he could hack it. He has to find the way to climb out of this hole: so welding it must be.

Hanging around on his break, squatting with a flask of tea on the edge of a pull-trolley, he observes a curious scene outside one of the workshops. Among the welders, in their green hard hats, overalls and pigskin leather coats, there seems a kind of camaraderie; but one among them is unmistakably getting stick as he works, the super gesticulating at his shoulder.

The welder stands back, flips up his lid, and Robbie realises that he is she.

'You no' see what I'm saying, sweetheart?'

She mutters something to the air that Robbie doesn't catch.

'Are you scared o' me, darlin'? D'you wannae speak up?'

'Are you deaf as well as daft? My name's Evie. I said, I let my welds do the talking. Look you at it now, you tell me what's wrong?'

The super is scowling but the other lads are enjoying the altercation, low jeers and cheers going round. This Evie sweeps by him, red spots on her pale cheeks, eyes clouded with displeasure, and Robbie clocks how tall she is, how much red hair has been stuffed down the back of her overalls.

'How d'ye like that attitude, eh?' the super offers to the lads. 'Fanny thinks it can weld.'

Robbie feels an old inner stirring, of taking sides, knowing which one he is on. Fighting it down, he gets up and goes back to his dog-work.

September 1972

Passion Projects

Aaron paces the floor of his silent house, mind ablaze with new possibility, pausing now and then to recheck the letter in his hand over which he has just pored with dawning delight. He has ghosted through this place ever since Heather left together with the removal lorry, and it has felt weirdly deserted, its emptiness accusing. *'Don't be lonely, pal,'* Robbie told him, feelingly, after it all fell apart. But then Robbie has become a little lonely, too, Aaron feels sure. After recent disappointments he has wanted so badly to throw himself into work, only to be thwarted at every turn. Might this be the perfect moment, then, for a change of career?

The letter is a formal approach, signed by Professor Maurice Ziskind, dean of a new college – Stoneybrook Institute of Technology, its campus currently under construction in parkland on the outskirts of Aberdeen. And Professor Ziskind wishes to discuss with Aaron the role of Director of a new School of Geoscience.

Newness *in excelsis*! Any return to an academic life has for so long felt to Aaron inadequate, an admission of defeat. But the letter is full of resonant phrases he could have wished to mint himself: *'bold new curriculum design . . . small state-of-the-art campus . . . you will shape this place from its inception'*. Aaron accepts no notion of providence, and yet here is something of which he has been in need yet afraid to admit, unable to ask for; delivered to him now in timely fashion – and with it, perhaps, a means to redeem decisions made and paths taken which he has since had cause to regret. Perhaps this path could even earn him some renewed esteem in the eyes of his ex-wife – and her father, his former mentor.

He is sure that his divorce from Heather has not sunk in him any sort of bitterness: there were no awful scenes, not between themselves nor before lawyers. He has credited himself with maturity in accepting a certain account of his deficiencies; also in wishing sincerely that life might be happier for Heather. For himself, he has tried to believe in a fresh start, with difficulty – until now.

In his mind, too, the offer in the letter is larger than him alone: concerning, moreover, *'the nation's need for more qualified scientists, and the proper encouragement of a rising generation . . .'* Here, Aaron has someone specific in mind.

During the chilly summer just gone, Aaron began to meet informally with Dottie Blair, M.Sc. student in geology at Aberdeen, who attended – and contributed so keenly to – the seminar he gave at the university back in the autumn of 1970. He remembered her the instant he heard her voice on the telephone, and meeting her for a cup of tea in the gothic shade of Marischal College he found her drive and purpose impressing him anew. Not just her readiness to take on summer work, or her yen to explore geological sites in Tanzania, Namibia, New Zealand. Not even the breadth of her research interests, now focused with some zeal upon petroleum geology.

Maybe above all these is her clear desire, modestly expressed, to work with him, for him. *'Not that I remotely have the knowledge to contribute to your research. But so that I could get better. Even just as a technician? I truly understand if you feel I'm not ready, but I'd be so glad if you would consider . . .'*

Hearing this, Aaron worried at once that if there were not some way for him to acknowledge her qualities, then he would upset her greatly. And yet he had to wonder if she was asking for more than he could offer.

He knows very well the value of a mentor – not necessarily a cloudless relationship, of course, but a vital one. And he sees that maybe the time of life has come for him to progress into such a steering role for others. But the case of Dottie Blair raises a delicate matter. What is the appropriate level of encouragement, of personal attentiveness? This question has started to prey on him.

The approach from Stoneybrook has at least clarified one thing. As much as Dottie has seemed to want to impress him, Aaron has wanted also to deserve her esteem; and lately it hasn't felt much like so. But as Director of Geoscience at Stoneybrook, he might properly supervise her academic development and encourage her to their mutual hearts' content.

Of course, then, he will meet with Maurice Ziskind.

This want of an exit strategy has been sharpened in Aaron by a recent summit over coffee with Clay Paxton, to which he trooped along in hope of an update on the plan for getting platforms planted out at sea, to start producing oil from Cetus. But the coffee never came; only bad news delivered like a dose of salts.

'Israelite, we've taken a long look at this thing from all ways round . . . and the upshot is we ain't doing it.'

'You mean, we'll not produce this field . . . ?'

'Oh, we'll produce, bet on it. I got a prize in my mind every morning I wake, and that's to beat the hell out of goddamn BP and get this oil onto land. But, a build even close to what they're doing up at Glinrock, a hundred miles of pipe . . . Jeez, there's no way an indie like us can make those numbers fly. So, we got to think a little harder, about some other means . . . You're lookin' gut-shot there, son.'

Aaron couldn't quite take his eyes from Paxton's liver-spotted hands clasped together before him on the desktop; somehow not quite the same cowboy of old, for once almost abashed.

'Aaron, remember, I gotta ride two horses here. I'm the drilling guy, hired for that service by a bunch of investors. And, sure, one of those investors is me. But my partners, they've got a whole lot more tied up in this, and they ain't gonna stand the big price-tag.'

'It just feels like such a short-term view, Clay. Don't they understand the potential of Cetus? I accept, as a field it's complex, unconventional—'

'Yep, and those just ain't the winning words in this business, son. People hear 'em and think it's gonna need a leap of faith, y'know?'

'Just like I kept faith in Cetus when everyone else said leave it.'

'Like I had faith in you, Israelite, even when you sent us down a dozen dry wells. You need to keep doing your job, Aaron, trust me to do mine.'

It felt to Aaron like his mere smidgen of dissent had done enough to revive Paxton's ornery style of reminding Aaron of his place. And he had felt a strong urge to show Paxton how perhaps he might be better valued – closer to his own estimation – in some other place.

In high anticipation, he drives to Stoneybrook Park, just a little leafy way out of the city centre near the banks of the Dee, proposed site of the new Institute.

It is indeed a construction site: dust in the air, site safety placards, hard-hat dispensation, the skeleton girders of a main building beside two hollow ten-storey towers of poured concrete with uniform blank gaps for fenestration. A gaunt Aberdeen sky does nothing to lift the scene.

Maurice Ziskind is coming at him across duckboards, beady-eyed and gaunt, short and black-suited. Aaron's hand is pumped hard. 'Aaron, welcome to the Institute. Cold today, huh?'

He leads Aaron to a Portakabin and hands across a desk some well-rendered artist's interpretations of how the finished Institute will look – thronged by slender student figures on some future sunlit day. Next, he is shown colour-coded site plans and layouts. He notes the meagre size of the library, finds himself wondering obscurely how different such a grid might look if it were laying out a prison.

'So' – Aaron ponders the larger blocks of colour – 'there are to be Schools of Geoscience, Engineering, Chemistry, Maths and Physics, and . . . ?'

'Business Science. Which I will direct.'

'The idea of a new geology lab is really exciting to me.'

'Yeah? That's terrific. Though, understand, we'd expect your gifts could be better deployed than in a classroom.'

'I'm a little confused, you mean — ?'

'The big excitement for us is oil, Aaron. How could it not be, right here and now? For me, career opportunities are what colleges are for. My vision is a place for vocational teaching that gives the oil industry a whole pipeline of new hires. An Academy for Oil, where students get boots on and see a working oil rig! Now, for that we've got to partner with businesses, and there your experience and contacts—'

Aaron has raised a hand; he just must. 'Professor, just how much research would you see me doing in this post?'

'Doctor Strang, it's up to you, but not "on" you. You get me? We don't want you to have to give up well-paid work you do elsewhere. But the oil companies are crying out for advice on solutions to immediate problems, advice you know how to give, and if you could give it here to our students—'

Not again. His spirits through the floor, all Aaron is thinking of now is how to remove himself from his room.

'So what do you think to the plans, Doctor?'

'In all honesty, Maurice? They look to me a bit like a nice walk spoiled.'

Sat in the tearoom by the Marischal Aaron has thought very hard about what to tell Dottie – an account that might not dismay her, might even repair his own hurt pride. But he is struggling. Now through the window he sees her in the street, exiting a Mini Cooper, at its wheel some mild fellow whom she kisses, before darting through the drizzle to Aaron's table.

'I'm afraid I misjudged, Dottie, I got carried away . . . I won't be joining this new institute. Meaning that I couldn't take you on and supervise you. In any case, that institute won't be the right environment for someone as talented as you. It can't compare with Aberdeen.'

It pains him to see her disappointment.

'But, Dottie, I shouldn't be supervising anyone . . . I'm not so sure any more how much I know myself. If you were with me you wouldn't flourish the way you should.'

He is conscious of feeling noble; but she shows him a shrugging, perplexed sort of a smile. 'Well, this is not . . . Sorry, I'm a bit upset, I suppose. I had hopes.'

'If you resent me now, you're right to. But please be assured you won't lose out. The best way I can help you is give you the best reference. I would only say – perhaps be wary of offshore? Think hard if it's the world for you.'

'I've a good idea how tough it is. I'm not deterred.'

'I know you have ambition. I'm saying, don't sell it cheaply. You don't belong to someone just because they pay your way.' But Aaron winces inwardly at the sound of this, and wonders if it is truly Dottie for whom he intends the advice.

'You're right, I have ambition. If you don't have that, then yes, you probably need to do something else.'

'You really want it? To get into that world?'

'Yes. Didn't you?' She smiles and shakes her head. 'You're a funny fish, Aaron.'

He realises something between them has shifted: she seems to be regarding him as somehow . . . not younger, of course, but perhaps less senior? She had wanted him for a thing that, when push came to shove, he could not provide. But she will move on – of that, he is sure. There is a maturity about her, of a sort he might still need himself? Aaron stands and offers his hand, and Dottie Blair does him the favour of shaking it.

September 1972
Castle Drummond

'Tovarich, if you're not busy on Friday I would love to get your eye on the work in progress. And your company, of course.'

Mark is free, as it happens, and he is undeniably curious. But there are also a few things he reckons they ought to discuss.

Beneath overcast, spit-spotting skies the drive is fairly dreary, miles of flat farmland after the Forth Bridge; but then – at last and as directed – Mark finds a long meandering lane hemmed by drystone walls and blackthorn, and around one final bend lies a sight to see: the wrought-iron entrance gate to Rathmullo Castle, drawn aside for a visitor.

Nosing the car up the muddy tree-lined track Mark is pleased to see the marks of disrepair to which Ally had referred ruefully in his invitation. Long grass and wild shrubbery are overgrown all around, scaffolding is erected, a forklift and a generator stand near. The stone walls have a well-weathered look, and really it seems more tower house than castle – a retreat for a lord rather than the fortress of a king. Still, it stands tall and broad and commanding, and it has parapets and battlements, and it is now the weekend residence of his properly wealthy old schoolfriend – who comes forward now from behind a big arched wooden entrance door, hand outstretched, clad in what Mark can only assume is his rural drag of cardigan, flat cap and baggy corduroys.

'Sadly we've not got a douce day, comrade, but you'll be able to see the basic shape of her. And the rain is good for the heather. Sure, a man goes mad if he sees not the heather once a year.'

'Och now, would those be the immortal words of . . . ?'

Ally removes the cap and claps it to his breast. 'Sir Walter Scott.'

Beckoning Mark in, he pauses at the doorway and digs a finger into the mortar of the wall, dislodging a thick cord of moss. 'This all needs doing before we can repoint. Perhaps you can give me a hand in the morning? I'm being urged to have it harled, but then it's going to look like some damn reformed church, not Castle Drummond . . .'

The grand tour does nothing to dispel Mark's wonder and mild envy. In the living room there is an odour of damp off the stone walls, and the fireplace is a charred shell with the wind moaning down its chimney. But the space is double-height, its ceiling vaulted, lit like a painting by tall windows. And there are antique Chesterfield sofas arranged around the hearth, a twenty-foot Persian rug across the stone floor, sawn logs stacked and ready to burn. The few pictures hung are hunting scenes, and a stuffed grouse stands perplexedly on a mahogany console table, leading Mark to suspect Ally is play-acting his role somewhat. But he is doing so with his usual elan, leading Mark up stone wheel stairs, past window openings with stone seats, to a terrace where a low iron brazier keeps watch over the battlements and the pastures of Rathmullo beyond. 'We should light the fire tonight,' says Ally, doffing his cap, 'so that our countrymen know to beware the warden of the English Marches.'

Upon their descent Ally remarks, 'Your sleeping quarters require a little fixing, but you'll be fine, just don't tell me you need hot water.'

'Such a challenge you've set yourself here.'

'I'm in danger of employing more people here than at the bank. But it's never boring. Now, I propose we go fetch fish and chips from the village, and I have a fine bottle or two picked out to get us merry.'

Soon they are strapped into the leather seats of the Spider coupé that Ally was keeping stashed behind the scaffolding; and within six seconds they have gone from nought to sixty. Great sport, for sure – though stirring again in Mark that uneasy feeling that for too long he has been riding on coattails. Still, he knows that in the spirit of the visit he ought to sit on his own news a while longer.

A mellow, smoky smell of burning wood is in the air, and Ally is sliding toward horizontal on the sofa, his glass of Chateau Angelus cradled on his chest. Mark decides the time is come.

'So . . .' And he rummages in the holdall at his feet to retrieve the cardboard tube, from which he produces and unfurls an A3 poster with a saltire emblem over the legend IT'S SCOTLAND'S OIL.

Under his fringe Ally's dark gaze exudes schoolmasterly disapproval. 'Are you telling me this is this your handiwork, Mark?'

'I just made a few suggestions . . .'

'Good grief.' Ally hauls himself upright.

'It's a fairly obvious slogan, I'd say. No sane man would deny the oil is the big issue for how Scotland gets governed from now. What it would mean—'

'Mark, I know some people want to argue these things ad nauseam. But I can tell you an awful lot of Scots really aren't that bothered.'

'But it bothers you . . . ?'

Ally's tone is patient, though. 'Listen, I'm sure what you've got there will get a lot of people good and riled. But when the oil was found, it didn't just suddenly annul the Act of Union. It had been there for a million years, it doesn't belong to Scotland, it belongs to the powers that be in the age that had the wit to go and get it. And that was never in a million years going to be Scotland.'

Then he sits back, sighing, avuncular again. 'I suppose I'm still just a little bewildered, Mark, that you've gone in so hard on this side.'

'What side are you on again, Ally?' Mark is trying to keep the mood puckish.

'My side, Mark.'

'Well then, you're not going to like this any better.'

'Oh lord . . .'

'A couple of the movers and shakers in the party have asked me if I'd fancy getting more involved. Putting myself forward as a candidate, even, for Westminster. I said I'd have a think, if that's what the executive wants.'

Ally is looking at him truly dubiously now. 'As bad as that? You're going to stand up and say what's on that poster like you believe it? Dear God, Mark . . . Seriously, we've to suffer you whizzing round shopping centres with a loudhailer?'

'I think I'll be quite adept at the hand-shaking and the baby-kissing.'

'You're a bit inexperienced on the baby front, no? I'm sure you'll know how to give an interview. But you're setting yourself up for a fall, tovarich.'

'Why? Seriously? You know I don't do things lightly. Why go on about the nonsense bit of it?'

'Mark, you're a journalist, a fine one, and you've made a name being intensely critical of politicians. How are you going to feel on the other side? It's not a debating society, it's a bloody dirty game. And tell me this – is Shona delighted by your plan?'

Mark is tempted to lie, to assert that his wife, yes, has her differences with the SNP but unshakeable faith in him – nothing close to Shona's actual and thoroughly sceptical position.

Instead he says, a little sullenly: 'Why does that matter?'

'Oh, Mark. Because the two of you have to be partners in an enterprise. That's the proper course of things – love, then children, then taking care of family business. Instead you want to make her a political widow.'

'I see little enough of her as it is, and that's her choice, actually.'

'And if you do this, Mark, then what'll be your collateral? If, God forbid, it weren't to go so well?'

'Al, I don't care, I just have to try it.' Mark is vexed: they are both tired and a little worse for wine, but the thought of a real rift with Ally is too terrible to contemplate.

'You know, I always remember, when we were at school we shared predictions with each other once – about the things we'd go on to do in life?'

Ally appears droll again. 'What, did we read each other's tea-leaves?'

'We were drinking Cokes laced with Scotch, as I remember. And you said to me, with great certainty, that I would write and debate and argue for ideas. It was so inspiring to me, I've never forgotten. Well, that's what I'm doing here, Al.'

'I said that? What did you predict for me?'

For a split-second Mark flounders, until the obvious answer descends, and he throws his arms wide. 'This!'

Ally grunts in amusement. Mark feels tension dissipated – surer now of his bed for night.

October 1972
Re-apprenticed

'Mate,' Bob enquires. 'Have you got any toenail clippers?'

Robbie does not. They are each getting prepared for the Saturday dance, only Bob is going about it a bit more determinedly – best jeans, wet comb, Old Spice – while Robbie stretches out on his bunk, smoking. He has cut down lately, enjoying them less, feeling that everyone at the Glinrock yard maybe smokes more than is good for them – the welders especially, their lungs taking the extra brunt of the evil heat and fumes made by all the work they do inside pipes.

He will troop down with Bob for the bus to the community hall. *You have to do something*; but he doesn't anticipate much of a night. He knows how unwelcome the hairy horde will be – gadgies after a fuck, some likely to settle for a fight, but most only after as much as they can pour down their necks, loading up for hungover Sunday purgatory. And Robbie sees himself apart from that horde; as an increasingly austere individual – head down, punch the clock, say little to very few, keep out of bother. Not quite Torrance McVey holed up in the manse, but still.

His mind, really, is fixed on Monday morning. The site contractor has posted a new rota for training up welders. A fair few boys have arrived from Clydeside lately, fleeing the shutdown yards, and a door has opened but could soon be closing. Robbie knows he must try to nip through it in time.

He stands before Mr Morrison in the personnel cabin, formally lodging his interest.

'I did a bit of welding on my dad's croft, and at Blaikdoon sawmill.'

'Aw aye? What kind of jobs?'

'I'd, y'know, fix a broke shaft on a hay-baler, the draw bar hold on a cart. Put a broke shovel back together.'

'Farmer's boy, eh?' Mr Morrison shakes his head tiredly. 'We've a muckle too many of them as it is . . .'

Morrison explains that he will need to get himself paired with a welder on site so as to get some learning on the job – someone willing to carry him, someone he won't annoy too much. And he is told to be sure and look in on a talk about current practices in the main workshop at lunchtime.

Robbie duly troops in to this session, finding several dozen disgruntled men already in the hut. He notes redheaded Evie Charlton, looking as narked as everyone else. The speaker has come up from the prestigious supplies firm of Baker Tools in Aberdeen: a gentleman named Sam Lietzske, a Yank in a check shirt and hunting jacket.

'Guys, my business in Aberdeen has been going great guns since oil got struck, and I love it here, I love my work. But, sometimes, what's good for me isn't necessarily what's best for the wider industry. Let me explain that. I sell a bunch of high-end tools, and one of these is a machine for gouging out a bad weld. And I have to tell you, I've been selling an awful lot of those machines to this yard . . .'

Robbie sees that Lietzske's patiently upbeat demeanour is in no way lifting the surly mood of the room.

'I wanted to know why, so I was real glad to be invited up today for a look-see at your weld shops here. Now, understand, I'm not casting aspersions on any one man's work. But I have seen some low-quality stuff – I'm talking substandard beads. And a yard this size can't afford to get a rep for poor workmanship, that's bad news for all of us, fellas. And, uh, ladies.'

Lietzske starts to expound on issues of weld spatter, porosity, inadequate fusion, shallow penetration. It sails over Robbie's head, but he takes the lesson that the yard needs to do better, and he will have to dedicate himself to this task, before he has even begun.

330

Robbie has kept his eye on Evie Charlton; as the meeting breaks up she is more or less the first one out the door, and he must put a step on to catch her up outside.

'Evie, aye? Could I have a wee word?'

'About what? You another one wanting to tell me how to weld, eh?'

'Naw, naw, you've got it round the wrong way . . .'

She stops as to hear him out. He explains his mission respectfully, asking if she would be willing to apprentice him. Judging by her face, though, each word seems to land worse than the previous.

'Aw God. Listen – Robbie? – I work by myself. That's my way, I dinnae want to be bothered. I'm not here to carry anybody. The Yank fella's right, there's too much bollox welding goes on here already.'

He had hoped a woman might be easy enough to reason with. Now, though, he feels himself faced by immovable resolution, underscored by her critical gaze, the bold set of her features, the brush-fire shade of her hair.

'Please, Evie? Give us a chance? I promise you I'm a grafter, I don't mess about. If I get up your nose you can bin me, no fear, I'll not cry about it.'

'Why's it got to be me? There's fifty lads you could bother with this.'

'Cos I've watched you work, I see how good you are. I just know I'll learn it right from you if you'll let me.'

Robbie has surprised himself by his own conviction; and he sees he has succeeded in making it a bit harder for Evie Charlton, who chews her lip unhappily.

'Will you listen? So long as you'll listen, we can give it a try, see how it goes. If Morrison's fine, come see me for my shift tomorrow.'

He pitches up on the stroke of seven in a padded jacket and boots, with gloves and iron visor issued him at the office, plus a stick welding kit of electrode and power-pack that feels familiar enough. Evie is already taking a grinder to the edges of a pair of two-inch pipe lengths, set up on stands as to mate. He spies what she has laid out nearby on a collapsible table – straight-edges and callipers and whatnot – and he reminds himself it is his wish to learn proper, no slacking, whatever the rigmarole.

She looks him up and down. 'If you're working wi' me, you work safe, okay?'

'I know safety, Evie, I've worked a sawmill, I was on the rigs.' He is surprised to have given away that fact having shielded it so carefully up to now. But Evie betrays no interest, her only concern that he don goggles plus an extra respirator mask, which snaps tightly around his face. He is beginning to feel encased, unrecognisable, even to himself.

'You've checked your leads? Okay, you see them there lengths? Drop your hood and strike me an arc, show me how you put them together.'

Robbie fires up his electrode and enjoins with confidence, sparks flying, old muscle memories stirring.

'Naw, naw . . .' She bats his shoulder with surprising brusqueness. 'Get closer, your arc's too long, that's how you spatter. Might do you for fixing a shovel, it'll no' pass with me.'

Chastened, he tries to do better. Moments later she grips him at the wrist, directing him. 'You've *got* to shift your angle more as you get into it.'

When his effort is complete, he is worried – by the state of the weld but as much by Evie's hard look as she measures him: the line of her mouth, the lift of her chin. She seems not to meet his eye, but he gathers he must be looking at her a bit persistently, for when she asks him what is the optimum current on his power-pack and he stands in a moment's perplexity, she scolds him: 'The answer's no' written on my nose, Robbie.'

'Watch this,' she counsels; then takes up her electrode and applies it. A sharp, steady frying sound arises from her labour. He notes her deftness, the capable speed in her hands, her finessing adjustments as she goes. Then she snaps up her hood and studies her handiwork, and he ceases his sidelong study of her, focusing instead upon her bead. Its ripples have a pleasing uniformity; her flair for molten metal clear by the subtlest evidence.

'You mind how it's good and shirred at the back end? A nice wee low oval? That's what you're after.'

'Aye.' Robbie nods. 'It's lovely, Evie.' He really means it.

She shrugs. 'Like anything, you get the feel of it by doing it.'

She swears by two hours on and then fifteen-minute breaks. So, after two hours she indicates he should get on his way over to the *Vergina*'s refectory, while she settles down on the grass with her flask and piece.

'I bunk in a caravan, yonder. I bring my own, I don't fetch for others.'

But he has no need for refreshment, only a few questions for her. So she suffers his company a while longer, the two of them side by side in their welding armour, looking out onto the Firth.

'How'd you get into this, Evie? The welding?'

She answers to the sandwich in her hand, in between bites. 'I always loved fire, even when I was wee. Loved to see stuff go up – bonfires and that. At school it bugged me how the lads got to do metalwork and the girls had to just bloody knit and cook. I kicked up such a fuss, they let me have a go. And I just carried on, y'know? Loved it.'

Robbie rather marvels at her resilience. 'It's a hard old job for you.'

'No harder for me than another.'

'But you get some stick, and for nothing. I've seen it.'

'I've heard worse. I've three brothers.'

'Used to being around the men, eh?' The moment he says this it sounds wrong; but Evie seems not to notice.

'It's girls who are weird to me. Can't figure them out. When we were bairns I'd to knock around with my brothers cos I'd no one else. Even at school I was just "Stevie's sister". But I don't need to be hanging round loads of people. Never have.'

'You're enough for yourself, eh? I've got a pal like you.'

This doesn't appear to interest her. And it is really starting to pain him now. He can tell she is a serious person, running her life on clear lines. He would wish her to see he is serious, too, if she only knew him a little better. So why is everything he says to her *so fucking shite*?

'What do your brothers do for work?'

'Jings, am I down the police station here or what? Will I be getting the life story of Robbie next?' She stands and brushes crumbs away. 'C'mon, let's get back to it. Check your gear, get your goggles on.'

He rises a bit more reluctantly. 'Listen, I understand it's safety and all, but have I really gotta wear the goggles *and* the visor?'

He instantly regrets the insubordination; yet she seems almost to smile. 'Your choice, pal, but if I'd eyelashes long as yours I'd no' want to be burning them off.'

Momentarily flummoxed, he has an urge to assure her there is nothing wrong with her lashes. But she is moving round him already, and he knows he must follow, for all his consternation – knows, too, that he must get his head on straight, concentrate, do better than the first time, if he's to earn the approval of this one.

Saturday night, and Robbie trudges off the *Vergina* gangway toward the minibus, trailing behind Bob in his best gear. By the door of the bus, some sixth sense moves him to look back whence he came – and he sees Evie Charlton coming down that same gangway, carrying a tartan cake tin under her arm.

He wonders, helplessly: *Was she looking for me? Did she bring me something?*

In the next moment that is made ridiculous, for one of the ship's Greek lads in his smart whites has appeared and is waving to her. She

334

waves back, then Robbie studies her retreating figure en route back to the caravan site.

'That chef boy, Adonis, he's a sly one.' The reprobate Jack has sidled up to join Robbie. 'Always giving that wee girl her dinner. Makes her the special moussaka. Oh aye, the special . . .'

'She's been teaching Robbie the welding,' Bob chips in.

'That so? You see them jugs on her? Pity she's a ginger. She'd still get it, but.'

Through the bus ride Robbie can barely manage his black mood. Younger guys around him act the idiot like they're off on a wild jaunt, and he can't be doing with them. At the dance he drinks whisky steadily, like medication, and dislikes every tune the band plays. He is approached very persistently by a girl who must be seventeen. 'Do you not like me?' she asks plaintively. He wants to be gentle with her, but he needs her also to understand what he knows too well: that the answer to that question can't always be the one the heart yearns for.

Meantime, it is kicking off at his table.

'SNP? Fuck *off*. "Everything'll be braw for Scotland!" Fuck *off*. We'll be a piss wee country trying to get by on fuck-all.'

'You say so?'

'Aye! It's like you talking your shite to a wee girl dinnae know any better, "It'll just be you for me, babe, no one else, all for you." All fucken *what*?'

'You say so?'

The fight might start early tonight. Robbie can't be bothered to stop it. If needs be, he will join in. It's not yet Sunday but he is certainly in purgatory.

PART VI
DIVISIONS

February 1973
A Breach

One of those dinners where it's a relief to see desserts if only to be done . . . Joe has stopped refilling his wine glass since drink is merely souring his mood. The evening had seemed to him ill-starred, and now halfway through it is not feeling to him like a success. Perhaps the failure is down to him: possibly he didn't wish it otherwise. And that suspicion of himself has got him feeling yet more out of sorts.

The setting has proved a factor, for sure. His choice that they reserve the private dining room of the Òrach, perfect for the size of the party; but clearly Andrew would have preferred somewhere more traditional. From the moment they crossed the threshold he has been looking around him very perplexed, at the chevron flooring, the Deco sconces, the strange chandelier. At table he has writhed a bit in his tall-backed chair.

Andrew surely can't take issue with the company. A table of nine, with the honouree and patriarch at its head; Sheila Balfour by his side; Garth and Bryony; Angela and Bodie; Joe and Isla; and Walter, unaccompanied. But maybe Andrew's own kin strike him now as an ill-sorted mob, maybe he would have wished for a few more cronies, the old timers from his new association. On this point Joe recognises a tincture of resentment in himself.

Ever since agreeing to be vice-president of a 'Federation of Trawler Owners' opposed to Britain entering the Common Market, Andrew has carried himself as if the Order of the Garter had been bestowed on him – even while he speaks freely of this new group as 'the resistance'. The whole bloody notion of a dinner to mark the distinction was Sheila's, suggested to Joe with both annoying persistence and the heavy implication he should take charge of the details. And now

Sheila sits there muttering into Andrew's ear, making resigned and displeased faces, his father's confidante. In Joe's view the situation with Andrew's long-time secretary is not appropriate; but he cannot say so, with Isla now by his side, acknowledged as his girlfriend, her hand on his lap and her own confidences in his ear . . . an arrangement at which Joe would have looked askance if anyone else were up to it.

But Isla is here to stay; whereas Joe and Bodie have for a while wanted Sheila out of her boardroom role, into which she was only slotted for convenience – one of those sprats to catch a mackerel. She has hardly grown into its functions, but has certainly made her nest there, with her worrying permanence and attentiveness to the dignities of 'Mr Killday'. Joe is aware he is not alone in misgivings over the Andrew-and-Sheila show. Only tonight over drinks he heard Garth and Bryony laughing mirthlessly at the idea of 'the second Mrs Andrew Killday'. To Joe it is no joke. Walter, typically, isn't saying anything, but Joe sees unease in his eldest brother's eyes, too.

For this dog-end phase of the night, though, Garth seems to be indulging their father's pet hatred, for they are in cahoots over brandies. Bryony is stifling a yawn: surely in her head she is already home and settling up with the babysitter. But her husband is cursing some tale he's been told about new Common Market compliances incumbent on skippers for reporting of catches. 'They're talking about fines, prison even.'

'I know, Garth, it's a disgrace.' Andrew nods, well pleased. 'You mind how it starts. First one wee step, then another. That's how they fool you. The road to perdition starts with a wee step . . .'

It is eating at Joe to say some things he knows he must never say. Bodie, too, when they make eye contact, has the look of one near the end of his tether. Right now, though, he is having some quietly discordant exchange with Angela.

'. . . and it astounds me, what the politicians will do for the sake of oil, when they'll not lift a finger for the fishermen. Disgrace is the word.'

340

Give away over with your last stand. The Common Market's the fact of it now. With all we're doing to get out of fishing it'll hardly matter anyway.

But then Bodie surprises Joe by getting to his feet, glass in hand. 'If I may be so bold – perhaps one more toast? To the Devane shipyard! Our success story of the year, now under our management and soon to have a new slipway.'

Amid the muted clinking Andrew does not drink. 'I'll call that yard a success,' he pronounces, 'the day we use it to build a fishing boat for ourselves.'

Bodie chuckles as if scolding. 'Och, Andrew! Is that really the spirit?'

'All very well people sitting round this fancy table slapping themselves on the back. It's hard-working fishermen make this business what it is. What do they get in return? Big money spent, aye – money won by fishing. But when they look at where it all goes, they might well ask why there's no effort made to improve the ships they go to sea in.'

Joe has decided: he does not want this row, not now. 'Da, if the budget will stand it next year we might look at a new boat for inshore. A deep-water boat isn't economical, we've discussed this.'

'So we own a shipyard but build no ships.'

'We are building ships, Andrew,' Bodie responds. 'Supply boats, for the rigs. That's the point of Devane.'

Joe winces at his phrasing, for he sees its effect on Andrew, who looks sharply at him. 'The purchase of that yard wasn't argued for that way. But then, I've wondered a while at how things get done if I'm not looking.'

The hush round the table is now indigestive. Angela is staring fixedly at her lap. Bryony is whispering in Garth's ear. But no one present seems to want to stop the dispute.

'Da, I've always said what's on my mind plain to your face, however daft it might sound . . .' Joe hopes to raise a smile. No such luck.

'I know you like your own mind well enough, Joseph. It would be handy if you'd more of a mind to others, them who raised you.'

Joe finds the old set of his father's face and that admonishing tone intolerable. 'I was raised, Da, not to freeze like a rabbit when a business decision needs taking. That's what I'm doing.'

'You're right, y'know, Andrew.' Bodie sails in blithely. 'An awful lot of things have conspired to make it harder and harder for fishing. It could make you weary of it.'

'Not me, boy, never,' Andrew scoffs.

Bodie leans forward sharply. 'But can you not see? Fishing is only going to be less and less of our economy from here – that's why we're moving out of it.'

Joe sees Garth throw a give-me-strength look to the ceiling.

Andrew, though, is looking only at Joe. 'You hear that, Joseph? Is that one of them things you said "plain to my face"?'

'Da, we're not doing that entirely. But in part, yes – it's for the good of the business—'

Andrew bangs the table, causing Sheila to flinch. 'What in God's name is Killday Fishing if we don't fish?'

Joe fires back at the same irate volume. 'If fishing were all we had then we'd have nothing. We'll not be bloody fishermen forever.'

'Joseph' – to Joe's horror Sheila has decided to weigh in – 'you know your father speaks from experience, and—'

'Sheila, your opinion's not required here.' The retort is from Bodie, and Joe knows it to be poison. Andrew puts his hand over Sheila's on the tabletop while glowering at Joe.

'Joseph, do you dare sit there and say I've not the right to argue for how things are done in my own company?'

Without looking aside from his father's eyes Joe can sense the nod of Bodie's head that says *Yes. Do it. Don't falter.*

'Argue all you want, Da. You put me here, you asked me to do this, when you knew damn well change was coming, and you promised I'd be given my head. All I've done is use it. But, Da, it's not your company any more, you're wrong to act like it is. I'm in charge, the board backs me. If you want to find that out a harder way then . . .'

'Do you imagine for one minute' – Andrew speaks slowly but fiercely – 'that you can kick me out of the company that bears my name?'

'Andrew, Andrew' – Joe sees the gleam now in Bodie's eye – 'I don't think you've been paying attention. We have a board now. Each man on it has a vote as good as the next.'

Joe feels all eyes upon him, and a sick, guilty flutter in his chest, telling him he must try to salvage something of the evening. 'Da,' he ventures, as equably as he feels capable, 'if you're so set against the strategy we've agreed, then maybe you should be putting your energies into other projects. Just like we're celebrating tonight . . .'

Andrew, though, is shaking his head, looking around the table as to ask if they have ever heard such claptrap. 'Thick as thieves, eh? Thick as thieves . . . My God, Joseph, if you were not my kin—'

'Then what, Andrew? What?' Bodie cuts in, still seeming to find this unholy mess amusing. 'It's a wicked world. We've all got to stake our claim in it, do what we need to get on. You know that, of course you do! You cut your own brother off at the knees just so you could have your way, and sure you've lived okay with that—'

Joe feels an inner lurch at the offence – Andrew shoves his chair back, is moving round the table to Bodie, ham fists clenched, and Garth, too, is up in an instant, but so is Bodie, even Walter – Joe is fractionally late to follow. Now Walter approaches Bodie, palms out in placation to bar the way, and Bodie lays hands on Walter's chest so firmly that Walter topples to the carpet, long limbs everywhere, his glasses pinwheeling away across the floor – a sight Joe might think comical if it weren't so terrible, semaphored by the hand Sheila claps to her mouth.

Garth has a staying arm on his father but with his other he jabs a finger at Bodie. 'Get out, you, y'bastard! I've never bloody liked you, and I was right. Get out!'

Joe can't tell if Garth's words have impacted Bodie at all, but then he looks to Joe, and Joe knows he has nothing to give. Now Angela rises, her pale face as woeful as Joe has ever seen. 'Ray, you must apologise to Da. You must!'

Joe nods. 'Angela's right, Ray.'

Bodie's brazen face is unchanged. 'But I can think them, right?' Then for a moment or so he contemplates the ceiling. 'Oh, let's not play this game. I think it's clear how we feel about each other.'

Briefly Joe fears Bodie will have yet more to say on that score.

'I'm a man for change, and that means ending things when they've run their course. If I can't take my own advice then I'm a regular hypocrite. And we can't be having that. It's clear we're at an end here.' Bodie looks at Joe closely then at his wife. 'Angela? You can leave with me now if you choose. It's really up to you.'

Angela's red-eyed look, the ragged line of her mouth, seem to say only that he should nevermore suggest such a thing.

Bodie half bows, hand on chest. 'Very well, my dear. I am going to the Gardner. For now. I'll be in touch in due course.'

Bodie straightens his wristwatch and exits.

Amid the wreckage Sheila is urging Andrew to sit and be calmed, and Bryony and Isla are half crouching and kneeling either side of a weeping Angela.

Garth, having helped Walter to his feet, catches Joe's eye and makes an irate gesture toward the door. Presently the three brothers are out in the narrow corridor, Walter massaging his chest frowningly, Garth pacing as if caged.

'What the hell possessed you, Joe? How did you let that happen?'

'Garth, it happened because people feel how they feel.'

'And how long's all that been your feeling, Joe? Did you not feel like sharing it with your own brothers?'

'It doesn't get shared so easy. Ask Uncle Allan.'

'Stop talking like Bodie, man! You were raised to know things are done by agreement.'

'Don't you be talking to me like Da.'

'Eh, you want to fight me and all, Joe?'

But there is no violence in Joe whatever, only the weary sense that there can be no end to their fruitless dispute.

Joe is sitting on an imitation Louis Quartorze banquette, in a secluded corner of the foyer when Isla's high-heeled pumps enter his low field of vision. He looks up.

'Ah . . . God. What happened?'

She nestles down beside him, very calm and assured, he feels.

'The right thing, Joe. Trust me, I've seen this in families. You get scenes, you get fights. People can be hurt, but . . . sometimes things get said and it's for the better for everyone.'

Then he feels his face cupped in both of her cool hands and she kisses him with a surprising force. He is taken aback, too, by the strength of her gaze.

'You've been very patient all this time. Your father's wrong. Sometimes you do have to keep a thing to yourself. Ray's got an idiot mouth on him. But that doesn't mean he's wrong.' She takes Joe's hand, firmly. 'You're clever. So keep being clever. Do what you have to, for the future. I want to be part of it, Joe. With you.'

Isla inclines her forehead to his until they touch. He feels an uncommon affinity with her. Selfishly, he has been feeling the loss of a real ally; now he is reminded that he has another.

April 1973

In the Springtime

Early to rise, attacking the day with purpose, Robbie takes two aspirin, wraps bandage gauze round his palms, knees and elbows, and inspects the small burn near his left eye – *What you get*, he rues, *for leaving off your goggles*. Then he straps on the lumbar support belt that makes him feel a fighter: middleweight champion welder of Glinrock Bay. He intends to be first through the door for the morning meeting with the foreman, first into the depot for supplies. It has been this way a while, and he doesn't kid himself that he has acquired the full set of skills over which his workmates have taken years. But it is the means by which he aims to prove to Evie Charlton that he is a serious person.

For the whole thing has turned serious, no question. He is not her assigned little helper any more, and once the blueprints are shared out the days don't tend to provide obvious work-based excuses for him to seek her company. He might see her often enough in passing; but so might anyone. And so often yearns to see her face and hear her voice that he must contrive to be near where she is – even while feeling a little sick about it. Amazing, and debilitating, that she has come to mean all this to him. Foolish, too? Is he off in the clouds, some gowk too blind to see? However you might cut it, it's how he feels.

The additional sting of the thing: never has a woman seemed so heedless of what he modestly reckons to be his charm. Possibly none of that means a damn to her. Baffled at first, he has been drawn into severe introspection and a whole new sense of unworthiness.

He must win her. He must have a plan that can work. He has tried everything, short of asking her out.

The trouble has been that there is never the time, never the privacy, the bantering and the scrutiny all too relentless. Her manners and habits have made it so much harder. His private investigations have established that no man around has a claim on her, not even Adonis of the 'special moussaka'. Still, he feels certain he must get her in private before making his case.

This Saturday, then. Big dance. Let the eejits get on the bus. He will stay home, and he will call on Evie – bearing some kind of offering, nothing too fancy or heavy but bespeaking his feelings – the precise item to be decided.

Dusk, and it is with unnerved and uncertain steps that he picks his way over the claggy ground to her caravan. The offering? Well, it just has to be two takeaway pasties from the Ferry Hotel.

'Alright, Evie?'

Low light and the radio on inside her sanctum. She in jeans and a red tee shirt, almost daringly unclad to his eyes, her work armour removed.

'Hullo, Robbie. You not for the dance?'

'Didnae fancy it. My back's acting up a bit. Too much welding, eh? All hunched up in them pipes.'

'That's cos you don't mind your posture.'

Yeah, yeah . . . 'I wondered if you might fancy something for your supper, I have these fresh.'

'That's awful good of you. Thanks.'

She accepts the paper bag but makes no other move at the top of the short steps; and he's unsure of how to read her face in the poor light, but feels a dire need to try some other gambit.

'And would you fancy a game of pool in the rec?' He knows she plays.

'Could do. Aye. Shall we have these first? I'll put the stove on for a brew.'

And with that she bids him entry to the sanctum, and after straightening up through the doorway he wipes his boots carefully

347

before taking another step across the vinyl floor. Her habitat is well-tended and fresh-scented, no clutter in the mini-kitchenette where Evie makes tea, her work overalls neatly hung between kitchen and living space. The most womanly thing in the caravan, maybe, is the raucous singer on the radio.

'You like that? Janis Joplin . . . Boy, she was something.'

'Didn't know you liked music.'

'You never asked. Asked me all else . . . Yeah, love it. My brothers always had records, all different stuff, rock, country, rhythm and blues . . .'

She hands him a mug and plonks down on her ottoman bed opposite the built-in chair onto which Robbie lowers himself, and she sets their supper between them. He smiles and looks about, wanting to seem appreciative.

On the boxy head-cum-bedside of her ottoman – next to a spray of wildflowers in a jam-jar – he sees a tall, framed photograph of a young man, dark-haired and open-shirted, the sight plunging Robbie's heart directly into his boots.

'Who's that?' he asks into his mug.

'That's Davie. My fella.'

'Davie . . . Welder, is he?'

'Engineer. He's out in Tanzania, been there five months. Mining for gold and diamonds.' She offers a fancy-that smile, then munches into her pastie.

'That's a serious thing to be doing.'

'He's a serious lad. He's a wee bit older than me. Savvy. Money's awful good. They give him a big house with a pool. Company town, y'know? Not like this one . . .'

'You didn't go out there with him?'

'We talked about it . . .'

Robbie, feeling the sharp trauma in his breast, would like to get up and pace about, run off the injury, free to curse out loud – rather than be nailed to this seat spouting niceties.

'So you want that game of pool?'

'Aye, quick one, Evie, eh?'

Evie plays pool with seriousness, too – plenty chalk on her cue-tip before every shot, eyes clouded by decision-making each time she stoops. And she strikes the white ball hard, frequently off a cushion. Robbie watches her in misery: so much a law onto herself. She's cheerful enough with him, but only about the game, which he rates as a waste of both their times while he stands there feeling a clown.

He is bent over a shot he hopes to sink to end the contest when she comes so close that she might take the shot for him.

'What's that round your neck?'

He misses the shot, then gives her a closer look at the trilobite fossil he wears on a silver chain, and he says a little of its provenance.

She seems bemused. 'However did you end up with a best pal like that?'

It nettles him, put like that; but he would like her to understand that much of who he is. As he relates a little of the story of him and Aaron, he realises anew how much of his life it amounts to. Their diving together as boys, their daft games, both of them losing their mothers young. How his cousin Morag got sweet on Aaron, to Aaron's blind panic. How Aaron was the dominie's son, and Mr Strang had helped Robbie at school. How they've always given one another a hand when in need – Robbie for Aaron most often on account of Aaron overreaching himself; Aaron for Robbie at times when Robbie has known he needed a kick up the backside.

Deeper into his rambling narrative Robbie becomes a little abashed; but it has seen them through a further frame, and Evie has listened more attentively and asked more of him than ever before.

'So different, the two of you. Funny.'

'Is it? Why does anyone get to be pals? Because you've a good opinion of someone. You're glad of their company. And you know they think the same and they'll do right by you.'

'Huh.' She looks at him so thoughtfully that he could believe all he said came as a terrific novelty to her. 'I don't think I've ever had a friend like that.'

'You could, Evie. You really could . . .' He has to chuckle, lousy as he feels. Truly she seems beyond his reach. And it is past time they returned their cues to the rack.

'What you up to tomorrow?' she asks at the kissing gate into the caravan site.

'Might have a wander up to Tarnwick. G'night, Evie.'

But come eleven the next morning Robbie has not summoned the energy to shift. He sits outdoors, quietly sorry for himself in the long grasses near the end of the spit, looking out on the Firth.

Then he sees her stomping toward him determinedly. Closer still and she is flushed, a colour in her cheeks not unlike the plum of her jersey, her whole demeanour suggesting agitation.

'Eh, Evie, y'alright?'

She summons a deep breath and glares at him. 'You picked your night, didn't you, just to – drop in on me, eh?'

'Are you angry wi' me? We'd an okay time, didn't we?'

'What right had you to go asking me so much about Davie?'

'Sorry, I just – I wanted to know, I suppose. I wish I'd known before.'

'Why?'

Robbie doesn't want to answer. He looks at her with all his heart – hopes she might understand, take pity. Possibly something registers, for she drops her shoulders and plonks down on the grass beside him.

'I've been walking around here all morning. Hardly slept last night. I'd to sit on my steps for a think, all the good that did . . .'

'Evie, what's—'

'I just called Davie. Okay? He's hard to get on Sundays but I got him. And I told him we'd to finish. Okay?'

'Okay,' says Robbie, believing this to be required of him.

'No, it's not okay. I feel rotten, right? Him six thousand miles away. But it's as well gettin' done. For the decision.' Her fingers worry at some blades of grass by her feet. 'Aw, I'm shit at this . . . Here's what. Sometimes, there's a thing you might like to happen. But instead you do stuff like . . . to near make sure it *doesn't* happen? You ever done that? Cos I've been doing it.' Now she looks directly at him. 'I like you, okay? I don't like many.'

'I like you, Evie,' he responds instantly, wholeheartedly.

'So?'

He is ill-prepared – and this is not proceeding in any way that he can recognise; yet the moment seems to call for some romantic gesture.

'Shall we maybe have a walk?'

He parks his cut-and-shut motor where the seafront cottages end, and they take the grassy coastal path north, progressing up the gentle slope, steadily attaining height over the water, their denimed legs brushing through overgrown reeds and ragwort. She links her arm in his. They have said little, and he is trusting she feels just as he does, which is that nothing needs saying that their closeness doesn't convey.

They reach the bluff, the gorsy clifftop overlooking the rocky basin where he and Aaron dived as boys. Below them the fretted sea seems to sparkle, and the shingle gleams. The sky has but a few stately clouds and birds swooping, playfully plummeting then rising. All is sunlit and quiet save for a sea-breeze that stirs the sward and carries the tang of salt to them.

'The sea's grand, isn't it? Don't you think?'

She smiles. 'I'm thinking how you did that job hundreds of miles out.'

She shivers slightly. He reaches and takes her hand. Her fingers close around his. He draws her to him, sharing their warmth, and they kiss gently.

'You're so bonny-looking,' she murmurs at his ear.

'You're lovely, Evie,' he whispers into hers.

'Don't say it just cos I've said it.'

'I mean it.'

She reclines in the grass, her red hair tumbling round her, chest rising and falling. He lowers himself next to her, kisses her mouth again, feeling her lips part; and the simple, joyous rush of desire as she presses her whole body into his.

Monday morning in the caravan, drawn curtains and weak yellowish light, oddly reminiscent to Robbie of his captivity on the Pecos . . . But today he feels liberated, awakened to soft rustling sounds in the room, tight for space yet at ease in the makeshift double bed. He studies the sight of Evie scooping herself into her sturdy brassiere, tugging her knickers up and over her lambent cluster of curls – the treasure he sought, the intimacy so much missed and coveted.

She brews them tea with her camp stove, fills up her thermos, and then they rush out to work, he with a breadcrust still in his mouth, his breeks barely zipped up. They start to run, she laces her fingers with his and clutches tight. As they race giddily across the ragged grasses Robbie feels as if together they might lift off the ground.

July 1973
The Consul-General

Mark doesn't care if his colleagues suspect he is slacking at his desk. It's not so uncommon to see his friend pictured in Edinburgh's top society gazette – tuxedoed and flute in hand amid bluebloods and muckety-mucks. But the company this time round is noteworthy.

Edinburgh's crème de la crème were out in force as the offices of the US Consulate in Regent Terrace played host to a Fourth of July party. The gathering had a dual purpose, marking a formal welcome to the new Consul-General, Mr Everett Wharton, the newest holder of an office open since 1798. Career diplomat Wharton has been seconded by the White House from Saigon . . .

CIA, thinks Mark instantly. Within seconds he is on the phone. Mr Drummond, though, is currently busy and will call back.

Amid balloons in the colours of the 'star-spangled banner', Mr Wharton's guests were treated to traditional American cuisine of corn dogs and T-bone steaks, with musical selections from the Tobacco Road Troubadours . . .

'You had a big night on July fourth, I see.'
'*Could you count my chins? Yes, that's me. It was a minor sort of occasion, I suppose.*'
'For quite a major figure.'
'*That consulate employs maybe three people and a dog. In the great sphere of American power I don't think it's a sought-after posting.*'
'Well then, a very big figure for a small post.'

'Forgive me, are you driving at something, tovarich?'

'Al, I'm just curious about this man.'

'We got along. He likes golf and whisky and salmon fishing. He's been all around the world, I daresay this job is his retirement treat . . . Listen, if you want an introduction I can make it, but you'll need to get yourself to Troon tomorrow.'

'What, the Open championship?'

'Third round. You've maybe forgotten the golfing promise of your youth, but surely the Scotsman still claims to cover games? Everett and I have an arrangement to watch the final pair together. If you can get yourself accredited you would be welcome to bump into us.'

'That . . . will be fine.' Mark is scribbling on the corner of a page, intending to hunt out a clippings file before day-end. He would bet money Wharton has been sent to keep an American eye on developments with oil, and the national question, to take a view on which dog the US ought to favour in the fight. This is exciting. Paris is worth a mass, and so Mark is going to the bloody golf.

'Just know, Mark, if you were to in any way disconcert the ambassador with inappropriate talk of politics then I'd take that poorly.'

'I will spectate respectfully, as a lover of the game, just hoping for a glimpse of the champion golfer of the year.'

'Piss off, Mark.'

On a drab morning, Mark parks up on a nearby beach, collects a pass from a busy hut and finds his way through the handsome stone clubhouse to the back of the bated crowd attending the first tee. Rain lies in puddles; anoraks, caps and shooting sticks abound. The board is up for the last pair: Weiskopf, nine under par, and Miller, minus six, both men beneath their striped umbrellas with an air about them of Ivy League varsity.

And there is Ally, stood by a smart gent who has, at his other flank, a very formidable fellow, likely armed. Mr Everett Wharton, surely, with a scholar's high forehead and the mouth and nose of a Roman bust. Ally gives Mark a munificent introduction, though Wharton looks preoccupied by the opening drives, on which he pronounces as they trudge off after the players.

'Miller's my man. Love his game. The aggression, how he attacks the stick. That confidence, you see it just in the way he strides the fairway.'

Instinctively Mark starts to favour the lanky, less cocksure Weiskopf. On the first green the fellow makes a hash of a too-delicate chip-shot, and Mark winces in sympathy to see a player of flair getting stymied and frustrated by the conditions.

'I sense,' says Wharton, 'you're rooting for Weiskopf?'

Mark shrugs. 'He swings the club beautifully for a tall lad. But I'd say he's playing against himself a bit, too? No disrespect to your man Miller.'

'None taken. My bet is Miller leads at day-end.'

'I'd say Weiskopf, by one.'

'Would you consider a small wager?'

'Oh, I'm just a penniless hack, Mr Wharton.'

'Everett, please.'

Ally intercedes. 'It's a day for whisky, how about the winner buys a round of the best malt in the member's bar after?' Mark, noting the least worst option, shakes on it.

Quickly reminded of the longueurs of golf spectating – the swishing over wet grass, the rituals of standing, waiting, and staring at sky – Mark sidles closer to Wharton and asks him very politely how he began in the ambassadorial game.

'Well, in my youth, about a hundred years ago, I thought I'd be an engineer of some kind. Then, Pearl Harbour happened, and it seemed an urgent thing to join the Air Force. Once that got settled, I got to thinking about State Department. And after the war, see, the position that the US then commanded – people all over the world were suddenly inclined to listen to any dope with my kind of a drawl.'

A certain rhythm is established in the drizzle. They stand as a trio

355

to watch the preppy young golfers trade blows, and on the longer treks from the tee-box Mark tries to extract intelligence without vexing the guest or their host.

'I understand you were in Saigon? What sort of job was that in wartime?'

'Well, particular to that war, which was a hearts and minds operation where we won neither. Obviously the Paris Accords have put an amen to it. But, a poor return on our efforts – which I feared from the outset. And despite, I should say, the integrity of those efforts.'

A tough character, Mark decides, not used to defeat. But on the links it is Mark's man Weiskopf who toughens up. At the last hole he makes an inspired save of par, while Miller's crucial putt lips the cup and stays out. Weiskopf by one, then, and Wharton is coming forward, his smile wry, his hand extended in defeat.

In the members bar they find deep armchairs for sore feet, and Wharton turns his thirty-year-old Dalmore round his glass.

'Gracious living, gentlemen. You know, I was in Paris a while, and the Quai d'Orsay is all-superior, I mean de Gaulle knows exactly where he thinks France ought to be in the world. But, after that came Gabon, and there I learned to put the correct price on comfort . . . I'd have come here any time, any weather. You'll know we've had ten US presidents of Scottish descent, half the signatories of the Declaration of Independence . . .'

Wharton's expansiveness, while enjoyable, is not quite what Mark drove to Troon for. 'We have oil on the way, too, of course. You've worked in that industry?'

He sees Wharton measuring him anew. 'Sure, there's a little Middle East on my curriculum vitae. Longer than I care to recall. But I was in Syria when the Suez went crazy . . . Oil, yes. It creates a big stir, political, economic, you name it.'

'Do you've a thought on what it will mean for Scotland?'

Mark can see Wharton weighing this like a handful of sand he doesn't care to spill; he senses, too, that Ally's affable smile has tensed.

'Oil makes things happen. Whether Texas or Biafra, right? Once the resource is proven, it can fuel a certain feeling, locally. You start to get arguments over which interests are paramount, what's to be protected, who gets what. I recall when Churchill started Anglo-Persian Oil. Wasn't so long before that got to be very unpopular on the Persian street . . . Yes, it could all get very interesting. A little too interesting for this long day. Gentlemen.'

And the Consul-General stands, his bodyguard rising near-simultaneous, in a manner that strikes Mark as very rehearsed. 'Thank you for sharing with me a little more of the culture of this country. If it were golf and whisky alone then, lord knows, those fine, fine things would suffice. And we've had the best of them today, along with good companionship.'

Ally, standing also, looks to Mark as if he might applaud. 'Thank you, Mr Ambassador. To a special relationship!'

'Hear hear.' Then Wharton is weaving from the room.

Yep, CIA, thinks Mark. 'So, I behaved myself,' he reasons to Ally as they sink back into their chairs, a little lingering asperity detectable in his friend's face.

'I'd say you just about passed. Since you tried every other angle, I'm amazed you didn't ask him about his time in Moscow . . .'

Mark only smiles – feeling himself to be a bit of a secret agent, too. After all, he is now an adopted candidate for the SNP, due to stand whenever the next by-election comes round. He simply hasn't yet seen fit to confirm as much to Ally, who won't care to hear it: of that, Mark is sure. Still, had he delivered the news sooner the invite to today's useful intelligence-gathering session would have been a far harder ask; and Mark couldn't have come away with this suggestive evidence that over in Washington, just like down in London, they are getting a little bit rattled by Scotland. Thus, mission accomplished, Mark raises his glass to his friend.

August 1973

On the Town

Aaron is waiting for his friends, toying innocently enough with a napkin and a cocktail olive; but he has been sitting alone over the martini for a while now, longer than planned, and has grown a little self-conscious of how he might be seen. The bar of the Òrach Hotel feels to him like a place made for assignations, illicitness of various kinds. There's something in the moodily pinkish light and the rounded space – all curves, fleshly – just like the red leather seat of the booth where he sits, a low lamp glowing on the tabletop before him as at all the other booths, enticing guests to incline to one another.

And then there are those seated on stools at the bar: waiting to be invited? Aaron has been glancing at one such in his line of vision: a woman with long blonde bangs and dark-lashed eyes, in a figure-hugging frock with heels. She seems uneasy, having burned through several cigarettes. He doesn't believe she is waiting for anyone special; rather, waiting for something to happen.

No sooner, though, has Aaron judged his theory sound than he sees a gentleman enter the bar and approach this woman, she gracing him with a toothy smile. Next, he's helping her into her coat to leave. An incongruous suitor, maybe – Brylcreem parting, grey double-breasted suit with a white handkerchief, donnish steel-framed glasses. *But what do I know?* thinks Aaron, rueful.

'Mr Killday?' The waiter has come round the bar to the couple. 'The lady said you would settle . . . ?' As the gentleman reaches into his jacket, it looks to Aaron as if he is a little shy about something. The surname resonates, for sure: Aaron supposes him to be one of those scions of the Killday fishing firm – but which, he cannot recall.

And now Robbie is entering, incongruous himself in a compulsory shirt and jacket, and with him his fiancée, of whom Aaron has heard so much, without a glimpse hitherto of this redheaded woman. It is almost as if Robbie has been shielding her. Aaron has wondered what kind of a match could be made up at Glinrock Fabrication Yard, and has formed only vague expectations of Evie Charlton. At first look she is nothing like even those; but he pushes such thoughts aside and aims to be of good cheer as the couple slide in beside him.

'How's the room?'

'Aw just grand, pal. So comfy. Bathtub big as the sea. And we'd a drink of that wine you had left for us, cheers for that!'

'It's all so swanky,' Evie says earnestly. 'Thank you ever so much for treating us. Really. Robbie's told me so much about you, I see why you've been pals so long, you're kind like he is.'

'Aye, we appreciate this, Aaron, me and her both.'

Aaron waves them away. 'An engagement deserves a present.'

'Nobody else has given us one,' Evie retorts. 'Though there's only so many as knows, I suppose. Just the ones worth telling our business to.' Aaron notes that 'we', as well as Robbie's placing of his hand over hers as in agreement.

It is an odd, quasi-parental feeling for Aaron to be treating his pal. Yet he feels he owes Robbie something near-incalculable, and that he hasn't always been so generous. Now he summons the red-jacketed waiter; Robbie orders a beer; Evie 'never knows what to drink'. Aaron suggests Cinzano and lemonade. In the process he steals a closer look at her: pale of complexion, robust of feature, a little hunched and uneasy in her myrtle-green dress, its buttons closely fastened up to the collar at her neck. Womanly for sure, suited to green, what with that hair . . . He might not have picked her for Robbie from a line; but, again, he knows very well just how little he knows.

He asks after their work, always glad to hear Robbie speak of his daily graft, that laconic smile about the parts that are a bit tough. This time, though, he seems deferent to Evie, evidently his mentor for the business they are both in. When their drinks arrive the waiter fusses over an addition of orange peel to the rim of Evie's glass, and to Aaron's surprise she lifts the fellow's hand and removes it. 'Naw, you're fine, leave be, eh?'

Then Robbie asks kindly after Aaron's situation, so Aaron prepares a face to relate how grim he is finding things at Paxton. 'Of course, what you guys are doing at Glinrock is all so BP's field can get connected to land by pipe. What *Paxton* wants to do is save money, get massive tankers out to the platform to fill up like at a petrol pump, then ferry the oil ashore.'

'Incredible.'

'Cowboy, really. That way he only has to spend big on tankers and an army of divers. All he's really after is being the first man who got North Sea oil ashore. No ambition for the field, the resource . . . It's shabby.'

'You found that oil, didn't you?' Evie addresses him respectfully. 'What you've done is so impressive.'

'Kind of you to say, Evie. It doesn't feel that way.'

Robbie has drained his pint and Aaron offers another round, but Evie wants the key to slip back to the room before their dinner reservation *à deux*. Robbie watches her all the way out of the pink-lit doorway.

'What d'you think, pal?'

'Seems a great girl. You look happy.'

'Aw she's a *woman*, I tell you. Like none I've known. Keeps me on my toes. She mightn't smile much, but see when you do get a smile off her, boy? Then you know you done good.'

Aaron can believe this: he sensed Evie was holding something of herself back. Robbie seems perhaps infected by some of the same: not wholly at ease, in any case.

'Things are good, then?'

'Me and her, aye. The job? S'okay. For now. Money's alright, they want the thing done quick, just like you say, so there's bonuses for them as wants it . . .'

'But . . . ?'

'It's no' gonna last. I keep thinking o' that. These platforms, once they're built? There'll no' be another. In another year I could be down the road again.'

'But even if it came to that – you're a welder now.'

'Naw, *she's* a welder, not me. I've gotta think about what my living is. For the good of the both of us, the things we're gonna want.'

'Robbie, don't wreck yourself thinking too far ahead.'

'I've *got* to, Aaron. This is serious. She's serious. The lad she was with before, he was a big earner, that was a big thing for her.'

'She's with you now.'

'Aye but she's not got with me so she can be the breadwinner. I just – I've got another chance here, man, I dinnae want to mess things up again.'

'This doesn't look to me at all like what you had with Marilyn.'

'I know. That's no' what I'm saying. I'm thirty-one, Aaron. I cannae keep living pillar to post. I've got to find the thing what I do in life. And stay at it, aye? Like what you've done, man.'

Don't do that is Aaron's doleful thought. And yet Robbie is looking at him like a man in need; and of more than a fancy hotel and a slap-up dinner. Aaron feels he must try to offer something more substantive.

'I wish I could be a help to you, Rob.'

'You're always that, Aaron.'

'I don't know . . . if you've ever given a thought to the offshore diving?'

Robbie looks down into the suds of his pint glass for a moment, then back at Aaron, with a distinct wariness. 'Aw, no' sure about that, pal. Seen some things there, y'know? We both have.'

'I know. But it's not the same game any more. And it's a job that's here to stay, now all the production is going ahead, like what Paxton's doing. They're all crying out for divers. Here's why I say it – they're training divers to weld and welders to dive, but you already do both,

361

Robbie. And there's terrific pay for that work, maybe the best money going, you can name your price.'

'Someone's always trying to tell you what's the best money. It never is.'

'This you can believe. Five hundred a week if you're good. It's not scuba and mask, you'd have to learn the deep diving where you go down in a bell. But you can do that. You can do anything, Robbie. You're a great diver, a natural, always were. Not like me, thrashing around like a fool, using all the air in his tank.'

'*Don't you be wasting my air, son!*' Robbie barks in what Aaron suddenly recalls as the army-camp style of McPherson, their examiner from years before.

'*Ye skinnymalink, ye!*' Aaron barks back, pleased to have put a grin back on his fretful pal's face – not least as Evie is headed back their way, looking a mite suspicious as Robbie grasps his shoulder with feeling.

'I'll have a think, eh? Listen, cheers, for everything, Aaron. You're a good man.' Aaron claps the back of Robbie's big hand in turn, touched by the sentiment, wishing that he shared it.

September 1973
The Creel Boat

Like a shot Joe wakes at the first *tring* of the alarm clock and claps a silencing hand upon it. Isla moans slightly at his side but does not stir under the covers. He slides clear, slips into the clothes he laid out, and he is washed and out of the door fifteen minutes later, a shade before six. He won't risk even a dry roll for breakfast: he is going to sea with his father, and he is determined to show an iron gut.

It is a peace-making mission: the need to restore the peace has dogged Joe's thinking these past months since Andrew's withdrawal from the day-to-day of the company – chairman in name only, his choice to retain even that perhaps chiefly to preserve his dignities and links to other things. But until yesterday, barring a brief exchange on his father's birthday, Joe had not spoken to Andrew for five months.

It was Garth who told him to make his trip. Part of the price of recent ructions for Joe is to tend toward Garth's wishes – to repair those relations also. *'He's on his own down there, Joe. He goes and sits by Ma's stone, he drinks whisky and he goes out on the creel boat. He's even asked me to go out with him on the damn thing. It should be you, but – the least you can do.'*

Thus it was agreed.

The sky has a pleasing aureate glow as Joe walks down the small wooden jetty at Stonehaven, easily spotting his father in ancient yellow oilskins and rubber boots on the deck of the twenty-seven-footer.

'So it's you, then,' Andrew grunts. 'Must be something awfy important, to get you on a boat.'

———

363

From a bench seat to one side of the wheel, Joe studies Andrew at the helm under the standing shelter, his dashboard messy as ever, driving the *Winnifred* out at thirty knots. There is a little low grey cloud over the steep-sided land a hundred yards off starboard, and as Andrew eases down the steady, hoarse chug of the engine, Joe realises they are passing – purposely? – close by the clifftop cemetery where Ma is buried. Andrew is studying the backs of his hands.

'You alright, Da?'

'So much of your mother still. Out here, in the house . . . I wish I was with her.'

'I understand.'

'Well you might. She nurtured all of you. You could have shown more feeling at the time, for your mother's memory.'

Joe is tempted to retort that these things go both ways. He refrains, knowing what he has come for, what would ensue.

A raucous shriek alerts Joe to a big herring gull hovering over the stern, as if sent to provoke and aggrieve, and he glares at it until it wheels away.

Once they are in range of the bobbing orange buoys marking where Andrew sank his creels down to the seabed, he takes up his gaff hook and snags the nearest buoy, drawing it up over the side of the vessel, trailing with it the basher rope by which the creels are linked.

Joe can see a flush of vigour about his father's white-bearded face, a kind of revival. But as he starts to yank on the rope, it doesn't come cleanly toward him. Snagged, maybe? Andrew yanks harder, agitated now, but to no avail. The deck is slick and his footing looks unsteady, the tread of his old boots so long worn down. Now Joe dons his gloves and steps forward.

'Da, let me—'

With one more brute pull, Andrew's balance is gone: he slips and topples back hard onto the deck. Alarmed, Joe darts to help him

364

up. But Andrew is fierce. 'Get that damn basher in!'

And so Joe seizes the rope. As soon as he begins to haul, the straining protest in his biceps reminds him of the stone weight that has kept the creels down there. He doubles his exertions, a paining tug of war with the water, his own borrowed boots squirming on the deck. He has a sense of being watched, weighed . . . so he feels a hard-won relief when the barnacled netting of the first creel breaks the surface, and he stoops to manhandle it over the side, glimpsing its seething crustacean captives.

His father is at his side, apparently none the worse, or else refusing to show it. 'Gettin' good and drookit there, that's a fisherman, eh, boy?'

Then Andrew is swiftly shifting the first creel roughly aside to the fixed worktop on the gunwale, delving into its netting.

'You never know what you'll get . . .'

His fist withdraws, and in its grasp is a lobster flapping its tail and flexing its pincers. Andrew inspects this creature critically, as if looking it right in the eye. Then with a flick of the hand – the dismissal of a meagre specimen – he tosses it past Joe's head and back over the side.

On the return journey, duty performed, Joe retakes a seat on the bench adjacent to where his father steers; and he tries to put a seal on his efforts.

'Da, look, I've wanted to say – that I'm sorry for the state things got into. I want you to know I've only respect for all you achieved . . . You're a winner, you built a great legacy.'

Andrew throws him only a cursory glance. 'So great, eh? Then why would you no' lift a hand to help keep it that way?'

'Because I want to win, too. I just wish you had some respect for my judgement . . .'

'I do see fault in myself, Joseph.' Still, Andrew does not look at him – only at the waters ahead. 'I was a poor judge of you. Me and you, we should have come to a crossroads a while before we did. But I let it be. I was waiting for you to take your shot at me. Because you had made up your mind to get me offside, I see that now.'

Joe feels a sudden lurch in speed; the boat is rocked.

'That's not true, Da. Yes, we argued . . . You wouldn't change, whatever you said. There were times I regretted letting myself get drawn into the business.'

'I gave you your choice in that. You do what you want for you, Joseph.'

'You had your choice of my brothers and all.'

'Huh. I should maybe have put Angela in charge.'

Futility creeps over Joe, and with it a familiar umbrage, as he studies his father's oilskinned back turned to him. 'It was yourself you wanted to pick, Da. Or your double. But anybody worth a damn would have told you what I told you. Angela, my eye – you didn't approve her pick of husband, you think you'd have let her do one thing for *your* company but what you said?'

'I was minded to refuse that bastard, right enough.'

'Da, you would fall out with anyone.'

'You defend the man still, eh?'

It is true, some days, of a given situation, Joe will find himself asking what Ray might do, and has taken instead to asking Isla.

At last, Andrew is looking at him, rancorous as ever was. 'Do you wish me dead and gone now, son, is that it? Did you come out here to finish me off?'

Believe what you want, thinks Joe. He tells himself he was a fool to think the breach could be repaired – it will just have to be lived with. He has had his fill of this little outing, and he brings his gloved hands up to his face so as to shut out any more of it.

November 1973
Honourable Member

Mark has for some weeks been living out of a suitcase in a cheap bed and breakfast in Pimlico, and his heart has grown fond for Edinburgh, home comfort, and those rare times when Shona is also in situ. But the important business of today puts an urgency in his stride down tree-lined Millbank toward the House of Commons. He knots his tie as he goes, trying to polish a few sentences that still seem short of their needful snap.

As he approaches St Stephen's Entrance he is presentable and has a marginally improved draft in mind. He rates the procedures of the parliamentary estate as antediluvian, inhibiting the figure he would prefer to cut around here as a marauding agent of change. But this place is ancient, while he is, as yet, relatively new and little-known. He flashes his laminated pass to the policeman at the gate.

'Mark Rutherford, Member for Glasgow South-West.'

He strides down corridors of tired carpet, wainscot and striped wallpaper, past closed doors to his office, a cupboard room with a stained-glass window that he's lucky to have. He bears half of a bacon sandwich, carefully wrapped in tissue, to offer to his newly hired researcher Claire Cushenden. She receives it coolly, as she does most things. Claire wears a black dress – her own deference, he supposes, to the notable business of the day. She has her fair hair pinned up like a nurse, and her dark hooded eyes seem critical; but then her smiles are reserved only for displays of conspicuous intelligence. Right now, she is frowning over his text.

'I think for a maiden speech it needs to be shorter.'

'I've done another fix-up. Read this one?'

She takes it, coolly. 'You know the convention is to be "non-controversial".'

'I don't think that's me, Claire. I don't think it's why I was sent here.'

What he learned from the short and highly successful by-election campaign was that his public speaking voice seems to carry people. He had good young SNP activist-volunteers supporting him, of course, but it seemed to Mark that the force of his convictions and the flair of his presentational style must have counted for something in the coup he pulled off. Up on the stage at his count, when his victory was declared, he felt a big sense of personal vindication. He outshone Labour in Glasgow by his eloquent support for the Upper Clyde shipbuilders and for decent standards of public housing, not the dreck he saw some working people having to put up with. And for his maiden speech he would like to keep faith with all of these burning issues.

Claire hands back his inky page. 'I just think you'll do best if you stick to one topic.'

'Which, though?'

'Isn't it obvious?'

In the chamber, called by the Speaker, he rises from the bench to face the long opposite lines of dreary Tories, grudgingly respectful in their silence.

'Let me begin with a tribute to my predecessor. Whatever our differences in outlook, we are both socialists and we both believe that Scotland should have its own democratic assembly.'

How do youse like that for starters? he thinks, hearing a low harrumph or two.

'Mr Speaker, while campaigning in the constituency I am proud to represent here, I saw bitter proof of the long-term economic and social injustices imposed upon Scotland, its slums and housing problems, the cancer of joblessness. Successive Scottish Office ministers have not managed to alleviate these. Now Scotland has a special and powerful resource sitting off its coast. The prospects for North Sea oil are ever improving. That oil is no panacea. But we have the prospect of an industry, and we should mind how it's to be run, in whose interest. The priority should be the long-term welfare of Scotland. Instead, we see a mad rush by multinational interests to extract the oil for the benefit of everyone but Scotland. I say we should take a little more time, and spare a thought for people, not just profit. Scotland's greatest resource is not the oil but its own folk – their talents and energies. The uses of oil should be properly planned, not subject to raids by bandits.

'Mr Speaker, for a time Scotland has maybe seemed to be on the periphery of the United Kingdom. But now the United Kingdom is on the periphery of Europe. And by any just measure Scotland should become one of the richest industrial areas in all of Western Europe. Whether that is as part of the United Kingdom or as a sovereign state – the SNP believes the Scottish people should decide.'

On his return to the little office he is rewarded by a smile: 'That was so good, Mark.' He feels massively energised, rather as it felt in his rugby-playing youth when he scored a solo try. Claire is young, yes, naïve, no. Her dad is a coal merchant, her mother a barmaid, and she a graduate in politics from Oxford. In truth she is the image of the party he wanted to get involved in, not like some of the eccentrics he has met in his wanders through it. Her opinion matters to him.

Mark feels, moreover, that he is maybe owed a share of the sort of favour Shona routinely bestows on her seeming hero, a Czech dissident named Pavel Bradáč, in whose every utterance she seems to find weight and moral courage. Bradáč is a playwright whose plays are *verboten*, who works instead as a railwayman and writes only samizdat diatribes. In photos Shona has shown him, Bradáč certainly looks more like a labourer than an artist: bearded with bloodhound eyes, clad in a scrofulous jumper and donkey jacket. He has been beaten with batons by cops in Wenceslas Square but refuses to call it bravery. 'He doesn't want to emigrate,' Shona asserted. 'He wants to stay and fight.' Mark, genuinely admiring of Bradáč's mettle, is none-theless sick of hearing about the guy, not least as it seems to him that his own entry into *engagé* politics ought really to be earning him the greater share of Shona's esteem.

For an hour or so he mulls over constituency mail, much of it pretty ditch-water stuff after the exuberance of his debut in the chamber. Finally, aware of stiffness in his back and legs, and pitch darkness outside the stained-glass window, he studies his gifted researcher, still gamely at her desk, similarly swathed in papers; but now her face looks a little wan above her black collar.

'Claire, you should head home now.'

'I'll only be doing the same thing in my flat. And' – she grimaces – 'there are mice in the kitchen . . .'

He is aware she still lives like an undergraduate; for a big chunk of his twenties he did the same. 'Look,' he says. 'Let me treat you to a square meal. A glass of wine, for God's sake. I owe you for all you've done.'

She appears content, even grateful to agree. He hopes to talk to her some more, earn perhaps a few more smiles; but to listen to her, too. There's a pleasing feeling in escorting a bright young woman out to dinner.

'It must be hard for you, Mark,' she remarks as they lock up. 'Stuck in London for the week, the late-night votes and all . . . I do feel sorry for you and Shona.'

'Me, too.'

November 1973
A Personal Favour

A strange thing for Joe to hear that voice over the phone for the first time in a while, the one he was used to hearing daily – even, at times, inside his own head.

'Joe, could I persuade you to meet me?'

'Why?'

'That sounds a little sharp, after all we've been through.'

'You must know why I'd ask, Ray.'

'There's a piece of business I'd like to explore with you.'

Less of a surprise now. Joe has glimpsed Bodie afoot around the harbour; he's gleaned a rumour or two.

'Do I hear right you're getting into the diving game?'

'That's right. As a contractor. Not so different to the game we know. The oil companies are pushing like hell out there, big demand for divers to fit and repair . . . Real money on the table.'

Joe considers. 'It's probably not a great idea if you come by the office, Ray.'

'I'd be glad if you'd come to mine.'

Joe replaces the receiver and looks out of his window at the dedicated industry of the Killday office. Isla's sleek head is lowered over her desk but she looks up now, uncannily, and favours him with a sly smile.

No harm in a meeting, to talk business, however speculative. Not while Killday are in the very act of completing the deal to partner with Cassels the Glasgow engineer, the 'next phase' that was Bodie's instigation. However mercurial, Bodie's ideas have always been worth hearing out. In truth, in spite of what fell, he wouldn't mind seeing the man again.

—

It is only a ten-minute stroll from Killday, a little way down a cob-bled by-street to the given address, which turns out to be a dismal four-storey stone facade with a cluster of insignia by the door, among these a small aluminium plaque reading *Triton 5 Diving Services Ltd.* Inside Joe mounts the stairs to the top of the building, where he is admitted with a nod by some unsmiling clerk and shown down an uncarpeted hall to the manager's office.

Ray Bodie is standing under a sloped ceiling, apparition-like in the glum light of a window looking onto a facing brick wall; seeing Joe, he starts to come jerkily around his cluttered desk and Joe sees that his right foot is in plaster to the ankle. Disconcerting, in a way, to see such a livewire man so hamstrung.

'It's good to see you, Joe. Sorry to be Hopalong Cassidy. Had a nasty prang in the car, fella drove right into my side at an intersection. His fault entirely, but I've got another fortnight of this. Please, have a seat.'

In an open-neck shirt and waistcoat Bodie looks a little peaky, his office a constricted lair, with a somewhat earthy odour that could almost persuade him Bodie has been sleeping here overnight.

Bodie seems to note his scrutinising look. 'These digs are a bit basic but it's temporary, fine just for now . . . I appreciate this, Joe. I worried you might tell me a flat no.'

'Like you say, we've been through a fair bit.'

'And how is Isla?'

'You're not in touch? She was your find.' Joe realises he would prefer that Bodie and Isla were no longer such pals.

Bodie waves a hand. 'I just went into Kaminsky's one day and saw this doll who looked like she was running the place from reception. Reminded me of me. No, she's your special friend now, Joe. I expect you'd have a bone to pick if I pinched her back over to Triton Five.'

Joe joins in the perfunctory chuckle. *No chance.*

'Joe, I won't dress it up. I know that I caused a rotten situation at Killday, I accept the blame for that. And it pains me that the first thing I do since is come begging. I'd never want to put you in a spot.'

'But still you ask.'

'Please understand, it's a difficult time for me. I'm under . . . enormous pressure here. I don't say you owe me anything, Joe. I just wonder if you'd feel you could do me a kindness, help me out of a big hole.'

'Well, I'm here, so you might as well say.'

'I bought a ship, good solid little supply boat, Dutch-made, called the *Rood-Maaier*. But it needs some work done on it, and quickly. Like I say, it's competitive out there, and I went in quite hard on price. I might have made a deal or two on the strength of assurances I wasn't entirely in a position to give.'

Joe looks askance. 'You don't change, Ray.'

'Oh, but Joe. *Joe.*' Bodie wags a finger, suddenly more like his old self. 'I do change. I realise it's part of the problem people can have with me. But changing and moving on is a prerequisite for success – otherwise people get the hang of you pretty sharpish. Next thing you know you're hanged by the neck. Now, I've got to get the *Rood-Maaier* into a dry dock and get a diving system fitted on her stern, for deep diving, right? So a diving bell and a chamber complex, with a compression centre. And I thought, where's the best yard I know?'

'There are a few good ones . . .'

'You're the best. And when you've worked with the best, you know it. But the other thing is . . . I'm really in need of the best price I can get.'

Joe sighs to see the sorry thing exposed to the light. 'Ray, you get what you pay for, right? I'm not saying it's a job we can't look at, but any kind of personal favour . . . that's on the wrong foot. Costings and quotes for this stuff are not just in my gift.'

'Come on. The business is all yours now.'

'Not that simple, as you know.'

The familiar intent set of Bodie's face seems to stiffen. His hand darts to his face and momentarily he gnaws at a knuckle, before recovering his composure.

'Joe, this just has to go right or I'm sunk before I start. One more push and I'll be off and away but . . . right now it's tough. This means everything. *Please . . .*'

Joe considers: so much they went through, shoulder to shoulder. Now the relationship might endure, albeit at arm's length. 'Ray, look – calm yourself. I will speak to Lennox Devane. We'll see what might be done.'

'Thank you, Joe.' The relief on Bodie's face appears genuine. Joe decides to reserve judgement on the prospect of a discount – wonders, even, if any arrangement they come to could be sweetened for the Killday Group by some share in Triton Five's business. In the past he sometimes fretted over the balance of power between them. Now that balance seems decidedly in his favour.

December 1973
Merry Christmas Everybody

Mark and Shona are a mite late through the door to Christmas drinks at Castle Drummond, but Mark likes to believe they retain the licence that comes with being the oldest of old friends, most valued of all guests – the only couple, surely, invited by Ally and Belinda to stay overnight?

Once over the threshold, though, and seeing their host very much engaged with others, Mark wonders if they should have sent apologies instead. Ally's greeting – 'Welcome, friends, to a final fling before the miners turn us all into Scrooges with our heat and light' – strikes him as Pooterish. If another miners' strike is on the way – as implied by the Tories' frantic orders for a three- or four-day working week come the New Year – it doesn't feel to Mark that anyone gathered in the castle tonight will suffer so terribly.

The place exudes splendour. Hired staff in black are coming and going with drinks and canapés. A fire fit for a hunting lodge is blazing in the hearth, its light glinting in all the crystal and jewellery round the room, and the Chesterfields are fully occupied by dressy guests balancing good china on their knees. Mark reflects that an evening with Ally has for some time now been not what it used to be. This one, evidently, is to be shared with a milling crowd of bankers and investors and golf bores from the Royal and Ancient club down the road.

Reluctant to enter this fray, Mark is struck by a conspicuous addition to the room's decor, fully occupying the generous corner space by an arch leading to what Ally calls 'the great hall'; and he wanders over to inspect. It is a sculpture of a horse, big as a shire pony, densely woven from dark willow twigs, martial and bull-like in aspect – one hoof raised as to strike. Closer, seeing that the beast stands on a wooden wheeled platform, the penny drops.

'The Trojan horse.' He gestures to Ally. 'Superb.'

'Isn't it? It's by the woman I found who did all the bits of wicker work about the place. When Tom saw it, he went doolally. Speaking of devils . . .'

Ally's two-year-old son, earnest-faced and smart in his pullover, is being led by Belinda down the stone wheel stairs from the upper quarters. The boy runs at Mark, and in an instant he is up on Mark's shoulders, drumming heels upon his chest. Mark feels delight all through himself at the child's glee.

'You're so good with him,' Belinda purrs. He feels a strong whim to plant the boy astride the Trojan horse; but even as he moves that way, Ally's hand is on his shoulder. 'Easy there, Mark, it won't take the weight.' And so he swings Tom down to the floor instead, and the boy sticks out his tongue peevishly at his father before turning a newly expectant face to Mark, who realises, cursing inside, that he ought really to have come bearing a gift. Tom is used to Uncle Mark producing from his coat, magician-like, some miniature Hot Wheels car or Dinky London bus.

He delves in his jacket pocket but all he has to hand there is one of the blue IT'S SCOTLAND'S OIL lapel badges he carries for all occasions. The instant he produces it, the look Ally shoots him is so reprehending that Mark feels suddenly and unhappily childlike himself.

'Please behave yourself, Mark,' Belinda murmurs in his ear after kissing his cheek, then she beckons both Shona and the boy away and Mark sees – in dismay – Gordon Fyfe bearing down on him with a big craggy sexagenarian in tow.

'Rutherford! I heard from Ally you'd a hand in all that "Scotland's Oil" stuff. Hell of a prank to pull.'

'A lot of my constituents tell me they agree, Gordon.'

'Oh, do they now? Do you know Clay Paxton, Paxton Oil?'

Seeing Paxton's sour face, Mark decides a simple nod of greeting will suffice. 'Mr Paxton. Actually we spoke some years ago, on the phone, way back when you started exploring here?'

'Oh yeah? I tell ya, if I'd thought it was "Scotland's Oil" I'd have stayed home.'

'Still, you found it, your black gold.'

'The hunt was horrendous. Basta! Like the Italians say . . .'

'Can I ask, how much oil do you think you've struck?'

'Well, that's the thing you politicians forever ask. Fact is I can't truly say yet. More's to the point, it's only worth what someone will pay for it.'

'But the price of oil is through the roof right now.'

'Everything's temporary, patriot. I'm saying don't go making laws on it. Don't take it down to the bank thinking it'll pay for whatever's your pet cause. Seems to me your coalminers are on strike so's they can get a Labour government that'll pay 'em whatever they ask. And we got Labour guys saying they'll take over the oil business and run it themselves? Well, if they start tearing up deals then I'll want to know how I'm to be compensated.'

'Forgive me, Mr Paxton, we've only the two Scottish Nationalists at Westminster, and I can't speak for Labour. But someone's going to have to settle with the miners.'

Fyfe butts in. 'Come on, Rutherford, we heard you say in parliament that the oil companies should be forced to hire Scottish workers and services, however long it takes to find people halfway competent.'

Paxton reddens. 'You said *what*? Listen, I got creditors, patriot, and they ain't gonna wait. You Brits said you wanted the oil real fast—'

'Not me, sir.'

'I mean lawmakers as was elected then. And oil is got out of the ground by oil men, not some big mouth shouting what's gotta be done when they ain't ever done it. Maybe all the Americans in Aberdeen ought to go on strike? How about that? You want us to just leave the oil down there under the seabed, let you Scots guys get your wrenches out?'

Mark can see the room has become aware of this choleric display; but he feels sure of what he speaks.

'The miners could say the same, right? "If you people want coal then you come dig for it." Listen, I hate to be Cassandra here but if there's not a benefit clear as day for Scotland out of all this oil found off our shores – I tell you, people are going to be furious. So we'll not be told we just have to take what others think we deserve, so long as we mind our bloody manners.'

Satisfied, Mark sips his wine, seeing that Paxton has not taken reproval half as easily as he dishes it out. Looking about him now for some more amenable conversation, ideally with Shona, Mark sees Ally glaring at him from ten paces.

His friend is not happy with him. So be it. The party is over and Mark is slumped alone on the Chesterfield with the eerie sensation of nobody wanting to sit next to him. Ally has been upstairs awhile. Shona is in the kitchen with Belinda, and when last they spoke she only gave him that helpless look that says he has made his own bed. When Ally reappears, his mood looks to be in no way improved.

'Just drink some more of my wine, why don't you, Mark?'

'C'mon, Al, that's not very friendly, I didn't come here to—'

'Pick a fight? I think you fail to understand how you've begun to sound? *Windy*, Mark. All talk for effect, little to do with the real world.'

'Come on, that's a dull thing to stick on me, no?'

'Not as dull as you sound when you kick off. Like Scotland's some poor bloody virtuous victim that needs a revolution to free it from the colonial master . . . and a few Jacobins like you to hand out the spoils.'

'When have I ever—?'

'That's the resentment in you that you're not hearing. And I don't know where it comes from, given the actual life you've led.'

Mark sees that Belinda and Shona are returning warily to the room. *Witnesses*, he thinks.

'It's possible, isn't it, Al, that you're not hearing things so clearly either? Not from the crowd you knock about with now?'

'Who, Mark?'

'I mean that unionist, Tory lot who can't see past Edinburgh and London, and the oil. Not one of them bothered a damn about Scotland.'

'I have just as strong a feeling about Scotland as you. But I don't need to beat my chest on it. I'm not for all of Scotland, but I am for this Scot, and selected others. Depending on how they behave.'

'Am I in that group?'

'Would you rather not be? You're going the right way about it.'

'Please, come on now,' Belinda cuts in, sounding more nervy than usual. 'I think we need to cool down before someone says something they really regret.'

But Mark is tired of minding his manners. 'The oil, Al – I'm sorry if you don't see it, but it's done something to you. Any time you smell that black gold now, you just dismiss any other consideration. I went up there to Glinrock, back when all the talk began of building yards, and land was changing hands like crazy. That geologist who works with you, he told me he'd put you on to that.'

'Strang? That's not his business.'

'Do you not think some of those landowners were ripped off? By speculators with not the slightest regard for what the people living there actually wanted?'

'Oh, get away. An awful lot of people did very well out of that.'

'Please stop,' Shona says urgently.

'No, we should get into it, since Mark's asking. Yes, we, Drummond Fyfe, had a part in developing that land for onshore works. We paid damn good money. The reason I started the bank was so that Scottish capital could have a part of oil, and I damn well did that, Mark.'

'Oh well, whatever's good for capital . . .'

'Can be good for labour, too. Oil is making things happen here no one could have imagined. Do you have anything to say about it that isn't just a schoolboy sneer?'

Mark feels a rankling so fierce that his words emerge through gritted teeth. 'In Glinrock I met a man named Caldwell, a farmer, widower, four children. He'd sold seventeen acres of land for ten thousand pounds. Was delighted by that. Four months later the speculator he'd sold to sold the land on again, for *two hundred thousand*.'

'I see that would be galling. But it's business.'

'A couple of days after he found out, he killed himself with a shotgun.'

'Oh for God's sake . . . that's awful, of course it is, but—'

'I spoke to his eldest son who he told me his dad was so crushed by the thought of what he could have done for his family, if he'd not been deceived—'

'Mark, are you trying to say I had some part in that man dying?'

'I'm saying stop justifying every damn thing done for oil when a blind man can see some people are coining it and others getting robbed.'

'You sanctimonious bastard. You think my money's dirty, Mark? You've kept that to yourself. Did I not help to pay for the bloody roof you sleep under?'

A fraught silence, broken by Shona. 'Sorry, I don't understand.'

Mark, rattled, resumes in a shakier manner. 'Shona, look, back when we bought the house in Leith . . . Ally offered me some help with the deposit, a loan, I was glad of it. He seems to think now is the time to make a thing of it.'

'Mark, *what*? Why on earth didn't you tell me?'

Mark clambers to his feet, replete with the bitter spirits of the evening. 'I'll tell you later. I think – clearly – we can't stay here tonight. Right? Can you drive us, Shona? I'm over the limit.'

'I'd be so grateful, Shona, if you would. Please just get him out of here.' The measured vehemence in Ally's voice hits Mark like a skelp to the cheek; and then the keeper of the castle is striding up the stone steps and away.

February 1974
Spaceman

Robbie awakens from a dreamless sleep to find himself sore and bone-weary, in his cramped coffin-like bunk, among strangers and shift-time at hand once again. On the day he first crawled headfirst into this spartan environment, the clang of the hatch closing behind him felt like incarceration, no question – a feeling that recurs.

And yet, Robbie is hopeful today, just as every other day of late, and every night when he crosses off another number on the calendar taped over the bunk. Six more to do on this stint. And all such time means good money – the whole reason why he let himself be locked up again.

He checks his watch and takes his customary moment to touch the hem of the tweedy scarf of Evie's he keeps knotted to the stanchion of the bunk – it retains her scent, and it is his ritual homage to the tenderness within, before he boxes this all up for one more day as a saturation diver with Charax Subsea Limited.

Then he is off, in just his Umbro shorts, pushing through the thin plastic curtain to the communal habitat: twenty feet long, seven feet wide, four fixed seats round an aluminium table where he and his colleagues sit like spacemen waiting to be fired into orbit. The porthole windows have cardboard taped across them, but outside is the deck of a ship, positioned quite precisely a hundred miles out at sea and six hundred feet above a wellhead in the advanced stages of being readied for production.

Barring the low mutters of his shipmates now stirring behind the curtain, the sole other sound is the low whir of the carbon dioxide scrubber. Their work here is a kind of experiment, but at times Robbie feels they are all being experimented on – like those monkeys that got fired into outer space in rockets before anyone dared send a human up there. In this controlled environment, this steel cocoon, he has the weird sense of living under observation, performance monitored, nourishment issued to him through the bars of a cage.

He turns to the regular morning palaver, going to the hatch to knock up the Topside crew for breakfast bacon and eggs, waiting for the bang of a spanner on the outer panel. Then the wait before the scran is sent through, pressurised in the airlock to match the divers' condition – fully saturated with inert heliox gases and thus robbed of their tastebuds, the food just a bland fuel to be shovelled down at given intervals.

Here come his oppos, Big Stu, Rowdy and Trev, hairy and semi-clad, blearily scratching their stomachs and poking around in their ear canals. Keeping his post by the hatch, Robbie turns his trilobite pendant between his fingers. A Celtic cross bobs about on a chain between Big Stu's chunky pectorals, whereas Rowdy, from Austin, Texas, sports a metal skull strung on a black bootlace. Trev from Dudley, a little older and tubbier, wears a vest and doesn't like jewellery on blokes.

There's a subdued air to the congregation that suits Robbie just fine. On the Pecos the tedium of close confinement made for a perpetual risk of punch-up. Here, they are pacified: all on the same clock, same focus. The helium in their bodies has made their voices comically squeaky, and it's hard to come on like Jack the Lad when you sound like Donald Duck. Any speaking aloud takes real effort, and small talk has perished among them: each in their own little worlds.

Once Robbie has played mother and handed around the food con-tainers, they fall to their reading matter. Robbie was given *Serpico*, a true story about corrupt police in New York, and it's pretty good. Rowdy has *Playboy* magazine and is taking it now to the 'wet pot' antechamber where the shitter is located. They will each take their turn in there soon, near-religiously.

Robbie opens his book where he's marked it, with a sunny snapshot of Evie sitting on the steps of her Glinrock caravan. He knows, he is going to break his rule and allow his mind to wander – to indulge the bittersweetness of missing someone, and to think of their future, the precious gift given just days before he went aboard, when Evie saw the doctor about her missed period. Such a huge and wondrous prospect – and with it, a sense of being blessed, of a fight to be together now vindicated, the conviction it was meant to be. It can feel too big to take in, but Robbie holds onto it like a charm.

Rowdy is calling to Topside for the shitter to be flushed. They are trained to such indignity now – grown men going about an adults-only job, but reduced daily to kids who must ask to be taken care of.

Then the voice of the diving super from the control room comes disembodied through the habitat's tannoy – the voice of God, telling Robbie and Big Stu that it is time to don rubber suits and take their instructions, then take the diving bell down to work. Robbie's turn to graft on the seabed – and the morning's task is familiar. Inspection of flanges on the oil flowlines, possible replacement of a gasket or two. Three, maybe four hours in the water?

Robbie dresses in the long-johns, thick socks and Aran sweater that are his first layer of insulation, then – feeling grossly swaddled – he takes his turn after Stu, like submariners, to pass through the tight round hatch into the wet pot. The seal closes behind Robbie with the finality he always feels in his gut. He inserts himself with usual difficulty into his heavy-duty rubber coverall, adding the belt and vest and big gloves until he knows he looks like the same queer armoured alien as his double Stu before him. He checks the vital hook-up points for life support about his person, does the same for Stu; then up through the next hatch into the diving bell, the two of them as constricted as if they were sharing a shower stall.

Stu squats down on the bellman's seat by the dashboard of switches and gauges, and Robbie takes the tiny perch opposite so Stu has room to shut them in. He tells Topside they are ready for the bell to detach from chambers – the nerve-straining 'transfer under pressure'. Robbie swallows hard, reads his own edginess in Stu. *Three, two, one...*

They are in motion, external hands and the hoisting winch carrying the bell over the edge of the ship; then the start of the descent to the lower depths. Robbie peers out of the window, seeking that short glimpse of natural light as they hit blue water. But soon the blue is chased away, turning dark grey then murkier still as they head down – a fleeting glimmer to the gas bubbles, then gone.

Stu's eye is fixed on the pressure gauge, and he counts out their depth. Robbie stares at his great gloved mitts over the five minutes it takes for them to sink six hundred feet.

The bottom door is lapping open, water sloughing in, and Stu draws it fully aside. Now Robbie accepts his oppo's help in getting attached to his umbilical lifelines of gas, power, heat, comms. The hot water starts to invade the crannies around his suit, at first pleasingly, then at scalding intensity.

'Topside!' Robbie barks into his comms. 'Cool the water, aye? Two degrees.'

'Roger that, diver.'

Finally Stu helps Robbie affix his spaceman's helmet firmly. And Robbie opens the valves on the gas he will breathe from here on.

'Okay, diver?'

'Roger, Topside. Diver down.'

A thumbs-up from Stu and Robbie hauls himself down and out through the trunking, into the North Sea.

He is sinking into space, Stu sending his umbilical tumbling out in his wake – and at once he is feeling the thickness of pressure all about him, the resistance of the water. He swallows steadily to clear his ears.

His boots land and plant in the muddy murk, stirring up a cloud of silt that rises menacingly all about him, killing visibility. But his helmet light is shooting a beam, radiating the particles around. The floodlights on the bell reassert as the silt settles, illuminating the gloom to maybe fifteen feet. All he hears is his own breathing. He feels the strange weightlessness. All colour has gone: fish and eels are like alien life around, he the spaceman among them. But Topside got its co-ordinates right: the wellhead is in view.

'*Diver, tools on their way down.*'

He wrenches his head upward, to where the tool rack is descending.

'See it, Topside . . .'

Then – alarmingly – a sudden tightness in his lifeline jerks him aside.

He looks upward again, and sees, aghast, that the rack has strayed into a tangle with his umbilicals, exerting a strain on the gas supply keeping him alive.

For a sickening instant he imagines the umbilical severed, cut ends tumbling toward him . . .

'Topside! Quit lowering them tools, you'll cut my gas! Tell the bellman he's gotta slack the umbilicals!'

Ghastly seconds: he hears himself breathing hard, tells himself *Fight it!*

The tray stops, suspended. As gently as he can manage by dulled touch, Robbie grasps his lifelines, feeling some give, and he moves them to and fro, shaking the tree.

He is hearing the counsels of this training, the gallows stuff. '*When things go wrong, they go wrong fast. They say you can only kill yourself. Not true. Someone might do for you accidentally.*'

But he is back in command now, he has his head. And he starts to take ponderous steps toward the worksite. He needs to piss – to rid the dose of fear just now injected into him – and without further ado he lets go inside his suit. All focus bent now on the job, the time, the money. The future.

PART VII

WAVES

February 1974
Unrecoverable

It is the morning of the special meeting of the Paxton Consortium, to be hosted in the Edinburgh offices of Drummond Fyfe. On the floor of his hotel room Aaron Strang struggles through three sets of ten push-ups, trying to drive out his nerves and steel himself for the confrontation ahead. He showers, towels himself roughly dry, then dons his suit and tie with care, vaguely oppressed by the spectral feeling that he is assuming a uniform in which to be buried.

Before the stern black door on Charlotte Square he stops to avail himself of the iron boot-scraper. The company brass plate is at his eye-level, harking him back to the melancholy legal meetings over his divorce. But Drummond Fyfe itself has had negative associations for Aaron since the morning when Alastair Drummond telephoned him to say, with baffling curtness, that Aaron's consultancy would not be renewed. The role had come to seem to him merely honorific; but his dismissal felt like a reproof – also an omen that change was afoot.

He has timed his arrival to the meeting to avoid small talk. With only a nod to Paxton and McGinn, he joins the group ambling from the banker's opulent reception space to its more sober boardroom. These are big guns: broad-shouldered men with steely handshakes and gravel voices, trading names easily – 'Cap,' 'Jim,' 'Gus.' Aaron intuits that the greying mousey fellow whose spectacles overwhelm his face must be the newspaper executive. In the boardroom, a dozen cowhide chairs are set precisely round a fifteen-foot walnut table topped with matching leather. Each place is laid with water glass and printed documentation. Taking his seat, Aaron notes a wary look exchanged between Paxton and Drummond as they ease into position at the opposing heads of the table.

'Gentlemen, let's get goin' here – my thanks to Lord Al not just for hosting this meet but also for agreeing to chair it.'

'Thank you, Clay. We meet in a fairly enviable position for our shared venture. The Pecos rig will soon come into dock for conversion to production purposes, and our target for first oil remains April of 1975. The main item of business today is less cheery, but essential nonetheless. We've all had the chance to review these estimates, made by Paxton Oil and Gas as operator, of the costs that will come with eventual abandonment of the Cetus field. Clay?'

'Sure thing.' Paxton clears his throat gruffly. 'Let's face it. Cetus is a small field, the smallest anyone's found out there so far. We've had to bust everything to get it to here. We win this and produce first? That's a hell of a claim. But, the downsides are a whole lot plainer to us, too. We know now, whenever we're done producing, what's gonna fall on us in terms of the shutdown costs and statutory requirements and all hell else that the government's gonna stick on us – whoever the hell is in government . . .'

Aaron notes the grim chuckles around the table but doesn't join in.

'We know we gotta seal up all the wells and clear our junk off the seabed . . . *and* reconvert all them tankers we refitted, which is a million dollars, easy. Some operators will never sink their own money in a well, but me, I've always wanted to look my partners in the face and know if we get lucky then we make a fair share of the spoils, and if we strike out then I'm out a whole lot personally, too. That's why we see it as time for a clear-eyed look at all the costs we got stacked against our payday.'

Gus of Texaco raises a hand. 'We don't expect any of those costs to be deductible from corporation tax?'

'Don't bet on it,' Paxton grunts.

'No,' Drummond eases in. 'It'll be classed as capital expenditure, and we accepted the clean-up as part of the licence to drill. So it's our duty and we can't – if I may borrow from Clay – "yellow out of it".'

'You said it, Al. So we know what we're in the hole for, and today I hope we can agree what production we expect out of Cetus. But also a hard date for us to plug it, clean up then get out and go hunting for another adventure . . .'

Paxton hands over to Charlie McGinn to unpick the documentation's calculations of how many barrels will be wrung from Cetus: millions, and yet rated as lamentably few. Aaron sits tight, brooding silently over a verdict on more than ten years of his life, and a bunch of paper he rates – in Paxton's terms – as bullshit. Aaron considers the figures McGinn is reciting to be self-fulfilling prophecy, cooked up by a conservative gang of reservoir engineers under the biased guidance of Erwin Shields. He imagines Shields would sooner drink a barrel of oil than allow Aaron's discovery to get its due.

Big Cap Maguire from Rio Tinto is nodding intently at McGinn's explanations. 'Of course, the consortium has made its own estimates of oil in place. And we see a pretty close conformity with the operator's figures.'

Drummond smiles. 'I wonder if I detect the promising signs of a consensus? Might it be unanimity?'

'It is not,' says Aaron, suddenly, as the table turns frowningly toward him. 'Obviously I bow before a majority, but I'd like to make a few observations, as the geologist who found this field.'

He looks to the chair; Drummond spreads his palms.

'Thank you. I was led to believe, on the basis of good geological evidence, that we would drill deeper into the beds beneath the Zechstein interval – to add more production wells beyond what was, after all, only the youngest, shallowest reservoir? I still insist – this field is bigger than it's been estimated. These figures are based purely on the performance characteristics of other reservoirs considered to be comparable, and I don't regard them as valid. I am utterly certain there is more oil to be found here – and we will rue the day we gave up looking for it.'

McGinn intercedes, tiredly. 'I have told Dr Strang his own calculations are way over-optimistic.'

'Well, I think Dr Shields's estimate is unduly pessimistic, deliberately low—'

'Let's not revisit old grudges, Aaron.'

'My problem isn't with Shields, Charlie, he's only obeyed orders here. Because the company wants to abandon. Because it's been decided, for rather perverse reasons, that the commercial life of the field should be brief. That is a waste of resource that I find staggering. Back when the oil price was in the cellar any number of discoveries got written off as "uneconomical" – well, now OPEC has quadrupled the price and that should make us—'

'If you'd been around this business a while longer, Aaron' – Paxton bites into Aaron's peroration – 'then you'd know that's not a dependable factor. For this consortium, Cetus is the only source of income – we got no other irons in the fire. We can't afford to drill our way out of that problem.'

The grousing, dismissive looks now trained upon him from all quarters are the only outcome that Aaron truly imagined. But the desire to make a last stand had been overwhelming; and that much now seems accomplished.

'Well,' he says finally, 'for the record, I am opposed.'

When Drummond calls a break Aaron finds himself in the excruciating position of having no one to talk to, wondering also – a worse sensation – whether he has anything left to say. He wanders to the front door, pulls it aside; and sees Drummond and Paxton standing together across the street by the black iron-railed perimeter of the square's gardens, both smoking cigars.

As if spotted thus, they recross the street, Drummond passing directly through the door with a circumspect look. Paxton, though, lingers.

392

'Clay' – Aaron gestures inside – 'am I needed from here?'

'Well, you ask that question and I wonder, Aaron . . .' It is Paxton's turn to use the boot-scraper, vigorously, as if something persistent there needed expelling. 'You know, you always struck me as a fella keeps a lot bottled inside. But I never heard you talk that way to me like you did in there. Now, if I had, I might've had to take you through a door and straighten you out some.'

A mite startled, Aaron sees in the next instant that Paxton is taking the tack more of sorrow than anger.

'See, Aaron, this business we're in is all about the future. Tomorrow. So long as the sun keeps coming up, that means you got one more shot. So what's it to be next? I gotta know the people who are with me are really *with* me, you understand?'

This is the way things end, Aaron knows. He has, at least, been bolder today than he hitherto thought capable; and so he girds himself to play the thing out.

'Clay, my question was, am I needed?'

'Naw, you're done.'

And Paxton is away back inside Drummond Fyfe. For a moment, on the threshold, Aaron contemplates his position. But he knows well enough that Paxton has called it correctly, and he closes the stern black door on himself.

February 1974

An Urgent Matter

Robbie cannot bear another minute longer, everything in him is pulled taut by the need to break his cage. He is watching the porthole, waiting for the promised release.

He will emerge from a lonely three-day decompression in the tiny hyperbaric chamber, and he is rank irritable: not just from the aches and pains but because he knows the ship is en route for Aberdeen; and that after the dreary days of life on pause, his liberty is now painfully close – real light, a real bed, a proper meal – but still not close enough.

This final stage of the torturous timed path back to surface pressure and breathing normal air he finds much the worst – being the slowest, a brute impediment to all he has been deprived of this fortnight past. His pregnant wife awaits him, needs him, and he her.

He could be running on tension and yearning alone. His features reflected in the chamber porthole are harrowed, leaner, just like the rest of him. Bored of his book, he has drawn diagrams of his habitat to show Evie, recording odds and sods of the work he does, thinking idly that there could be something there to interest a child, too.

At last, encouraging noises from outside: the porthole opens and he exits into the fresh air of the deck, ungainly, feeling like one of his father's baby lambs coming into the world forelegs first. Responding to greetings, he gets the proof that his proper voice is returned. The ship's doctor stands ready to check him over, but with a look of greater concern on his face than usual. Behind him is not just the dive superintendent but also the skipper, who asks that Robbie go to the bridge to return a call from his wife at her parents' home.

———

'Evie, love?'

He hears troubled breath, the catching sound of someone who has been weeping.

'Robbie, I've lost the baby. I've lost it, the pregnancy, it's finished.'

Within him he feels the sudden stopping of a clock.

'Oh, darling . . . what happened?'

'It was a couple of days ago, I—'

'You could have reached me then, love—'

'I didn't see any good in it, Robbie, you stuck out there. Not how it happened.'

'But *what* happened, love?'

'I got pains, I was bleeding. I went to the doctor and he examined me and he said he was sorry but I'd miscarried.'

'Oh, love, love . . . You were bleeding?'

'I'd been feeling bad in my head and stomach, and it got worse, then in my knickers I saw these bloodspots. Really red. I knew it wasn't right. Then it got, oh, just so heavy, Robbie . . . I called the doctor then but it was too late . . .'

'Could the doctor tell you nothing of why?' The line crackles, causing Robbie an unwelcome flare of irritation. 'I'm sorry, love, I couldnae hear.'

'He said it's still got to pass, but, the tissue . . . He said I've a few more days of this.'

'Aw God, love, I gotta get off this fuckin' ship.'

'Robbie, no—'

'Evie, I cannae just sit here.'

'Come when you can, I'll be so glad to see you. But there's nothing you can do now.'

Hating the sound of that, he tries to collect himself – to do better, as a man, in his part of this woebegone exchange.

'Listen, love, this . . . it happens, right? It won't stop us. You did all you could. Your work's so hard on you—'

'It was nothing to do with work, Robbie.'

395

He wonders anew at this gift for saying always the wrong fucking thing.

'All I mean is, it just wasn't meant. Not this time. But we can try again in a wee while.'

'*Aye. Maybe . . .*'

'For sure, darlin'. For sure we will.'

'*It's not a thing to just fix, Robbie. I've to get over this first. It's gonna take me a bit of time, to think this over . . .*'

'Think what over?'

'*I need to not be bleeding.*' There's an edge in her voice now, it hits him; but he sees now how she has been hit harder. *Was pregnant. Now not.* He is aching with the uselessness of his wish to be with her, the dead hope of all he would try to lift her, reassure her, make her believe no setback can't be overcome.

But it's not going to happen. He realises the two of them must be apart a while longer, feeling awful, bearing their loss separately. He looks around the dull, grey, hostile North Sea, and feels consuming hatred for it.

Fuck this, man. I cannae do this any more. He puts fingers like pincers to his pulsing temples.

'You alright, son? Eh, y'okay?' But the superintendent's hand on his shoulder has none of the gentleness he needs, and he throws it off.

February 1974
Friday

Joe parks good and close to the office, Isla by his side: Friday, and he looks forward to the weekend, to time with her. He turns to her, sees her composing her hair in the rear-view, smoothing the front of her belted Lanvin dress; and he feels contentment in having found this fit, this chemistry – to make with her such a presentable couple. She smiles and he kisses her, curls an arm around her. He thinks of their lovemaking this morning – so satisfying to him, such a part of it being that heated, reaching look on her face at climax, so divorced from her usual poise that, if he didn't know better . . . But no, surely not?

Isla breaks from him, jabbing a finger at the windscreen and he sees that Ray Bodie has stepped out of the office doorway and is watching them intently. *Inappropriately.*

Striding out from his vehicle, sending Isla indoors to open up, Joe can see Bodie looks better than the wounded ghost of their last meeting, which is handy, for he feels a nagging urge to jab a finger in the man's chest.

'What can I do for you, Ray?'

'Can we speak inside?'

'Let's get started here.'

'Joe, I need another job out of your yard, there's no time to waste.'

'Another favour, eh?'

'There's a problem, with the dive bell you put on my ship.'

'You're trying to say it's our problem?'

'Not as such, but we need to go back to the drawing board.'

'For starters it's Devane you need to speak to.'

'It's more complicated, Joe, the urgency is part of it. I've a contract to provide my ship and divers to Paxton out in the Cetus field, and he's given me an ultimatum, but first I've got to get this design fix on the bell or the whole thing is fucked.'

'We don't design system here, Ray.'

'No, my people have designed something. We just need it fitted.'

Joe shakes his head in frustration. Friday had looked better than this.

After lunch Joe drives to the Devane yard to find out the damage, knowing that Bodie will already have had his audience there. Sitting down with Lennox Devane is never Joe's favourite recreation. Devane is but a few years younger than Andrew, but still commandingly at the head of his business, the industry of which is plain on the workshop floor that his office overlooks.

'I believe,' Devane says slowly, 'you're wanting to keep a close eye on this job, on account of the gentleman concerned.'

'Not too close. But I know Bodie, I know his game.'

'This isn't quite his game, is it? I must say, he turned up here today mobhanded like he expected a fight – had his boat's engineer with him, his skipper, his diving super . . .'

'What did you think of them?'

Devane sucks his teeth, and Joe doesn't suppose he is wracking his brains for another way of saying *First-rate*. Finally, he says: 'I had some questions.'

'What are they asking for?'

'Oh, they've taken the *Rood-Maaier* out to sea and tried to launch the dive bell from the stern – in conditions plenty rough, of course – then they struggled to get the damn thing down through the waves. It just jerked about on the end of its wire, like a kiddie's yo-yo. The obvious fix is just to pile on more weight. And that's what they're asking.'

'Do they have a design you can approve?'

'I see we can build it and fit it. I daresay it's what they should have had from the start – a proper clump-weight tray under the bell. Two

398

tons of metal. We'd sling it underneath with chains, so it sits on the seabed and the bell floats above.'

'Right. Like an anchor. Simple as that?'

'No, Joe. Not simple. We'd have to fix their winch for them, too, so it can take all that weight. Then they'd need to test the thing bloody carefully before they took divers out. I told Bodie all this, and that if we booked in now he could expect delivery first week of April. But he's not happy, says he needs it quicker. And that's the trouble I have with this man.'

Joe mulls the weight of Devane's reservations. Bigger and burlier than Andrew, he has some of the same silvery asperity about his looks, and he occupies his desk chair formidably, censoriously, such as to make Joe feel abashed for having got back into business with Ray Bodie. He is contemplating what backing out now would mean, the somehow weaselly feel of it, when Devane's secretary steps delicately through the doorway – it is Joe she addresses with wary eyes.

'So sorry to disturb but, Mr Killday, your sister is on the telephone, she says it's urgent.'

That is a bother. Angela has been at Netherdown of late, minding Andrew, and it hasn't been her wont to call for assistance. Devane indicates that Joe may certainly take the call from his desk.

'Joe, I'm worried about Da. He went out on the creel boat first thing and he's not back, he should be in by now.'

'Angela, I wouldn't worry just yet. Not on a day as fine as this, while it's light. Da knows what he's doing, he'll sometimes take most of the day out there.'

'Not lately, Joe. That's my worry. I'm sorry, could you speak to the watch officer at the coastguard?'

Joe weighs the options. Garth is at sea, Walter up at Mo Seiche . . . 'Angela, we can't be summoning the coastguard for no reason when they've rigs and trawler boats to worry about. If Da was in trouble he'd send a mayday. Let's just keep our heads, keep in touch – I'm sure he'll be in soon enough.'

Joe is conscious of Devane's eye on him as he replaces the receiver; but he knows he is doing the rational, responsible thing.

Joe returns to his own office, and no sooner is he through the door than Isla is chasing him up the aisle with messages from Bodie. Friday's promise is draining away further. He sits down to return the call without delay.

'*Devane's given me a load of haver, Joe. The job's not what they're saying it is, they're bolting in things I'm not asking for.*'

'Ray, you're welcome to go elsewhere.'

'*Why should I? Why should this job run to more than five thousand, when Devane's telling me ten?*'

'Ray, then take it to tender. Don't try to dictate terms to me. If you want to discuss financing options then speak to Walter.'

'*He's not damn well there, is he?*'

'No, but you can get him Monday.'

'*I can't wait that long—*'

But Joe doesn't care, for his other line is flashing red and Isla has come through the door, ashen. 'Joe, you need to take this . . .'

Joe makes the ten-mile drive in fifteen minutes and dashes from his car as soon as he has pulled it over on a narrow grassy track at Portlethen Village, high over the bay below. He is in the grip of foreboding. It is the same spot where as boys he and his brothers gathered to watch Andrew sailing out to the Faroes. Now, as he starts to scrabble down the slope to access the bay, he sees the rocky reef of Craigmaroinn at its southernmost end – and a boat's wreckage, overturned and broken on the rocks, its shattered creels strewn around amid other flotsam. The *Winnifred*'s life raft bobs hopelessly close by. There are policemen on the sands, and by them the slight figure of his sister. Against hope Joe is scanning for a glimpse of his father, bundled up in a blanket, there to be scolded that he gave them such a terrible fright . . . But of Andrew there is no trace.

Once it is clear that their attendance at the scene will achieve nothing for no one, the depleted clan gather at Netherdown. Walter has driven in haste from the cottage in Pennan Bay, wearing his gardening clothes and looking painfully pale. Joe clutches the hand of Angela, who is drained from weeping, but has yet to reproach him for his earlier response to her anxiety. The facts of the case have a stony cast: Joe feels wretched in the face of them, scarcely believing the disaster could have unfolded as it appears.

Just before ten o'clock Sergeant Peck of Stonehaven Police Station arrives at the door, youthful and grave in demeanour.

'The coastguard got the call around five from the gentleman who spotted the wreckage, and they'd a boat out within the half-hour. But clearly the window for rescue had already passed.'

'What hope have we got now?' Angela looks up from her hands.

'Boats are still out over ten square miles, a chopper's out, too. All vessels in the area are alerted. But the dark will soon make anything more impossible tonight.'

'But what chance is there of finding my father?'

'We'll get at it again come first light, madam, be assured. It's only right to say, though, you might need to – prepare yourselves for the worst.'

'But I don't understand,' says Joe, groaning, 'how it could have happened. If anyone knew these waters it was Da – he's gone out there a thousand times.'

'I understand you, Mr Killday. But at sea, of course, an accident can be the work of an instant. From what we can make of the wreckage, it looks like the basher rope got tangled with the propeller. That could have been a problem for your father.'

Now Joe is recalling his last unhappy excursion with Andrew on the *Winnifred*. Those worn old seaboots, that drastic tumble he took . . . What if this time out he had yanked on a rope that was never going to budge? Coming up fast, footing lost, the next instant pulled off deck . . .

'I wonder,' Joe says finally. 'Last time we went out I'd to haul in his creels for him . . . he wasn't managing so well.'

'You never told us that, Joe.' Angela seems consternated.

Sergeant Peck has his pencil poised. 'You've been on that boat with him, sir?'

'Of course, we all have, since we were children.'

'But when was that last time, sir?'

'Oh God, it was all of six months ago.'

The sergeant contemplates his notebook. 'Did your father have any ill-wishers? Who might want to do him harm? Forgive my asking – I do it just to rule it out.'

He saw enemies everywhere is the thought that flashes in Joe's head as he studies the floor. But he knows he will leave it there. When he looks up, though, he has the sense of eyes trained expectantly on him, Angela's and Walter's most especially – the familiar court of his family's opinion. And he does not care for the seeming implication.

February 1974
Glasgow South-West Decides

'I'm sure you know our position,' Mark assures his prospective voter. 'It's Scotland's oil. And we intend to do something with that wealth, for the benefit of everybody.'

'Are we's gonna be rich? You hear that, Gregor?' Dawn is a large young woman, doleful of feature, and she fills the door of her twenty-first-floor flat in Govan's Crowhall Court, stroking the head of the wide-eyed child who nestles into her hip.

'Naw, naw,' Mark responds with a candidate's smile. 'But we'd be richer as a society. Better housing, better jobs—'

What's really bugging Dawn, though, are these letters she's had from the council about unpaid rent when she'd rung them to say she'd been in hospital.

'Give me your surname and I'll look into it,' Mark proposes, meaning it, hoping, too, that his word will mean one vote in the bag.

A general election has forced him back into the fray of campaigning, the fight to retain his by-election seat won just four months previous. Currently Mark has sizeable problems of a personal nature to manage, but he hopes that doesn't show too much on his face. He has been trying to throw himself into his work.

On his way back down the corridor at Crowhall, Mark worries about Gregor. Mark himself has no vertigo issues but – when it comes to young ones – a worry about the extreme high-rise of these towers. The distressed state of some of the flats he has glimpsed into is another demoralising matter. No place for pets, either. Still, nearing the lifts he clamps a hand over his nose and readies to sidestep where somebody's dog has left its foul business.

Mark has known better than to sit on his laurels. Last time out his newness, his lack of experience, proved advantageous: he was not some clapped-out veteran towing a baggage train of unkept pledges. Hoping to reprise the same fortune he has got out canvassing houses street by street, tower blocks floor by floor. He has done loudspeaker flybys in shopping centres. His adeptness at this, at politics in the raw, is, for one thing, a way of silently telling Ally Drummond to get stuffed.

Can he point to substantive achievements, solving constituents' problems? He has made a lot of calls for people – not just Dawn Mathieson. His office is not yet festooned by thank-you notes; but he doesn't think he has offended many. He's been told MPs don't enjoy a 'personal vote'; but Mark does believe a fair few people came out on the strength of his performance and will do so again.

He has grown used to party activists asking him if he's okay, and he knows he must wear a hangdog look, but he can't let on why.

Nothing has been right since the night he came home and realised Shona was there already, sooner than expected, and had opened the mail, including the small blue envelope that, to his horror, was addressed in Claire's handwriting and marked 'Private & Confidential' with a line underneath.

She was in the kitchen, looking very dispiritedly at him. 'Is this another thing you were planning not to tell me, Mark?'

'Don't . . .'

But she had the letter in hand and she read. '*I will always admire you for your eloquence in our cause. But I must also consider*' – Shona raised three fingers, counting off – '*my own best interests, the differences between us, and what is right and proper. I realise you must have problems in your marriage, but I am not so naïve as to become part of them. For sure, I know I am not the solution to them.* Oh, she's a smart one, Mark, I'll give you that.'

'Shona, will you let me explain? Nothing has happened.'

'Nothing?'

Not a thing. Yes, they had been together in his hotel room, working after hours. Yes, they had ended up perched across from each other on the bedspread, papers spread between them. A softness had come over Claire's face as she said, *'It's funny, I've wanted to tell you something, since we started working together, but I've been afraid to . . .'* With a rising heartbeat he had urged her, gently: *'Go on.'* But she couldn't, oh no. Then, seeing his need, she gave in. *'You just seemed so full of yourself, like it was all just a one-man show? I thought, "God, he's sort of awful . . ." Will you forgive me? I know better now . . .'* And with that, she seemed her usual self, having bestowed her version of a compliment. Unwilling to let it pass – idiot! – he lifted her hand from the bedspread, and her look turned uncertain: enough for him to incline to her, but she moved away, and instantly he had known his error, its size. Moments later she was leaving in haste, clearly right to have felt trespassed against.

'I realise it looks bad,' he told Shona. 'I'm sorry. I was lonely. I think maybe things were misconstrued.'

'Let me guess, my fault, is it?' She put a hand to her chin and shook her head at him, almost pityingly. He didn't ignore that he had hurt her. It was only that she somehow wore the look of a magistrate newly in receipt of some clinching evidence to conclude a difficult case.

'Labour has let you down,' he tells the pensioner pushing her shopping cart down rainy red-brick Elder Street. 'Look around. Aren't you tired of the same old politics? Tired of waiting for the government in London to do something that's for you?'

He fears it might sound like he is telling her she must be tired of life. But he's not sure she's listening too closely. 'Och I don't know. The Sedley fella is my usual vote, I've always voted Labour. But I'll think about it.'

Mark knows that means no. The idea that Glasgow is Labour and Labour is Scotland persists; they have forty-three seats to his team's two. His party insist they have 'momentum' and he has been no small part of that – they have Labour on the run! But Mark comes too easily by reminders of the forces against him, in depressed places resistant to the change he is offering – more comfortable with the service they've had before. Ally's prejudice of old: sometimes, in some places, you might stick a red rosette on a corpse and it could carry the day.

In the Vital Spark pub he tries his luck with some men from Birtleshaw, the Sheffield-owned engineering firm across the street. They seem a thoughtful set of swiggers and smokers, agreed about London's negligence, at least.

'You've a fair point on the oil, I gi' you that. If things don't get better up here now sure they never will. But you talk about the working class and all. What's your own work been, Mr Rutherford?'

'Thon leaflet of yours, but? I wish you wouldnae be sayin' *"Rich Scots or Poor British"*. Like it's easy as that. How many jobs in oil, but? You say all what it's worth. By the time the money's all in, sure how much is for us? We's each get a fiver?'

'It cannae work the way yousens are sayin'. Scotland cannae go it alone.'

Mark rates it necessary to persuade this last man – the most sceptical – above all. 'My party is arguing for independence but, let's be honest, it's not happening tomorrow. Vote SNP here and you'll not be voting for a government.'

'Aw I know. Just for you, eh? Listen, son, I'll have a think.'

Midnight, and he stands in the ranks of the prospective tribunes once again, hands clasped and hair combed, on the municipal stage of his recent triumph.

'I, Fraser Macdonald, Returning Officer for the Glasgow

South-West constituency, declare that the total number of votes given to each candidate was as follows . . .'

Mark knows turnout was high, even the Tory vote up. *But who's up by most?*

'Rutherford, Mark, nine thousand nine hundred and seventy-one . . .'

Up by plenty! His heart lifts.

'Sedley, George, ten thousand . . .'

Defeat, short, sharp and cruel – bringing heat to his cheeks. He feels abrupt exposure, trusted sureties falling off him – his job, his wage, his dignity, a huge investment of personal time and energy. By contrast, the merriment all around is extraordinary, Labour's lot wagging their fingers at him, chanting – 'You only had it on loan!' And Mark has to stand there and take it.

Being a professional, he has prepared a few gracious words in the event of defeat, and he stumbles through these, numbly.

The phone call with the party leader is more excruciating still – a great night for the SNP, eight seats in all, the tide truly is with them! Except not in Glasgow South-West. To be assured of his part in a wider success is of zero consolation.

'We'll sort you out for getting back to London to pack up, Mark. On the upside, we'll still have need of your staff, so you'll not have to let anyone go.'

True: if he has fallen, Claire still has a future to make. Chagrined, he realises she has shown him that politics must be a team game, and for now he has been taken off the pitch.

It is 2 a.m. when he returns to home, expecting to find it empty, feeling that such an insubstantial presence as his would hardly stir a soul from sleep in any case. But from the door he sees the kitchen light is on at the back of the house, and at the threshold he sees Shona sitting.

'I'm sorry, Mark.'

'The sorry one is me.' He lowers himself into the seat opposite.

'Are you dreadfully disappointed?'

'I didn't really get the time to love it. But . . . it feels like quite the rejection, yeah. I really worked for this. Put so much into it. Maybe I was blind, maybe it fell in my lap . . . I just don't know what happens now is all.'

'There's a question,' she says simply.

'Maybe Ally was right, the bastard.'

'About what?'

'Plenty of things. He'll be laughing now.'

'I doubt that. Have you never thought about trying to patch it up?'

He has, and has resented himself for not doing it, thus ending up more depressed. 'No. No point pretending your old pal is the same person as when you were boys.'

'You, neither.'

'Maybe.' He sighs tiredly. 'Maybe I can do something else now. I can't go back to just being a scribbler. I don't mean you, Shona. You're far more than that. Obviously.'

He is only saying what he has always felt, and yet she is looking at him with mild surprise, considerately, even, as one given a rare compliment.

'You know, I never really thought of you as a politician, Mark.'

'Did you think of me as a writer?'

She doesn't seem to rise to that; he wishes she would. Professional resentment has surely festered somewhat in a corner of their affairs. He has long felt under some onus to measure up to her nuanced views of things.

'I always wanted us,' she says now, 'to be two writers. Two thinking minds, in our garret, sharpening each other's pencils . . . each other's arguments. That's why we've not had kids, don't you think? Knowing the time they'll take from you when there's so much else to crack on with.' She smiles, unusually weakly. 'I just think the balance of our life has been wrong, Mark. From the start.'

She is sounding much too reflective, like too much thinking has already gone on.

'Can we change it, do you think? Have I messed up too bad?'

She picks at the edge of the table. 'Oh . . . I don't think you're some shit. It's not like I'm perfect. I don't know what to say. Too much time apart has cost us, anyone can see . . .'

No: Mark can't bear it for Ally to be right about everything. Shona reaches out and touches his hair. 'I think we're going to need to try something different, Mark. Might sound silly to call it time apart. But maybe so?'

June 1974

Celebration Day

The feat is accomplished. Now, for better or worse, he cannot deny its scale.

Torrance McVey sits astride his Triumph motorcycle at the dusty top of the refurbished road running down to Glinrock yard. There, below, is the invincible evidence under the sun: the so-called Black Isle Jacket Number One, that great skeletal steel beast that has dominated the view from above for so long – now complete and ready to serve. However brutal in aspect, it has a majesty of sorts, like some ancient pyramid, resting in its purpose-made concrete basin, waiting to be towed into the Firth for its great reckoning with the seabed a hundred miles out.

Thus the party – the big day out going on down there, to which Torrance has felt drawn almost despite himself. All local people have been warmly invited, welcomed into the yard and its environs; but folk have come from all over, judging by the parked cars dotted around the shores. Torrance can make out marquee tents, bunting flapping atop scaffolds; he can hear the squawk of a tannoy as at a fairground, and bagpipers striking up. There will be plenty of company men, great-and-goods in attendance, no doubt; but also the yard's regular workers, their families, wives and kids, feeling some well-earned pride, deserving of the company's treat under the pure blue sky and the warm sun.

Such was the project Torrance tried to resist. That effort could hardly seem more futile; and it occurs to him that he might have overlooked the manner in which the task would bring people together. Maybe, then, the occasion and these people deserve their bit of nature's blessing?

He is tempted to take his bike down further for a closer look, even a mingle. He would like to run into Robbie Vallance and his lady love, the newlyweds, whose feelings on the day might not be a million miles from his own. But in his heart he doesn't feel wholly welcome.

He turns and looks around, at the quiet fields under the fineness of the day. And it strikes him that a ramble a mile or so east would take him up to Glinrock Hill and its monument, a spot he hasn't looked at for a year or two, where he always finds solace – in its view, unsurpassed, as far as Dunrobin to the north and Ben Rinnes to the south; also in the pleasure of being alone in peace, amid a part of the landscape that remains, at least, unchanged.

He trundles the Triumph round the side of a low wall unseen by the road, and then he sets off on foot.

A well-trodden grassy track skirts the hill on the low north side, and Torrance starts to feel the good resistance of the rising slope in his calves and his cheeks and a refreshing breeze on his face, like cool water. He rounds a small loch, and steps over brush and felled branches into a strip of forestry guarding the hill's upper reaches. Picking through the shaded gloom, beyond the trees he can make out the wide, open space he has sought – the panorama of a plain five hundred feet over the Firth, slowly declining toward it. He sees, too, the monument, that weathered sandstone slab that juts out of the plain – maybe a thousand years old, tall as a man and veined with quartz. Local lore deems it the burial marker of some Viking chief, and the side of the stone facing Torrance as he passes is adorned with carved characters of a Norse nature – a rearing sea-creature and a hooded hunter wielding a bow. On the obverse, though – and to Torry's satisfaction – is an ornate Christian cross.

A further hundred yards down the slope, with smaller sounds muted by the elevation and the breeze, Torrance's field of vision is dominated by the panorama of the Firth, its twin headlands making that long channel of the placid waters. He sidles down to an overhang and fancies that he will take the stony little winding descent to the plateau below; but first he peers over the drop – whereupon his eye falls at once upon two figures, lying entwined, gently shaded and seemingly asleep on the grassy slope.

Robbie Vallance, Evie Charlton: no question. Her shirt is pulled up at the waist, his head is on her belly, cradled there by her hands, and Robbie's lips are pressed to the curve of her pale skin.

Of course, he reasons. Not at the party. Happier things to do.

To Torrance it is a curious, intimate sight, also a touching one, as if the lap of the earth has welcomed two of its own, two bodies twisted artfully into one flesh. He is struck by something lovely, indeed enviable: two lovers, so much alive and bonded to one another. It elicits a pang in his chest.

But creeping across him now is a feeling that he should not be intruding here; how awkward he would feel to be caught like some snake in the grass. Glancing aside from the lovers he realises that near Robbie's trailing leg is a wooden cross, looking as if newly fashioned and planted upright in the earth – two spartan branches bound with twine. It seems like some humble little thing that Robbie and Evie have erected of their own. But he thinks no more than that – instead, turns and steals away a little guiltily whence he came.

July 1974
An Invalid

Joe has never much cared for Mo Seiche, the family cottage up in Pennan Bay. But Walter has been holed up there for weeks, now becoming months. *'You gotta go see him, Joe,'* Garth urged. *'Talk sense into him.'* Joe – accepting that he is the big talker, vexed only by his brother's ever more paterfamilias manners – had been meaning to go anyway.

Getting there is its own trial, not least the sharp bends of the narrow give-way track down to the village, where Joe is required to park near a stretch of bothies and then hack his way back up a steep path to where Mo Seiche perches on the hillside. Walter opens the door wearing a dressing gown, sallow and unshaven, his spectacles halfway down his nose; and he seems to Joe uncommonly embarrassed by his disarray.

'Joe, will you give me a moment to dress?' His tongue seems somehow slow in his mouth. But Joe is left frowning on the doorstep, and so he paces the small paved front area, studies the small boats bobbing in the bay below, the gulls shrieking on the stone quay.

Then the door is reopened and Walter, now in shirt and slacks, embraces Joe, causing him nearly to flinch.

'It's good to see you, Joe.'

'You, too. You okay? You look peaky still, man.'

Walter waves a resigned hand, but he moves back into the cottage as if he aches all over. Following, Joe observes that his brother could be a ghost in the place, so little has it changed from when he saw it last – the duck-egg blue wallpaper, scanty and careworn soft furnishings, tablecloths and curtains a mite frayed. While Walter shuffles around the kitchen galley, Joe takes one of the two armchairs beside the picture window onto the sea. Propped on the sill is the card invite made

413

for their father's memorial service. *'Andrew Killday. Unexpectedly died at sea on Friday 22 February 1974, aged 67 years'*. Walter returns with a tray of tea and toast with orange marmalade.

'Are you managing, Walter?'

'I get along. It's restful here.'

'Handy enough, this place . . . I'd wondered, actually, whether we should hold on to it much longer? I've meant to ask both Garth and yourself.'

'I'm finding it very good for me at present. I'd wish for us to hold off on any decision for now.' Walter sips tea slowly and then offers Joe his first smile of the day. 'How is Isla?'

'She's well, thank you. We're, uh . . . getting on.'

'She's now the company secretary proper, yes? Sheila is off the payroll?'

'That's right, yes.' Joe hadn't considered Walter to be quite so down on Sheila as himself, but he senses now that he could be wrong. At any rate, he has been given his chance at a segue. 'Forgive me, Walter, but we do need to discuss the business, your position.'

'No getting away from business with you, Joe.'

Joe ignores the jibe. 'We've managed, of course. But when do you think you might be fit to return to work?'

Walter sets down his cup and saucer. 'I wonder . . . maybe never? Being here has made me thoughtful, Joe. On top of all else lately, of course. I've wondered about what I have left in me.'

'Are you talking about retirement? At forty?'

'I've had a shock, Joe. As we all have. I've been reminded of, oh – the limits of what we're given, what we might still do about it . . .'

Surprised by this, Joe is finding it not unwelcome, reminded of Bodie's perennial jibe about Walter being made of not quite the right stuff. He decides to speak the words he had prepared on his way.

'I understand, Walter. It's just, you've been integral to the company, through all the changes we've seen. And now we're on the verge of another—'

414

'Well, that's just it, Joe. Since you're on the point of establishing this group structure, if the oil's on one side and fishing another . . . it seems like a moment for someone new to take the reins of the finance. For me I feel it could be too much.'

'You'd be greatly missed.'

'Good of you to say . . . I'm not sure I ever had the drive for the business you have, Joe. Let's not pretend, eh?'

'In which case' – Joe steps delicately – 'how much longer might we have you for?'

'I really hope to be ready very soon. In another week or two, perhaps, I would come in to start squaring things away for a handover. That business, by the way, with Bodie's firm, Triton Five? That's all fine and well, don't you worry about it.'

'I'd no such worries,' Joe responds instantly.

'I'd appreciate also an eye on the choice of my successor.'

'Absolutely.'

'It's a strange time. But you've been full of ideas, Joe, I'm sure you'll have more, you've brought in all sorts.'

'I know my judgement hasn't been perfect. Bodie . . . But, y'know, he was our brother-in-law. We should blame Angela.' Joe sees that Walter is not smiling. 'But, of course, he was my hire.'

'Yes. You must have seen something particular in him.'

'I have regrets about that now.'

'I'm sure we all have those. You know, it's true that when the policeman asked if Da had enemies – you crossed my mind, Joe, I can't deny it.'

Joe is, for a moment, speechless in the face of his brother's silent, clouded gaze, and the hardest words he has ever heard Walter utter.

Then from above, through the thin ceiling, comes the unmistakeable creak of an ageing floorboard. Joe, perplexed, glances back to Walter and sees a strange, tense look now meeting him.

'Walter, is there someone else here?'

'It's . . . private, Joe. Will you understand?'

415

Joe sits back, turning over what has felt like a disconcerting minute.

'I'd be grateful if you could leave me to myself now, Joe. What we've discussed, I will take it in hand.'

'Walter, what I—'

'Please, Joe. If you would.'

Joe walks back down the garden path, very unhappily – uneasy, too, feeling sure he is being observed from the upstairs. But, turning and glancing upward, he sees nothing but the frayed curtain in the small, darkened window.

September 1974

Aaron and Robbie and the Volcano

Aaron is waiting on the main concourse of Aberdeen railway station, his Volvo parked outside, the light of day not yet gone. He knows straight away the strapping figure, rucksack on back, who disembarks with purpose out of the three o'clock from Inverness and heads his way.

'Eh, man!'

Up closer, though, Aaron grasps a notable change, for Robbie's hair is cut strikingly short at the back and sides.

'What's with the hair? You've the look of some soldier boy off to Belfast.'

'Evie cuts it for us. With clippers. Like I'm one of my dad's lambs. Is it bad?'

'Of course not. Just different.'

'It's itchy, I'll tell you that. I'd fancy it more round my ears like yours.'

Aaron has let his hair grow, as seems to be the style for men. Still, he doesn't suppose he's begun to resemble Mick Jagger; whereas Robbie still has those lean good looks, needing no embellishment.

Driving them back to his house, Aaron is vexed by the vehicle ahead of him at a roundabout, seemingly shy of sticking its nose out into rush hour, and he slams his hands on the steering wheel – then glances to Robbie, who grins.

'What?'

'Just lookin' at you. Angry Aaron . . .'

Aaron smiles. In fact, his spirits are good. He is feeling the lively lightness of one who has made an important decision, who is hopeful of newness at hand after so much torpor. So now he just wants to be on the road, moving forward.

Robbie avails of the living room telephone to talk to Evie, who is with her parents in Cumbernauld, while Aaron busies in the kitchen, baking potatoes in foil and grilling a couple of steaks. Robbie's rucksack is propped in the hall and Aaron has the strongest intimation that Evie packed it for him, so snugly assembled does it seem, with Robbie's pyjamas folded neatly on top for instant access.

He brings the hot food to the dining room and they sit at the teak table, the TV news on with the sound down, Robbie still at work on a cigarette.

'Evie okay?'

'Aye. Sorry, I hate the goodbye stuff, y'know? Gets me in the back of the throat a bit. She'd rather I was there. But, it means a lot to know she's okay.'

It is a little plaintive to Aaron: how clearly Robbie will miss her, she him.

'Anyhow, I'm earning for three now. So, listen, the morrow – it's your field I'm heading out to. Cetus, aye?'

'You're working for Paxton?'

'The diving contractor's called Triton Five. And the fella in charge is old Ray Bodie out of Tarnwick. You remember that boy?'

Aaron clucks his tongue. 'The entrepreneur . . . Yeah, I've run into him once or twice in Aberdeen. What about the last place, I thought you were well in there?'

'Aw, they've no' been the same for me since Evie had her trouble, y'know? I thought they could have shown us more consideration. Didnae sit right.'

'Well, I hope Ray Bodie is more considerate.'

'Tarnwick boys, eh? We've gone far. He's going out with us on the vessel tomorrow, sounds like he's mad keen to get it done before all the winter foulness and that.'

'Give him my regards.'

'I will. Last shift I'll do before Christmas anyways. When I get back Evie will be six months . . .'

Aaron smiles. 'You ready for it?'

'I've a wee bit of nerves. After last time. I worry more. You have to, but, when you care about something. She's a wary one, Evie. It rubs off a bit . . .' Robbie is looking all of a sudden almost blushful. 'I tell you, pal, I've not laid a finger on her in weeks. Like I don't want to hurt the baby. Mad, eh?'

Aaron pats Robbie's denimed knee. 'I'm sure it's quite common.'

'Sometimes she'll come up close to me and just rub that belly of hers into me . . . Pretty hard to resist, I tell ye.'

Aaron, feeling his maladroitness in a conversation of this sort, can nevertheless see and feel very well what Robbie is driving at. 'What the two of you have, Rob, it's wonderful.'

Robbie looks abashed. 'Eh well. We's might be happy yet.'

'Are you not happy now?'

'Eh, you gotta look ahead, but, Aaron. Or you get caught out. Big year for us next year. The place we've got in Tain, it's no' ideal.'

'Well, you could make more use of this place. Maternity hospital fifteen minutes away, Evie could have the baby there. I'd be glad of it.'

'Aaron, you're so decent, man, but we cannae intrude on you that way.'

'Robbie, the thing is – I won't be here. I'm going abroad a while, for work.'

'Aaron, where?' Robbie looks so affected by his news it is nearly comical. Aaron might have supposed he was kidding, if he didn't know his friend far better.

'New Zealand,' he says, feeling his own big news as nearly a revelation to himself. 'I've been needing a change of air, change of work. It's a place called Dunedin, they've an excellent university, outstanding for geology. The whole town's basically on the remains of a volcano.'

'Jesus, man. Is it *safe*?'

'Oh the last eruption was eleven million years ago. A hell of a landscape, but.'

'Interesting rocks, eh?' Robbie smiles softly.

Aaron nods. 'Lot of interesting igneous rocks. I read about a research opening there, to look into this thing called geothermal. How you might get heat, energy, from rocks – even a dead volcano? I just felt it was right for me. They were after guys who know seismology and drilling – and I know them awfully well now, maybe more than I'd like. So, I applied and . . .'

Robbie whistles. 'Big move.'

'We'll see. Just two years, for starters.'

Robbie clasps Aaron's arm gently and shakes it. 'Don't be lonely, eh, pal?'

It is Aaron's turn, taken by surprise, to feel something in the back of his throat. 'I don't want to be . . . I don't need that much, not if I believe in what I'm doing . . . But, listen, I'm sad I'll not be here to see your wean born. And, you know – if it's a boy's name you're after then I'd say a really strong choice would be "Aaron".'

This elicits the broad grin Aaron hoped for. He knows well he is not so naturally ebullient as Robbie; but then his friend is not him – that's always been the point. And his friend has always been so good for him, not least in lifting his spirits. Aaron, too, knows what it's going to mean to miss someone.

October 1974
The Weight

'What time is it?' Robbie asks thickly.

'Ah it's close to the midnight hour, sir.'

'Feels stormy out there.'

'Windy gauge is forty, sir. Hit fifty earlier.'

The night shift awaits; and Robbie has just awakened. He has regained his head, run his checklist, and emerged into the submarine ambience of the living quarters to confer with his young Texan bellman, Marvin Sparks. Marvin is twenty-two, gawky-looking with a nimbus of hair, pale eyes and bloodless lips; he jabbers on a bit, but that's not the worst in a bellman, and the lad is rigorous and polite, almost excessively.

Robbie is feeling dogged by the dismal, unnatural cast that hangs over night-work, conscious of the blackness outside the chamber, and this torrid weather. The ship has been pitching and rolling ever since they left Peterhead.

He and Marvin sip water and listen to the brief piped in from the super in the control room. *'Looks like we've got a leak to a pipeline connection. Diver, you'll locate and inspect. Plan on making a weld.'*

'Topside, what do you make of this weather?'

'Not ideal. Not terrible. But, it looks a bit worse tomorrow. So we go now and we see where we are then.'

The argument is, to Robbie's mind, imperfect. He ponders.

'Do you want your bed, eh, diver? Look, we've to keep on schedule, there's no good reason not to from where I'm sitting.'

'Is that cos the boss is breathing down your neck?'

The dead-air pause is long enough to be an answer in itself.

'Mr Bodie's not in this room, diver, lucky for you. And he's not that big a guy. C'mon now, let's go.'

421

'Topside, can I ask we not get too close to that wellhead, not when we're banging about like this. I'd rather not have the worry for my lifelines.'

'*Diver, we got five thrusters on this ship giving us position, we'll put you down where you like it. We got two tons of heft under the bell, that'll keep you straight.*'

Marvin shoots Robbie his pale, nervy smile. Being the relative veteran, Robbie aims to project assurance.

The launch of the bell is rocky. Outside the porthole is nothing but night. Robbie feels the brute burden on the deck crew as they push and shove the bell out and over the stern. He has noticed the powerful reinforcements bolted into the winch; still, the vessel is pitching up and down madly. Finally, the winch achieves full extension and, after a sick lurch upward, Robbie feels descent commence. The passage through the water is maelstrom-like, the bell shifting in the teeth of great forces upon it – Robbie seizes the grip rail tight and looks to see Marvin is doing the same. But then the great dead-weight beneath is bearing them surely downward through pitch-black waters to the lower depths.

Marvin's pale eyes are fixed on the gauges. Robbie can still feel those gales up on the surface being transmitted down the drop-cable; he is minded of the most turbulent, fist-clenching chopper rides he has known. Still, this feels more like a cocooning within a very heavily armoured system.

'Topside! Slow descent,' Marvin calls out. 'We're at two-fifty feet.' Robbie sees and feels seawater, the old, cold enemy, trickling in through the bottom of the bell.

Then a resonant, shaking thump felt through the bell tells Robbie the weight tray has settling on the seabed. He gets himself hooked to the thick twisted spools of umbilicals. Soon he feels that sweet circulation of hot water round his person.

'Topside, you read me?' He counts to five; no response. 'You read me, Topside?'

'*Go again, diver.*'

He repeats, until he hears: '*Five on five, diver.*'

'I'm ready for off.'

'*Got it, diver. You're twenty feet from the wellhead.*'

'Okay, far enough.'

'*Maybe not close enough. See what you see.*'

Robbie gives the thumbs-up, slides out of the hole and through the trunking – falling, falling into the netherworld, swallowing hard, until he is planting his feet down on the lead-lined weight tray.

He surveys the dark beyond the halo of light emanating from the bell, then hops down onto the sea-floor. Immediately he senses strangeness – the bed under his fins feels clinging and claggy – whether with spilled crude or old diesel mud he can't tell. But no silt is raised as he steps out uneasily across the mired surface. He can see nearly ten feet in front of him – already a dark mass coming clear, the looming monolith of the wellhead, a skeletal totem adorned with valves, fittings and connectors. A few more feet away, the start of the pipeline is visible, and Robbie begins to trudge down its length.

'Topside, diver is out, you read me . . . ?' Now Robbie worries anew. 'Topside, are you hearing me or no?'

'*Diver, sorry, we've got some cut-out. You're getting near the end of your umbilical.*'

'*Received, tell the bellman to keep a hold on it and I'll go direct as I can.*'

With a few paces more Robbie can make out the leaky connection ahead – a poisonous little cloud of black, issuing in puffs. In the next instant he feels a threatening tightness that lets him know he is at full extension – but the target remains several feet yet from the reach of his gloves.

He thinks quick. The bell will need to move.

'Topside, I'm out full, aye, just not close enough to the leak.'

Silence. Now a proper worry. *Fuck this.* He imagines himself telling Evie how shoddily this job got done; and knows in the next instant he must never, ever breathe a word of any such thing.

'Topside, eh? I'm returning to the bell, we need to sort this.'

He is retracing his steps through the murk when the voice in his helmet returns. *'Diver, you read me? Listen, I've talked to Mr Bodie, we're going to move the boat.'*

'Topside, aye, I bloody know. Are you hearing me or what?'

Fuelled by agitation, the lit-up bell looming above now, Robbie gets a footer onto the weight tray and starts to climb, hand over hand, up the cord of his umbilical, back through the trunking, until he is able to press his head through the bottom door. Marvin is startled. Robbie gestures for help in unclamping his helmet.

'The comms are hashed, man. Tell Topside they've to shift the bell maybe five, ten feet starboard, and be bloody careful about it.'

The bell's speaker splutters to life. *'Bellman, you got the diver's umbilical in hand, we're about to move.'*

'Uh, Topside, diver has returned to the bell.'

'Okay, we got to adjust the winch then we're gonna hoist the bell, hold on tight.'

Noise and vibration come emanating down from the surface. The bell shakes. Robbie is braced for the sensation of lift. He glances below and sees the tensing of the chain-wires down to the weight tray, thick mephitic clouds rising from around the two-ton block, the proof of the mighty task of shifting it.

But the tray is not shifting – it is staying obstinately settled on the bed, as if concreted into mud, resisting the colossal draw exerted on it, like some elemental, stirring creature of the sea-floor refusing to give up a captive.

The strain on the chain-wires is – alarming. The water is alive with vibrating tension, a creaking sound that seems suddenly on the edge of ripping.

'Topside, stop!' Robbie shouts. Marvin echoes him, frantic.

Robbie can hear the fearful torsion of metal contorting – the noise it makes before it breaks. His heart lurches.

'Diver, we got a red light up here, what the hell's—?'

A ghastly grinding noise – then the horrific finality of a *snap*. Robbie sees one chain-wire break loose and lash away into the water like some riled serpent. Instantly the bell is thrown violently to one side, and he is clinging to the rim of its bottom hole. One second more, another hard *snap*. The bell light burns out. And Robbie feels himself blasted from a cannon, a sudden and terrible velocity shooting the bell up to the surface, dragging him with it, the fingers of one hand gripping desperately on, furies of bloating gas bubbles all around his stunned head.

Suddenly he feels both of Marvin's arms clamped onto his taut forearm, trying to drag him wholly back inside the bell, but he is not shifting as the bell rockets crazily upward.

And now Robbie feels extraordinary pain in his chest: fast spreading, suffocating fullness radiating into his shoulders and spine. Marvin is shouting but the sound is pitiful as wailing. Robbie realises he is staring directly at doom: powerlessness cleaves into him and through him. Nausea rises, his throat tight, his whole body assailed by merciless pressure. How can this be? Consciousness is leaving him. He is leaving Evie. With terrible clarity her face is in his head, the wary scrutiny he came to know as her tenderness for him. *I don't like many . . .* The pain is blinding and must end. His vision reddens drastically, darkens like blood through water, then he is engulfed.

October 1974

A Formal Communication

Dear Mrs Evelyn Vallance,

Please allow me on behalf of Triton 5 Diving to express our deepest condolences for the loss of your husband Robert. In the brief period of his association with our company, he proved himself a hard worker and a trusted and personable individual. He will be missed. We mourn with you.

I am personally sorry that it was not possible for us to speak sooner, that I was unavailable when you contacted the office, and I understand the strength of your feeling. I am told that you received the news of Robert's passing very early yesterday from a newspaperman who turned up at your door. I can imagine how distressing this must have been, and I deplore the irresponsibility. It was natural that we should try to return the vessel back to Aberdeen as quickly as possible, and regrettably the necessary presence of police at the harbour also attracted reporters, who can be unscrupulous.

Be assured this company will co-operate with the Diving Inspectorate and any inquiry that might be judged necessary. It is painful to know that despite our best efforts there was nothing that could be done to save Robert. Tragically, in this work, accidents – acts of God – can befall even trained and experienced divers. At such depths there are also things we may never know. Certainly, irresponsible speculation in the press is helpful to no one.

We appreciate that at these very difficult times of life no words will be sufficient, and we wish you strength in the days ahead. You are in our prayers.

Yours sincerely,
Raymond Bodie

October 1974

A Proper Apportioning

Joe sits behind his desk feeling paralysed, confounded by the dilemma before him – every option equally unpalatable. But as he watches Isla's approach through the glass he knows there is no escape. Then she is through the door.

'Lennox Devane for you.' She takes the seat opposite, and he knows by the set of her face that she is with him, his partner.

'Joe, I need you to get down here, I've got Mr Bodie on the premises being difficult. His Rood-Maaier *is back in harbour but he's asking to bring it into dry dock with us, for more work. "Urgent," he says.'*

'No, no. Nothing hasty gets done here. There's a diver died and a man who was with him looking bad, too. I've already had a call from the procurator fiscal wanting my view on what went wrong.'

'I've had the same, Joe.'

'So what the hell's Bodie saying?'

'He wants his old system putting back on the bell, the old doughnut weight they had?'

'Why, do you think?'

'To get the whole thing seaworthy again? Obviously that heavy tray we fitted for them is lost on the seabed now.'

'God almighty, how do you think it happened, Lennox?'

'Maybe the bed just held onto it, wouldn't let go – too much suction. A fault in design, maybe. But it wasn't our design.'

'We didn't propose different, though?'

'Our job was just to execute.' Joe is unsettled by that form of words. *'Let's not forget, we had a very particular client, name of Raymond Bodie, and his watchword was speed.'*

Joe is trying hard to ensure Devane cannot hear how frightened he is that this bad piece of business will ruin the company.

'We need to take care here, Lennox. We have to be clear about what we did and when we did it and why. You and me need to speak again together before we say any more to the police.'

'*Bodie wants to speak to you, of course.*'

'No point in that until I know exactly what I can say.'

'*Okay but don't be surprised if he's on your doorstep soon enough.*'

Hanging up, Joe sees the intensity in Isla's eyes, fixed on his. 'What am I going to do?'

'Joe, you need to talk to someone straight away – the smartest person you know. Get a hold on this before it turns to chaos.'

'It *is* chaos, Isla. A man's dead.'

She gets out of her chair, comes round to him, grasps him by both forearms. 'You can't dwell on that. It wasn't your fault. You know what your responsibility is, and to who.'

She is so close and so intent, her fragrance and breath so strong . . . he sees no right answer but to say he is going to do just as she says.

'I'll talk to the company solicitor now.'

'Joe, is that really the smartest person you know?'

Joe looks at his watch. He feels, as so often with Bodie before, that she has seen inside his head.

'Alastair, I'm sorry if I pulled you out of anything.'

'You seemed to be in need, and I do understand.' Drummond, attentively at the leather-topped desk in his Charlotte Square office, is already giving Joe some succour by his manners. 'Also, this sorry matter – it's Killday business but also that of the Paxton consortium, in which we have a significant interest. And corporate law is where I began. So, tell me the story from your side, leave nothing out.'

This much Joe endeavours to do. There is no part of the deal with Triton Five that embarrasses him until its terrible end. He retains a hollow of unease about Bodie's attempts to barter with him; but then he purposely left the numbers to Walter, who had no reason to placate Bodie. On concluding his tale, he worries mainly that it speaks, on his part, of culpable buck-passing leadership.

Drummond ponders. 'You agreed with Triton Five a full build specification?'

'We agreed to build what they asked. Devane's view was that it was viable.'

'But it wasn't. Forgive me, Joe, I must pick out the parts of the case that don't look so great. They will inspect for evidence of proper process. I daresay the worst way this could sound would be if it were presented as a slightly hooky deal done as a favour for a friend.'

'I know. There's history there. But it didn't influence the deal.'

'They will ask whether you exercised a reasonable duty of care, whether the client was right to have confidence in what you provided. Was this weight-tray thing tested?'

'It was tested in our yard. Not on the seabed under three hundred feet of water. That was their duty, surely.'

'You think?' For a moment the arch of Drummond's brow panics Joe. 'You might be right. But in determining individual responsibility . . . Did you provide the correct instructions for operation? Yes? Was it then operated correctly? Bodie, as the owner – he was on the boat at the time of the accident, in the control room, right? So, it could be asked if the man knew what he was doing.'

'I see that, Alastair.'

'You do? Good. It's the shape of your defence.' He rummages in his drawer and produces cigar and cutter. 'Forgive the habit, I just find it keeps me alert.'

Cigar lit, Drummond steps to the big arched window, and looks out onto Charlotte Square's fading sunlight.

'Joe, we have so many young businesses in the North Sea right now, doing very new and dangerous work. Diving contractors are at the sharp end of that. And in all candour? The safety regulations around diving just aren't very tight – for better or worse. As I see it, it's Triton Five who dropped the ball here. I expect it's the end of the road for them with Paxton. But I see no grounds for complaint with you.'

For the first time in this long, fraught day, Joe feels hope. 'I want to be clear, Alastair, I'm not trying to shirk responsibility here, or go after anyone else.'

'No need for either, I'm sure. My bet is that very little will come of this.'

Joe weighs the verdict. 'Except, of course, that a man has died.'

'Yes. Dreadful. Shouldn't happen. But it wasn't because of you, Joe. Keep your nerve, eh?'

And then Drummond is seeing him out, and telling Joe that he must come up to Rathmullo for dinner with him and Belinda some time.

In the firm grasp of Drummond's hand Joe feels a precious infusion of reassurance but also, perhaps more importantly, a sending gesture of personal support – and from someone he once considered a rival. There is, he has decided, rather a merciless side to this man; but for sure, in a tough spot, it's the side you would want to be on.

Joe is back in Aberdeen a shade after five, and as he comes through the door at Killday Fishing he is unsurprised to see Ray Bodie awaiting him, seated amid the philodendrons in the reception area, looking as if the blood has been drained from his body. Joe had known the curse was not so easily rid.

Isla stands tensely by her desk. With a nod in her direction, Joe steers Bodie into his private office.

'You've been busy today, Joe. Not avoiding me, I trust.'

'I'm sure we've both had a lot to think about. The work you want on the *Rood-Maaier*? We can consider it. It just needs to be properly assessed and scheduled. You realise things can't be done hastily.'

'Joe, I've already had a letter from the Department of Energy, a Mr Kynaston of the Petroleum Directorate, telling me the *Rood-Maaier* can't go to sea again until it has the proper system installed.'

'Are you sure that's the priority, Ray? When there's a good chance of an inquiry into what just happened?'

'My lawyers think otherwise. So does the Association of Contractors. I've been busy just like you, Joe. Obviously we are going to review that incident, see what lessons can be learned, so there's no repetition. Meantime, though, you owe me to put things right on the *Rood-Maaier*.'

'Not "owe", Ray. You're implying the work was wrong in the first place. I don't recognise that. Did you ever test the installation out at sea, at depth?'

For some long moments following Joe's question, Bodie merely stares at him. Joe resolves to sit tight, hold on to his mettle, sure that he is in the final stage of a war of nerves. At last, Bodie breaks the silence.

'Joe, in the end, it's not for me or you to judge on things like blame and liability, is it? Maybe we were both a bit naïve? Just trying to get things done. But I do think you and I should see what we have here as a shared problem that we ought to help each other get free of. After all we've been through.'

Looking at Bodie now, considering the implication of his words, the thought of their long association – Joe feels repulsion stealing over him.

'You know what I find galling, Joe? You didn't even give me the damn deal you promised.'

'What do you mean?'

'The price on the job. The invoice, when it came in – every damn line item was more, stuffed with extras. Sharp practice, Joe.'

Joe is disoriented. 'The accounts are all Walter's area, not me.'

'The dark horse, eh? You might want to look at that, Joe. Have a look, eh? I told you, didn't I?'

After Bodie has gone, Joe goes directly to Walter's office. He scans the box files on the shelves. Isla is soothingly at his shoulder, ready for home, but he tells her she should take the car and go, this cannot wait. He sits down to read, head under the desk-lamp, and he is there for some time.

October 1974
Disclosures

Approaching the door of the cottage Joe feels the stealth and racing pulse of the thief. He has not forewarned Walter. And it is as if someone else's hand were about to rap the knocker, cross the threshold, to another place where things will henceforth be different. He can hear movement from behind that wooden door – shuffling feet, a low voice . . . voices?

'You asked me, Walter, about my relations with Da, about bad blood between us.'

They are seated together again by the picture window. Walter is dressed, has more colour than last time, but no more relish for talk.

'Joe, do you really want to rehash that?'

'Me and Da, we bashed heads, no question. Over the business, and maybe things that went before, too. I grant, I never settled with him over the pain I caused him. Me and Ray both.'

Walter grimaces as if to say, again, why revisit this?

'Walter, I asked you before, do you think I was in some way responsible for Da's death?'

There is a pause, marginally longer than Joe had bargained for. 'No, Joe. You're a better soul than that.'

'I am?'

'I know you fancy you're a hardnosed businessman, but you're not so tough, whatever disagreements you and Da had . . . And in a way, in a business, where there's a dispute, and one wins and another gets shoved aside . . . there's a violence there. A kind of a killing.' He shakes his head. 'But, Joe, you're not guilty for things in your head. Even if you might want to be.'

'Want to be?'

'Sometimes I think people want to be punished, they walk around permanently guilty. You have to watch out, they might confess to anything. But it's our deeds alone that matter. I know you had regard for Da, there was love there. Even when you fought . . .'

'We all saw sides of him. I remember times Da was plenty hard on you.'

Walter plays with an arm of his spectacles, and sighs. 'Again, Joe—?'

'See, I thought you could manage, that it was okay by you, you were better than that. But I've realised now how much you had to put up with.' Joe leans forward, wondering by Walter's eye if the intent is being read. 'Did you feel properly esteemed by Da, Walter? Valued by him?'

'I know Da knew that I . . . had my particular abilities.'

'He trusted you always, especially with the finance side.'

'He did that, whatever my abilities there.'

'Was he right to?'

Walter shifts abruptly in his chair. 'What's on your mind, Joe?'

'We have a very grave problem, over the business with Triton Five – Bodie said something to me—'

'Oh Bodie, good lord . . .'

'So I went into your files, Walter. I found some things that concerned me. Made me look back a bit further, even, at a few other jobs, just random. But I saw a kind of pattern that was very alarming to me. Invoices not tallying with quotes. Signs of the books having been reconciled, after the fact. Some very odd-looking debits and credits.'

'Have a care, Joe, what you say to me. This is hardly your—'

'Walter, it's plain as day to me you've been taking money out of the company. For a while, no? Going to a lot of trouble to cover your tracks. But not enough. Now, I have to know the full picture. Because I have a duty to protect the business.'

Walter shakes his head and looks aside, through the picture window to the North Sea. Joe lets the unhappy silence lengthen.

Then his brother snaps back abruptly. 'The way things went, how we each were treated – how do *you* think I felt, Joe?'

'Walter . . . I only saw what I saw.'

'I can't begin to tell you, as a son, how much I was failed by my parents. Da most of all. I was never encouraged, never supported. Not valued, no. I was just belittled and taken for granted. So many disappointments, Joe. A fundamental failure of consideration.'

Walter's voice is cracking, his eyes misting. Joe wonders suddenly if his tactics for this confrontation were advisable.

'And, realising that the consideration would never come – I did think, yes, that I deserved something for myself. Da trusted me on where to move the money. So I did.'

'Why, Walter? What did you do with it? Was it for something or – ?'

'I have somebody. Someone I have made plans with. To go away together, abroad. A place of our own. That was our idea for the money . . .'

Joe sits back, absorbing the fresh revelation. So many questions; and still, only one essential matter before them. 'Did you not think it would come out? Didn't you fear what it could do, to us, to the company?'

'Oh, it was you gave me the courage, Joe. Your vehemence.'

'What does that mean?'

'I could see, so clearly, the things you wanted for yourself. How dead set you were on what it took to get them. You're selfish that way. It's not that you don't see another man's view, but you damn well know your own comes first. You're just like Da. He couldn't even see that. In the end I thought, is that *really* not me, too? Not even a bit? Could I not strike back at him, too? Why not?'

A horrible notion arises in Joe. 'By "strike", Walter, you don't mean – '

'I didn't kill Da, Joe, no, of course not. But I admit . . . I had thoughts.'

'Walter – what?'

'Insane, I know that. But I got into such a fear that Da might marry Sheila – that she'd inherit? That was utterly unacceptable. I did get pictures in my head, some sort of "accident" I might contrive . . .' He cracks a weak, pained smile. 'But you know me, Joe. I don't do that sort of thing. Da did for himself, God help him. By accident. Because he was too old to keep going out alone, but he wouldn't change . . .'

Joe feels himself breathe again, but with no relief in it. 'Walter, you are going to have to come clean. What you've told me you'll have to tell others.'

'No. I won't do that.' Walter's voice is on an edge. 'Joe, you owe me something, for all I've been through. Something just for me. I've still got a chance in this. I can't give it up. Just give me what I deserve, Joe. Your silence.'

Joe shakes his head without a stroke of hesitation. 'Walter, this can't be hidden.'

'Yes it can. Who needs to know? You can look the other way.'

'Impossible. What you've done is embezzlement, false accounting. It has to come out now, or else the business is going to face—'

'Can you never think for a moment about one other damn thing? That I'm your *blood*, Joe?'

Joe absorbs this. He is not indifferent to the catch in his brother's voice, the crisis on his face. He thinks; and can see but one poor way out.

'Walter, answer me this – can you at least return the money you took?'

'No. No, it's all but spent. A property, in Almeria, Spain . . .'

Joe exhales heavily. 'Aw, Walter, it's hopeless. This has to be for the police, or else we—'

'I won't go to prison.' He speaks now with a low force Joe hadn't expected. 'That can't happen. Don't doubt what I can do if I have to, Joe. You say you'll do what you must, so will I.'

Excruciated, Joe struggles to respond. Finally, Walter stands. 'I need . . . I must have a moment, Joe. Will you let me be?'

Joe stands, warily. 'You're not going to do anything daft, Walter?'

'Worse, you mean? No. Please. Only a moment.'

'Alright. I'll be outside.'

Joe steps out the door into the small paved area, desperate for air and for a clear head amid this morass. The modest, familiar fixtures in his field of vision seem unreal to him – the little boats still bobbing, the gulls still shrieking, heedless on the quay below.

Through the door he can make out the thump of footfalls descending stairs. He bends an ear, to a voice, female, addressing his brother, at first too low to be distinct, but then alarmingly loud: *Don't say that! You can't say that!*

Then he hears those steps aimed at the door and he steps back, on edge, as it opens inward.

The woman standing there appears slight and swamped in a thick cabled rollneck sweater and denims, her dyed-blonde hair showing the roots of growing out. The face she shows Joe is pallid and sore-eyed.

'What are you ganna do?' she asks.

Her voice, though wracked, is familiar. Yes, they've met, he can see it. From the bar of the Òrach Hotel, when everything about her was painted, frosted, applied. Now she is au naturel and her eyes, big and green in his memory, look wanly grey. He'd thought her younger, but she must be his age, if not quite Walter's.

'I'm askin', what are you ganna do?'

She produces a cigarette from her sleeve and lights it, shakily.

'It was for you, then, all this . . . ?'

'It's not about me. Don't hurt him. Please. Help us out?'

'I'm sorry, but . . . it's not your business.'

'Course it's my business. It canna *not* be. I love him.'

'I'm afraid that's not what matters now . . . Things can't just be put away and buried.'

'Can they not? Is it really so bad? That everything has to get ruined?'

437

'I'm not going to argue this —'

'He deserves better. He's not had it easy like you.'

For Joe this is too much. 'C'mon. You don't know what you're talking about.'

'You know it, so do I.' She seizes Joe's arm, so hard she scratches him through his sleeve. 'Please. Will you not let this be? I'm beggin' you, *beggin'* —'

'Sheryl, stop.' Walter's voice, from the doorway, loud enough to carry, though to Joe his brother looks resigned, vacated of spirit.

Joe removes Sheryl's hand as calmly as he can, and stares at her until at last she withdraws to Walter's side, under his consoling arm, in the sunlit doorway of their parents' cottage.

Joe is trying to imagine what sort of togetherness the two of them have shared, so covertly, for however long, by whatever arrangement. What future they can have, he has no clue. Evidently he has known so little, and what's before him now is more of a tangle than he can possibly unpick. Rueful, he meets Walter's eye and shakes his head, then turns away and starts the difficult hack back down the steep path.

Back in the office, alone, Joe contemplates the telephone – contemplating disgrace. There is no more thinking that will change the facts, no one else to talk to now. Alastair Drummond told him he would have to hold his nerve. He can feel calamity at hand, though, bearing down implacably. He's not certain he can face it.

And yet he knows that he has faced other things before that were unknown and frightening to him. He can't feign to unlearn what seemed then to be the lesson: not to run from fear like a rabbit, but to face what must be faced. He lifts the receiver and dials.

November 1974

A Girl

Aaron has sat at the wheel of his parked car for some time, conscious of a numbing weight within, resisting entry into the proceedings of what he fears to be the lowest day of his life. Finally, the steady procession of mourners going past his window tells him he must also put a foot forward.

His father is there to meet him at the church gate, as arranged. David Strang, hollow-eyed, looks as badly as Aaron feels. He clasps Aaron's shoulder while shaking his hand. Aaron realises that today they must support one another.

'Weather's decent,' Aaron offers.

'Perhaps,' replies David, 'someone had a word.'

There are maybe a hundred mourners. But Aaron can see only Evie, flanked by her parents and her three brothers – the flame of her hair, her gravid figure in her black dress and coat, red-eyed and staring straight ahead as if not truly seeing. She is a picture of heartbreak, and it cuts into Aaron – as bad as his conscience in the knowledge that all he has said to her since the news was in a single condoling phone call, one in which his own words had pained him by their lousy inadequacy.

Now the Charltons are being approached by the Gallaghers, those staunch attendees of all community occasions – Juliet taking Evie's hand, Marilyn and her husband Richard Mount at their back, he whispering something cautiously into his wife's ear, appearing to Aaron as they always have, two co-conspirators.

Aaron sees the Reverend McVey coming forward onto the steps of the kirk, in the shadow of the church's harled walls, under the high lancet windows.

Seated in the front row looking up at the large dark pulpit

and the three long windows in the south wall, hearing Torrance McVey begin the prayers, remembering Torrance's father so often performing the same impersonal rituals – Aaron begins to feel cut adrift from the present moment, haunted too strongly by the past, the incomparable force of its reality; set against which whatever lies ahead now seems insubstantial. Despondently he reflects that for so long he was drawing on his friend's reserves – constancy, principle, guts – steering by them, even; but that now, some vital part of his own life has been extinguished.

The ritual concluded, Aaron follows the elders heavy-footed to where Robbie's coffin is revealed at the church door, where Evie waits. He wonders now if Evie took a last look inside, before it was closed; or whether she chose to remember him from life. He risks a glance at her, hoping she might sense that he is thinking of her.

He joins the cortège in taking up the casket and proceeding up the slope to where the grave is dug. The physical effort in the task is much simpler than he feared – as nothing compared to its meaning. He knows he will carry out his role to its end, but after that he will not stay another moment. He knows where he is going.

Two o'clock. The old sea fret is in the air. Aaron, sitting on the rocks and staring out to sea, shivers a little. The sea still teems as if with life. *But the sea doesn't care.*

He runs a finger round the collar of his shirt, like a coil upon his neck, feeling a clamminess there – a tired, sordid sort of a feeling.

He has been sitting for some time, emptied of resolve, vaguely oppressed by the God-fearing sentiments of the service. The way it seems to him: the experiment is complete, it has not been successful, the results have not surprised, but must be known and reckoned with it. Was it ordained to have turned out this way? No, he thinks. No such excuses are credible. A coward's way out.

He recalls the fantasies he entertained as a boy, about the water as a realm into which one might merge and vanish. The folly of that – as if there were something there that awaited, and cared, enough to bear one away. It seems to him that Robbie always knew, intuitively, what the sea meant; and how much better it was to be alive in a body. But still he was claimed by the sea.

Something in Aaron is telling him insistently that he ought to follow – throw himself into the water and under, have done. But he simply can't face that fate.

He gets to his feet, off the rocks. He turns, and up on high he sees the figure of Evie.

Squinting in the sun, he realises she has not seen him. He wonders now whether or not she is seeing anything? She is, he feels sure, much too close to the edge of the cliff. An awful apprehension crawls over him.

'Evie!' He shouts and waves his arms around his head. She sees him now – that much he can tell – though she doesn't move at all. He starts to run, up the steep and circuitous stony track toward the top of the coastal bluff. He is gripped by urgent compunction, unable to keep Evie in his sights, heart rate rising with the strange fear that when he gets up there she will be gone.

When he surfaces, she is there – stepping slowly toward him, nothing in her expression other than the grief so clear at the church.

'Evie, are you alright?' He realises immediately how that must sound. 'What's got you up here?'

'Same as you, maybe? I came here with Robbie.' And she lowers herself with care onto the ground, one hand splayed below her, one hand on her bump. He moves to her side and stays there, on his knees.

'He'd bring me here. I feel him here. This comes from here, right?' She reaches and lifts out from her collar the trilobite fossil Aaron once bestowed on Robbie.

Aaron smiles. 'Hereabouts.'

'His things are so dear. This is extra-precious.'

He nods. 'I'm sorry we didn't speak, at the church? I've wanted to.'

441

'What else did you want to say?'

'A million things . . . To know how you're feeling.'

She pulls at some blades of grass, quiet for a moment. 'There's been so much to do, and I've just had to do it, on my own. And every moment now, when I'm thinking about what I'm meant to do next, I only get so far and then it just hits me – Robbie's dead. How can that have happened? It's not fair.' Her throat is clotted: she lowers her head and sobs shortly into her chest. 'We were supposed to be together.'

Aaron is silent, wanting very much to lay a comforting hand on her, unsure of how it would be received.

'There I go, eh?' She gulps bitterly. 'Didn't want to be like this today . . .'

'I'm so sorry, Evie, so sorry.'

'What do *you* think happened? Down there when he died?'

'I think someone was careless. Not him. Only he's the one paid for it.'

'Will anyone else pay?'

'I just don't know. There are procedures. But people get away with an awful lot of things. If there was anything I could do, I would. He did so much for me.'

He feels her gaze on him more closely, critically, even. Now she says: 'I always wished we'd get on, me and you.'

His response tumbles out of him. 'I know you did, you had a right to. If you haven't felt that then I apologise, Evie, truly. The lack was in me, not you. The only thing that was wrong was me.' She is looking at him perhaps still a little reprovingly. He isn't sure. 'Please know, if I can be any help to you now, do anything for you . . .'

'But you're going away, aren't you? New Zealand?'

'Soon, yes. Not just yet.'

She sighs, looks away and out to the fretted surface of the sea.

'I'm not sleeping . . . It was hard enough before, since I got big and all. I've no appetite to speak of . . . and I don't think anyone knows how to help me with them things. But, I can manage. I have to. I have to, don't I? For this one.'

She encircles her belly, a gesture that seems also to Aaron like self-comfort.

'I just want to cry that he'll never see her, hold her . . . But when I'm alone, see, I don't have to pretend like I'm okay to anyone. No brave face. I don't want anyone else around me but him. And I can't have that, Aaron, can I?'

She is looking him in the eye, but he is simply taken aback by her; then, to his great surprise, she reaches and takes his hand in hers.

'Will you walk me back to the village?'

Unquestioning, he helps her get back up onto her feet. Brushing themselves down, they start to walk, away from the edge, along the grassy coastal track high over the water.

'Back then, you said "her",' Aaron remarks into the breeze, glancing at her. 'Have you been told you'll be having a girl?'

'Och no. I just think she is. Don't ask why.'

He smiles. 'It should be a girl. I mean, it ought to be.'

'Why?'

Now he has to pause, struggling again. Why indeed did he say that?

A moment later, like mercy, the right answer falls upon him.

'If it's a girl then you'll be her role model. I mean, she'll have some of Robbie, of course, no doubt, but . . . she'll take after you, I'd expect. Which would be a fine thing.'

'Thank you, Aaron,' she says, after a moment. 'There's a lot she'll have to be told about her father.'

'Well, you'll have so much to tell her.'

'So will you.'

Epilogue
October 1982

Dusk, and the lights burn in the battlement windows of Castle Drummond. Outside, a storm, lashing rain and high wind. Ally can nearly suppose how a soul might feel out at sea or marooned on one of those infernal oil platforms. This place, though, is secure and defended.

In his upstairs office-cum-library he sits drafting a speech, in the after-dinner business mode; but it is causing him uncommon difficulty. He is hunting for the early joke, the relaxing first laugh that permits pretty much any sort of serious or felt comments to follow. He has always prided himself on his lightness of touch, having put so much of life's work into appearing unruffled. But it's a mask at times – false by nature. And tonight he is feeling a mite challenged by the notion of his audience.

He and Belinda will be receiving Japanese visitors, executives from Mitsubishi, and so none of the usual protocols of entertaining apply. For an hour he has been toying with punning variations on 'yen', 'sake', 'samurai', 'microchip', 'solid state', how smaller can be better . . . But nothing is working.

'No, you're not very much like anyone else, are you?' he murmurs to his scribbled and scored page.

Japanese investment has been moving steadily into East Lothian, searching out greenfield sites on which to house factories; and Ally has been happy to advise these investors on the incentives and tax efficiencies available to them. Conveniently, this work has been to the benefit of some of his own real estate investments in East Lothian. But he is pleased also to be supporting jobs in a Scottish electronics industry, however much it is Japanese-owned. *We're buying it in*, he thinks. If he had his druthers there would be more local firms rushing into the fray; but that is just not the Scotland Ally knows and loves. A little disappointing; but there's always hope.

He has, at least, completed his homework for tomorrow on greetings, bowings, toasts, the importance of punctuality and the order of whom you speak to about what. He has prepared remarks on the last Open at Troon, and the decent performance there by Japanese players. He has hired in catering: there will be fish and steak, a taste of Scotland! And he expects to be on solid ground when the delicate moment comes to turn to business.

One further unresolved matter, though – the proffering of gifts. He has yet to figure out what is appropriate to present to the top man, to Kurahara-san. What to give someone with so many toys at his disposal already? Ally, too, has a microwave oven in his kitchen, a Betamax VCR in his den, a Commodore computer looking blankly at him across his desk. He uses precisely none of these things, but he imagines Kurahara does. What could impress the man?

Ally has long known that having the answers to these sorts of questions is a big part of his currency, of what has made him into the panjandrum who sits on so many boards, is consulted on so many ventures, and listened to with such seriousness. Openness to innovation, taking bold steps, has been his life's work.

That idea of newness . . . it gets him onto his feet and over to his shelves, overcrowded as always. But he has a notion. Sitting there is a little ceremonial token once placed in his hand, never opened: a little glass globe, coloured smoky by a sample of North Sea oil. No bigger than a dram, but black as the oil of imagination, and engraved for that day back in July of 1975 when Paxton brought oil ashore in Kent – oil from the Cetus field, Aaron Strang's eccentric discovery.

Ally holds the globe up to the light, growing steadily more pleased with himself, and with this souvenir of the great North Sea adventure, this drop of wildness domesticated. It has a tale to it, a bit of magic in it.

Settled, then: he will place it on his dining table and offer it humbly to Kurahara-san.

He re-boxes the globe and carries it with care, descending the steep stairs onto the floor given over to bedchambers – his and Belinda's master suite, also the room of young Tom, home from Kilmuir for half-term.

Looking in, Ally sees his eleven-year-old son bent owlishly over his desk, and he has the sense of disturbing a habit ever so slightly furtive. Has that age arrived? Could he be writing up a storm in a diary, or working on some private collection of candid photography . . . ? But before he can fret any further, Tom has turned queryingly in his chair. Ally lowers himself onto the boy's narrow bed.

'Hullo, Tom-Tom. What have you got your head stuck in there?'

'I got a letter from Uncle Mark.'

'Oh really? Did he send you any money?'

'He sent me a book.' Tom waves a paperback in the air, long enough for Ally to read ORWELL on its cover – typically Mark, less so Tom.

'I daresay a fiver might have been handier, eh? What else has he got to say for himself?'

'Just asking what I'm up to. The usual . . .'

'You say that, Tom, but I never know what that is. Might I have a glance at the letter?'

The boy looks uncomfortable. 'It's private, Dad.'

'So private I shouldn't see, Tom?'

'We don't talk about you, Dad, don't worry . . .'

'I won't, Tom, fear not. I just wonder what in hell the two of you have in common to be swapping little notes.'

Ally moves off and out, a little unhappy at himself for the flash of temper. He has not resented Mark having a part of the boy's life, in spite of his estrangement from the parents' affections. He knows that were he to see Mark now, they would only argue all over again, very unprofitably. He has learned – from Belinda the spy, sometimes in back-channel exchanges with Shona – that Mark is back in the Labour

Party, trying to grind out self-rule for Scotland by that useless route, the SNP having proved insufficiently pure for him just as everyone else. He would like to sit his old schoolfriend down and point out that the Tories still govern Scotland and distribute the fruits of the oil; ask him, too, if he yet understands why? An idle fantasy, though. A waste of time.

Memory of all that he and Mark used to share can still rouse a rush of affection in him; but it's so long ago, and they were simply different souls then. Better, Ally feels, that their disagreements came to a head, tough as it felt at the time: two people can't rub along with such divergent views. *Irreconcilable differences . . .* Ally does wonder how the thoroughly sane Shona has put up with Mark's flakiness, his umpteen about-faces, through all their ups and downs. *No kids*, he supposes. Only each other, to chivvy and indulge. Maybe, too, why Mark keeps up his feeble fly-by-night godfathering.

Down the hallway Ally finds Belinda standing before the vanity table, evidently not entirely happy either, long black skewers through her pinned-up hair as she attempts to dress herself in a kimono of plum-coloured silk. The garment rather fascinates Ally with its criss-cross lapels and wizard-like sleeves – but clearly the fastening of the belt to hold the package all in place is causing his wife great vexation.

'Oh bother!' she exclaims, casting the long length of cloth to the ground. 'Bloody fucking thing . . .'

'You know, you don't need to do this, darling. It's not the point of the evening.'

'It was your idea, Alastair. I am but humble, dutiful wife.' She fake-bows, her hands pressed together, but scowling – and Ally realises that his little whim might have been ill-considered; also that he has sounded snappish again. His temper really is not quite what it was; Belinda keeps telling him.

'I'm sorry, darling. Look, they'll love it. They love us adopting their stuff. And you look glorious.'

'I suppose it'll be a lark. It's just so damn fiddly.'

'Perhaps I can help.' He collects the cloth from the floor, attempts to re-straighten its many folds, and steps around behind her.

'Mind you don't poke your eye out . . .'

He encircles her waist, she instructs him briskly in how to drape a length over her shoulder, and they begin to work toward some rudimentary closure.

'Now we're getting somewhere . . .'

'It still feels like parading round in my bathrobe. You should see what I'm wearing underneath.'

'Something French? Séduisante?'

'No, I mean I am slightly padding my arse. Can't you tell?'

He kisses the cool nape of her neck and leaves her to finish. Then he heads down to the kitchen, brews a pot of tea, and raids the refrigerator for a sandwich of cold cooked sausages and mustard – the finest food! – which he carries through to the Great Hall where the dining table is already place-set for tomorrow's feast. His simple repast reminds him: they live in such profusion, more even than they know how to use. But still, Ally doesn't feel his drive and appetite are sated. There must still be something more – if only to keep the game afoot, and boredom at bay.

The globe! He remembers that he put it down in Tom's room and forgot, in his pique, to carry it off. He goes back to the foot of the stone wheel stairs and shouts up.

'Tom? Be a dear and fetch me down the little box I left on your bed?'

No reply. Typical. Yet, moments later, he watches the boy a little disgruntledly trooping down toward him; and it is on Ally's mind to tell him to cheer up and use both hands – this in the same moment as Tom stumbles on the fourth step up, falling spectacularly the remainder of the way. The box tumbles from his hand, the globe thrown out on impact, hitting the flagstones and smashing instantly, its small payload of oil spilling in a meagre trickle.

For a moment Ally is speechless. Then he goes to drag Tom up off the floor, the boy rubbing his sore knees with sore palms, looking as though he has been smacked.

'Damn it, are you hurt?'

'I'm fine. I'll go get a cloth.'

'Forget it.' The boy's mere glumness is suddenly and colossally irksome to Ally. 'Could you not have been more careful?' he barks.

'I'm sorry, I didn't know it was such a thing—'

'It was *irreplaceable*, Tom. Some things can't be replaced, you know that? God *damn* it.' The ideal gift, the perfect notion, ruined. Ally rubs at his face, despondent over the sheer unthinking carelessness.

'I'm *sorry*, Dad. Really, really sorry . . .'

He has got through to the boy, at least. The lip is trembling. Tom really needs to be tougher, as well as less clumsy.

Now he sees Belinda looking down from the stairs, in her Japanese drag. He can read her: he must look to himself, too. Be proportionate. Make peace.

'Tom, look – forgive me, you're right, son. I'm sorry. It's only a thing. Please, just be more careful, eh? We can't just go around smashing things, can we? Remember, something small to us could be very precious to others.'

He hugs the boy lightly and sends him on his way up to his mother. Then, with a sigh, he goes to make a start on cleaning up the sorry mess.

Acknowledgements

I am hugely grateful to Ruth McCance, with whom I first discussed the notion of a North Sea fiction; to my agent Matthew Hamilton for his encouragement, and to Lee Brackstone, who supported the project from the start at Faber; to Alex Bowler and Aisling Brennan, who read the work in progress with great care and finesse, and who helped me editorially to see so many places where it could be improved; to Joanna Harwood, Louise Pearce and Nate Rae for rigorous shepherding of the text through pre-press; to Robbie Porter and Pete Adlington for the inspired design and art direction of the cover; to Kate Burton, for her expertise in publicity; and, always, to Rachel, Cordelia and Lucy, whom I love.

The now vanished era of North Sea exploration was captured at the time by some superb non-fictional accounts, and in my research I was especially indebted to a number of these, as well as some others that came later – in particular, *Cromarty: The Scramble for Oil* by George Rosie (Canongate, 1974); *The Oil Rush* by Mervyn Jones, illustrated by Fay Godwin (Quartet Books, 1976); *Offshore* by A. Alvarez (Sceptre, 1986); *Requiem for a Diver* by Jackie Warner and Fred Park (Brown, Son & Ferguson, 1990); and *Trawler* by Redmond O'Hanlon (Hamish Hamilton, 2003).